Do you e...
step into s...

IN HE...

Modern-day Cinderellas get their grooms!

Our modern-day Cinderellas
swap glass slippers for stylish stilettos!

So follow each footstep,
through makeover to marriage, rags to riches,
as these women fulfil their hopes and dreams…

Look out for more *In Her Shoes…* stories, coming soon!

OH-SO-SENSIBLE SECRETARY

BY
JESSICA HART

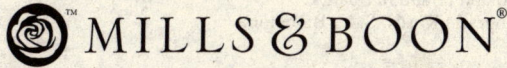

DID YOU PURCHASE THIS BOOK WITHOUT A COVER?

If you did, you should be aware it is **stolen property** as it was reported *unsold and destroyed* by a retailer. Neither the author nor the publisher has received any payment for this book.

All the characters in this book have no existence outside the imagination of the author, and have no relation whatsoever to anyone bearing the same name or names. They are not even distantly inspired by any individual known or unknown to the author, and all the incidents are pure invention.

All Rights Reserved including the right of reproduction in whole or in part in any form. This edition is published by arrangement with Harlequin Enterprises II BV/S.à.r.l. The text of this publication or any part thereof may not be reproduced or transmitted in any form or by any means, electronic or mechanical, including photocopying, recording, storage in an information retrieval system, or otherwise, without the written permission of the publisher.

This book is sold subject to the condition that it shall not, by way of trade or otherwise, be lent, resold, hired out or otherwise circulated without the prior consent of the publisher in any form of binding or cover other than that in which it is published and without a similar condition including this condition being imposed on the subsequent purchaser.

® and TM are trademarks owned and used by the trademark owner and/or its licensee. Trademarks marked with ® are registered with the United Kingdom Patent Office and/or the Office for Harmonisation in the Internal Market and in other countries.

First published in Great Britain 2010
Harlequin Mills & Boon Limited,
Eton House, 18-24 Paradise Road, Richmond, Surrey TW9 1SR

© Jessica Hart 2010

ISBN: 978 0 263 87334 4

Harlequin Mills & Boon policy is to use papers that are natural, renewable and recyclable products and made from wood grown in sustainable forests. The logging and manufacturing process conform to the legal environmental regulations of the country of origin.

Printed and bound in Spain
by Litografia Rosés, S.A., Barcelona

Jessica Hart was born in West Africa, and has suffered from itchy feet ever since, travelling and working around the world in a wide variety of interesting but very lowly jobs, all of which have provided inspiration on which to draw when it comes to the settings and plots of her stories. Now she lives a rather more settled existence in York, where she has been able to pursue her interest in history, although she still yearns sometimes for wider horizons. If you'd like to know more about Jessica, visit her website www.jessicahart.co.uk

For Nikki at 2DC,
with many thanks for all her work on the website

CHAPTER ONE

EVERYTHING was in place. A sleek computer sat on my desk, humming gently. A notebook and freshly sharpened pencil were squared up to one side of a high-tech phone, but otherwise the desk was empty, the way I like it. I can't bear clutter.

There was only one thing missing.

My new boss.

Phin Gibson was late, and I was cross. I can't bear unpunctuality either.

I had been there since eight-thirty. Wanting to make a good impression, I'd dressed carefully in my best grey checked suit, and my make-up was as subtle and professional as ever. Rattling over the keyboard, my nails had a perfect French manicure. I was only twenty-six, but anyone looking at me would know that I was the ultimate executive PA, cool, calm and capable.

I might have *looked* cool, but by half past ten I

certainly wasn't feeling it. I was irritated with Phin, and wishing I had bought myself a doughnut earlier.

Now, I know I don't look like the kind of girl with a doughnut fetish, but I can't get through the morning without a sugar fix. It's something to do with my metabolism (well, that's my story and I'm sticking to it), and if I don't have something sweet by eleven o'clock I get scratchy and irritable.

OK, even *more* irritable.

Chocolate or biscuits will do at a pinch, but doughnuts are my thing, and there's a coffee bar just round the corner from Gibson & Grieve's head office which sells the lightest, jammiest, sugariest ones I've ever tasted.

I'd fallen into the habit of buying one with a cappuccino on my way into work, and waiting for a quiet moment to get my blood sugar level up later in the morning, but today I'd decided not to. I wasn't sure what sort of boss Phin Gibson would prove to be, and I didn't want to be caught unawares with a sugar moustache or jammy fingers on our first day working together. This job was a big opportunity for me, and I wanted to impress him with my professionalism.

But how could I do that if he wasn't there?

Exasperated, I went back to my e-mail to Ellie, my friend in Customer and Marketing.

No problem, Ellie. To be honest, I was glad of something to do. There's a limit to what you can do as a PA without a boss—who STILL hasn't appeared, by the way. You'd think he could be bothered to turn up on time on his first day in a new job, but apparently not. Am already wishing I was back in the Chief Executive's office. I have a nasty feeling Phin and I aren't going to get on, and unless

——Original Message——
From: e.sanderson@gibsonandgrieve.co.uk
To: s.curtis@gibsonandgrieve.co.uk
Sent: Monday, January 18, 09:52
Subject: THANK YOU!

Summer, you are star! Thank you SO much for putting those figures together for me—and on a Friday afternoon, too! You saved my life (again!!!!!).
Any sign of Phin Gibson yet??? Can't wait to hear if he's as gorgeous as he looks on telly!
Exx

'Well, well, well...Lex must know me better than I thought he did.'

The deep, amused voice broke across my exasperated typing and my head jerked up as I snatched my fingers back from the keyboard.

And there—at last!—was my new boss. Phinneas Gibson himself, lounging in the doorway and smiling the famously lop-sided smile that had millions of women, including my flatmate Anne, practically dribbling with lust.

I'd never dribbled myself. I'm not much of a dribbler at the best of times, and that oh-so-engaging smile smacked a little too much of I'm-incredibly-attractive-and-charming-and-don't-I-know-it for my taste.

My first reaction at the sight of Phin was one of surprise. No, thinking about it, surprise isn't quite the right word. I was *startled*.

I'd known what he looked like, of course. It would have been hard not to when Anne had insisted that I sit through endless repeats of *Into the Wild*. It's her flat, so she gets control of the remote.

If you're one of the two per cent of the population fortunate enough never to have seen it, Phin Gibson takes ill-assorted groups of people to the more inhospitable places on the planet, where they have to complete some sort of task in the most appalling conditions. On camera.

According to Anne, it makes for compulsive viewing, but personally I've never been able to see the point of making people uncomfortable just for sake of it. I mean, what's the point of hacking through a jungle when you can take a plane?

But don't get me started on reality TV. That's another thing I can't bear.

So I was braced against the extraordinary blue eyes, the shaggy dark blond hair and the smile, but I hadn't counted on how much bigger and more *immediate* Phin seemed in real life. Seeing him on the small screen gave no sense of the vivid impact of his presence.

I'm not sure I can explain it properly. You know that feeling when a gust of wind catches you unawares? When it swirls round you, sucking the air from your lungs and leaving you blinking and ruffled and invigorated? Well, that's what it felt like the first time I laid eyes on Phin Gibson.

There was a kind of lazy grace about him as he leant there, watching me with amusement. So it wasn't that he radiated energy. It was more that everything around him was energised by his presence. You could practically see the molecules buzzing in the air, and Phin himself seemed to be using up more than his fair share of oxygen in the room, which left me annoyingly short of breath.

Not that I was going to let Phin guess *that*.

'Good morning, Mr Gibson,' I said. Minimising the screen just in case, I took off the glasses I wear for working at the computer and offered a cool smile.

'Is it possible that *you're* my PA?' The blue eyes studied me with a mixture of surprise, amusement and appreciation as Phin levered himself away from the doorway and strolled into the room.

'I'm Summer Curtis, yes.'

A little miffed at his surprise, and ruffled by the amusement, I pushed back my chair so that I could rise and offer my hand across the desk. *Some* of us were professional.

Phin's fingers closed around mine and he held onto my hand as he looked at me. 'Summer? No.'

'I'm afraid so,' I said a little tightly. I can't tell you how many times I've wished I was called something sensible, like Sue or Sarah, but never more than at that moment, with those blue eyes looking down into mine, filled with laughter.

I tried to withdraw my hand, but Phin was keeping a tight hold on it, and I was uncomfortably aware of the firm warmth of skin pressed against mine.

'You are *so* not a Summer,' he said. 'I've never met anyone with a more inappropriate name. Although I did know a girl called Chastity once, now I come to think of it,' he added. 'Look at you. Cool and crisp. Conker-brown hair. Eyes like woodsmoke. What were your parents thinking when they called you Summer instead of Autumn?'

'Not about how embarrassing it would be for me to go through life named after a season, anyway,' I said, managing to tug my hand free at last. I sat down again and rested it on the desk, where it throbbed disconcertingly.

'I must thank Lex,' said Phin. To add to my discomfort, he perched on my desk and turned sideways to look at me. 'He told me he'd appointed a PA for me, but I was expecting a dragon.'

'I can be a dragon if required,' I said, although right then I felt very undragon-like. I was suffocatingly aware of Phin on the other side of the desk. He wasn't anywhere near me, but his presence was still overwhelming. 'I'm fully qualified,' I added stiffly.

'I feel sure Lex wouldn't have appointed you if you weren't,' Phin said.

He had picked up my pencil and was twirling it absently between his fingers. It's the kind of fiddling that drives me mad, and I longed to snatch it from him, but I wasn't that much of a dragon.

'What's your brief?' he added, still twirling.

'Brief?'

The look he shot me was unexpectedly acute. 'Don't tell me Lex hasn't put you in here to keep an eye on me.'

I shifted uncomfortably.

'You're the most sensible person around here,' had been Lex Gibson's exact words when he offered me the job. 'I need someone competent to stop that idiot boy doing anything stupid. God knows what he'd get up to on his own!'

Not that I could tell Phin that. I admired Lex, but I wondered now if he was quite right. Phin didn't seem like an idiot to me, and he certainly wasn't a boy. He wasn't that much older than me—in his early thirties, perhaps—but he was clearly all man.

'Your brother thought it would be helpful for you to have an assistant who was familiar with the way the company operates,' I said carefully instead.

'In other words,' said Phin, interpreting this without difficulty, 'my brother thinks I'm a liability and wants you to keep me in order.'

I'd leapt at the chance of a promotion, even if it did mean working for Lex Gibson's feckless younger brother. Perhaps I should just explain, for those of you who have just jetted in from Mars—well, OK, from outside the UK—Gibson & Grieve is a long-established chain of department stores with a reputation for quality and style that others can only envy. The original, very exclusive store was in London, but now you'll find us in all the major British cities—setting a gold standard in retail, as Lex likes to say.

The Grieves died out long ago, but the Gibsons still have a controlling share, and Lex Gibson now runs the company with an iron hand. As far as I knew, Phin had never shown the slightest interest in Gibson & Grieve until now, but, as heir to a substantial part of it, he was automatically a member of the board. He was coming in right at the top, and that meant that his PA—me—would be working at the most senior level.

I gathered the idea was for Phin to spend a year as the public face of Gibson & Grieve, so even though the job wasn't permanent it would look very good on my CV. And the extra money wouldn't hurt, either. If I was ever going to be able to buy my own place I needed to save as much as I could, and this promotion would make quite a difference to my salary. I'm someone who likes to have a plan, and this job was a major step on my way. I might not be thrilled at the thought of working for Phin Gibson, but it wasn't an opportunity I was prepared to lose.

I couldn't dream about a future with Jonathan now, I remembered sadly, and that left buying my own flat the only plan I had. I mustn't jeopardise it by getting on the wrong side of Phin, no matter how irritatingly he fiddled.

'I'm your personal assistant,' I assured him. 'It's my job to support you. I'm here to do whatever you want.'

'Really?'

'Of course,' I began with dignity, then saw that his eyes were alight with laughter. To my chagrin, I felt a blush steal up my cheeks. It was just a pity my plan involved working with someone who was clearly incapable of taking anything seriously. 'Within reason, of course.'

'Oh, of *course*,' Phin agreed, eyes still dancing.

Then, much to my relief, he dropped the pencil and got up from the desk. 'Well, if we're going to be working together we'd better get to know each other properly, don't you think? Let's have some coffee.'

'Certainly.' Making coffee for my boss. That I could do. Pleased to be back in proper PA mode, I swung my chair round and got to my feet. 'I'll make some right away.'

'I don't want you to make it,' said Phin. 'I want to go out.'

'But you've just arrived,' I objected.

'I know, and I'm feeling claustrophobic already.' He looked around the office without enthusiasm. 'It's all so...sterile. Doesn't it make you want to shout obscenities and throw rubbish everywhere?'

I actually winced at the thought.

'No,' I said. Gibson & Grieve had always been noted for its style and up-market image. The offices were all beautifully designed and gleamed with the latest technology. I loved the fact that this one was light and spacious, and free as yet of any of the clutter that inevitably accumulated in a working office. 'I like everything neat and tidy,' I told Phin.

'You know, I should have been able to guess that,' he said in a dry voice, and I suddenly saw myself through his eyes: crisp and restrained in my grey suit, my hair fastened neatly back from my face. In comparison, he looked faintly unkempt, in jeans, a black T-shirt and a battered old leather jacket. He might look appropriate for a media meeting, but it was hardly appropriate for an executive director of a company like Gibson & Grieve, I thought disapprovingly.

Still, I had no doubt he was even less impressed by me. I would have bet on the fact that he thought me smart, but dull.

But then maybe all men thought that when they looked at me. Jonathan had, too, in the end.

I pushed the thought of Jonathan aside. 'We can go out if you'd rather,' I said. 'But don't you at least want to check your messages first?'

Phin's brows rose. 'I have messages?'

'Of course. You're a director and a board member,' I pointed out. 'We set up a new e-mail address for you last week, and you've been getting messages ever since. I'm able to filter them for you, and you have another address which only you will be able to access.'

'Great,' said Phin. 'Filtering sounds good to me. Is there anything important?'

'It's all important when you're a director.' I couldn't help the reproving note in my voice, but Phin only rolled his eyes.

'OK, is there anything *urgent*?'

I was forced to admit that there wasn't. 'Not really.'

'There you go,' he said cheerfully. 'I didn't think

I'd need a PA, but Lex was right—as always. You've saved me wading through all those e-mails already. You deserve a coffee for that,' he told me, and held open the door for me. 'Come on, let's go.'

It was all going to be very different now, I thought, stifling a sigh as we headed down the corridor to the lift. I was used to working for Lex Gibson, who barely stopped working to sip the coffee Monique, his PA, took in to him.

Lex would never dream of going out for coffee, or bothering to get to know his secretaries, come to that. I was fairly sure he knew nothing about my private life. As far as Lex was concerned you were there to work, not to make friends, and I was perfectly happy with that. I didn't want to get all chummy with Phin, but for better or worse he was my boss now, so I could hardly refuse.

'Where's the best place for coffee round here?' Phin asked when we pushed through the revolving doors and out into the raw January morning. At least it wasn't raining for once, but I shivered in my suit, wishing I'd bothered to throw on my coat after all.

'Otto's is very good,' I said, hugging my arms together. 'It's just round the corner.'

'Better and better,' said Phin. 'Lead the way.' He glanced down at me, shivering as we waited to cross the road. 'You look cold. Would you like to borrow my jacket?'

The thought of his jacket, warm from his body, slung intimately around my shoulders, was strangely disturbing—quite apart from the fact that it would look very odd with my suit. 'I'm fine, thank you,' I said, clenching my teeth to stop them chattering.

'Let's step on it, then,' he said briskly. 'It's freezing.'

The warmth and the mouth-watering smell of freshly baked pastries enveloped us as we pushed through the door into Otto's. Inside it was dark and narrow, with four old-fashioned booths on one side and some stools at a bar in the window.

The coffee and sandwiches were so good that first thing in the morning and at lunchtime there was always a long queue out of the door, but it was relatively quiet now. We lined up behind three executives exuding testosterone as they compared bonuses, a German tourist, and a pair of middle-aged women carrying on a conversation that veered bizarrely between some terrible crisis that a mutual friend was enduring and whether a Danish pastry was more or less fattening than a blueberry muffin.

Phin picked up a tray and hustled me along behind them. 'What about something to eat?' he said. 'I'm going to have something. I'm starving.'

I eyed the doughnuts longingly, but there was no way I was going to eat one in front of him. 'Just coffee, please.'

'Sure?' I could almost believe he had seen the yearning in my eyes, because he leant suggestively towards me. 'You don't want a piece of that chocolate cake?' he said, rolling the words around his mouth suggestively. 'A scone with cream? One of those pastries? Go on—you know you want to!'

I gritted my teeth. 'No, thank you.'

'Well, you're a cheap date,' he said. 'I'm going to have one of those doughnuts.'

I had to press my lips firmly together to stop myself whimpering.

Ahead, Otto's ferocious wife, Lucia, was making coffee, shouting orders back to Otto, and working the till with her customary disregard for the service ethic. Lucia was famous for her rudeness and the customers were all terrified of her. I've seen senior executives reduced to grovelling if they didn't have the correct change. If the coffee and the cakes hadn't been so good, or if Lucia hadn't been so efficient, Otto's would have closed long ago. As it was, she and the café had become something of a local institution.

'Next!' she snarled as we made it to the top of the queue, and then she caught sight of me and smiled—a sight so rare that the executives now helping themselves to sugar stared in disbelief.

'Back again, *cara*?' she called, banging out old coffee grounds from the espresso machine. 'Your usual?'

'Yes, thanks, Lucia.' I smiled back at her, and then glanced at Phin, who was watching me with an oddly arrested expression. 'And...?' I prompted him.

'Americano for me,' he supplied quickly, before Lucia got impatient with him. 'No milk.'

'Why are you looking at me like that?' I asked Phin as I slid onto a shiny plastic banquette. Otto's wasn't big on style.

'I'm curious,' he said, transferring the cups to the table and pushing the tray aside.

'Curious?'

'Perhaps intrigued is a better word,' said Phin. 'You know, I've dodged guerrillas in South America, I've been charged at by a rhino and dangled by a rope over a thousand-foot crevasse, but I found Lucia pretty scary. She had every single person in that queue intimidated, but you she calls *cara*. What's that about?'

'Oh, nothing,' I said, making patterns in the cappuccino froth with my teaspoon. 'I wrote her a note once, that was all.'

'What sort of note?'

'I noticed that she wasn't here one day, mainly because the queue doesn't move nearly as fast when she's not around. I asked why not, and she told me she'd had to go back to Italy because her father had died. I wrote her a short note, just to say that I was sorry. It wasn't a big deal,' I muttered. I was rather embarrassed by the way Lucia had never forgotten it.

Phin looked at me thoughtfully. 'That was a kind thing to do.'

Feeling awkward, I sipped at my coffee. 'I didn't do much,' I said. 'Anyone can write a note.'

'But only you did.'

He picked up his doughnut and took a big bite while I watched enviously. My mouth was watering, and I was feeling quite light-headed with the lack of sugar.

'Want a bit?' he asked, offering the plate.

I flushed at the thought that he had noticed me staring. 'No...thank you,' I said primly.

'Sure? It's very good.'

I *knew* it was good. That was the trouble. 'I'm sure.'

'Suit yourself.' Phin shrugged, and finished the doughnut with unnecessary relish.

The more he enjoyed it, the crosser I got. What sort of boss was this, who dragged you out to coffee, tried to force-feed you doughnuts and then tortured you by eating them in front of you?

Scowling, I buried my face in my cappuccino.

'So, Summer Curtis,' he said, brushing sugar from his fingers at last. 'Tell me about yourself.'

It sounded like an interview question, so I sat up straighter and composed myself. 'Well, I've been working for Gibson & Grieve for five years now, the last three as assistant to the Chief Executive's PA—' I began, but Phin held up both hands.

'I don't need to know how many A levels you've got or where you've worked,' he said. 'I'm sure Lex wouldn't have appointed you if he didn't trust you absolutely. I'm more interested in finding out what makes you tick. If you're going to be my personal assistant I think we should get to know each other personally, and your work experience won't tell me anything I really need to know.'

'Like what?' I asked, disconcerted.

Phin sat back against the banquette and eyed me thoughtfully. 'Like your pet peeves, for instance. What really irritates you?'

'How long have you got?' I asked. 'Sniffing. Jiggling. Mess. Smiley faces made out of punctuation marks. Phrases like "Ah…bless…" or "I love her to bits, but…" Men who sit on the tube with their legs wide apart. Unpunctuality. Sloppy spelling and misuse of the apostrophe—that's a big one for me.' I paused, aware that I might have been getting a bit carried away. 'Do you want me to go on?'

'I think I might be getting the picture,' he said, his mouth twitching.

'I'm a bit of a perfectionist.'

'So I gathered.' I could tell he was trying not to laugh, and I was beginning to regret being so honest.

'You did ask,' I pointed out defensively.

'I did. Maybe I should have asked you what you *do* like.'

'I like my job.'

'Being a secretary?'

I nodded. 'Organisations like Gibson & Grieve don't work unless executives have proper administrative back-up. I like organising things, checking details, pulling everything together. I like making sure everything is in its right place. That's why I like filing. I find it satisfying.'

Phin didn't say anything. He just looked at me across the table.

'I'm sorry,' I said, putting up my chin. 'I do. Shoot me.'

He grinned at that. 'So...an unexpectedly kind, nitpicking perfectionist with an irrational prejudice against poor punctuation and a bizarre attachment to filing. I think we're getting somewhere. What else do I need to know about you?'

'Nothing.'

'Nothing? There must be more than that.'

I drank my coffee, unaccountably flustered. I was more thrown than I wanted to admit by the blueness of his eyes, by that lazy smile and the sheer vitality of his presence. There was a whole table between us, but I was finding it hard to breathe.

'I really don't know what you want me to tell

you,' I said. 'I'm twenty-six, I share a flat in south London with a friend, and my life is the exact opposite of yours.'

His eyes gleamed at that, and he leant forward. 'What do you mean?'

'Well, you come from a wealthy family whose stores are a household name,' I pointed out. 'You make television programmes doing the kind of things the rest of us would never dare to do, and when you're not skiing down a glacier or hacking through a jungle you're at all the A-list parties— usually with a beautiful girl on your arm. The closest *I* get to an A-list party is reading about one in *Glitz*, and I'd rather stick pins in my eyes than set foot in a rainforest. We don't have a single thing in common.'

'You can't say that,' Phin objected. 'You don't really know anything about me.'

'I feel as if I do,' I told him. 'My flatmate, Anne, is your biggest fan, and after listening to her talk about you for the past two years I could take a quiz on you myself.' I pushed my empty cup aside. 'Go on—ask me. Anything,' I offered largely, and even gave him an example. 'What's your latest girlfriend called?'

A smile was tugging at the corner of Phin's mouth. 'You tell me,' he said.

'Jewel,' I said triumphantly. 'Jewel Stevens.

She's an actress, and when you went to some awards ceremony last week she wore a red dress that had Anne weeping with envy.'

'But not you?'

'I think it would have looked classier in black,' I said, and Phin laughed.

'I'm impressed. Clearly I don't need to tell you anything about myself, as you know it all already. Although I think I should point out that Jewel *isn't*, in fact, my girlfriend. We've been out a couple of times, but that's all. There's no question of a real relationship, whatever the papers say.'

'I'll tell Anne. She'll be delighted,' I said. 'She's got a very active fantasy life in which you figure largely, in spite of the fact that she's very happy with her fiancé, Mark.'

'And what do you fantasise about, Summer?' asked Phin, his eyes on my face.

Ah, my fantasies. They were always the same. Jonathan realising that he had made a terrible mistake. Jonathan telling me he loved me. Jonathan asking me to marry him. We'd buy a house together. London prices being what they were, we might have to go out to the suburbs, and even pooling our resources we'd be lucky to get a semi-detached house, but that would be fine by me. I didn't need anywhere grand. I just wanted Jonathan, and somewhere I could stay.

I realise a suburban semi-detached isn't the stuff of most wild fantasies, but it was a dream that had kept me going ever since Jonathan had told me before Christmas that he 'needed some space'. He thought it was better that we didn't see each other outside the office any more. He knew how sensible I was, and was sure I would understand.

I sighed. What could I do but agree that, yes, I understood? But I lived for the brief glimpses I had of him now, and the hope that he might change his mind.

Phin was watching me expectantly, his brows raised, and I had an uneasy sense that those blue eyes could see a lot more than they ought to be able to. He was still waiting for me to answer his question.

Jonathan had been insistent that we keep our relationship a secret at the office, so I hadn't told anyone. I certainly wasn't going to start with Phin Gibson.

'I want a place of my own,' I said. 'It doesn't have to be very big—in fact I'll be lucky if I can afford a studio—but it has to be mine. It has to be somewhere I could live for ever.' I glanced at him. 'I suppose you think that's very boring?'

'It's not what I was expecting, and it's not a fantasy I understand, but it's not *boring*,' said Phin. 'I don't find much boring, to tell you the truth. People are endlessly interesting, don't you think? Obviously not!' he went straight on, seeing my sceptical expression.

'Well, *I* find them interesting. Why is it so important for you to have a home of your own?'

'Oh...I moved around a lot as a child. My mother has always been heavily into alternative lifestyles, and she's prone to sudden intense enthusiasms. One year we'd be in a commune, the next we were living on a houseboat. When my father was alive we had a couple of freezing years in a tumbledown smallholding in Wales.'

It was odd to find myself telling Phin Gibson, of all people, about my childhood. I didn't normally talk about it much—not that it had been particularly traumatic, but it was hard for most people I knew to understand what it was like growing up with a mother who was as charming and lovely and flaky as they come—and there was something about the way he was listening, his expression intent and his attention absolutely focused on me, that unlocked my usual reserve.

'Wales was the closest we ever got to settling down,' I told him. 'The rest of the time we kept moving. Not because we had to, but because my mother was always looking for something more.

'Basically,' I said, 'she's got the attention span of a gnat. I lost count of the schools I attended, of the weird and wonderful places we lived for a few months before moving on.'

I turned the cup and saucer between my fingers.

'I suppose it's inevitable I grew up craving security the way others crave excitement. My mother can't understand it, though. She's living in a tepee in Somerset at the moment, and for her the thought of buying a flat and settling down is incomprehensible. I'm a big disappointment to her,' I finished wryly.

'There you are—we've something in common after all,' said Phin, sitting back with a smile and stretching his long legs out under the table. 'I'm a big disappointment to my parents, too.'

CHAPTER TWO

I LOOKED at him in surprise. 'But you're famous,' I said. I'd known Lex wasn't impressed by his younger brother, but had assumed that his parents at least would be pleased by his success. 'You've had a successful television career.'

'My parents aren't impressed by television.' Phin smiled wryly. 'They think the media generally is shallow and frivolous—certainly compared to the serious business of running Gibson & Grieve. Lex and I were brought up to believe that the company was all that mattered, and that it was the only future we could ever have or ever want.'

'When did you change your mind?'

'When I realised that there wasn't really a place for me here. Lex is older than me, and anyway he had Chief Executive written all over him even as a toddler. Gibson & Grieve was all he ever cared about.'

It was my turn to study Phin. He was looking quite relaxed, leaning back against the banquette, but I sensed that this wasn't an easy topic of conversation for him.

'Didn't you ever want to be part of it, too?'

'As a very small boy I used to love going into the office,' he admitted. 'But as I got bigger I didn't fit. I was always being told to be quiet or sit still, and I didn't like doing either of those things. I wanted to skid over the shiny floors, or play football, or fiddle with the new computers. After a while I stopped going.'

Phin's smile was a little crooked. 'Of course it's easy now to see that I was just a spoilt brat looking for attention, but at the time it felt as if I were reacting against all their expectations. Lex was always there, doing what he should, and there never seemed any point in me doing the same. I got into as much trouble as I could instead,' he said. 'My parents were beside themselves. They didn't know what to do with me, and I didn't know what to do with myself. I don't think they ever thought I would get a degree, and I took off as soon as I'd graduated. I suspect that they were glad to be rid of me! I mean, what would they have done with me at Gibson & Grieve? I didn't fit with the image at all!'

No, he wouldn't have done, I thought. In spite of its commitment to style, Gibson & Grieve was at heart a very solid, traditional company—it was one of the reasons I liked it—and Phin would have been too chaotic, too vibrant, too energetic to ever properly fit in.

'So what did you do?' I asked, wondering how he was going to fit in now that he was back.

'I messed around for a few years,' he said. 'I worked my way around the world. I didn't care what I did as long as I was somewhere I could keep my adrenalin pumping—skiing, sailing, white-water rafting, climbing, sky-diving...I tried them all. I spent some time in the Amazon and learnt jungle survival skills, and then I got a job leading a charity expedition, and that led onto behind the scenes advice on a reality TV programme.'

He shrugged. 'It seems I came across well on camera, and the next thing I knew they'd offered me my own programme, taking ill-assorted groups into challenging situations.'

And I knew what had happened after that. It had taken no time at all for Phin Gibson to become a celebrity, almost as famous as Gibson & Grieve itself.

'And now you've joined the company,' I said.

'I have.' Phin was silent for a moment, looking down at his hands, which lay lightly clasped on the table, and then he looked up at me and the blueness of his eyes was so intense that I actually drew a sharp breath.

'Last year I took a group of young offenders on a gruelling trek through Peru,' he said.

I remembered the programme. I had watched it with Anne, and even I had had to admit that the change in those boys by the end of the trek was extraordinary.

'I recognised myself in them,' Phin said. 'It made me think about how difficult it must have been for my parents. I guess I'd grown up in spite of myself.'

His mouth quirked in a self-deprecating grin, then he sobered. 'My father had a stroke last year as well. That put a new perspective on everything. It seemed to me that it was time to try and make some amends. My mother has got it into her mind that all Dad wants is for me to settle down and take up my inheritance at Gibson & Grieve.'

He sighed a little. 'To be honest, it's a little hard to know exactly what Dad wants now, but he did manage to squeeze my hand when my mother told him what she had in mind. Basically, a certain amount of emotional blackmail is being applied! In lots of ways it's worse for Lex,' Phin went on thoughtfully. 'He stepped into my father's shoes as Chief Executive, and he's been doing a good job. Profits are up. Everyone's happy. The last thing he wants is me muddying the waters. In the end he suggested that we capitalise on my "celebrity", for want of better word, and make me the new face of Gibson & Grieve. You know we've just acquired Gregson's?'

He cocked an eyebrow at me and I nodded. The acquisition had made the headlines a few months ago when it happened.

'Supermarkets are a change of direction for us,' Phin went on. 'Our brand has always been upmarket, even exclusive, and we need more of a popular, family-friendly image now. Lex seems to think I can help with that, and I agreed to see how it went for a year initially, on condition that I could finish a couple of filming commitments.'

I smoothed my skirt over my knees. I was feeling a bit bad, if you want the truth. I'd dismissed Phin as a spoilt celebrity and assumed that he was choosing to dabble in the family business for a while. I hadn't realised that he was under some pressure.

'It makes sense for you to be Director of Media Relations,' I offered.

'I think we all know how little that means,' said Phin, leaning across the table, and I found myself leaning back as if pushed there by the sheer force of his personality. 'Lex's idea is to shunt me off and just wheel me out to be photographed every now and then. As far as he's concerned all the media relations will be done by his PR guy…what's his name? John?'

'Jonathan Pugh.'

Just saying his name was enough to bump my heart into my throat, and my tongue felt thick and unwieldy in my mouth. I wondered if Phin would notice how husky I sounded, but he didn't seem to.

'Yep, that's him,' was all he said, sitting back again. 'A born suit.'

I bridled at the dismissive note in his voice. I'd been quite liking Phin until then, but I was very sensitive to any criticism of Jonathan. At least Jonathan dressed professionally, unlike *some* people I could mention, I thought, eyeing Phin's T-shirt disapprovingly.

'Jonathan's very good at his job,' I said stiffly.

'Lex wouldn't employ him unless he was,' said Phin. 'But if he's that good there won't be much left for me to do, will there? I'm not going to spend a year opening stores and saving Lex the trouble of turning up at charity bashes.'

'Then why come back if you're not going to do anything?' I asked, still ruffled by his dismissal of Jonathan.

'But I am going to do something,' he said. 'Lex just doesn't know it yet. If I'm going to be part of Gibson & Grieve, I'm going to make a difference.'

Oh, dear. I had a nasty feeling this was the kind of thing Lex had meant when he had told me to stop Phin doing anything stupid.

'How?' I asked warily.

'By increasing our range of fair trade products.

Promoting links with communities here and overseas. Being more aware of environmental issues. Developing our staff and providing more training. Making *connections*,' said Phin. 'We're all part of chain. It doesn't matter if we're picking tea in Sri Lanka, stacking it on the shelves in Sheffield or buying it in Swindon. We should be celebrating the connections between people, not pretending that the only thing that matters is underlying operating profit or consensus forecasts.'

I was secretly impressed that Phin even knew about consensus forecasts, but I couldn't see any of this going down well with Lex.

I nibbled my thumb. It's a bad habit of mine when I'm unsure. 'And you haven't discussed any of this with your brother yet?'

'Not yet, no,' he said. 'I wanted to get to know you first.'

'Me?' I was taken aback. 'Why?'

'Because if I'm going to get anything done I need a team. I need to be sure that we can work together, and that we share the same goals.'

The blue, blue eyes fixed on me with that same unnerving intensity. 'You've been working for Lex, and I know his staff are all very loyal to him. I'm not trying to take over, but there's no use pretending he's going to share my ideas, and I don't want to put you in a difficult position. If you'd rather not work with me to change things, this is the time to say, Summer. I'm sure Lex would give you your old job back if you wanted it, and there'd be no hard feelings.'

I'll admit it. I hesitated. There was part of me that longed to go back to the Chief Executive's office—which buzzed with drive, where everyone was cool and efficient, and where there was no Phin Gibson with his unsettling presence and alarming ideas about change. I didn't like change. I'd had enough of change as a child. I wanted everything to stay the same.

But this was my big chance. When Anne got married I was going to have to move out of the flat. With my new salary I might be able to save enough to put down a deposit on a place of my own by then. It was only for a year, too, I reminded myself. When it was up, I'd be in a good position to get another job at the same level in spite of my age. It would be worth putting up with Phin until then.

So I met the blue eyes squarely. 'I don't want my old job back,' I said. 'I want to be part of your team.'

I was sorting through the post the next morning when Phin appeared. Late again. Hadn't he ever heard of a nine-to-five day at work?

He had spent no more than a couple of hours in

the office after we had got back from Otto's, before disappearing to a meeting with his producer.

'But I've read all my e-mails, you'll be glad to hear,' he said as he left. 'I take back everything I said about never being bored. All that corporate jargon puts me to sleep faster than a cup of cocoa. I'm never going to make it through a meeting if these guys actually talk like that.'

It would be nice to think he would ever be there to *go* to a meeting, I thought crossly.

It was after ten, and I had been in a dilemma about when to have the doughnut I'd bought earlier at Otto's. Having forgone my treat the day before, I was determined not to miss out again, but I wanted a few minutes to myself, so that I could enjoy it properly. I needed Phin to be in his office, so that I knew where he was.

Not knowing when he might appear had been making me twitchy, so when Phin strolled in and wished me a cheerful good morning I glared at him over the top of my glasses.

'Where have you been?' I demanded.

'You know,' Phin confided, 'that librarian thing you've got going really works for me.'

'What librarian thing?' I asked, thrown.

'The fierce glasses on the chain, the scraped back hair, the neat suit…' He grinned at my expression, which must have been dumbfounded. That's certainly how I felt. 'Please say you're about to shake out your hair and tell me you're going to have to be very strict with me for being late!'

I'd never met anyone like Phin before, and I was completely flummoxed. 'What on earth are you talking about?'

'Never mind,' he said. 'I was just getting a bit carried away there. What was it you wanted to know again?'

'I was wondering where you'd been,' I said tightly. 'It's after ten. I was expecting you here an hour ago at least.'

'I went into the Oxford Street store to see how things are going,' said Phin casually, picking up the post from my desk and leafing idly through it. 'I thought it would be an idea to meet the staff and hear what they think, and it was very useful.' He looked up at me, his eyes disconcertingly blue and amused. 'Why? Should I have asked permission?'

I pressed my lips together. 'It's not a question of permission,' I said. 'But there's no point in having a PA unless you let me know where you are. I need to be able to make appointments for you, and I can't do that if I've no idea when you're going to turn up.'

'Who wants an appointment?'

'Well, no one, as it happens,' I was forced to admit. 'But they might have done. It's a matter of principle.'

'Principle? That sounds serious.' Phin dropped

the post back onto the desk and without thinking I squared up the pile, looking up when he sucked in his breath alarmingly.

'What's the matter?' I asked, startled.

'I don't know…' He was squinting at the pile I'd tidied. 'I think those papers at the bottom might be half a millimetre out of alignment.'

'Sarcasm—excellent,' I said. Sarcastically. That was all I needed. 'Thank you so much.'

He held up his hands. 'It's nothing, honestly. Just one more service we offer.'

My lips tightened. I tried to pick up the conversation. 'Perhaps we should agree a system.'

'A system,' said Phin, testing the word as if he'd never heard it before. 'Fine. What sort of system?'

'If you let me have your mobile number, so that I can get hold of you if I need to, that would be a start. And then perhaps we could sit down and go through your diary.'

'Absolutely. Let's do it.' He clenched his fist and punched it in the air, to demonstrate an enthusiasm I was perfectly aware he didn't feel. 'Let's do it now, in fact.'

'Fine.'

We exchanged mobile numbers, and then I carried the diary into his office. I would put all the details on the computer later, but it was easier at this stage to use an old-fashioned hard copy.

I sat down with the diary on my knee, while Phin fished out a personal organiser and leaned back in his chair so that he could prop his feet on the desk.

'What do you want to know?'

'I'd better have everything.' I smoothed the page open, admiring in passing how nice my hands looked. I take care of my nails, and today they were painted a lovely pale pink called Dew at Dawn. 'If you're the face of Gibson & Grieve, you'll be expected to appear at various functions and I'll need to know when you're available.'

'Fair enough.'

He had an extraordinarily complicated social life, with two or three events an evening as far as I could make out. I couldn't help comparing it with my own, which largely consisted of painting my nails in front of the television, watching Anne getting ready to go out with Mark and feeling miserable about Jonathan.

'This is great,' said Phin when we'd finished. 'I never need to remember anything by myself ever again. Maybe I won't mind being an executive after all. What else is there to do?'

'There's a meeting to discuss the new media strategy at half past ten,' I said, handing him a folder. 'Your brother suggested you went along if you were here on time. I've noted all the salient points, and included copies of recent minutes so you know the background.'

'Salient points?' he echoed, amazed. 'I didn't realise people still said things like that any more!'

I chose to ignore that, and looked pointedly at my watch instead. 'You should get going. You've only got a couple of minutes and you don't want to be late.'

'You mean *you* don't want me to be late,' said Phin, but he swung his legs down from the desk.

I could hardly wait for him to go. I practically shoved him out of the door towards the lifts. Lex's office was on the floor above, and as soon as I saw him step into the lift I scurried down the corridor to the kitchen to make myself some coffee.

My office, and Phin's of course, was in a prime location on the corner of the building, with fabulous views of Trafalgar Square, but more importantly we were at the end of the corridor, which meant that nobody dropped in just because they were passing.

Even so, I closed the door as a precaution and prepared to enjoy my doughnut in private. I settled happily behind my desk with my coffee and cleared a space. Eating a doughnut could be a messy business. Perhaps that was why it always felt faintly naughty to me.

At last. I pulled out the doughnut and took a bite, mumbling with pleasure as my teeth sank into the sugary dough.

And then froze as the door opened and Phin came in. 'I forgot that file—' he began, and then it was his turn to stop as he took in the sight of me, sitting guiltily behind my desk, doughnut in hand and mouth full.

His eyes lit with amusement. 'Aha! Caught red-handed, I see.'

Blushing furiously, I dropped the doughnut and brushed at the sugar moustache I could feel on my top lip. 'I thought you'd gone,' I blustered, mortified at having been caught in such an unprofessional pose.

'Now I know why you were so keen to get rid of me,' said Phin. 'This is a new side to you. How very, very unlikely. Who would have thought that sensible Summer Curtis would have a doughnut addiction!' He leant conspiratorially towards me. 'Does anyone else know?'

'It's not an *addiction*,' I said, trying for some dignity. 'I just work better if I've had some sugar in the morning.'

'Well, I'm delighted to find that you've got a weakness. I was finding all that perfection just a little intimidating.' He grinned. 'It's good to know that when it comes down to it you can't resist temptation either.'

Of course, then I had to prove him wrong.

The next day, when I called in to buy my usual

cappuccino on my way into work, I refused the doughnut Lucia offered and felt virtuous. This would be the start of a new regime, I vowed. I didn't need a sugar fix, anyway. That was just silly. I would stick to coffee—a much less embarrassing habit and one that was less likely to lead to humiliation.

And I made it all the way to the lifts before I started to regret my resolution. Why shouldn't I have a mid-morning snack? It wasn't as if eating a doughnut was immoral or illegal. I blamed Phin for making me feel guilty about it. It was more satisfying than blaming myself.

Already I could already feel the craving twitching away in the pit of my stomach, making me tense. It didn't bode well for the rest of the day, and I hoped everyone would give me a wide berth. I wasn't known for my easygoing attitude on the best of days, and I had a feeling this most definitely wasn't going to be a good one.

At least Phin managed to turn up before ten o'clock, looking distinctly the worse for wear.

'I hope I get a gold star for turning up early,' he said.

I thinned my lips, still illogically determined to blame him for my doughnut-less day. 'I'd hardly call ten *early*,' I said repressively.

'It is for me.' Phin yawned. 'I had a very late night.'

I wondered how much his lack of sleep was due

to the beautiful Jewel Stevens. According to last night's *Metro*, the two of them were 'inseparable'. Not that I was scouring gossip columns for news of my new boss, you understand. In spite of taking a book to read on the tube every day, I somehow always ended up devouring the free paper on the way home. When it's pressed into your hand, it seems rude not to.

Phin's name just happened to catch my eye—honest. There had even been a picture of him at some party, with Jewel entwined around his arm. I know I'm in no position to talk about stupid names, but really…Jewel? I'd put money on the fact that she was christened Julie. In the picture Phin had a faintly wary look, but that might have been the flash. He certainly didn't look as if he were pushing her away.

Why would he? She was dark and sultry, with legs up to her armpits, a beestung mouth and masses of rippling black hair. Every man's fantasy, in fact.

I felt vaguely depressed at the thought, and then worried by the fact that I was depressed—until I realised it must just be the lack of sugar getting to me.

'No, really, though. I'll be fine,' said Phin, when I failed to offer the expected sympathy. 'There's no need to make a fuss.'

I sighed and narrowed my eyes at him.

'I can tell that deep down you're really worried,'

he said, and when I just looked back at him without expression he wisely took himself off into his office.

'I'll survive,' he promised, just before he shut the door. 'But if I don't, you're not to feel bad, OK?'

All was quiet for nearly an hour. I was betting that he had gone to catch up on his sleep on one of those sofas, but frankly I was glad to get rid of him for a while. I tried to soothe myself with a little filing, but a few days wasn't long enough to generate much of a backlog, and I couldn't stop thinking about how good a doughnut would taste with a cup of coffee.

Perhaps Phin was right. Perhaps I really was addicted, I fretted. I even considered sneaking out to Otto's, but couldn't take the chance of Phin waking up and finding me gone. I'd never hear the end of it.

The more I tried not to think about doughnuts, the more I wanted one, and it was almost a relief when Phin buzzed me. Yes, buzzed me—like a real executive! Maybe he would get the hang of corporate life after all.

'It's almost eleven,' came his voice through the intercom. 'Am I allowed to have coffee yet?'

'Of course,' I said, glad of the distraction from my doughnut craving, and relieved to be able to act as a normal PA for a change. 'I'll bring you some in.'

'Bring yourself some, too. We need to do some planning. You'll like that.'

Planning. That sounded more like it. I switched my phone through, wedged my notebook under my arm, and took in a pot of coffee and two cups on a tray.

I half expected to find Phin lying on one of the sofas, but he was sitting behind his desk, apparently immersed in something he was reading on the computer screen. He looked up when I pushed open the door with my elbow, though, and got to his feet.

'Let's make ourselves comfortable,' he said, guiding me over to the sofas and producing a familiar-looking paper bag from a drawer. 'I thought we'd have a little something with our coffee,' he said, waving it under my nose.

He'd brought two doughnuts.

It was all I could do not to drool. I've no idea what my expression was like, but judging by the laughter in the blue eyes it was a suitable picture.

'*Now* aren't you sorry you weren't more sympathetic?' he asked as he set the doughnuts out on a paper napkin each.

I eyed them longingly. 'I've just decided to give them up,' I said, but Phin only clicked his tongue.

'You can't do that just when I've found a weakness I can ruthlessly exploit,' he said. 'Besides, you told me yourself you needed a sugar fix in order to concentrate. You'll just get grumpy otherwise.'

Unfortunately that was all too true.

'Take it as an order, if that helps,' he said as I hesitated. 'Keeping me company on the doughnut front is compulsory. If I'd been able to appoint my own PA I'd have put it in the job description.'

What could I do? 'Well, if you insist…' I said, giving in.

I sat on one sofa, Phin sat on the other, and we bit into our doughnuts at the same time.

I can't tell you how good mine tasted. I laughed as I licked sugar from my fingers. 'Mmm…yum-yum,' I said, and then stopped as I saw Phin's arrested expression. 'What?'

'Nothing. I was just realising I hadn't heard you laugh yet,' he said. 'You should do it more often.

My eyes slid away from his. 'It's easy to laugh when you're being force-fed doughnuts,' I said after a tiny pause. I was very aware of him watching me, and I licked sugar from my lips with the tip of my tongue, suddenly uncomfortable as the silence stretched.

I cleared my throat. 'What exactly did you want to plan?' I said.

'Plan?' echoed Phin, sounding oddly distracted.

'You said we needed to do some planning,' I reminded him.

'Oh, yes…' He seemed to recover himself. 'Well, I had a chat about my role here with Lex last night, and we discussed things in a civilised manner.'

'Really?'

'No, not really. We had a knock-down-drag-out fight, and shouted at each other for a good hour. It didn't quite come to fisticuffs, but it was touch and go at one point. Just like being boys again,' he said reflectively.

I couldn't imagine anyone daring to shout at Lex, but then Phin was a self-confessed adrenalin junkie and obviously thrived on danger.

'What happened?' I asked a little nervously. I hoped Phin hadn't enraged his brother so much that we would be both be out of a job.

'I'd like to claim utter victory, but I'd be lying,' Phin admitted. 'Lex wasn't budging when it came to renegotiating our suppliers, but he did agree eventually that I could start to build up links with communities overseas. In return I had to promise to co-operate fully on the PR front. Apparently he's lined up a feature in *Glitz* already.'

Phin shrugged as he finished his doughnut and brushed the sugar from his hands. 'So, not everything I wanted, I'll admit, but it's a start.'

'Well...good,' I said, feeling a little uncertain. 'What happens next?'

'We'd better keep Lex quiet about the PR,' he decided. 'Make arrangements for that interview, and talk to Jonathan Pugh about what they want.'

Talk to Jonathan! *Talk to Jonathan*. My stomach

clenched with excitement. I had a reason to go and talk to Jonathan! My handwriting was ridiculously shaky as I made a note, although there was no chance of me forgetting that particular task.

Phin was talking about a trip to Cameroon he was planning but I hardly listened. I was too busy imagining my meeting with Jonathan.

This would be my first chance to talk to him properly since that awful evening when he had told me it 'wasn't working' for him. I had seen him around the office, of course, but never alone, and I was sure that he was avoiding me. I'd been holding onto the hope that if we could just spend some time together again he would change his mind.

I would play it cool, of course, I decided. Surely he knew that I was the last person to make a fuss? I would be calm and reasonable and undemanding. What more could he want? *I've missed you, Summer,* I imagined him saying as the scales dropped from his eyes and he realised that I was just what he needed after all. *You've no idea how much.*

But if he had missed me, why hadn't he told me? I puzzled over that one. OK, maybe he had just been waiting for the right moment. Or he'd thought I was busy.

It even sounded lame in my fantasy, which wasn't a good sign.

I suddenly realised that Phin had stopped talking

and was looking at me enquiringly. 'So what do you think?' he asked.

'Um...sounds good to me,' I said hastily, without a clue as to what he'd been talking about. 'Great idea.'

His brows lifted in surprise. 'Well, that's good. To be honest, I didn't think you'd go for it.'

'Oh?' I regarded him warily. That sounded ominous. 'Er...what exactly didn't you think I'd like?'

'Staff development in Cameroon,' he prompted, but his eyes had started to dance.

'What?'

Phin tried to look severe, but a smile tugged at the corner of his mouth. 'Summer, is it possible you weren't listening to a word I was saying?'

I squirmed. 'I may have got distracted there for a moment or two,' I admitted feebly.

He tutted. 'That's not like you, Summer. After I gave you sugar, too! I've just explained about my plan to take a group from Head Office to Cameroon for a couple of weeks, to help build a medical centre in one of the villages I know there. It's a great way to start forging links between the company and a community, and everyone who goes will get so much out of it. But you don't need to worry about it yet. You'll have plenty of time to prepare.'

'Hold on,' I said, alarmed by the way this was going. 'Me? Prepare for what?'

'Of course you'll be coming, too,' said Phin, with what I was sure was malicious pleasure in my consternation. 'We're a team, remember? This is our scheme. It's important that you're really part of it. What better way than to go as part of the first group, to find out what it's like out there?'

CHAPTER THREE

'YOU'RE not serious?'

'I'm always serious, Summer,' said Phin. His face was perfectly straight, but I've never seen anything less serious than the expression in the blue eyes right then.

I stared at him, aghast. 'No way am I going to Africa!'

'Why on earth not?'

'I don't like bugs.'

'There's more to the rainforest than bugs, Summer.'

'The rainforest?' My eyes started from my head. How much had I missed here? 'Oh, no. No, no, no. The jungle? No way. Absolutely not.'

'You'd like it.'

'I wouldn't,' I said, still shaking my head firmly from side to side. I'd seen him leading those poor people through enough rainforests on *Into the Wild* to know just what it would be like. They spent their whole time struggling through rampant vegetation, or slithering down muddy slopes in stifling humidity, so that their hair was plastered to their heads and their shirts wringing with sweat.

There was almost always a shot of Phin taking off his shirt and rinsing it in the water. Anne's favourite bit, in fact. Whenever they reached a river she'd sit up straighter and call out, 'Shirt alert!' and sigh gustily at the glimpse of Phin's lean, muscled body.

I didn't sigh, of course, but I did look, and even I had to admit—although not to Anne, of course—that it was a body worth sighing over if you were into that kind of thing.

But I certainly wasn't prepared to trek through the rainforest myself to see it at first hand.

'It sounds awful,' I told Phin. 'Hot and sweaty and crawling with insects…ugh.'

He leant forward, fixing me with that unnerving blue gaze. 'You say hot and sweaty, Summer,' he said, rocking his hand in an either/or gesture. 'I say heat and passion and excitement.'

Heat. Passion. Excitement. They were so not me. But something about the words in Phin's mouth made me shift uneasily on the sofa. 'And what on earth makes you think I would like that?' I asked, with what I hoped was a quelling look.

'Your mouth.'

It was a bit like missing a step. I had the same

lurch of the heart, punching the air from my lungs, the same hollowness in the stomach. My eyes were riveted to Phin's, and all at once their blueness was so intense that I felt quite dizzy with the effort of not tumbling into it.

'It just doesn't go with the rest of you,' he went on conversationally, while I was still opening and closing the mouth in question. 'You're all cool and crisp and buttoned up in your suit. But that mouth…' He put his head on one side and studied it. 'It makes me think there's more to you than that. It makes me think that you might have a secretly sensual side… Am I right?'

'Certainly not,' I blustered, unable to think of a suitably crushing reply. 'I can assure you that there isn't a single bit of me that wants to go to the rainforest.'

Phin clicked his tongue and shook his head sadly. 'Summer, Summer…I never thought you'd be a coward. Isn't it time you stepped out of your comfort zone and explored a different side of yourself?'

'I'm not into exploration,' I said coldly. 'That's the thing about comfort zones. They're comfortable. I've got no intention of making myself *un*comfortable if I don't have to.'

'But I'm afraid you *do* have to,' said Phin. 'You're on my team, and my team is going to

Cameroon, whether you want to or not. So you'd better get used to the idea.'

I looked mutinously back at him. He was smiling, but there was an inflexibility to his jaw, a certain flintiness at the back of the blue eyes, that gave me pause and, like the coward Phin called me, I opted out of an argument just then.

I was sent off to liaise with Human Resources and find candidates for the first staff development trip. Phin said that he would organise everything at the Cameroonian end, but it would be my job to sort out flights, insurance, and all the other practicalities involved in taking a group of people overseas.

I didn't mind doing that as long as I didn't have to go myself. Still, he could hardly force me onto the plane, could he? I would be able to get out of it somehow, I reassured myself, and in the meantime I was much more excited about organising the *Glitz* interview. This was the chance I had dreamed about. At last I had a real reason to be in touch with Jonathan again.

Putting Africa out of my mind, I sat down to compose an e-mail to him. My heart was beating wildly at the mere thought of seeing him again, and I didn't trust my voice on the phone.

All I had to do was suggest that we meet the next day to discuss the *Glitz* feature, but you wouldn't believe how long it took me to produce a couple of lines that struck just the right balance between friendliness and cool professionalism.

I knew Jonathan would want to get involved. *Glitz* was stacked at every supermarket checkout in the land, and a positive piece about Phin taking up a new role at Gibson & Grieve would be fantastic publicity for us. Jonathan wouldn't let a PR opportunity like this go past without making sure Phin's office—i.e. me—was onboard.

Sure enough, he came back straight away.

Good idea. 12.30 tomorrow my office? J

Not a long message, but I read it as carefully as the floweriest of love letters, desperate to decipher the subtext.

Good idea… That was encouraging, wasn't it? I mean, he could have just said *OK*, couldn't he? Or *fine*. So I chose to see some warmth there. Also, he'd signed it with an initial. That was an intimate kind of thing to do. Not as good as if he'd added a kiss, of course, but still better than a more formal *Jonathan*.

But the bit that really got my heart thumping with anticipation was the time. Twelve-thirty. Was it just the only time he could fit me in, or had he chosen it deliberately so that he could suggest lunch?

Naturally I spent the entire afternoon composing a suitable reply. The resulting masterpiece ran as follows: 12.30 tomorrow fine for me. See you then. S. And, yes, my finger did hover over the *x* key for a while before I decided on discretion. I didn't want to appear too pushy. Jonathan would hate that.

I discarded the idea of suggesting lunch myself for the same reason. But just in case Jonathan *was* thinking that we could discuss a PR strategy for Phin over an intimate lunch somewhere, I was determined to be prepared. Normally I'm very confident about putting outfits together, but I spent hours that night, dithering in front of my wardrobe, unable to decide what to wear the next day.

'What do you think?' I asked Anne.

I had dragged her away from yet another repeat of *Into the Wild*—wasn't there anything else on television?—so she wasn't best pleased. She sprawled grouchily on the bed.

'What I *think* is that you're wasting your time,' she said frankly. 'Face it, Summer, Jonathan's just not that into you. He's already made that crystal-clear.'

'He might change his mind,' I said, and even I could hear the edge of desperation in my voice.

'He won't,' said Anne, who had never liked Jonathan. 'Why can't you see it?' She sighed at my stubborn expression. 'For someone so clear-thinking, you're incredibly obtuse when it comes to Jonathan,' she told me. 'It's not like he ever made any effort for you, even when you were seeing each other. Why was he so keen to keep your affair a secret? It wasn't like either of you were involved with anyone else.'

'Jonathan didn't think it was appropriate to have a relationship in the office,' I said primly.

'You weren't *having* a relationship,' said Anne, exasperated. 'That was the whole point. You weren't even having much of an affair. You were just sleeping together when it suited Jonathan. If he'd been really keen on you he wouldn't have cared who knew. If he'd loved you he would have wanted to show you off, not hide you away as if he was ashamed of you.'

'Jonathan's not the kind of person who shows off,' I said, aware that I sounded defensive. 'I like that about him. He's sensible.'

'I think you're mad!' she said, throwing up her hands. 'I can't believe you spend every day with a hot guy like Phin Gibson and you're still obsessing about Jonathan Pugh!'

'Phin's not that hot,' I said, dismissing Anne's objections as I always did. 'And anyway, he's my boss. And we all know his idea of commitment is making it through to dessert without feeling trapped. I'm certainly not going to waste my time falling for him. That really would be mad! Now, concentrate, Anne. This is important. The twinset or the jacket?'

I held them on hangers in each hand. The cropped jacket was one of my favourites, a deep red with three-quarter-length sleeves, a shawl collar and a nipped-in waist. 'Too smart?' I asked dubiously. 'I don't want to look as if I'm trying too hard. But maybe the cardigan is a bit casual for the office?'

I'd bought the twinset with my Christmas bonus. A mixture of angora and cashmere, it was so beautifully soft I hadn't been able to resist it. I liked to take it out and stroke it, as if it were a kitten. To be honest, I wasn't sure that the colour—a dusty pink—was quite *me*, and I never felt entirely comfortable with the prettiness of it all, so I'd never worn it to the office. It was very different from my usual smartly tailored look, but perhaps different was what I needed.

Anne agreed. 'The twinset,' she said without hesitation. 'It's a much softer look for you, and if you leave your hair loose as well it'll practically scream *touch me, touch me*. Even Jonathan won't be able to miss the point.'

The hair was a step too far for me. If I turned up at work with my hair falling to my shoulders *everyone* would get the point. I might as well hang out a sign saying 'On the Pull'. So I tied my hair back as usual, but made up with extra care and painted my nails a pretty pink: Bubblegum—

much nicer than it sounds. I wore the twinset, with a short grey skirt and heels just a little higher than usual.

Phin whistled when he came in—late, as usual—and saw me. 'You look very fetching, Summer,' he said. 'What's the occasion?'

'No occasion,' I said. 'I just felt like a change of image.'

'It's certainly that,' he said. 'You look very... touchable. How many people have stroked you to see if that cardigan is as soft as it looks?'

'A lot,' I said with a sigh. I'd lost count of the women who'd stroked my arm and ooh-ed and aah-ed over its softness. I couldn't blame them, really. Wearing it was like being cuddled by a kitten. 'It's a bit disconcerting to have perfect strangers running their hands down your arm.'

'But you can understand why they do,' said Phin. 'In fact, I'm sorry, but I'm just going to have to do it myself. I don't count as a perfect stranger, do I?' Without waiting for my reply, he smoothed his own hand down from my shoulder to my elbow, and I felt it through the fine wool like a brand. 'Incredibly soft,' he said, 'and very unexpected.'

Funny—I'd never felt anyone else's stroke quite like that. My skin was tingling where his fingers had touched me. I swallowed.

'I think I'll go back to a suit tomorrow.'

'That would be a shame,' said Phin. 'I like this new look a lot.'

Now all I needed was for Jonathan to like it, too. If the cardigan had the same effect on him, it would be worth feeling self-conscious now.

For the first time I realised that Phin didn't look quite his normal self either that morning. There was a distinctly frazzled air about him, and his shirt was even more crumpled than usual. Probably partying all night again with Jewel, I thought unsympathetically.

I was sure of it when he suggested having coffee immediately. 'In keeping with today's theme, I've bought Danish pastries for a change,' he said. 'I'm badly in need of some sugar!'

'Hangover?' I asked sweetly.

'Just a very fraught morning,' said Phin with a humorous look. 'I never thought I'd be glad to say I had to go to the office!'

He didn't say any more, and I didn't ask. I was too busy checking the clock every couple of minutes and willing the hands to move faster.

I decided that if Jonathan didn't suggest lunch, I would. I would make it very casual. *Do you want to grab a sandwich while we're talking?* Something like that.

I mouthed the words as my fingers rattled over the keyboard. The trouble was that I didn't do casual very well. Look how astounded everyone was when I appeared in a cardigan.

I knew the words would come out sounding stiff and awkward if I didn't get it right, but how was I supposed to practise when Phin was in and out of my office every five minutes, asking how to send a fax from his computer, wanting to borrow my stapler, giving me the dates for the Cameroon trip—about which I was still trying to keep a *very* low profile.

'You know, you could just buzz me and I'd come in to you,' I said, exasperated, in the end.

'I'd rather come out,' said Phin, picking up a couple of spare ink cartridges from my desk and attempting to juggle them. 'I feel trapped if I have to sit down for too long.'

I detoured back from the photocopier to snatch the cartridges out of the air. I put them in a desk drawer and shut it firmly as I sat down.

'Why don't you go for a walk?' I suggested through clenched teeth.

'It's funny you should say that. My producer just e-mailed me to say that we're going back to finish filming in Peru next week, so I'll be doing the last part of the trek again. I'll be away about twelve days.' Now he had my stapler in his hand, and was holding it out to me like a microphone. 'Do you think you'll miss me?'

'Frankly, no,' I said, taking the stapler from him and setting it back on the desk with a click. I glanced at the clock. Just past midday! I didn't have long. 'Are you going out for lunch?' I asked hopefully.

'I haven't got any plans,' said Phin. 'I might just—'

That was when my mother rang. As if I didn't have enough to cope with that morning!

'I just *had* to tell you,' she said excitedly. 'A new galactic portal is opening today!'

I love my mother, but sometimes I do wonder how we can possibly be related. I'd suspect a mix-up in the hospital if I hadn't been born into a commune, with who knows how many people dancing and chanting and shaking bells around my mother. It must have been the most godawful racket, and if had been me I would have told them all to go away and leave me to give birth in peace. But of course Mum—or Starlight, as she prefers to be called nowadays—was in her element. The wackier the situation, the more she loves it.

I pinched the bridge of my nose between thumb and forefinger. I knew better than to ask what a galactic portal was.

'That's great, Mum,' I said. 'Look, I can't really talk now—'

But she was already telling me about some ceremony she had taken part in the night before, that apparently involved much channelling of angels and merging of heart chakras.

'Such a beautiful spiritual experience!' she sighed. 'So empowering! The energy vibrations now are quite extraordinary. Can't you *feel* them?'

I resisted the urge to bang my head against my desk.

'Er, no—no, I can't just this moment,' I said, aware that Phin was eavesdropping. I couldn't imagine him caring about the fact that this was obviously a personal phone call, but I hoped he couldn't hear anyway. My mother was deadly serious but, let's face it, she could sound nuts.

'That's because you're not open to the energy, darling,' my mother told me reproachfully. 'Have you been entering the crystal the way I showed you? You must let the love flow through your chakras.'

'Yes, yes, I will,' I said, one eye on the clock. After dragging all morning, it was suddenly whizzing round. If I wasn't careful, I'd be late for Jonathan. 'The thing is, Mum, I'm actually quite busy right now. Can I call you later?'

I'd finally managed to give her a mobile phone, which I paid for by direct debit. I knew she would never keep it topped up herself. My mother preferred spiritual forms of communication to the humdrum practicalities of paying phone bills or keeping track of credit.

'That would be lovely, darling, but I'll be seeing you soon,' she said. 'I'm coming to London, so we can talk properly then.'

Another time I would have been alarmed at her casual mention of a London visit, but I was desperate to get her off the phone before my meeting with Jonathan.

'That's great,' I said instead. 'Bye, then, Mum.'

I caught Phin's eye as I put the phone down. 'That was my mother,' I said unnecessarily.

'Is everything OK?'

'Oh, yes, fine,' I said airily. 'A new galactic portal is opening. You know how it is.'

'Blimey.' Phin sounded impressed. 'Is that good or bad?'

'I've no idea. Whatever it is, it seems to be keeping my mother busy.' I glanced at the clock again. Twelve-fourteen. I should think about getting ready.

I gathered my papers into a file and stood up. Only sixteen minutes and I'd be alone with Jonathan for the first time in weeks. I couldn't wait.

Edging round the desk, I opened my mouth to tell Phin that I was going to a meeting, but before I could make my escape I saw consternation on his face as he looked over my shoulder. I turned to see Jewel Stevens framed in the doorway.

To say that she came in wouldn't do her justice.

You could tell that she was an actress. I felt that there should have been a fanfare—or possibly the theme tune from *Jaws*—as she waited until all eyes were on her before making her entrance.

'Hi, baby,' she cooed, her sultry brown eyes on Phin. I was fairly sure that she hadn't registered my existence.

'Jewel!' The appalled expression I had glimpsed had vanished, and he was once more Mr Charm. 'What are you doing here?'

She pouted at him, sweeping a glance up from under impossibly long lashes. 'I just wanted to make sure you weren't too cross with me after this morning.'

'No, no,' said Phin easily. 'I never liked that dinner service anyway.'

Jewel laughed, delighted at her own power, and then her voice dropped seductively. 'I came to make it up to you. To see if you missed me after last night.'

You had to hand it to her. Completely ignoring my presence, she wound her arms around his neck and kissed him on the mouth. And I don't mean a casual peck. I mean a full-on passionate kiss with tongues—well, I assume with tongues. It certainly looked that kind of kiss.

Anyway, by the time she had finished she was plastered all over him and twirling her tongue in his ear. Yuck. I can't bear anyone touching my ears—I'm funny like that—and it made me queasy just looking at her. Just as well I hadn't had my lunch yet.

I averted my gaze. No wonder Phin was looking tired this morning!

'What say we go back to my place?' Jewel was saying huskily. 'We can spend the afternoon together. Just wait until you see what I've got for you, tiger,' she whispered suggestively in his ear, and then—and I swear I'm not making this up—she growled.

Oh, please. I rolled my eyes mentally, only to catch Phin's gaze over her shoulder. He grimaced at me and mouthed an unmistakable *Help!*

I was half tempted to leave him to it, but there was such naked appeal in his eyes that I relented. 'You haven't forgotten your twelve-thirty meeting, have you?' I asked clearly.

'God, yes, I have!' Phin sent me a grateful look as he disentangled himself from her—which took some doing, I can tell you. Managing to free a hand, he slapped his head. 'I'm sorry, Jewel. I can't.'

Jewel's beautiful face darkened. 'Do you have to go? Meetings aren't important. What's it about?'

Another agonised look at me. 'You need to discuss PR strategy,' I supplied obediently.

'Yes, that's right. PR. So I'm afraid it *is* important.' Phin spread his hands disarmingly.

'Then I'll wait for you in your office.' She was twining herself around him again. Honestly, the woman was like an octopus. Phin would just manage to prise one of her hands away and the other would already be sliding round him.

'I think you'd get very bored, Jewel,' he said. 'It's likely to be a long meeting. We're going out to lunch. In fact, we'd better go—hadn't we, Summer?'

I looked at the clock. 'Definitely,' I said, picking up the file. I didn't care what he did with Jewel, but I was meeting Jonathan at twelve-thirty if it killed me.

Jewel's beautiful sullen mouth was turned down. 'When will you be finished?'

'I'm not entirely sure,' said Phin, steering her towards the door. 'I'll give you a ring, OK?'

Still pouting, Jewel insisted on another kiss before she would let him go. 'See you later then, tiger.' She smirked, and sashayed off towards the lifts.

There was silence in the office. I looked at Phin. 'Tiger?'

He had the grace to squirm. 'Believe me, Jewel's the tiger. I'm the baby antelope here.'

'I'm sure you fought madly.'

'If I'd known what I was getting into I would have done,' he said frankly. 'I mean, she's gorgeous, and I've got to admit I was flattered when she made a beeline for me, but she gives a whole new meaning to high-maintenance. Talk about a prima donna! I must have withdrawn my attention for about ten seconds this morning, while I made myself some toast, and my eardrums are still ringing! She was throwing plates at the walls—it was like Greek night down at the local kebab shop. I'm buying plastic ones next time. I never thought I'd say it, but it was a real relief to come into the office and find you as cool and calm as ever.'

I certainly hadn't been feeling cool and calm, I thought, but could only be glad my fluttery nerves hadn't shown.

'Anyway, I owe you one,' he said. 'If you hadn't rescued me I'd have been dragged back to her lair and spat out later, an empty husk of a man.'

'Call it quits for the doughnuts,' I said. I looked at my watch and my heart gave a lurch. Twelve twenty-five. 'I'd better go.'

Phin peered round the doorway to check if Jewel was still waiting for the lift. Apparently she was, because he withdrew his head hastily. 'I might as well come, too,' he said.

I looked at him in dismay. I didn't want him muscling in on my *tête-à-tête* with Jonathan! 'I don't think you'll find it very interesting,' I tried, but Phin was already hustling me down the corridor away from the lifts.

'We'll take the stairs,' he muttered. 'Isn't your

meeting about PR, anyway?' he went on once safely out of Jewel's sight. 'I should know what's going on.'

'I'll fill you in on the details afterwards,' I tried.

'No, I'd better come. I wouldn't put it past Jewel to come back and surprise me,' said Phin, with an exaggerated grimace of fear. 'And where would I be without you to rescue me?'

If I resisted any more, Phin would start wondering why I was so keen to be on my own with Jonathan, and that was the last thing I wanted. I could hardly refuse to take my own boss to a meeting, after all, but I was rigid with disappointment as we made our way up to Jonathan's office on the floor above.

Not that Phin seemed to notice. He was in high good humour, having escaped Jewel's clutches, and he breezed into Jonathan's office and completely took over the meeting. I had no need to bring out my line about grabbing a sandwich.

'Let's talk over lunch,' said Phin, and bore us off to a wine bar tucked away in a side street between Covent Garden and the Strand.

So much for my date with Jonathan. I walked glumly beside Phin, listening to him setting out to charm Jonathan, who was obviously delighted at Phin's unexpected appearance. I was feeling pretty miserable, if you want the truth. I couldn't fool myself that there had been even a flash of disappointment from Jonathan because he wouldn't be meeting me alone.

Still, I found myself grabbing onto pathetic crumbs of comfort—like the way he arranged for me to sit next to him at the table. Later, of course, I realised it was so that he could sit face to face with Phin, on the other side, but at the time it was all I had to hang on to.

Not that it did me much good. I wanted to concentrate on Jonathan, but somehow I couldn't with Phin sitting across the table exuding such vitality that even after what had obviously been a heavy night with Jewel everyone else seemed to fade in comparison to him. Whenever I tried to slide a glance at Jonathan my eyes would snag instead on Phin's smile, or Phin's solid forearms, or his hands that fiddled maddeningly with the cutlery as he talked and gesticulated.

The two men couldn't have been more of a contrast. Jonathan was in a beautifully cut grey suit, which he wore with a blue shirt and dotted silk tie. Anne would have looked at him and said conventional and boring, but to me he was mature and professional. Unlike Phin, whose hair could have done with a cut and who was wearing a casual shirt and chinos in neutral colours and yet still managed to look six times as colourful as anyone else in the room.

'*Glitz* are planning a major spread,' Jonathan was

explaining to Phin. 'It's a great opportunity for us to promote a more accessible image. Market research shows that Gibson & Grieve are still seen as elitist, so for the new stores we need to present ourselves as ordinary and family-friendly. Your image as a celebrity will be very valuable to us, but up to now you've been associated with the wild. What we want is to associate you with the home, and we'd like *Glitz* to interview you at your house, so that their readers get an idea of you in a domestic setting.'

Jonathan paused delicately. 'If you have a girlfriend, it would be very good to get her involved as well—perhaps even give the impression that you're thinking of settling down. I did hear that you're going out with Jewel Stevens…?' He trailed off, more than a touch of envy in his tone.

Phin's eyes met mine. 'I'm not involving Jewel,' he said with a grin. 'It might give her all the wrong ideas—and besides, I wouldn't have any crockery left by the time *Glitz* turned up. I'm reduced to eating off paper plates as it is!'

'She sounds very feisty,' said Jonathan. I don't know if he was aiming for a man-about-town air or humour, but either way it didn't quite work.

I glanced at Phin and away again.

'Feisty is one way of putting it,' he said. 'Sorry, Jonathan, but I'm going to have to do this as single guy.'

Jonathan looked disappointed. I got the feeling that he would have liked to have talked more about Jewel. 'Well, perhaps you could give the impression that you're thinking of settling down without mentioning any names,' he suggested.

'I'll do my best.'

'What about your house? Do we need to redecorate for you?'

'Redecorate? I thought the article was supposed to be showing me as I am at home?'

'No, it's to show you at the kind of home we want readers to associate with Gibson & Grieve,' Jonathan corrected him. He turned to me. 'Summer, you'd better check it out. You'll know what needs to be done.'

'She'll just tidy me up,' Phin protested.

'Summer's very competent,' said Jonathan.

Competent. You know, when you dream of what the man of your dreams will say about you, you think about words like *beautiful, amazing, sexy, passionate, incredible.* You never long for him to tell you're competent, do you?

'No redecorating,' said Phin firmly. 'If you make it all stylish it'll look and seem false, and that would do our image more harm than good. Summer can come and keep me on the straight and narrow in the interview, but I'm not changing the house. If you want readers to see what my home is like, we can show them. It's not as if I live in squalor.'

My only hope was that Phin might leave us after lunch, but, no, he insisted on walking back with us. So I never had one moment alone with Jonathan. I had to say goodbye to him in the lift as Phin and I got out on the floor below.

And that was my big date that I'd looked forward to so much. A complete waste of make-up. Jonathan hadn't even commented on my cardigan.

Phin looked nervously around the office when we got back. 'She's gone—phew!' He wiped his brow in mock relief. 'Thanks again for earlier, Summer. It's good to know you can lie when you need to! If Jewel comes in again, I'm not here, OK?'

I was too cross about Jonathan to be tactful. I was even beginning to feel some sympathy for Jewel. At least she had the gumption to go for what she wanted. Jonathan evidently found her feistiness appealing. Perhaps I should have tried smashing a few plates.

'If you don't want to see her again, you should tell her yourself…tiger,' I said sharply, and Phin winced.

'I'll try,' he said. 'But Jewel isn't someone who listens to what she doesn't want to hear. Still, I'm going away in a few days,' he remembered cheerfully. 'She'll soon lose interest if I'm not around.'

CHAPTER FOUR

HE LEFT for Peru a week later. 'How long will you be away?' I asked him.

'We should be able to wrap it up in twelve days.' Phin looked up from the computer screen with a grin. 'Why? Do you think you'll miss me after all?'

'No,' I said crushingly. 'I just need to know when to arrange a date with *Glitz*.'

But the funny thing was that I *did* miss him a bit. I realised I'd got used to him being in the office, managing to seem both lazy and energetic at the same time, and without him everything seemed strangely flat.

I told myself that I enjoyed the peace and quiet, and that it was a relief to be able to get on with some work without being teased or constantly interrupted by frivolous questions or made to stop and eat doughnuts—OK, I didn't mind that bit *so* much. I had a whole week without Phin juggling with my stapler and my sticky note dispenser, or messing around with the layout of my desk, which I know quite well he only did to annoy.

He was always picking things up and then putting them down in the wrong place, or at an odd angle, and he seemed to derive endless amusement from watching me straighten them. Sometimes I'd try and ignore it, but it was like trying to ignore an itch. After a while my hand would creep out to rearrange whatever it was he had dislodged, at which point Phin would shout, 'Aha! I knew you couldn't do it!'

I mean, what kind of boss carries on like that? It was deeply unprofessional, as I was always pointing out, but that only made Phin laugh harder.

So all in all I was looking forward to having the office to myself for a few days, but the moment he'd gone I didn't quite know what to do with myself.

That first morning on my own I went down to the kitchen to make myself some coffee. I'd got out of the habit of buying myself a doughnut, I realised. Phin always bought them now, and I'd forgotten that I wouldn't have anything to have with my coffee. It wouldn't kill me, but the lack of sugar just added to my grouchiness as I carried my mug back to my desk.

Khalid from the postroom was just on his way out of my office. 'I've left the mail on your desk,' he told me. 'You've got a Special Delivery, too.'

I'd ordered a scanner the day before. The

supplies department must have moved quickly for once, I thought, but as I set down my mug I saw a small confectionery box sitting in front of my keyboard. 'Summer Curtis, Monday' was scribbled on the top. Not a scanner, then.

Puzzled, I opened it up. Inside, sitting on a paper napkin, was a doughnut.

There was a business card, too. I pulled it out. It had Phin's name and contact details on one side. On the other he had scrawled, 'I didn't want to think of you without your sugar fix. P x'

My throat felt ridiculously tight. Nobody had ever done anything as thoughtful for me before.

Of course it didn't mean anything, I was quick to remind myself. It was just part of Phin's pathological need to make everyone like him. His charm was relentless.

But still I found myself—annoyingly—thinking about him, about where he was and what he was doing, and when I picked up the phone and heard his voice my heart gave the most ridiculous lurch.

'Just thought I'd check in,' said Phin. 'I hardly know what to do with myself. I'm so used to you telling me what to do and where to be all day. I've got used to being organised. Are you missing me yet?'

'No,' I lied, because I knew he'd be disappointed

if I didn't. 'But thank you for the doughnut. How on earth did you organise it?'

'Oh, that was easy. I had a word with Lucia—who, by the way, smiled at me the other day, so you're not the only favourite now—and I asked her to send you a selection, so that you get something different every day I'm away. I think we're in a doughnut rut.'

'I like my rut,' I said, but I might as well have spared my breath. Phin was determined that I would try something different.

Sure enough, the next day an apricot Danish arrived at half past ten, and even though I was determined not to like it as much as a doughnut, I had to admit that it was delicious.

The next day brought an almond croissant, and the one after that an apple strudel, and then an éclair. Pastries I'd never seen before appeared on my desk, and I found myself starting to glance at the clock after ten and wondering what I'd have with my coffee that day. I'd try and guess what would be in the box—vanilla turnover? *Pain au chocolat?*—but I never got it right.

Inevitably word got round about my special deliveries. I wasn't the only one who was guessing. I heard afterwards they were even taking bets on it in Finance.

'I wish my boss would send me pastries,' my

friend Helen grumbled. 'You'd think in Food Technology it would be a perk of the job. You are lucky. Phin's so lovely, isn't he?'

I heard that a lot, and although I always said that he was a nightmare to work for, the truth was that I was finding it hard to remember just how irritating he was. When he walked into the office the following Tuesday, my heart jumped into my throat and for one panicky moment I actually forgot how to breathe.

He strolled in, looking brown and fit, his eyes bluer than ever, and instantly the air was charged with a kind of electricity. Suddenly I was sharply aware of everything: of colour of my nails flickering over the keyboard—Cherry Ripe, if you're interested—of the computer's hum, of the feel of the glasses on my nose, the light outside the window. It was as if the whole office had snapped into high definition.

'Good morning,' I said, and Phin peered at me in surprise.

'Good God, what was that?'

'What was what?' I asked, thrown.

'No, no…it's OK. For a moment there I thought I saw a smile.'

'I've smiled before,' I protested.

'Not like that. It was worth coming home for!' Phin came to sit on the edge of my desk and picked up the stapler. 'I'm not going to ask if you missed me because you'll just look at me over your glasses and say no.'

'I would have said a bit—until you started fiddling,' I said, removing the stapler from his grasp and setting it back into its place. 'But now I've remembered how irritating you are.'

Deliberately, Phin reached out and pushed the stapler out of alignment with one finger. 'Irritating? Me?'

'Stop it,' I said, slapping his hand away. I straightened the stapler once more. 'Haven't you got some other trip to go on? I'm sure they must need you in Ulan Bator or Timbuktu or somewhere.'

'Nope. Next time you're coming with me.' He had started on the scissors now, snapping them at me as he talked. 'So, what's the news here?'

'We've set up your *Glitz* interview for Thursday,' I told him. 'The interviewer is called Imelda Ross, and she's bringing a photographer with her. They'll be at your house at ten, so can you please make sure you're ready for them?'

'That's an appointment, not news,' he said. 'What's the gossip? Has Lex run off with a lap dancer? Has Kevin been caught siphoning funds to some offshore bank account?' Kevin was our Chief Financial Officer and famously prudent.

'Nothing so exciting, I'm afraid. Everyone's been doing what they always do.'

Actually, that wasn't *quite* true. Jonathan was looking much more relaxed these days. I had shared a lift with him a few days earlier, and instead of being stiff and awkward he had smiled and chatted about the spell of fine weather.

I'd replayed the conversation endlessly, of course, and was hugging the hope that he might be warming to me again. Between that and Phin's pastries I'd been happier than I'd been for ages—but I didn't think that would be of much interest to Phin, even if I had been prepared to confess it, which I wasn't.

'According to the gossip mags, Jewel Stevens has got a new man,' I offered instead.

'*Has* she? Excellent! I was hoping she'd lost interest.'

'She rang looking for you a couple of times, but I didn't think you'd want to speak to her in Peru, so I said you were out of contact.'

'Summer, you're a treasure,' he told me, putting down the scissors at last and digging around at his feet. 'So, even though you haven't missed me, you deserve a reward,' he said as he produced a paper bag. 'I've brought us something special to celebrate my return.'

The 'something special' turned out to be a cream doughnut each. 'I didn't feel we knew each other well enough to tackle one of these before,' he said as I eyed it dubiously, wondering how on earth I was going to eat it elegantly.

'I defy you to eat one of these without making a mess,' Phin added, reading my expression without any difficulty.

I couldn't, of course. I started off taking tiny nibbles, until he couldn't bear it any more.

'Get on with it, woman,' he ordered. 'Stop messing around at the edges. Take a good bite and enjoy it! That's not a bad recipe for life, now I come to think of it,' he said, watching as I sank my teeth obediently into the middle of the doughnut and cream spurted everywhere. 'The doughnut approach to living well. I might write a book about it.'

'Make sure you include a section on how to clean up all the mess,' I said, dabbing at my mouth with my fingers, torn between embarrassment and laughter. I spotted a blob of cream on my skirt. 'Ugh, I've got cream *everywhere!*'

'The best things in life are messy,' said Phin.

'Not as far as I'm concerned,' I said, as I carefully wiped the cream from my skirt. 'But maybe I'll make an exception for cream doughnuts. It was delicious!'

With a final lick of my fingers, I got to my feet. 'I'd better get back to work,' I said.

Phin got up, too. His smile had faded as he watched me eat the doughnut, and his expression was oddly unreadable for once. He was looking at me so intently that I hesitated.

'What?' I asked.

'You've missed a bit,' he said and, reaching out, he wiped a smear of cream from my cheek, just near my mouth. Then he offered me his finger to lick.

I stared at it, mesmerised by the vividness with which I could imagine my tongue against his finger. I could practically taste the sweetness of the cream, feel the contrast between its smoothness and the firmness of his skin, and a wave of heat pulsed up from my toes to my cheeks and simmered in my brain. For one awful moment I was afraid that the top of my head would actually blow off.

Horrified by how intimate the mere idea seemed, and about Phin—my boss!—of all people, I found myself taking a step back and shaking my head at the temptation.

Phin's eyes never left my mouth as he licked the cream off himself.

'Yum, yum,' he said softly.

I know, it doesn't sound very erotic, but my heart was thudding so loudly I was sure he must hear it. My pulse roared in my ears and I had a terrible feeling that I might literally be steaming. I had to get out of the room before Phin noticed.

I cleared my throat with an effort. 'I...er...I should let you get on. Haven't you got a meeting now?'

'I have?'

'Yes, in HR. You wanted me to set it up for you, to talk to Jane about staff development and the Cameroon trip. It's in the diary.' I could feel myself babbling as I backed away towards the door. 'I'll forward the e-mail to you…'

Somehow I made it back to my desk, and had to spend a few minutes just breathing very carefully.

I felt very odd, almost shaken. I had never thought about Phin that way before. I had never thought about Jonathan like that either, to be honest. I loved Jonathan, but he was safe. This wild pounding of my blood felt dark and rude and dangerous, and I didn't like it.

I pulled myself together at last. A momentary aberration, I told myself. A huge fuss about nothing. I mean, we hadn't even touched. A flick of Phin's finger against my cheek. That was all that had happened. Nothing at all, in fact.

I was just…hot. Was this what a hot flush was like? I wondered wildly. If so, I wasn't looking forward to the menopause at all.

Jittery and unsettled, I took myself off to the Ladies' to run cold water over my wrists. Someone had once told me that was the best way to cool yourself down, and I had no intention of splashing cold water all over my make-up. I wasn't in *that* much of a state.

I met Lex's PA, Monique, on her way in at the same time. Typical, isn't it, that the moment you're desperate to be alone people you don't normally see for ages start popping out of the woodwork? This wasn't even Monique's floor.

I was afraid that she would comment on how hot and flustered I looked, but fortunately she didn't seem to notice anything amiss. Reassured, I stopped to chat.

See, I told myself, all I needed was a little normality. It was a relief to talk about ordinary stuff, and I began to feel myself again.

'So what's the gossip?' I asked Monique, remembering Phin's question earlier. Monique was famously discreet, but if she did have any news it would be good to be able to pass a titbit on to Phin. At least it would be something to say other than *Could we try that cream on the finger thing again?*

'Funny you should say that.' Monique glanced around and lowered her voice, even though there was no one else in there with us. 'Have you seen Jonathan recently?'

Phin and the cream were instantly forgotten. 'A couple of times,' I said, as casually as I could. My poor old heart was working overtime this morning. Now it was pattering away at the mention of Jonathan. 'Why?'

'He's a changed man, isn't he?'

I thought of how relaxed he had looked the last time I'd seen him. 'He seems to be in a good mood.'

'Yes, and we all know why now!'

'We do?' I asked cautiously.

Monique grinned. 'Our steady, sensible Jonathan is in love.'

Not content with pattering, my heart pole-vaulted into my throat, where it lodged, hammering wildly. 'In love?' I croaked.

She nodded. 'And with Lori, of all people! I wouldn't have thought she was his type at all, but they're all over each other and they're not even bothering to try and hide it. Oh, well, at least he's happy.' She looked at her watch. 'I'd better get on. Lex will be wondering what's happened to me.'

There was a rushing in my ears. I think I must have said something, but I've no idea what, and Monique waggled her fingers in farewell as she hurried off, oblivious to the fact that my world had come crashing down around me.

Shaking, feeling sick, I shut myself in a cubicle and put my head between my knees. *I mustn't cry, I mustn't cry, I mustn't cry,* I told myself savagely. I had the rest of the afternoon to get through, and if I cried my mascara would run and everyone would know my heart was broken.

I don't know how long I sat there, but it can't have been that long. I knew I had to get back.

Lifting my head, I drew long, painful breaths to steady myself. I could do this.

Thank God for make-up. I reapplied lipstick very carefully and studied my expression. My eyes held a stark expression, but you'd have had to know me very well to spot that anything was wrong. Inside I felt ragged and raw, and I walked stiffly, so as not to jar anything, but outwardly I was perfectly composed.

I made it back to my desk and sank down in my chair, staring blankly at the computer screen. I just had to sit there for another few hours and then I'd be able to go home. Phin had gone out to his lunch with Jane, the director of HR, so I was spared him at least. Those blue eyes might be full of laughter but they didn't miss much.

By the time he came back it was after four, and I had had plenty of time to compose myself. I ached all over with the effort of not falling apart, and my brain felt as if it had an elastic band snapped round it, but I was able to meet his gaze when he came in.

'How was your meeting?' I asked, knowing Phin would never guess what it cost me to sound normal.

'Very useful. Jane's great, isn't she? We talked about Cameroon and she's all for a trial visit to see—' He broke off and frowned. 'What's the matter?'

'Nothing.' My throat was so tight I had to force the word out.

'Don't try and deny it,' said Phin. 'That stapler is a millimetre out of alignment. And...' he peered closer '...yes, I do believe that's a chip in your nail polish!' The laughter faded from his voice and from his face. 'Come on, I can see in your eyes that something's wrong. What is it?'

'It's...nothing.' I couldn't look at him. I stared fiercely away, pressing my lips together in one straight line.

'You're not the kind of person that gets upset about nothing,' he said gently. Going back to the door, he closed it. 'Tell me,' he said.

There was a great, tangled knot of hurt in my throat. I knew if I even tried to say Jonathan's name I would break down completely, and I wasn't sure I could bear the humiliation. 'I...can't.'

'OK,' he said. 'You don't need to say anything. But we're going out. Get your coat.'

I was too tired and miserable to object. He took me to a dimly lit bar, just beginning to fill with people leaving work early. Like us, I supposed. We found a table in a corner and Phin looked around for a waiter.

'What would you like?' he asked. 'A glass of wine?'

God, I was so predictable, I realised. No wonder Jonathan didn't want me. Even Phin could see that I was the kind of girl who sensibly just had a small glass of white wine before going home. I was boring.

'Actually, I'd like a cocktail,' I said with a shade of defiance.

'Sure,' said Phin. 'What kind?'

I picked up the menu on the table and scanned it. I would love to have been the kind of girl who could order Sex on a Beach or a Long Slow Screw Against a Wall without sounding stupid, but I wasn't. 'A pomegranate martini,' I decided, choosing one at random.

His mouth flickered, but he ordered it straight-faced from the waiter, along with a beer for himself.

When it came, it looked beautiful—a rosy pink colour with a long twirl of orange peel curling through it. I was beginning to regret my choice by then, but was relieved to take a sip and find it delicious. Just like fruit juice, really.

I was grateful to Phin for behaving quite normally. He chatted about his meeting with Jane, and I listened with half an ear as I sipped the martini which slipped down in no time. I even began to relax a bit.

'Another one?' Phin asked, beckoning the waiter over.

About to say that I shouldn't, I stopped myself. Sod it, I thought. I had nothing to go home for. 'Why not?' I said instead.

When the second martini arrived, I took another restorative pull through the straw and sat back. I was beginning to feel pleasantly fuzzy around the edges.

'Thank you,' I said on a long sigh. 'This was just what I needed.'

'Can you talk about it yet?'

Phin's voice was warm with sympathy. The funny thing was that it didn't feel at all awkward to be sitting there with him in the dim light. Maybe it was the martini, but all at once he felt like a friend, not my irritating boss. Only that morning the graze of his finger had reduced me to mush, but it was too bizarre to remember that now.

I sighed. 'Oh, it's just the usual thing.'

'Boyfriend trouble?'

'He's not my boyfriend any more. The truth is, he was never really my boyfriend at all,' I realised dully. 'But I loved him. I still do.'

In spite of myself, my eyes started to fill with tears. 'He told me before Christmas that he wanted out, that he didn't think it was working,' I went on, my voice beginning to wobble disastrously. 'I'd been hoping and hoping that he'd change his mind, and I let myself believe that he was beginning to miss me, but I just found out today that he's going out with Lori and he's mad about her and I don't think I can bear it.'

I couldn't stop the tears then. It was awful. I hate crying, hate that feeling of losing control, but there was nothing I could do about it.

Phin saw me frantically searching for tissue, and

silently handed me a paper napkin that had come with the bowl of nuts.

'I'm sorry, I'm sorry,' I wept into it.

'Hey, don't be sorry. It sucks. Who is this guy, anyway?' he said. 'Do you want me to go and kill him for you? Would that help?'

'I don't think Lex would be very pleased if you did.' I sniffed into the napkin. 'He'd have to find a new PR person.'

Phin's brows crawled up to his hairline. 'Are we talking about *Jonathan Pugh*?'

I could see him trying to picture Jonathan's appeal. I know Jonathan isn't the sexiest looking guy in the world, but it was about more than looks.

'Jonathan's everything I ever wanted,' I told him tearfully. 'He's a bit older than me, I know, but he's so steady, so reliable. He seems reserved, but I always had the feeling that he'd be different in private, and he is. I never thought I'd have a chance with him, but then there was the summer party…'

I'll never forget my starry-eyed amazement when Jonathan came over to talk to me, and suggested going for a quiet drink away from all the noise. I'd been bedazzled by all my dreams coming true at once.

'I was so happy just to be with him,' I told Phin. Now I'd started talking, it was as if I couldn't stop.

I had to blurt it all out. I gulped at my martini. 'I'd never been in love before, not like that, and when I was with him it felt like I had everything I'd ever wanted. I didn't mind that he wanted to keep our relationship a secret—to me that was just him being sensible, and I loved him for that, too. But he's not being sensible with Lori,' I said bitterly. 'He's not keeping *her* a secret. He doesn't care who knows how he feels about her.'

My mouth began to tremble wildly again. 'It wasn't that he didn't want to have a proper relationship. He just didn't want *me*. He wanted someone like Lori, who's pretty and feminine.'

'I bet she isn't prettier than you,' said Phin.

'She is. If you saw her, you'd know.'

I'd never liked Lori. She's the kind of woman who gives the impression of being frail and shy and helpless, but who always manages to get her own way. Men hang around, asking her if she's all right the whole time. As far as I knew Lori had no female friends—always a bad sign, in my opinion—but even I had to admit she was very pretty. She was tiny, with a tumble of blonde curls, huge blue eyes and a soft, breathy little voice.

Phin wouldn't be able to resist her any more than Jonathan had.

'OK, maybe she's pretty,' Phin allowed, 'but you're *beautiful*, Summer.'

'I'm not.' I blew my nose on the napkin. 'I'm ordinary. I know that.'

He laughed at that. 'You are so not ordinary, Summer! You've got fantastic bones and beautiful skin and your eyes are incredible. And don't get me started on your mouth... Your trouble is that you don't make the most of yourself.'

'I do,' I protested, still tearfully. 'Look at me.' I gestured down at my suit. Even in the depths of my misery I knew it was better not to draw attention to my face right then. I'm not a pretty crier. Maybe the likes of Lori can cry without their skin going blotchy and their eyes puffy and their nose running, but I couldn't. 'I always take trouble over my clothes,' I pointed out. 'I never go out without make-up. What more can I do?'

'You could let your hair down sometimes,' said Phin, lifting a hand as if to touch it, but changing his mind at the last minute. 'It looks as if it would be beautiful, thick and silky. It would make you look more...' he searched for the right word '...accessible,' he decided in the end, and I remembered what Anne had said about changing my image by letting my hair hang loose.

But what difference would it have made? 'What's the point in looking accessible when I'm boring?' I asked despairingly. 'Jonathan still wouldn't want me.'

'He must have wanted you at some point or he wouldn't have got involved with you in first place.'

'No, he didn't.' I was just starting to accept the truth. 'I flung myself at him, and I must have been convenient, but he never meant it to be more than that. He didn't want *me*. And why should he? I'm boring and sensible and practical,' I raged miserably, remembering now—too late—some of the things Jonathan had said. In hindsight, it was all so obvious. Only I hadn't wanted to see the truth before.

'Jonathan doesn't want someone as competent as he is. He doesn't want someone who can look after herself. He wants someone needy and feminine—like Lori. Someone he can look after. But I can't do needy. I'm too used to dealing with everything, ever since I was child. I can't help it, but Jonathan thinks it makes me bossy. He used to make comments about it. I thought he was being affectionate, but now I wonder if it really bothered him. Funny how a man is never bossy, isn't it?' I added in a bitter aside. 'A man is always assertive or controlling, but never, ever bossy.'

'I don't think you're bossy,' said Phin. 'You're practical, which is a very different thing.'

'Jonathan thinks I am. He just got bored with me. All that time I was telling myself how much I loved him, he was losing interest. I should have realised that he hadn't invested anything in the relationship. He didn't even leave a toothbrush at my flat. When he ended it, there was nothing to discuss.'

Oh, dear, here came the tears again. I groped around for the wet napkin until Phin found me another, and I scrubbed furiously at my cheeks before drawing a shuddering breath.

'When Monique told me about Lori today, it just made me realise what a fool I've been about everything,' I said. 'I'd had this dream in my head for so long, and it was all wrapped up with being with Jonathan and feeling safe, but I should have known it was too good to be true,' I said wretchedly. 'He'd never want someone like me.'

'But you still want him?'

I nodded. 'I love him,' I said, my voice catching.

'Then I think you should go out and get him back,' said Phin. 'I didn't have you down as someone who would give up as easily as that. What have you been doing since you split up?'

'Nothing.'

'Precisely, and look where it's got you. You're miserable, and Jonathan's dating a woman named after a truck. Lori? I mean, how serious can he be?'

I looked at him. 'That's a pathetic joke,' I said, but I managed a watery smile even so.

'I'm just saying you shouldn't give up,' Phin said. 'Your trouble is that you're too subtle. I had lunch with you both the other day, and I didn't have a clue that there had been anything at all between you. I wouldn't be surprised if Jonathan thinks you don't care one way or the other. I suggest we have another drink,' he went on, gesturing for the waitress to bring another round, 'and plan your strategy.'

I considered that, my brow creased with the effort of thinking after two martinis. 'You think I should tell Jonathan how I feel?'

'Absolutely not!' Phin tutted. 'Really, Summer, you haven't got a clue, have you? If you get heavy on him he'll panic and think you're about to drag him off to the suburbs via the nearest registry office—which is what you want, of course, but this is not the time to tell him that. You've got to reel him in first.'

'Well, what do you suggest, if you're such an expert?' I asked, wiping mascara away with the napkin. What was the point of waterproof mascara if you couldn't cry? I would have to write and complain. 'If I tell him how I feel, I'm too intense. If I don't, he won't notice because I'm so boring and predictable.' I lapsed back into gloom once more.

Another beer and a fresh martini were placed on the table. Phin pushed my glass towards me. 'For a start, you've got to get this idea that you're boring out of your head,' he told me sternly. 'You're smart, you're funny—not always deliberately, I'll grant you—and you're sexy as hell.'

CHAPTER FIVE

I STARED at him. *Sexy?* I was sensible, practical, reliable. Not sexy.

Jewel was sexy, pressing herself against him and sticking her tongue in his ear. Not me, with my glasses on a chain and my neat suits. Phin was either being kind or making fun of me.

For a fleeting moment I remembered the way I had felt as he'd wiped that blob of cream from my cheek, but then I pushed the memory aside. It was too incongruous.

'All you've got to do is make Jonathan appreciate what an incredible woman you are,' said Phin.

Yeah, right. 'How?' I asked, with a trace of sullenness. 'He never appreciated how "incredible" I was before.'

'Make him jealous,' said Phin promptly. 'I know guys like Jonathan. Hell, I *am* a guy like Jonathan, and if I saw you with another man I'd be intrigued at the very least. I guarantee Jonathan would start to remember what he saw in you if there's another guy sniffing around and making it obvious that he thinks you're incredible.'

'Well, yes, brilliant idea,' I said, picking up my glass. The third martini was definitely kicking in now. 'There's just one problem. I don't have another guy.'

'Start dating again,' said Phin, as if it was obvious.

'Oh, sure,' I said sarcastically. The martinis had made me bolshy, but it was better than snivelling. 'That's easy. I'll just snap my fingers and produce a man.' I patted my pockets. 'I'm sure I left one or two lying around somewhere…'

Phin looked at me appreciatively. 'I see you're feeling better,' he said. 'Look, it can't be that hard for a girl who looks like you to find a guy. Go and stand at the bar and smile, and I bet they'll be falling over themselves. Better still, eat a cream doughnut.'

There was a tiny silence. I flickered a glance at Phin. He was smiling, but the blue eyes held that odd expression again—the one that made me feel as if the world was tilting out of kilter.

'You have no idea, do you?' he said.

I swallowed. I didn't want to remember that disconcerting wave of heat. I didn't want to think about what it meant.

'I don't think it would be that easy,' I told him, my eyes sliding away from his. 'And even if I *did* find a boyfriend who wouldn't mind the fact that I don't actually want to be with him, when would Jonathan ever find out?'

'I see what you mean. Someone at work would be better.'

'Except if it was someone at work Jonathan would just feel sorry for him.' My confidence was crumbling again. Quick, it was time for another gulp of pomegranate martini.

'Not if it was obvious he was mad about you.'

'Oh, so now I have to find a boyfriend who can act, too? I'd have to hire him, and where do you suggest I look?'

'What about right here?'

I looked around the bar. 'How do I know if any of these guys can act? Well, the barmen are probably resting actors, but I'd never dare talk to them—they're far too cool.'

'No, *here*,' said Phin, tapping his chest.

My jaw dropped. *'You?'*

'There's no need to look like that! I'm perfect.'

'I know you think so,' said the third martini, and Phin grinned.

'I do think so, and so will you if you think about it,' he said. 'Jonathan can hardly not notice if you're with me, and I think you'll find I'm not a bad actor. They still talk about my Ugly Sister in the school pantomime and, according to my mother, I stole the show in the nativity play as the sheep that fell over when it tried to kneel in front of the manger.'

'I don't know why you're not in line for an Oscar,' I said, 'but why would you want to squander your great talent on me?'

'I like you,' said Phin simply, 'even if you are a bit sharp with me sometimes. If I can help you, I will. Besides, it might work out quite well for me from a PR point of view.'

I frowned. 'How do you work that out?'

'Think about it. Jonathan was very keen to push my family credentials in the *Glitz* interview. How better to do that than pretend I'm about to settle down with you? You can hang around and look good for the article, which means that even if Jonathan hasn't got the idea before, he definitely will then. A double whammy.'

He sat back smugly while I sipped my martini and considered what he had said. Surely it couldn't be as easy as Phin seemed to believe?

'What about Jewel?' I prevaricated.

'What about her? You said yourself that she's been going out with someone else, poor guy. I'm well out of that one!' said Phin. 'I wouldn't have had a plate left in the house. But now I come to think of it,' he went on, 'it might not be a bad idea to let her see I'm unavailable now. Just in case she's thinking she might pick up where we left off before I went to Peru.'

'I can't believe you'd have much trouble finding someone else to make sure she gets the point,' I demurred. 'There must be much more likely types who would give the impression that you're ready to settle down.'

'I wouldn't want to give anyone the wrong idea,' said Phin, not bothering to deny it. It would have been annoying if he had, but I was annoyed anyway. 'I'm not the settling down kind,' he said. 'At least with you we'd both know it was just a pretence.'

I blame it on the pomegranate martinis, but it was starting to make a weird kind of sense.

'No one would believe that I was really your girlfriend,' I said. 'You're used to going out with actresses and models.'

'Which is why they'll think I'm serious if they see me with you.'

My, this was doing wonders for my ego.

'It would only be for a few weeks,' Phin was saying. 'You wouldn't have to do much. Just be seen out at a few parties with me and hang around looking like a girlfriend for the interview. Then we can seem to break it off later, so I can carry on avoiding commitment while you walk off into the sunset with Jonathan.'

'Do you really think it would make a difference with Jonathan?' I asked wistfully.

'Listen, do you really want him back or not?'

'I really do.'

'Even though he's made you feel boring and unlovable?'

'I love him,' I said, dangerously close to getting weepy again.

'OK,' said Phin, 'if Jonathan is what you really want, then I think you deserve what you want. The first thing is to make him realise that you're not boring at all, that you're quite capable of being spontaneous when you've got the right incentive. Make him think that it's *his* fault you never had much fun with him—which it probably is, by the way. We're going to convince him that we're having a raging affair, and he's sure to sit up and take notice.'

'How do we go about having an affair?' I said doubtfully. I couldn't see myself being convincing as someone in the throes of a raging affair somehow. It wasn't the kind of thing I would do. It wasn't the kind of thing I liked, to be honest. It smacked too much of losing control and abandoning yourself. I liked things calm and steady and *safe*.

'Well, let's see,' said Phin with a grin. 'I could take you back to my place. We'll say it's just for a drink, but we won't be able to keep our hands off each other. The moment we're through the front door I'll start kissing you, and you'll kiss me back. You'll fall back against the door and pull me with you—'

'I don't mean really have an affair,' I interrupted, scarlet. I was horrified at how vividly I could imagine it, and there was a strange thumping deep inside me. Jonathan had never lost control like that. I was beginning to feel very odd, but I hoped very much that was down to the martinis. 'I meant... how would we make everyone believe it? We can hardly send round an e-mail announcement that we're sleeping together.'

Phin didn't seem to think that would be a problem. 'We'll go to a couple of parties, maybe leave work together—or even better arrive together—and word will get round in no time. If you can contrive to blush whenever my name is mentioned in the Ladies', or wherever you girls all congregate, so much the better. And remember how besotted I'm going to be with you,' he went on. 'I won't be able to keep my hands off you— especially when Jonathan is around. I don't think it will take long before he gets the point.'

I buried my nose in my martini, trying not to wonder what it would be like to have Phin putting his arm around me, sliding his hand down my back. Would he twine his fingers around mine? Would he stroke my hair?

Would he *kiss* me?

The breath rushed out of my lungs at the thought. *Would* he? And if he did what would it be like?

My heart was thudding painfully—ba-*boom*, ba-*boom*, ba-*boom*—and I had to moisten my lips before I could speak. This was about Jonathan, remember?

'But if Jonathan thinks I'm with you, he'll assume I'm not interested in him any more,' I objected.

'Once he starts paying attention—and he will—you'll have to let him know that you just might be tempted away from me. If you can do it without seeming too keen. You might have to spend some time alone together…' Phin snapped his fingers. 'Of course! Jonathan can come to Cameroon. If you can't seduce him back on a steamy tropical night, Summer, I wash my hands of you!'

I thought about it as I sucked on the long curl of orange peel which was all that was left at the bottom of my glass. Apart from the reminder of Cameroon, which I'd been rather hoping he'd forgotten about, I was struggling to think of a good argument as to why Phin's idea wouldn't work.

The third martini wasn't helping. I was feeling distinctly fuzzy by now, and finding it hard to concentrate.

Phin followed my gaze to the empty glass. 'Had enough?' he asked, and I bridled at the humorous understanding in his voice.

A sensible girl would say yes at this point, but being sensible hadn't got me anywhere, had it?

'No,' I said clearly. Well, it was *meant* to sound

clear. Whether it did is doubtful. 'I'd love another one.'

One of Phin's brows lifted. 'Are you sure?'

'Absho—abs*o*lutely sure.'

'It's your hangover,' he said, the corner of his mouth quirking in that lop-sided smile of his. He beckoned the waitress over. 'Another pomegranate martini for my little lush here, and I'll have another half.'

I waited until she had set the glasses on the table. Part of me knew quite well that Phin's plan was madness, but I hadn't been able to come up with a single argument to convince him how ridiculous the idea was.

'Do you really think it would work?' I asked, almost shyly.

'What's the worst that could happen if it doesn't?' Phin countered. 'You'd be in the same situation you are now, but at least you'll know you did everything you could to make your dream come true. That has to be better than just sitting and watching it disappear, doesn't it? And, if nothing else, we'll have promoted the family image of Gibson & Grieve with this interview. As a good company girl, I know you'll be glad to have done your bit!'

He was watching my face.

'It's a risk,' he said in a different voice, 'but

you don't get what you really want without taking chances.'

I looked back at him, biting my lip.

'So,' he said, lifting his glass, 'do we have a deal?'

And I, God help me, chinked my glass against his. 'Deal,' I said.

'Good morning, Summer!' Phin's cheery greeting scraped across my thumping head.

'Not so loud,' I whispered, without even lifting my head from the desk, where I'd been resting it ever since I'd staggered into work twenty minutes earlier. Late, for the first time in my life. I would have been mortified if I had had any feelings to spare. As it was, I had to save my energy for basic survival. Breathing was about all I could manage right then, and even that hurt.

'Oh, dear, dear, dear.' I could picture him standing over me, blue eyes alight with laughter, lips pursed in mock reproach. 'Is it possible you're regretting that last martini?'

I groaned. 'Go away and leave me to die in peace!'

'Aren't you feeling well?' Phin enquired solicitously.

'How could you possibly have guessed that?' I mumbled, still afraid to move my head in case it fell off.

'I'm famed for my powers of deduction. The

FBI are always calling me up and asking me to help them out.'

I didn't even have the energy to roll my eyes. 'How many martinis did you make me drink last night?'

'Me? It wasn't me that insisted on another round, or the next, or the next... I asked you if you were sure, and you said that you were. Absolutely sure, you said,' he reminded me virtuously, and I hated the laughter in his voice.

I only had the vaguest memory of getting home the night before. Phin. A taxi. Anne's astonished face as I reeled in the door.

'Oh, God...I'm going to be a statistic,' I moaned into the desk. 'I'll be one of those moody binge drinkers we're always hearing about who throw away their entire careers.'

'You don't think you might be exaggerating just a teeny bit?' said Phin. 'Letting your hair down once in a while isn't the end of the world.'

It certainly felt like the end of the world to me. I'd never been closer to pulling a sickie. I couldn't even *imagine* a time when I would feel better. My forehead stayed where it was, pressing into the desk. 'If you knew how awful I felt, you wouldn't say that.'

'You were great fun,' he offered, but that was no consolation to me then. 'You were the life and soul of the bar by the time I managed to bundle you into a taxi. It's one of the best nights I've had in a long time. I think I'm going to enjoy going out with you.'

'I'm not going out ever again,' I vowed.

'You'll have to. How else will everyone know how in love we are?'

Very cautiously, I turned my head on the desk and squinted up at him. 'Please tell me last night was all a bad dream.'

'Certainly not!' said Phin briskly. 'We had a deal. You drank to it—several times, if I recall. Besides, we're committed. I met Lex on my way in and asked if I could take you to some drinks party he's having on Friday.'

'What?' Horrified, I straightened too suddenly, and yelped as my head jarred.

'Our cunning plan is never going to work if you hide away,' Phin pointed out, sitting on the edge of my desk and deliberately pushing a pile of square-cut folders aside. I was in such a bad state that I didn't even straighten them, and he looked at me in concern.

'Jonathan will be there,' he added, to tempt me, but I was beyond comfort by then.

'Oh, God.' I collapsed back onto the desk. 'What did Lex say? He must have been horrified.'

'Not at all. He was surprised, sure, but he said falling for you could be the most sensible thing I'd ever done.'

'I can't believe I let you talk me into this,' I moaned.

'Now, come along—you'll feel better when you've had some sugar,' said Phin, jumping off the desk. 'I'll go and make some coffee, and you can have your doughnut early.'

Oddly enough, I *did* feel a bit better after something to eat. My head was still thumping, but at least it didn't feel as if it was about to fall off my neck any more.

Gingerly, I settled down at my computer and managed a few e-mails, although the clatter of the keyboard made me wince and I had to type very, very slowly, while Phin drip-fed me coffee and tried to rouse me by pretending to put files away in the wrong drawer.

'Don't torture me,' I grumbled. 'I thought you were supposed to be in love with me?'

'That's true. I should think of a truly romantic gesture to show what you mean to me. I could start putting my books in alphabetical order, or using a square rule to tidy my desk.'

'Why don't you try leaving *my* desk alone, for a start?' I said, swatting his hand aside as he made to pick up my calculator.

'Aha, I see you're feeling better!'

'I'm not. I'm a sick woman. I can't take any more.'

The words were barely out of my mouth

before 'more' arrived—much more—in the shape of my mother.

She wafted in the door, beaming. 'Summer, darling, *there* you are!'

'Mum!'

It was Phin's turn to gape. *'Mum?'*

I couldn't blame him for looking staggered. No one ever believes she's my mother. You'd never think she was in her forties. She's got long red hair, shining eyes and a clear happy face. There's something fey, almost childlike, about her. I've never seen her in a scrap of make-up, she wears sandals and flowing ethnic skirts, and she always looks wonderful.

And, while she may be deeply into all things spiritual, she's not immune to flattery either. The smile she gave Phin was positively flirtatious. 'I hope I'm not interrupting?'

'Of course not,' said Phin, leaping forward to shake her hand. 'I'm Phin Gibson.'

'And I'm Starlight,' she told him.

They beamed at each other. I judged it was time to put a stop to their mutual love-in.

'I wasn't expecting you,' I said.

'I did tell you I was coming to London,' she reminded me.

She *had* said something, I remembered too late. 'I didn't realise it would be so soon.'

'It was an impulse.'

When had it ever *not* been an impulse? I thought wearily.

'We were gathered the other evening, channelling, when we were all seized by the same idea. It was the most extraordinary coincidence, so we knew that it had to be meant! Each of us felt our guardian angels were telling us to follow the ley lines into London...and now here we are!'

'What about the shop?' I asked, my heart sinking. A couple of years ago she had decided that she would open a New Age shop in Taunton. I'd been all for the idea of her settling to a job, so I'd helped with the practicalities of arranging the lease and sorting out a set-up loan. Mum had been full of enthusiasm for a while, but I hadn't heard much about it recently. Obviously she was into something else now.

Sure enough, she waved all talk of the shop aside. 'This is more important, Summer. We've been walking between the worlds at the powersites along the ley line. The earth needs it desperately at the moment. Only by channelling the energy and letting the Divine Will flow through us can we help to heal it.'

'Someone told me there's a ley line running right along the Mall to Buckingham Palace,' said Phin, sounding interested. 'Is that right?'

'It is.' She beamed approvingly at him. 'And this building sits on the very same line! I'm getting good vibes here.'

I dropped my head into my hands. My hangover had come back with a vengeance. I wasn't up to dealing with my mother today. I wished Phin would stop encouraging her.

Meanwhile my mother had turned her attention back to me. 'Your aura is looking very murky, Summer. Haven't you been using the crystals I sent you? If only I had some jade with me. That's very calming for irritability.'

'I'm not irritable, Mum,' I said—irritably. 'I've just got a bit of headache.'

'I sense your energy is all out of balance.' She tutted. 'You need to realign your chakras.'

'Right, I'll do that. Look, Mum, it's lovely to see you, but I have to get on. Where are you staying? We could meet up this evening.'

Her face fell. 'Jemima is going to regress tonight. Her spiritual journeys are always *so* interesting,' she told Phin. 'Last time she was reborn as one of Cleopatra's maids. It was quite an eye-opener.'

'I can imagine,' he said. 'You wouldn't want to miss that, so why don't I take you both out to lunch?'

'Oh, but—' I began in dismay, but neither Phin nor my mother were listening.

'I know a vegan restaurant just round the corner,'

he was telling her, having accurately guessed her tastes. 'They do a great line in nut cutlets.'

How Phin came to know a vegan restaurant I'll never know, as I'd had him down squarely as a steak and chips man, but sure enough, tucked away a block or two from the office, there was a little café. Before I knew it, we were tucking into grilled tofu, bean ragout and steamed brown rice, and my mother, blossoming under Phin's attention, was well into her stride with stories about my childhood. I gazed glumly into my carrot juice and wished for the oblivion of another martini.

'She was such a funny little thing,' Mum told Phin. 'Always worrying! Ken and I used to joke that her first words were "Have you paid the electricity bill?"' She laughed merrily.

'Ken was my father,' I explained to Phin. 'He died when I was nine.'

'Such a spiritual man!' My mother sighed. 'I know I should be glad he's moved on to a higher astral plane, but I still miss him sometimes. We were totally in harmony, physically and spiritually.'

'You're lucky to have had that,' said Phin gently. 'It's quite rare, I think.'

'I know, and I'm so glad dear Summer is going to have the same feeling with you.'

I looked up from the alfalfa sprouts I was pushing around my plate, startled. 'Er, Mum, I think you've got wrong end of the stick. Phin's my boss.'

I might as well have spared my breath. 'His colours are very strong,' she said, and turned to him. 'I'm getting a lot of yellow from you.'

'Is that good?' asked Phin, as if he was really interested.

'In positive aspects, absolutely. Yellow is a warm colour. It relates to the personality, the ego.'

'No wonder you've got so much of it,' I said snippily, but Phin held up a hand.

'Hold on, I get the feeling your mother really understands me.'

'Yellow is how we feel about ourselves and about others.' Did I tell you Mum is a colour therapist? 'It tells me that you're confident and wise and positive about life.'

'And you thought I was just like everyone else,' Phin said to me. 'What about Summer? Is she as wise as me?'

'Summer has a cool aura,' said Mum, well away now. 'She's got a lot of indigo and blue. That means she's fearless and dutiful and self-sacrificing, but she's also kind and practical.'

Phin nudged me. 'Bet you wish you were wise, like me!'

'You're a very good match,' Mum said, and I scowled.

'How do you work that out? Yellow and blue are quite different.'

'But when you put them together they make green,' said my mother. 'That's the colour of balance and harmony.' She smiled at us both. 'Green relates to the heart chakra, too. When it comes to giving and receiving love, it's the perfect combination.'

'Thank you for not laughing at her,' I said to Phin when my mother had drifted off to prepare for the evening's regression. I fingered the clear crystal pendulum ("Very good for energy tuning") that she had pressed on me before she left. 'I know she's a bit wacky, but…'

'But she's so shiningly sincere you can't help but like her,' said Phin. 'What's not to like about someone who loves life as much as she does?'

As we walked back to the office I tried to imagine Jonathan sitting down to grilled tofu with my mother. I'd never really talked to him about my childhood. I'd had the feeling he'd be appalled by her flaky ideas, and I was absurdly grateful to Phin for seeing her good side.

'It must have been hard for you, losing your father when you were so young.' Phin broke into my thoughts. 'Did you miss him?'

'Not that much,' I said honestly. 'We were living in a commune then, and there were lots of other people around. Besides, we weren't allowed to be sad. We had to rejoice that he had ascended to a higher plane.'

I shook my head, remembering. 'I think it must have been much harder for my mother. They do seem to have really loved each other, and I suspect she threw herself into the spiritual side of things as a way of coping. She's got a very flimsy grasp on reality, and sometimes she drives me mad, but at least she's happy.' I sighed. 'And who am I to say what she should or shouldn't believe?'

'I can't see you in a commune,' Phin commented.

'I hated it, but, looking back, it was the best place for Mum,' I said reflectively. 'I wish she'd join another. At least then someone else would worry about the day-to-day things.'

'Like paying the electricity bill?'

'Exactly. They were both hopeless with money, and just couldn't be bothered with things like bills, so the electricity was always getting cut off. They thought it was funny that I used to fret, but if I didn't sort out the practicalities no one else would.'

'Sounds like they were the opposite of my parents,' said Phin, as we waited to cross the road at the lights. 'They were both obsessed with financial security. They thought that as long as they could pay for us to go to "good" schools and we had everything we wanted they would have done their duty as parents.'

He grinned at me suddenly. 'We're an ungrateful generation, aren't we? My parents did their best, just like yours did. It's not their fault that we want different things from them. Mine drive me mad, just like your mother does you, but that doesn't mean I don't love them. The truth is that there's part of me that still craves their approval. Why else would I be at Gibson & Grieve, getting in Lex's way?'

'At least you're trying,' I said. 'My mother would be delighted if I gave up my job to channel angels or dowse for fairy paths. I don't think she even knows what "career" means.'

We were passing a burger bar just then, and as the smell of barbecued meat wafted out Phin stopped and sniffed appreciatively. 'Mmm, junk food…!' His eyes glinted as he looked down at me. 'Are you still hungry?'

'What? After all those delicious alfalfa sprouts? How can you even ask?'

We took our burgers away and sat on the steps in front of the National Gallery, looking down over Trafalgar Square. It was a bright February day, and an unseasonal warmth in the air taunted us with the promise of spring.

I was certainly feeling a lot better than I had earlier that morning. I was still a bit fuzzy round the edges but my headache had almost gone. Perhaps my mother's crystal was working after all.

'What are you doing?' Phin demanded as I unwrapped my burger and separated the bun carefully.

'I don't like the pickle,' I said, picking it out with a grimace and looking around for somewhere to dispose of it.

'Here, give it to me,' he said with a roll of his eyes, and when I passed it over he shoved it into his own burger and took a huge bite.

'See—we're like a real couple already,' he said through a mouthful.

I wished he hadn't reminded me of the crazy pretence we'd embarked upon the night before. I couldn't believe I'd actually agreed to it. I kept waiting for Phin to tell me that it was all a big joke, that he'd just been having me on.

'Did you really tell Lex that we were going out?'

'Uh-huh.' He glanced down at me. 'I told him that we were madly in love.'

I wanted to look away, but my eyes snagged on his and it was as if all the air had been suddenly sucked out of my lungs. Held by the blueness and the glinting laughter, I could only sit there and stare back at him, feeling giddy and yet centred at the same time.

It was a very strange sensation. I was acutely aware of the coldness of the stone steps, of the breeze in my face and the smell of the burger in my hands.

I did eventually manage to wrench my gaze

away, but it was an effort, and I had to concentrate on my breathing as I watched the tourists milling around the square. They held their digital cameras at arm's length, posing by the great stone lions or squinting up at Nelson on his column. A squabble erupted amongst the pigeons below us, and my eyes followed the red buses heading down Whitehall, but no matter where I looked all I saw was Phin's image, as if imprinted behind my eyelids: the mobile mouth with its lazy lop-sided smile, the line of his cheek, the angle of his jaw.

When had he become so familiar? When had I learnt exactly how his hair grew? When had I counted the creases at the edges of his eyes?

There was a yawning feeling in the pit of my stomach. Desperately I tried to conjure up Jonathan's image instead, but it was hopeless.

'What did Lex say?' I asked, struggling to sound normal. 'Did he believe you?'

'Of course he did. Why wouldn't he?'

'You've got to admit that we make an unlikely couple.'

'Your mother doesn't think so,' Phin reminded me.

'My mother believes that fairies dance around the flowers at dawn,' I pointed out. 'The word "unlikely" doesn't occur in her vocabulary.'

'Well, Lex didn't seem at all surprised—except

maybe that you would fall in love with me.' Phin crumpled the empty paper in his hand. 'He seemed to think that you were too sensible to do anything like that. He's obviously never seen you drinking pomegranate martinis!'

I flushed. If I never touched a martini again, it would be too soon.

'I would have thought he'd be more surprised that you'd be in love with *me*,' I said, finishing my own burger.

Phin shrugged. 'I'm always falling in and out of love. I suspect he's more worried that I might hurt you. He knows I'm not the settling down type. When you dump me for Jonathan, he'll probably be relieved.'

CHAPTER SIX

THE *Glitz* interview was scheduled for the next day.

Phin lived just off the King's Road, in one of those houses I have long coveted, with painted brick and colourful doors. That morning, though, I was in no mood to admire the prettiness of the street, or the window boxes filled with early daffodils that adorned the cottages on either side. I was feeling ridiculously nervous as I stood on the steps outside his door—a bright red—and I wasn't even sure why.

Except that's not quite true. I *did* know why. It was because of this crazy pretence we had agreed on. I couldn't understand how I had let myself get sucked into it. It was utter madness. *And* it would never work. I should just accept that Jonathan didn't love me and move on.

But instead I was committed to pretending to be Phin's girlfriend. It was too late to change my mind. Phin had told Lex that we were madly in love—just imagining a conversation like that with our dour Chief Executive made my mind boggle—and now everybody knew.

Phin had rested his hand against casually against my neck as we'd waited for the lifts on our way back from Trafalgar Square. I knew he was only doing it so that Michaela at Reception would see and pass the word around—she had, and I'd only been back at my desk five minutes when Ellie was on the phone demanding to know what was going on—so there was no reason for my nape to be tingling still, no reason for me to be tense and jittery.

But I was.

Well, I had to get on with it. Drawing a deep breath, I rang the bell.

The door opened as suddenly as a slap, and there was Phin, smiling at me, in faded jeans and a T-shirt. His feet were bare, his hair rumpled, and he was in need of a shave. He looked a mess, in fact, but all at once there wasn't enough air to breathe and my mouth dried.

I badly wanted to retreat down the steps, but pride kept me at the top. 'Hi,' I said, horrified to hear how husky my voice sounded.

'Hey,' said Phin, and before I realised what he meant to do he had kissed me on the mouth.

It was only a brief brush of the lips, the casual kind of kiss a man like Phin would bestow a hundred times at a party, but my pulse jolted as if from a massive bolt of electricity. So that's what it's like being struck by lightning. I swear every hair on my body stood up.

'What was that for?' I asked unsteadily.

'Just getting into character,' he said cheerfully. 'I hadn't realised the perks of promoting G&G's family-friendly image until now. Who would have thought it would be so much fun keeping Lex happy?'

He stood back and held the door open. 'Come on in and see where we're having our wild affair.'

We won't be able to keep our hands off each other. I remembered Phin answering my stupid question about how we would go about having an affair. *The moment we're through the front door I'll start kissing you, and you'll kiss me back. You'll fall back against the door and pull me with you...*

Now I couldn't help glancing at the door as I passed, couldn't help imagining what it would be like to feel the hard wood digging into my back, the weight of Phin's body pressing me against it, his mouth on mine, his hands hot and hungry.

I swallowed hard. I had no intention of giving Phin the satisfaction of knowing how that casual kiss had affected me, but it was difficult when I still had that weird, jerky, twitchy, shocked feeling beneath my skin.

It wasn't a very big house. Clearly it had once

been a cottage, but the kitchen had been extended at the back with a beautiful glass area, and on a sunny February morning it looked bright and inviting.

'Nice house,' I managed, striving for a nonchalant tone that didn't quite come off.

'I can't take any credit for it,' said Phin. 'It was like this when I bought it. I wanted somewhere that didn't need anything doing to it. I'm not into DIY or nest-building.'

'Or tidying, by the looks of it,' I said as I wandered into the living room. Two smaller rooms that had been knocked into one, it ran from the front of the house to the back, where dust motes danced in the early spring sunshine that shone in through the window.

It could have been a lovely room, but there was stuff everywhere. A battered hat sat jauntily on the back of an armchair. The sofa was covered with newspapers. Books were crammed onto a low table with dirty mugs, empty beer cans and a water purification kit.

I clicked my tongue disapprovingly. 'How on earth do you ever find anything?'

'I've got a system,' said Phin.

'Clearly it doesn't involve putting anything away!'

He made a face. 'There never seems much point. As far as I'm concerned, this is just somewhere to pack and unpack between trips.'

'What a shame.' It seemed a terrible waste to me. 'I'd love to live somewhere like this,' I said wistfully. 'This is my fantasy house, in fact.'

'The one you're saving up for?'

The chances of me ever being able to afford a house in Chelsea were so remote that I laughed. '*Fantasy*, I said! I'm saving for a studio at the end of a tube line, which will be all I can afford. And I'll be lucky if I can do that with London prices the way they are. But if I won the Lottery I'd buy a house just like this,' I said, turning slowly around and half closing my eyes as I visualised how it would be. 'I'd paint the front door blue and have window boxes at every window.'

'What's wrong with red?'

'Nothing. It's just that when I was a kid and used to dream about living in a proper house it always had a blue door, and I always swore that if I ever had a home of my own the door would be blue. I'd open it up, and inside it would be all light and stripped floorboards and no clutter...like this room could be if there wasn't all this mess!'

'It's not messy,' Phin protested. 'It's comfortable.'

'Yes, well, comfortable or not, we're going to have to clear up before Imelda and the photographer get here.'

I started to gather up the papers scattered over the sofa, but Phin grabbed them from me. 'Whoa—

no, you don't!' he said firmly. 'I'll never find anything again if you start tidying. I thought we agreed the idea was to let readers see me at home?'

'No, the *idea* is that readers have a glimpse of what their lives could be like if only they shopped at Gibson & Grieve all the time,' I reminded him. 'You're a TV personality, for heaven's sake! You know how publicity works. It's about creating an image, not showing reality.'

Ignoring his grumbles, I collected up all the mugs I could find and carried them through to the kitchen. I was glad to have something to do to take my mind off the still buzzy aftermath of that kiss. I was desperately aware of Phin, and the intimacy of the whole situation, and at least I could try and disguise it with briskness.

'We'll need to offer them coffee,' I said, dumping the dirty mugs on the draining board. 'Have you got any fresh?'

'Somewhere…' Phin deposited a pile of newspapers on a chair and opened the fridge. It was like a cartoon bachelor's fridge, stacked with beers and little else, but he found a packet of ground coffee, which he handed to me, and sniffed at a carton. 'The milk seems OK,' he said. 'There should be a cafetière around somewhere, too.'

It was in the sink, still with coffee grounds at the bottom. I dreaded to think how long it had been there. Wrinkling my nose, I got rid of the grounds in the bin and washed up the cafetière with the mugs.

'What sort of state is the rest of the house in?' I asked when I had finished.

'I haven't quite finished unpacking from Peru,' Phin said as he opened the door to his bedroom.

'Quite' seemed an understatement to me. There were clothes strewn everywhere, along with various other strange items that were presumably essential when you were hacking your way through the rainforest: a mosquito net, a machete, industrial strength insect repellent. You could barely see that it was an airy room, sparsely but stylishly furnished, and dominated by an invitingly wide bed which I carefully averted my eyes from.

Phin had no such qualms. 'That's where we make mad, passionate love,' he said. 'Most of the time,' he added, seeing me purse my lips and unable to resist teasing. 'Of course there's always the shower and the sofa—and remember that time up on the kitchen table…?'

'It sounds very unhygienic,' I said crisply. 'I'd never carry on like that.'

'You would if you really wanted me.'

'Luckily for you,' I said, 'I'm only interested in your mind.'

'Don't tell *Glitz* that,' said Phin, his eyes dancing. 'You'll ruin my reputation.'

'They're not going to be interested in our sex life, anyway.'

'Summer, what world are you living in? That's *exactly* what they'll be interested in! They're journalists on a celebrity rag. I can tell you now this Imelda won't give two hoots about our minds!'

I lifted my chin stubbornly. 'The interview is supposed to be about you as a potential family man, not as some sex symbol.'

'You know, sex is an important part of marriage,' he said virtuously. 'We don't want them thinking we're not completely compatible in every way.'

'Yes, well, let's concentrate on our compatibility in the living room rather than the bedroom,' I said, closing the bedroom door. 'We'll just have to hope that they don't want to come upstairs.'

Anxious to get away from the bedroom, with all its associations, I hurried back downstairs.

'We're going to have to do something about this room,' I decided, surveying the living room critically. 'It's not just the mess. It looks too much like a single guy's room at the moment.'

I made Phin clear away all the clutter—I think he just dumped it all in the spare room—while I ran around with a vacuum cleaner. It didn't look too bad by the time I'd finished, although even I thought it was a bit bare.

'It could do with some flowers, or a cushion or

two,' I said. 'Do you think I've got time to nip out before they get here?'

'Cushions?' echoed Phin, horrified. 'Over my dead body!'

'Oh, don't be such a baby. A couple of cushions wouldn't kill you.'

'Cushions are the beginning of the end,' he said mulishly. 'Next thing I know I'll be buying scented candles and ironing my sheets!'

'Sheets feel much nicer when they're ironed,' I pointed out, but he only looked at me in disbelief.

'I might as well be married. I've seen it happen to friends,' he told me. 'They meet a fabulous girl, they're having a great time, and then one day you go round and there's a cushion sitting on the sofa. You know it's the beginning of the end. You can count the days before that wedding invitation is dropping onto your mat!'

I rolled my eyes. I was feeling much better by that stage. I always find cleaning very comforting.

'Oh, very well, it's not as if we're supposed to be married,' I conceded. 'You'll just have to look as if you're keen enough on me to be considering a cushion some time soon.'

'I think I can manage looking keen,' said Phin, and something in his voice made me glance at him sharply. Amusement and something else glimmered in the depths of those blue eyes. Something that made my breath hitch and my heart thud uneasily in my throat. Something that sent me skittering right back to square one.

I moistened my lips, and cast around wildly for something to say. 'Shouldn't you go and change?' To my horror, my voice sounded high and tight.

'What for?' said Phin easily. 'They want to see me at home, don't they?'

'Well, yes, but you might want to look as if you've made a bit of an effort. You haven't even got any shoes on. You look as if you've just rolled out of bed,' I said, and then winced inwardly, wishing I hadn't mentioned bed.

'That's what we want them to think,' said Phin. 'And, now you come to mention it, I think you're the one who needs to do something about your appearance.'

'What do you mean?' Diverted, I peered anxiously into the mirror above the mantelpiece. Anne and I had spent hours the evening before, going through the clothes heaped on my bed and trying to pick just the right look. It had to be sexy enough for me to be in with a remote chance of being Phin's girlfriend, but at the same time I wanted it to fit with Gibson & Grieve's new family-friendly image.

'And you mustn't wear black or white next to your face,' Anne had said bossily. 'It's very draining in photographs. You want to look casual, but sophisticated, elegant, but colourful, sexy, but sensible.'

In the end we had decided on a pair of black wool trousers with a silky shirt I had worn to various Christmas parties the previous December. It was a lovely cherry-red, and I had painted my nails with Anne's favourite colour, Berry Bright, to match. I had even clipped my hair up loosely, the way I wore it at the weekend. I thought I looked OK.

'What's wrong with how I look?' I asked.

'You look much too neat and tidy,' said Phin, putting his hands on either side of my waist. 'Come here.'

'What are you doing?' I asked nervously as he drew me towards him.

'I'm going to make you look as you've just rolled out of bed, too. As if we rolled out of bed together.'

Lifting one hand, he pulled the clip from my hair so that it slithered forward. 'You shouldn't hide it away,' he said, twining his fingers through it. 'It's beautiful stuff. I thought it was just brown at first, but every time I look at it I see a different colour. Sometimes it looks gold, sometimes chestnut, sometimes honey. I swear I've even seen red in there…it makes me think of an autumn wood.'

I was speechless—and not just because of his closeness, which was making me feel hazy. No one had ever said anything like that to me before.

I didn't want to look into his eyes to see if he was joking or not. I was afraid that if I did I would lose what little grip I still had on my senses.

'Very poetic,' I managed.

'But it'll look even more beautiful tousled up,' said Phin—and, ignoring my protests, he mussed up my hair before turning his attention to my shirt. 'And, yes…I think we'll have to do something about this, too. There are just too many buttons done up here, and they're all done up the right way! That won't do at all.'

Very slowly, very deliberately, he undid the first two buttons and looked down at me, his eyes dark and blue.

'No, you still look horribly cool,' he said, which must have been a lie because my heart was thundering in my chest and I was burning where those blunt, surprisingly deft fingers had grazed my skin. I opened my mouth, but the words jammed in my throat, piling into an inarticulate sound that fell somewhere between a squeak and a gasp. He was barely touching me, but every cell in my body was screaming with awareness and I couldn't have moved if I had tried.

'I may have to work a bit harder on this one…' he went on and, bending his head, he blew gently just below my ear. The feel of it shuddered straight down my spine and clutched convulsively at its base. In spite of myself, I shivered.

'Mmm, yes, this may just work,' said Phin, pleased, and then he was trailing kisses down my neck, warm and soft and tantalising.

I really, *really* didn't want to respond, but I couldn't help myself. It was awful. It was as if some other woman had taken over my body, tipping her head back and sucking in her breath with another shudder of excitement.

My heart was thudding in my throat, and I could hear the blood rushing giddily in my ears.

'You see where I'm going with this,' murmured Phin, who was managing to undo another couple of buttons at the same time. 'I mean, we did discuss how important it was to make it look as if we found each other irresistible, didn't we?'

'I think that's probably enough buttons, though,' I croaked as he started on the other side of my neck. His hair was tickling my jaw and I could smell his shampoo. The wonderfully clean, male scent of his skin combined with the wicked onslaught of his lips was making my head spin, and I felt giddy and boneless.

Perhaps that was why I didn't resist as Phin steered me over to the great leather sofa. There was no way my legs were going to hold me up much longer, and as we sank down onto the cushions I felt as if I were sinking into a swirl of abandon.

'OK, no more buttons,' he whispered, and I could

feel his lips curving against my throat. 'But…I…don't…think…you…look…*quite*…convincing…enough…yet.'

Between each word he pressed a kiss along my jaw until he reached my mouth at last, and then his lips were on mine, and he was kissing me with an expertise that literally took my breath away. Since I'm being frank, I'll admit that it was a revelation. I'd never been kissed so surely, so thoroughly, so completely and utterly deliciously. So irresistibly.

I certainly couldn't resist it. I wound my arms around him, pulling him closer, and kissed him back.

It wasn't that I didn't know who he was or what I was doing, but I thought… Well, I don't know what I thought, OK? The truth is, I wasn't thinking at all. I was just *feeling*, the slither of the satiny shirt against my skin, the hardness and heat of his hands on me as he pushed the slippery material aside.

Just tasting…his mouth, his skin.

Just hearing the wild rush of my pulse, the uneven way he said my name, my own ragged breathing.

Just *touching*—fumbling at his T-shirt, tugging it up so that I could run my hands feverishly over his smoothly muscled back, marvelling at the way it flexed beneath my fingers. I let them drift up the warmth of his flanks and felt him shiver in response.

What can I say? I was lost, astonished at my own abandon, and yet helpless to pull myself back.

Or perhaps I'm not being *entirely* honest. I was aware at one level of my sensible self frantically waving her arms and ordering me back to safety, but Phin's body felt so good, so lean and hard as it pressed me into the sofa, and his mouth was so wickedly enticing, that I ignored her and let my fingers drift to the fastening of his jeans instead.

Afterwards, I could hardly believe it, but the truth is that there was a moment when I *did* know that I'd regret it later, and I still chose the lure of Phin's hands taking me to places I'd barely suspected before. I succumbed to the excitement rocketing through me, and if Imelda and the photographer hadn't arrived just then who knows where we would have ended up?

Except I do know, of course.

What I don't know is whether that would have been a good thing or a bad thing. I'm pretty sure I would have enjoyed it, though.

As it was, the piercing ring of the doorbell tore through the hazy pleasure and brought me right back to earth with a sickening crash.

I jerked bolt upright. 'Oh, my God, it's them!'

Frantically I tried to button up my shirt and shove it back into my trousers at the same time as pushing my hair behind my ears. 'What were we *doing*?'

Phin was infuriatingly unperturbed. He was barely breathing unsteadily. 'Well, I don't know about you, but *I've* been doing my bit for our pretence—and with all due modesty, I think I've excelled,' he said, and grinned as his eyes rested on my face. I dreaded to think what I looked like. 'Now you really *do* look the part.'

The bell rang again, more stridently this time. 'Ready?' asked Phin, and without waiting for me to answer strolled to open the door.

I could hear him exchanging chit-chat with Imelda and the photographer in the narrow hallway as I desperately tried to compose myself. I was horrified when I looked in the mirror to see that my hair was all over the place, my eyes huge and my lips swollen. I hardly recognised myself. I looked wild. I looked wanton.

I looked *sexy*.

I looked the part, just like Phin had said.

The next moment Phin was ushering Imelda into the room. She stopped when she saw me. 'Hello,' she said, obviously surprised.

'Hello,' I said weakly, and then remembered—far too late, I know—that I was the one who had set up this interview. I cleared my throat and stepped forward to shake her hand. 'We've spoken on the phone,' I said. 'I'm Summer Curtis—Phin's PA.'

'Ah.' Imelda looked amused, and when I followed her gaze I saw that she was looking at my shirt, which I had managed to button up all wrong in my haste.

Flushing, I made to fix the top button, and then realised that I was just going to get into an awful muddle unless I undid them all and started again. As Phin had no doubt intended.

'Not just my PA,' said Phin, coming to put his arm round my waist and pulling me into his side.

'So I see,' said Imelda dryly.

Her elegant brows lifted in surprise. I didn't blame her. She must have known as well as I did that I wasn't exactly Phin's usual type, and I lost confidence abruptly. We'd never be able to carry this off. Not in front of someone as sharp as Imelda.

'Shall I make coffee?' I asked quickly, desperate to get out of the room. My heart was still crashing clumsily around in my chest, and I was having a lot of trouble breathing. I felt trembly and jittery, and I kept going hot and cold as if I had a fever.

Perhaps I *did* have a fever? I latched onto the thought as I filled the kettle with shaking hands. That would explain the giddiness, the way I had melted into Phin with barely a moment's hesitation. My cheeks burned at the memory.

Not just my cheeks, to be honest.

When I came back in with a tray, having taken the opportunity to refasten my shirt and tuck myself in properly, Phin was leaning back on the sofa, looking completely relaxed. He pulled me down onto the sofa beside him. 'Thanks, babe,' he said, and rested a hand possessively on my thigh.

Babe? Ugh. I was torn between disgust and an agonising awareness of his hand touching my leg. It felt as if it were burning a hole through my trousers, and I was sure that when I took them off I would find an imprint of his palm scorched onto my skin.

'So, Phin,' said Imelda, when we had got the whole business of passing around the milk and sugar out of the way. 'It sounds as if you're making a lot of changes in your life right now. Does your new role at Gibson & Grieve mean you're ready to stop travelling?'

'I won't stop completely,' he said. 'I've still got various programme commitments, and besides, I'm endlessly curious about the world. There are still so many wonderful places to see, and so many exciting things to do. I'm never going to turn my back on all that completely. Having said that, my father's stroke did make me reassess my priorities. Gibson & Grieve is part of my life, and it feels good to be involved in the day to day running of it. It's time for me to do my part, instead of leaving it all to my brother.

'And then, of course, there's Summer.' He lifted my hand and pressed a kiss it. His lips were warm and sure, and a shiver travelled down my spine. I did my best to disguise it by shifting on the sofa, but I saw Imelda look at me. 'She's changed everything for me.'

'You're thinking of settling down?' She made a moue of exaggerated disappointment. 'That's another of the most eligible bachelors off the available list!'

'I'm afraid so,' said Phin, entwining his fingers with mine. 'I was always afraid of the idea of settling down, but since I've met Summer it doesn't seem so much like giving up my freedom as finding what I've been looking for all these years.'

You've got to admit he was good. No one could have guessed he'd been ranting about cushions and commitment only a few minutes earlier.

Imelda was lapping it all up, while I sat with a stupid smile on my face, not knowing what to do with my expression. Should I look besotted? Shy? Smug?

'You're a lucky woman.' Imelda turned to me. 'What's it like knowing that half the women in the country would like to be in your place?'

I cleared my throat. 'To be honest, it hasn't sunk in yet. It's still very new.'

'But it feels absolutely right, doesn't it?' Phin put in.

He was doing so much better than me that I felt I should make an effort. 'Yes,' I said slowly, 'funnily enough, it does.'

And then, bizarrely, it didn't seem so difficult. I

smiled at him, and he smiled back, and for a long moment we just looked at each other and there was nothing but the blueness of his eyes and the thud of my heart and the air shortening around us.

It took a pointed cough from Imelda to jerk me back to reality. With an effort, I dragged my eyes from Phin's and tried to remember what I was supposed to be talking about. Phin, that was it. Phin and me and our supposed passion for each other.

'We're so different in lots of ways,' I told Imelda, and the words seemed to come unbidden. 'Phin isn't at all the kind of guy I thought I would fall in love with, but it turns out that he's exactly right for me.'

'So it wasn't love at first sight for you?'

'No, he was just…my boss.'

'And what made the difference for you?'

Images rushed through my head like the flickering pages of a book. Phin smiling. Phin wiping cream from my cheek. Phin pulling the clip from my hair. Phin's mouth and Phin's hands and the hard excitement of Phin's body.

'I…I don't know,' I said hesitantly. 'I just looked at him one day and knew that I was in love with him.'

I thought it was pretty feeble, but Imelda was nodding as if she understood and looking positively dewy-eyed.

I was all set to relax then, but that was only the

beginning. I still had to endure an excruciating photo session, posing cuddled up to Phin or looking at him adoringly, and my nerves were well and truly frayed by the time it was over. I tried to get out of the photographs, pleading that the article was about Phin, not me, but Imelda was adamant.

'All our readers will want to see the lucky woman who has convinced Phin Gibson to settle down,' she insisted.

I can tell you, I didn't feel very lucky by the time we'd finished. I was exhausted by the effort of pretending to be in love with Phin, while simultaneously trying to convince him that all the touching and kissing was having no effect on me at all.

But at last it was over. We waved them off from the steps, and then Phin closed the door and grinned at me. 'Very good,' he said admiringly. 'You practically had me convinced!'

'You didn't do badly yourself,' I said. 'You weren't lying when you said you were a good actor.'

No harm in reminding him that I knew he *had* been acting.

'If you can fool a hard-boiled journalist like Imelda, you should be able to fool Jonathan,' Phin said.

Why hadn't I remembered Jonathan before? I wondered uneasily. Jonathan was the reason I was doing this. I should have been thinking about him all morning, not about the sick, churning excitement I felt when Phin kissed me.

'Let's hope so,' I said, as coolly as I could. I looked at my watch. 'We'd better get back to the office.'

'What's the rush? Let's have lunch first,' said Phin. 'We should celebrate.'

'Celebrate what?'

'A successful interview, for one thing. Promoting Gibson & Grieve's family image. And let's not forget our engagement.'

'We're not engaged,' I said repressively.

'As good as,' he said, shrugging on his jacket and slipping a wallet into the inside pocket. He held the door open for me. 'You're now officially the woman who's convinced me to settle down.'

'You may be settling down, but I'm certainly not spending my life with anyone who calls me babe!'

Phin grinned at me as he pulled the door closed behind him. 'It's a mark of affection.'

'It's patronising.'

'Well, what would you like me to call you?'

'What's wrong with my name?'

'Every self-respecting couple has special names for each other,' he pointed out.

We walked towards the King's Road. 'Well, if you have to, you can call me darling,' I allowed after a moment, but Phin shook his head, his eyes dancing.

'No, no—darling is much too restrained, too

ordinary, for you. You're much sexier than you realise, and we need to make sure Jonathan realises, too. Shall I call you bunnikins?'

'Shall I punch you on the nose?' I retorted sweetly.

He laughed. 'Pumpkin? Muffin? Cupcake?'

'Cupcake?'

'You'd be surprised,' said Phin. 'But you're right. I don't see you as a cupcake. What about cookie?'

'Oh, please!'

'Or—I know! This is perfect for you, and in keeping with the baking theme...cream puff?'

'Don't you dare!'

'Cream puff it is,' said Phin, as if I hadn't spoken. 'All crispy on the outside, but soft and delicious in the middle. It couldn't be better for you,' he said. 'That's settled. So, what are you going to call me?'

I looked at him. 'You really—*really*—don't want to know,' I said.

CHAPTER SEVEN

PHIN only smiled and took my hand. 'Come along, my little cream puff. Let's go and find some lunch. If you don't want to celebrate our non-engagement, let's just celebrate the fact that it's a beautiful day. What more reason do we need, anyway?'

I tried to imagine Jonathan suggesting that we celebrated the fact that the sun was shining, but I couldn't do it. It wasn't that he was a killjoy. Jonathan would celebrate a promotion, a rise in profits, a successful advertising campaign, perhaps. But a lovely day? I didn't think so.

And if he did celebrate he would want to plan it. Jonathan would book the very best restaurant, or order the most expensive champagne. He wouldn't just wander along the King's Road the way Phin did, and find the first place with a table in a sunny window.

But that was why I loved Jonathan, I reminded myself hastily. I loved him precisely because he *wasn't* spontaneous, because he was the kind of man who would think things through and plan them sensibly, instead of dropping everything when the sun came out, and because he didn't act on a whim the way my mother and Phin did.

On the other hand, I have to admit that I enjoyed that lunch—although that may have been largely due to the large glass of wine that came with it. I asked for water, but the wine came, and then it seemed too much of a fuss to send it back, so I ended up drinking it. I'm not used to drinking in the middle of the day, and I could feel myself flushing, and laughing a lot more than I usually do.

Perhaps it was relief at having got through the interview. Perhaps it was the sunshine.

Or perhaps it was Phin sitting opposite me, making me believe that there was nowhere else he would rather be and no one else he would rather be with. Having spent months having to be grateful for any time Jonathan could spare me, it was a novel sensation for me to be the focus of attention for a change.

It was so little, really—to feel that Phin saw *me* when he looked at me, that he was listening, really listening, to what I was saying—but I'd have been less than human if I hadn't responded, and I could feel myself unfurling in the simple pleasure of having lunch with an attractive man on a sunny day.

It was very unlike me. I'm normally very puritanical about long lunches in office time. I wasn't myself that day.

I felt really quite odd, in fact. Fizzy, is the best way to describe it, as if that kiss had left all my senses on high alert. I was desperately aware of Phin opposite me, scanning the menu. I could see every one of the laughter lines around his eyes, the crease in his cheek, and that dent at the corner of his crooked mouth which always seemed on the point of breaking into a smile.

I was supposed to be looking at the menu, too, but I couldn't concentrate. My eyes kept flickering over to him, skittering from the prickle of stubble on his jaw to his hands, to his throat and then back to that mobile mouth. And my own mouth dried at the memory of how excitingly sure his lips had been.

My whole body still seemed to be humming with the feel of his hands, of his mouth, but at the same time it seemed hard to believe that we could have kissed like that and yet be sitting here quite normally, as if nothing had happened at all. I shifted uncomfortably as I remembered how eagerly I had kissed Phin back. What must he think of me?

On the other hand, it hadn't been a *real* kiss, had it? It hadn't meant anything. Phin had made it clear enough that he had only been kissing me for effect, and I wondered if I ought to make it clear that I had been doing the same. And, yes, I know, that wasn't exactly how it was, but a girl has her pride.

Or perhaps I should pretend to ignore the whole issue?

I was still dithering when Phin looked up from the menu. 'Have you decided? I'm going to have a starter, too. I don't know about you, but all that kissing has given me an appetite!'

Now that he had raised the subject, I thought I might as well take the opportunity to make my position quite clear.

'Speaking of kissing,' I said, and was secretly impressed at how cool I sounded, 'perhaps we ought to discuss what happened earlier. I understand *why* you kissed me—' I went on.

Phin's brows lifted and his smile gleamed. 'Do you, now?'

'Of course. It created a convincing effect for Imelda, and I can see that it worked, but I hope there won't be any need to repeat it,' I said, at my most priggish.

Much effect it had on Phin. 'Now, there we differ, cream puff, because I hope there *will*. I enjoyed that kiss very much. Didn't you?'

My eyes darted around the table and I longed for the nerve to lie.

'I just don't want to lose sight of what we're

trying to do here,' I said evasively. 'And don't call me cream puff.'

'That wasn't quite an answer to my question, though, was it?' said Phin with a provocative smile.

I might have known he wouldn't let me get away with it.

We locked eyes for a mute moment, until he gave in with a grin and a shake of his head.

'Look, don't worry. I haven't forgotten that for you this is about getting Jonathan back.'

'And it's promoting Gibson & Grieve,' I added quickly, not wanting it to be all about me. 'Not to mention keeping Jewel at arm's length!'

'All very fine causes,' Phin agreed with a virtuous expression. 'But since we're going through this pretence, it seems to me we might as well enjoy it. We're not going to look like a very convincing couple if we never touch each other, are we? Touching is what couples do.'

Jonathan and I had never touched in public. But then we hadn't been a real couple, had we?

'OK,' I said, 'but only when necessary.'

'Only when necessary,' he confirmed, and held up crossed fingers. 'Scout's honour. Now, let's get serious and talk about lunch…'

I felt that I had made my point, and after that I was able to relax a little. I suppose that glass of wine helped, too. I don't remember what we talked about—just nonsense, I think—but I was still in an uncharacteristically light-hearted mood when we made it back to the office.

We waited for a lift in the glossy atrium, with the sun angling through the building to lie across the floor in a broad stripe. Phin was telling me about a disastrous trip he'd been on for one of the *Into the Wild* programmes, where everything that could possibly go wrong had done, and I was laughing when the lift pinged at last and the doors slid open to reveal Lex and Jonathan.

There was a moment of startled silence, then they stepped out. I had a sudden image of myself through Lex's eyes, flushed and laughing and dishevelled. Somewhere along the line I had mislaid my clip, and my hair was still tumbling to my shoulders. In my silky red shirt I must have looked almost unrecognisable from my usual crisp self.

My smile faded as I encountered first Lex's stern gaze, then Jonathan's astounded look.

'Hello,' said Phin cheerfully. 'Don't tell me you two are sloping off early?'

'We've got a meeting in the City.' Pointedly Lex looked at his watch and, like Pavlov's dog, I looked at mine, too. My eyes nearly started out of my head when I saw that it was almost three o'clock. How had it got that late?

'I see you're not letting your new position here

change your work ethic,' he added, with one of his trademark sardonic looks.

Phin was unperturbed. 'Less of the sarcasm, please,' he said. He was the only person I knew who wasn't the slightest bit intimidated by Lex. I suppose it helped that Lex was his brother. 'I'll have you know we've been busy promoting Gibson & Grieve all morning.'

'It's some time since morning,' said Lex, less than impressed.

'We've been recovering from the stress of persuading the media of my family friendly credentials. Summer did an absolutely brilliant job.'

I wished he hadn't mentioned me. Lex's cold grey gaze shifted back to me, and it took all I had not to squirm. I was unnervingly aware of Jonathan's astounded gaze fixed on me, too. I managed a weak smile.

'Remarkable,' was all Lex said.

'Isn't she?' said Phin fondly, putting an arm around me and pulling me against him. I could feel the heat and weight of his hand at my waist, making the slippery material of my shirt shift over my skin. 'That's just what I've been telling her.'

'We're so late,' I wailed as soon as we got in the lift. I could feel myself winding rapidly back up to my usual self. I was *never* late. Well, there had been yesterday, after the pomegranate martinis, but that had been exceptional circumstances. I couldn't believe that I had actually sat there in the sun and let time tick by without even thinking about getting back to the office.

'We're not late,' said Phin. 'We haven't got any appointments this afternoon.'

'I should have been back earlier,' I fretted, remembering Jonathan and Lex's raised brows. 'I wish they hadn't seen me like this,' I said as I tugged my shirt into place. 'I look so unprofessional.'

'Nonsense. You look fantastic,' said Phin. 'We couldn't have planned it better if we had tried. Did you *see* Jonathan's expression?'

I nodded. 'He was horrified,' I said gloomily.

'He wasn't horrified. He was absolutely amazed.' Phin spoke with complete authority. 'He looked at you and saw exactly what he could have had if he'd ever taken the trouble to kiss you senseless on a sofa and then take you out to lunch. He didn't like me touching you either,' he added.

'How on earth do you know that?'

'It's a guy thing.' Phin smiled smugly. 'Trust me, Summer, our little plan is working already.'

I know I should have been delighted, but actually I spent the rest of the afternoon feeling scratchy and unsettled. It was impossible to concentrate. It wasn't fair, the way Phin could be so casual about it all. How could he kiss me like that and then turn round and sound pleased at the idea of handing me on to someone else?

Easily, of course. It was a guy thing, just like he had said. Phin was perfectly happy to enjoy a kiss, or a long lunch, as long as there was no suggestion of any long-term commitment.

I'm not the settling down type, he had said. Well, no surprises there. And no reason for his cheerful admission to leave me feeling not *depressed*, exactly, but just a bit…flat.

I told myself not to be so silly.

So there we were, in this ridiculous situation, working together as boss and PA during the day, and at night pretending to be madly in love.

Whenever I stopped to think about what we were doing I wondered what on earth had possessed me to agree to such a thing, so it was easier to carry on as if it were perfectly normal to spend your days talking to your boss about brand marketing or strategic development or the logistics of taking twenty people to Africa to help build a medical centre, and your nights holding his hand and leaning into his warm, solid body as if you knew it as well as your own.

It was a strange time, but the funny thing was it really did seem quite normal after a while. I couldn't understand why everybody else didn't see through the pretence right away, but they all seemed to accept it without question. It was bizarre.

I was so unlike Phin's normal girlfriends, most of whom he still seemed to get on excellently with. To a woman, they were lushly glamorous and prone to extravagant kisses, with much 'mwah-mwah' and many 'darlings' scattered around. Next to them, I felt prim and boring. I tried to loosen up, but every time Phin put his arm around me or took my hand my senses would snarl into a knot and I would prickle all over with awareness. It wasn't exactly relaxing.

The first night we appeared as a couple we went to a party, to launch some perfume, I think. Something unlikely, anyway. I can remember wondering why on earth Phin had been invited, but he seemed to be on hobnobbing terms with all sorts of celebrities. That was also the first time I realised quite how many ex-girlfriends he had, and I was glad I hadn't done anything silly like let myself wonder if that kiss might have meant something to Phin, too.

Still, I was nervous. It was all so strange to me, and I was feeling very self-conscious in a short dress with spaghetti straps which I had borrowed from Anne. It showed rather more flesh than I was used to, and when Phin let his hand slide down my spine I shivered.

He clicked his tongue. 'You're too tense,' he

murmured in my ear. 'You're supposed to like me touching you.'

'Anyone would be tense, meeting all your ex-girlfriends like this,' I said out of the corner of my mouth, while keeping my smile fixed in place. 'They're all wondering what on earth you're doing with me.'

'Their boyfriends aren't.' His smile glimmered as he ran a knuckle along the neckline of my dress. 'You look delectable, in a behind-closed-doors kind of way.'

I hated the way every cell in my body seemed to leap at his touch. It made it very hard to remember that I was in control.

'What kind of way is that?' I asked, squirming at the breathlessness in my voice.

'You know—all cool on the surface, but making every man feel that if only he were lucky enough to get you on your own you'd be every hot-blooded male's fantasy.'

'Oh, please,' I said edgily, moving away from him. 'And stop stroking me!'

'Nope,' said Phin as he pulled me easily back against him. 'You're my girlfriend, and I can't keep my hands off you!'

'You've clearly got the same problem with your ex-girlfriends too,' I said waspishly. 'I notice you're still very touchy-feely with them.'

'Could it be that you're jealous, cream puff?'

'I'm hardly likely to be jealous, am I? I'm just keeping in character, like you. I'm sure if I really was your new girlfriend I wouldn't want to see quite how chummy you still are with them.'

'I'm just saying hello to old friends.'

I sniffed. 'I can manage to say hello to friends without sticking my tongue down their throats!'

'You do exaggerate, Summer—' Phin began, amused, and then broke off. 'Uh-oh. Do you see who I see?'

I followed his gaze to where Jewel Stevens was wrapped around a young guy who looked vaguely familiar to me. I wondered if I'd seen him on television. He was very pretty, but had a vacuous look about him.

'That's Ricky Roland,' said Phin in my ear. 'He's a rising star, they say, and just as well if he's going to get involved with Jewel! He'll be able to afford a new dinner service. I wonder how many plates he's got left?'

'She's coming over,' I hissed as Jewel somehow spotted Phin and made a beeline for him, abandoning poor Ricky with barely a word. Phin promptly put his arm around my waist and pulled me closer, so that I was half in front of him like a shield.

'Phin, darling, where have you *been*?' she cried as she came up—and, completely ignoring my existence, she gave him a smacking kiss on the lips.

'Peru,' he said, keeping a firm hold of me.

'What on earth for?' said Jewel, but didn't bother to wait for his reply. She glanced languidly around at the party. 'This is all very tedious, isn't it? We're all going on to a club after this if you want to come.'

'Not tonight, thanks, Jewel,' said Phin, his smile steady but inflexible. 'I'm taking Summer home. You remember Summer, don't you?'

Jewel's eyes flicked over me as if I was something unpleasant Phin had brought in on the bottom of his shoe. 'No.'

Charming, I thought. 'I'm Phin's PA,' I reminded her.

'And so much more than that, too,' said Phin.

At that, Jewel's gaze sharpened, and she looked from Phin to me, and then back to Phin again. 'You and…Sunshine, or whatever her name is?' she said incredulously.

'Yes,' said Phin blandly. 'Me and Summer.'

Disconcertingly, Jewel began to laugh. 'You and your little secretary…isn't that a bit of a cliché, darling?'

Phin's arm tightened around me, but his voice was admirably even. 'That's the thing about clichés,' he said. 'They're so often true.'

'Well, if you say so.' Jewel was evidently unconvinced. Her brown eyes rested speculatively on me once more, and I could practically hear her thinking that I was too boring to hold Phin's attention for more than five minutes. 'How very odd,' she said.

And then she leant forward to Phin and did her ear licking trick again. *Bleuch*. 'When you're bored and want some excitement again, give me a call,' she said huskily, only to shriek and leap back as I moved, managing to stand on her foot and spill my glass of champagne all down her fabulous dress at the same time.

It was quite a clever move, even if I say so myself. Subtle, but effective.

'Oh, I'm *so* sorry,' I said insincerely as she glared at me. I could feel Phin's body shaking with suppressed laughter. 'How clumsy of me.'

I could see Jewel debating whether to make a scene, but in the end she just sent me a poisonous look and kissed Phin once more. On the mouth, this time, which was a fairly effective retort of her own.

'You know where to find me when you change your mind, darling,' she said to him.

My lips thinned as she prowled off to reclaim Ricky Roland, who was making the big mistake of talking to a pretty girl about his own age. I didn't fancy his chances of keeping the rest of his plates intact.

'When!' I huffed. 'She's got a nerve, hasn't she? Not even *if* you lose interest in me!'

'Yes, but the round definitely went to you, with

the champagne spilling trick,' said Phin, letting me go at last. 'That was an excellent impression of a jealous girlfriend, Summer. I didn't think you had it in you!'

'I don't think it convinced Jewel,' I said. 'She clearly didn't believe for a moment that you'd be interested in anyone as boring as me!'

'No? Well, her style is much more obvious than yours.'

'You can say that again!'

He studied me for a moment. 'Personally, I think that restrained look is good for you. It's classy. On the other hand, it *would* look more natural if you could be a little more relaxed.'

'What do you mean?'

'We may have to do something about making you look a *little* less like a librarian who's strayed into an orgy,' said Phin. 'It works for me—don't get me wrong!—but other people might wonder eventually why you're so tense with me.'

'Maybe they'll think I'm shy,' I said, on the defensive. I knew I looked uptight—I *felt* uptight—but then so would you if you had to snuggle up to Phin while Jewel stuck her tongue down his ear, and I wasn't used to parties where you fell over a celebrity every time you turned round.

'You can get away with being shy tonight, but the next time we go out you'll need to loosen up a bit.'

'How do you suggest I do that?' I snapped, annoyed because I knew he was right.

'I'm not sure yet,' said Phin. 'I'll give it some thought.'

But, apart from Jewel, everyone seemed to accept our supposed relationship with an extraordinary lack of surprise. Monique, Lex's PA, whom I'd always admired for her perspicacity, even told me that she thought Phin and I were a perfect match!

'You're just right for each other,' she said when we met in the corridor one day, on my way back from making coffee. 'He's so lovely, isn't he?' she went on, while I was still boggling at the idea that anyone could think Phin and I were right for each other when it must be blindingly obvious that we were completely different.

'Lex is always baffled by him, but Phin is a huge asset to Gibson & Grieve if only he'd recognise it. He's one of those people that just has to walk into a room and everyone relaxes, because you know he'll be able to defuse any situation and charm everyone so they'll all go away feeling good about themselves, whatever's been decided.'

I did some more boggling then. Relaxed was the last thing I felt with Phin. He was too unpredictable. One minute he'd be sitting lazily with his feet up on the desk, the next he'd be fizzing with energy. I never knew when he was going to appear or what he was going to do.

Whenever Phin was around I felt edgy, jittery. My pulse was prone to kicking up a beat at the most inexplicable moments. All he had to do was stretch his arms above his head and yawn, or look at me with that smile twitching at his mouth, and my heart would start to thump and an alarming shivery feeling would uncoil in my belly and tremble outwards, until my whole skin prickled with awareness. It was very disturbing.

Relaxed? Ha!

'How are *you* anyway, Monique?' I asked, sick of being told how wonderful Phin was.

'Fantastic,' she said, beaming. 'In fact...' She checked to make sure no one else was around. 'I'm not telling many people yet, as it's early days, but I'm pregnant!'

I was delighted for her. I knew that Monique and her husband had been hoping for a baby for a while now. 'Monique, that's wonderful news! Dave must be thrilled.'

'He is. Lex is less so, of course,' she said, with a wry roll of her eyes.

Monique adored her boss, but she had no illusions about him. With Lex it was business all the way, and babies just didn't enter the equation.

'He was grumbling just this morning that if I'd

told him earlier he would never have let you go and work for Phin—and what a shame that would have been!' She hesitated. 'I don't suppose you'd want to go back to Lex's office now, but he'll be looking for someone he trusts to cover my maternity leave, so if you're interested there might be an opening in a few months.'

'*Really?*'

'The baby's due in September, so I'll work up until August,' she said. 'Talk it over with Phin and see what he thinks. If you're spending all your time together, it might not be a bad thing to work in different offices...but you'd obviously want to vet any new PA!' Monique could obviously see the thoughts whirling in my brain. 'Maybe I shouldn't have said anything? I was just being selfish. It would make it so much easier for me if I could reassure Lex that you'd look after him while I'm away, that's all.'

'I'll definitely think about it,' I promised.

Thoughtfully, I carried the coffee back to my office. To be Lex's PA—the most senior in the company...! Only temporarily, of course, until Monique came back. But what a thing to have on my CV. It would be an extraordinary opportunity, and one I could only ever have dreamed of up to now.

It was hard to believe that only a month ago I had felt utterly hopeless. Now I not only had the prospect of a fantastic promotion, but there was even a real chance of getting back together with Jonathan. Or so Phin seemed to think—and, much as I hated to admit that he was right, I had to admit that Jonathan had been much more friendly the last few days. He had taken to dropping by the office on the slimmest of pretexts, and telling me how nice I looked if we met by the lifts.

It was all very confusing. Everything was changing so quickly I didn't know what to think any more.

I should be excited. I knew that. In a few months' time I could be back with Jonathan and working with the Chief Executive—and Phin... Well, this had only ever been meant as a temporary exercise anyway. Phin would move on. He'd go back to making television programmes and I wouldn't see him any more. There would be no more jitteriness, no more exasperation, no more teasing. No more doughnuts. And that would be fine, I told myself. It would all work out perfectly.

But there was a sick feeling in the pit of my stomach all the same.

'What's up?' said Phin, when I took in his coffee. It was uncanny the way he always knew if something had happened, no matter how smooth I made my expression.

So I told him what Monique had said. 'Typical Lex,' was his comment, when he heard about his brother's response to the news that his PA was having a much longed for baby. 'He's got no idea. You'd think he could be happy for her before he thought about how her pregnancy will affect Gibson & Grieve!'

'Monique doesn't really mind,' I said, a little uncomfortably. 'She knows what he's like. The normal rules don't apply to someone like Lex.'

'Well, they should,' said Phin. He was leaning back, twirling a pen between his fingers. 'So what about you?' he asked, blue eyes suddenly intent. 'Do you really want to work for a man who wouldn't know what a doughnut was, let alone think about buying you one?'

'It would be a good career opportunity for me.' Unable to bear it any longer, I held out my hand for the pen, and after a stubborn moment he surrendered it, dropping it into my open palm.

'At least I wouldn't have to put up with your endless fiddling any longer,' I said, putting the pen back into its holder. 'And it might be easier when our supposed romance falls through,' I added. 'It would look a bit odd if we carried on working together perfectly happily when…if…'

'When you're back with Jonathan?' Phin finished for me.

There was an unusual note in his voice that made me look sharply at him.

'Even if that doesn't happen, we can't carry on like this indefinitely,' I pointed out.

'Then we'll have to make sure it does happen,' he said, swinging his feet off the desk abruptly. 'Maybe it's time to intensify our campaign. When's the launch party for the *Charmless Chef*?'

The *Charmless Chef* was Phin's own title for a series of TV food programmes that Gibson & Grieve were sponsoring that spring. It was actually called *Hodge Hits*, after the presenter, celebrity chef Stephen Hodge. Hodge was famously rude, and prone to the most appalling temper tantrums. Very early in his career he had discovered that the worse he behaved, the more audiences would want to watch him and the more he would be paid.

This meant Gibson & Grieve would get even more publicity from their sponsorship of the programme, and a fabulous party had been planned to mark the launch and appease his monstrous ego. All senior staff were on a three line whip to turn up and do whatever it took to keep Stephen Hodge happy. Except Lex, of course. He hated socialising, and only went out when absolutely necessary. On this occasion Phin was lined up to represent him and make a speech.

'It's on Friday,' I said.

'Jonathan will be there, won't he?'

'Of course. He negotiated the deal with Stephen Hodge,' I reminded Phin.

'In that case you'll have to pull out all the stops. You always look smart, but on Friday you've got to look stunning. Take tomorrow off and buy a special dress if you have to, but wear something that will knock Jonathan's socks off.'

'He'll be too busy with Stephen Hodge to notice me,' I protested, but Phin refused to listen to any objections.

'If you get the right dress he'll notice you, all right,' he said. 'Besides, I have a cunning plan up my sleeve to relax you.'

'What sort of plan?' I asked suspiciously. I had tried to loosen up whenever we'd been out together, but it was almost impossible when every cell in my body jolted if Phin so much as grazed me with his touch.

'I'll explain on Friday,' he said. 'The launch is at seven, isn't it? We might as well go straight from here.'

Which is how I ended up changing in the directors' bathroom that Friday evening. I'd brought my dress in on a hanger, and carried shoes and make-up in a separate bag.

I had put the need to look stunning to Anne, who had borne me off late-night shopping the night before, and bullied me into buying the most expensive dress I'd ever owned. Even though I felt faintly sick whenever I thought about my credit card bill, I couldn't regret it. It was *so* beautiful.

I don't really know how to begin to describe it. It was red, but not that hard pillarbox red that's so hard to wear. This was a softer, deeper, warmer red—a simple sleeveless sheath, with a layer of chiffon that floated and swirled as I walked. I wasn't used to such a plunging neckline, and with bare shoulders and a bare back I felt a lot more exposed than usual, but it was the kind of dress you couldn't help but feel good in.

I'd painted my toenails a lovely deep red—Ruby, Ruby—to match my fingers, and slipped my feet into beautiful jewelled sandals. My hair was swept up into a clip, and I thought it looked elegant like that, but I hesitated as I studied my reflection, remembering Phin's librarian comment. On an impulse I pulled the clip out and shook my hair free, and then I walked back into the office before I could change my mind.

Phin was there, adjusting his bow tie, but his fingers froze when he saw me. There was a moment of stunned silence. 'Dear God,' he said blankly.

My confidence promptly evaporated. 'What's wrong with it?' I asked, looking down at my lovely dress. I'd been so sure he would like it.

'Nothing's wrong.' Phin cleared his throat. 'Nothing at all. You look…incredible.'

He sounded a bit odd, I thought, but he had said I looked incredible. 'Shall I order a taxi?' I asked after a moment.

'No, it's all sorted,' he said, still distracted. 'A car's waiting downstairs.'

'Oh. Well, shall we go, then?'

Phin seemed to pull himself together. 'Not quite yet, CP,' he said, making a good recovery. 'We need to put my cunning plan into action first.'

'CP?' I echoed blankly.

'Cream...' He waited expectantly for me to supply the rest.

Puff, in fact. I sighed.

'Oh, for heaven's sake,' I said crossly. 'Will you *stop* with the silly names? Now, what *is* this plan of yours?'

'It's really quite simple,' said Phin, coming towards me. 'I'm going to kiss you.'

CHAPTER EIGHT

'KISS me?' The world titled disconcertingly beneath my feet, and it took me a moment to realise that the air was leaking out of my lungs. I drew in a hissing breath, glad of the steadying effect of the oxygen. We had been through this before, I remembered. 'What kind of plan is that?'

'A good one,' said Phin.

'We agreed that you would only kiss me again if it was necessary,' I reminded him, backing away. My voice was embarrassingly croaky, but under the circumstances—i.e. pounding heart, racing pulse, entrails squeezed with nerves or, more worryingly, anticipation—I didn't think I did too badly.

'I think it *is* necessary,' he said.

I had ended up against the desk, the wood digging into the back of my thighs. 'There's no one else here,' I pointed out bravely. 'How can it be necessary?'

Phin kept coming until he was right in front of me. 'That's the whole point,' he said.

'I've been thinking about it. If we kiss before we go out every time you'll get used to it. It'll just seem part of the evening, like putting on your lipstick—although you might think about doing that *after* we kiss next time. You'll look much more relaxed after a kiss,' he went on. 'Remember how well it worked before the *Glitz* interview?'

'We're not kissing like that again!' My eyes went involuntarily to the sofas on the other side of the room. If we ended up on one of those we'd never get to the party.

'Maybe not *quite* like that,' Phin agreed. A smile hovered around his mouth. The mouth I was doing my level best not to look at. 'Not that it wasn't very nice, but what we want now is for you to feel more comfortable. Once kissing me feels normal, you'll stop feeling so tense whenever I touch you.'

'It's not going to feel normal tonight.'

'No, but I can tell you that if you go to the party in that dress, looking thoroughly kissed, it won't just be Jonathan I'll be fighting off with a stick,' Phin promised.

Jonathan. The thought of him steadied me. Jonathan was the reason I was wearing this dress... wasn't he?

'Go on, admit it,' said Phin. 'It's a good plan, isn't it?'

I eyed him dubiously. I couldn't help remembering the last time we had kissed. I had got carried away then, and I didn't want that to happen again. On the other hand, I didn't want to admit to Phin that I was nervous about losing control. Somehow I had to pretend that it wasn't that big a deal.

'It might work,' I conceded, and he grinned.

'Come along, then—pucker up, cream puff,' he said. 'The sooner we get it over with, the sooner we can get to the party.'

'Oh, very well.' I gave in. 'If you really think it'll help.'

Maybe it *would* help, I told myself. Instead of constantly wondering what it would be like to touch him again, I would know.

So I stood very still and lifted my face for Phin's kiss, pursing my lips and closing my eyes.

And willing myself not to respond.

Nothing happened at first, and, feeling foolish, I opened my eyes again in time to see him brush my hair gently back over my shoulders. Then very slowly, almost thoughtfully, he slid his hands up the sides of my throat to cup my face. His eyes never left mine, and I felt as if I were trapped in their blueness. My heart was slamming against my ribs.

My mouth felt dry, and I had moistened my lips before I realised what an inviting gesture it was.

Phin smiled. We were so close I could see every eyelash, every one of the tiny creases in his lips, the precise depth of the dent at the corner of his mouth, and I felt dizzy with the nearness of him.

By the time he lowered his head and touched his mouth to mine my blood was thumping with anticipation, and I couldn't help the tiny gasp of relief that parted my lips beneath his.

I willed myself to stay still and unresponsive. All I had to do was stand there for a few seconds and it would be over. How difficult could it be?

You try it. That's all I can say. Try not responding when a man with warm, strong hands twines his fingers in your hair and pulls you closer. When a man with warm, sure lips explores your mouth tantalisingly gently at first, then more insistently. When he smells wonderful and tastes better.

When every kiss pulls at a thread inside you, unravelling you faster and faster, until the world rocks and your bones melt and the only way to stay upright is to clutch at him and kiss him back.

'That's better,' murmured Phin when he lifted his head at last.

I was flushed and trembling, but I was glad to see that his breathing wasn't quite steady either.

'There—it wasn't so bad, was it?' he added, sliding his hands reluctantly from my hair.

'It was fine,' I managed, hoping my legs were going to hold me up without him to hang on to. I was very glad there was a car waiting downstairs.

It was going to take all I had to get to the lift, and I was in no shape to trek to the tube—even if my shoes had been up to it.

For reasons best known to the television company, the launch party for *Hodge Hits* was being held in the Orangery at Kew Gardens. I'd never been before, and it looked so beautiful with that row of high arched windows that I actually forgot my throbbing lips and crackling pulse as I looked around me.

The room was already crowded, but I caught a glimpse of Stephen Hodge, surrounded by groupies as always, wearing his trademark scowl. He had long hair that always looked as if it could do with a good wash, and he was very thin. There's something unnatural about a thin chef, don't you think? I suspected that Stephen Hodge never ate his own food and, having seen some of his more innovative recipes, I didn't blame him.

'Now, be nice,' said Phin, seeing my lip curl.

'That's good, coming from you,' I countered. 'Are you sure you've got the right speech with you?'

He'd tried a scurrilous version on me earlier, which had been very funny but which was unlikely to go down well with either Hodge or Jonathan, who had been instrumental in setting up the sponsorship. I was hoping that he had a suitably bland alternative in his pocket somewhere, but with Phin you never knew.

'Don't worry, I've got the toadying version right here,' he said, patting his jacket. 'Besides, you're not in PA mode tonight. You're my incredibly sexy girlfriend and don't you forget it. Talking of which—' he nudged me '—look who's heading our way. Or rather don't look. You're supposed to be absorbed in me.'

I risked a swift glance anyway, and spotted Jonathan, pushing his way through the crowd towards us. He had Lori with him, looking tiny and delicate in a sophisticated ivory number. I immediately felt crass and garish in comparison, but it was too late to run away.

'Remember—make him jealous,' Phin murmured in my ear.

There was no way Jonathan would even notice me next to Lori, I thought, but I turned obediently and slid my arm around Phin's waist, snuggling closer and smiling up at him as if I hadn't noticed Jonathan at all.

Perhaps that kiss had worked after all. It felt oddly comfortable to be leaning against Phin's hard, solid body—so much so, in fact, that when Jonathan's voice spoke behind me I was genuinely startled.

'I'm glad you're here, Phin,' Jonathan began. 'I just wanted to check everything's under control. We want to kick off with your speech, and then Stephen's going to—'

He broke off as his gaze fell on me, and I gave him my most dazzling smile. 'Summer!'

'Hi, Jonathan,' I said.

Gratifyingly, he looked pole-axed. 'I didn't recognise you,' he said.

Beside him, Lori raised elegant brows. 'Nor did I. That colour really suits you, Summer.'

'Thank you,' I said coolly. 'You look great, too.'

Jonathan was still watching me with a stunned expression. Funny, I had dreamt of him looking at me just that way, but now that he was doing it I felt awkward and embarrassed.

'You look amazing tonight,' he said, and all I could think was that it wasn't fair of him to be talking to me like that when Lori was standing right beside him.

'Doesn't she?' Phin locked gazes with Jonathan in an unspoken challenge, and slid his hand possessively beneath my hair to rest it on the nape of my neck.

I could feel the warm weight of it—not pressing uncomfortably, but just there, a reassuring connection—and I had one of those weird out of body moments when you can look at yourself as if from the outside. I could see how easy we looked together, how right.

Jonathan and Lori had no reason not to believe that we were a real couple. They would look at us and assume that we were used to touching intimately, to understanding each other completely. To not knowing precisely where one finished and the other began, so that there was no more me, no more Phin, just an us.

The thought of an 'us' made the world tip a little. Abruptly I was back in my body, and desperately aware of Phin's solid strength beneath my arm, of the tingling imprint of his palm on my neck.

There *was* no us, I had to remind myself. I only just stopped myself shaking my head to clear it. Everything about the party seemed so unreal, but I was bizarrely able to carry on a conversation with Jonathan and Lori while every cell in my body was straining with Phin's closeness.

True, it wasn't much of a conversation. Some small talk about Stephen Hodge and his vile temper. I complimented Lori on her earrings, she mentioned my shoes, but all I could really think about was the way Phin was absently stroking my neck, his thumb caressing my skin.

Every graze of his fingertips stoked the sizzle deep inside me, and I was alarmingly aware that it could crackle into life at any time. If I wasn't careful there would be a *whoosh* and I would spontaneously combust. That would spoil Stephen Hodge's party all right.

I had to move away from Phin or it would all get

very messy. Straightening, I made a show of pushing my hair behind my ears. 'Um…isn't it time for your speech?' I asked him with an edge of desperation.

'I suppose I'd better throw a few scraps to the monster's ego,' sighed Phin. 'He hasn't been kowtowed to for all of thirty seconds! Where would you like me to do it, Jonathan?'

'We've set up a podium,' said Jonathan. 'I'd better go and warn Stephen that we're ready to go.'

'Lead on,' said Phin, and held out his hand to me. 'Are you coming, CP?'

Jonathan looked puzzled. 'CP?'

I smiled uncomfortably as I took Phin's hand. 'Private joke,' I said.

After that, we had to kiss every time we got ready to go out. 'Come here and be kissed,' Phin would say, holding out his arms. 'This is the best part of the day.'

I was very careful to keep reminding myself that those kisses didn't mean a thing, but secretly I found myself looking forward to them. I always tried to make a joke of it, of course.

'Oh, let's get it over with, then,' I'd say, putting my arms briskly around his neck, but there was always a moment when our determined jokiness faded into something else entirely, something warm and yearning—the moment when I succumbed to the honeyed pleasure spilling along my veins, to the tug of longing and the wicked crackle of excitement between us.

I would like to say that it was me who put an end to the kiss every time, but I'd be lying. It was almost always Phin who lifted his head before I remembered that it was only supposed to be a quick kiss and thought about pulling away.

'We're getting good at this now,' Phin would say. I noticed, though, that the famous smile looked a little forced, and he was often distracted afterwards.

The theory had been that the more we kissed, the easier it would get. But it didn't work like that. It got more and more difficult to disentangle those kisses from reality, harder and harder to remember that I wanted Jonathan, that Phin was just amusing himself.

To remember why we had to stop at a kiss.

And the worst thing was that there was a bit of me that didn't want to.

Whenever I realised that I'd give myself a stern ticking off. This would involve a rigorous reminder of all the reasons why it would be stupid to fall for someone like Phin. He wasn't serious. He wasn't steady. He didn't want to settle down. I'd end up hurt and humiliated and I'd have no one to blame but myself.

Much—*much*—more sensible to remember why

I had loved Jonathan. Why I *still* loved him, I'd have to correct myself an alarming number of times.

Jonathan was everything Phin wasn't. He was everything I needed.

I just couldn't always remember why.

Ironically, the harder I tried to remind myself of how much I wanted Jonathan, the more often Jonathan found excuses to drop into the office.

'You can't tell me our plan's not working now,' Phin said to me one evening as we sipped champagne at some gallery opening. 'Jonathan's always sniffing around nowadays. I trip over him every time I come into office. I notice he was there again this afternoon.'

He sounded uncharacteristically morose, and I shot him a curious look.

'He just came to see what I knew about the Cameroon trip,' I said uncomfortably, although I had no idea why I felt suddenly guilty.

'Ha!' said Phin mirthlessly. 'Was that all he could think of as an excuse?'

'It wasn't an excuse,' I said.

I had the feeling Jonathan was looking forward to going to Africa about as much as I was. I'd tried everything I could to get out of the trip, but Phin was adamant. The flights were booked for the end of March, and I was dreading it.

It was so *not* my kind of travelling. I like city

breaks—Paris or Rome or New York—and hotels with hairdryers and mini bars, all of which were obviously going to be in short supply on the Cameroon trip. We'd had to be vaccinated against all sorts of horrible tropical diseases, and Phin had presented us all with a kit list so that we'd know what to take with us. Hairdryers didn't appear on it. I would be taking a rucksack instead of a pull-along case, walking boots in place of smart city shoes.

'And don't bother with any make-up,' Phin had told me. 'Sunblock is all you'll need.'

I was taking some anyway.

I don't suppose Jonathan was bothered about the make-up issue, but he was clearly anxious about the whole experience. Phin had presented the trip as a staff development exercise, and I suspected Jonathan didn't want to be developed any more than I did.

'I'm really glad you're going to be in same group when we go to Africa,' he had said to me, only that afternoon.

Phin was eyeing me moodily over the rim of his champagne glass. 'Nobody could be *that* worried about going to Africa. He just wants to hang around and talk to you.' He scowled at me. 'I hope you're not going to give in too easily. Make him work to get you back!'

'Look, what's the problem?' I demanded. 'Isn't

the whole idea that Jonathan starts to find me interesting again? Or did you want to spend the rest of your life stuck in this pretence?'

'It just irritates me that he's being so cautious.' Phin hunched a shoulder. 'If you'd been mine, and I'd realised what an idiot I'd been, I wouldn't be dithering around talking about malaria pills, or whether to pack an extra towel, and how many pairs of socks to take. I'd be sweeping you off your feet.'

It wasn't like Phin to be grouchy. That was *my* role. The worst thing was that there was a bit of me that agreed with him. But I had no intention of admitting *that*.

'Yes, well, the whole point is that you're *not* Jonathan,' I said. 'Yes, he's being careful—but that's only sensible. As far as he knows I'm in love with his boss. It would be madness to charge in and try and sweep me off unless he was sure how I felt.'

I lifted my chin. 'And I wouldn't *want* to be with someone that reckless,' I went on. 'I'd rather have someone who thought things through, who saw how the land lay, and then acted when he was sure of success. Someone like Jonathan, in fact.'

And right then I even believed it.

Or told myself I did, anyway.

Now, I know what you're thinking, but you have to remember how clear Phin always made it that he would never consider a permanent relationship.

He liked teasing me, he liked kissing me, and we got on surprisingly well, but there was never any question that there might be more than that.

I'm not a fool. I knew just how easy it would be to fall in love with him. But I knew, too, how pointless it would be. I might grumble about him endlessly, but it was fun being with Phin. Much to my own surprise, I was enjoying our pretend affair.

But I wouldn't let myself lose sight of the fact that the security I craved lay elsewhere. I was earning better money now, and could start to think about buying a flat. Lori, I'd heard, was back with her old boyfriend and, whatever I might say to Phin, I knew Jonathan was definitely showing signs of renewed interest in me. Somewhere along the line I'd lost my desperate adoration of him, but he was still attractive, still nice, still steady. I could feel safe with Jonathan, I knew.

I had never had a better chance to have everything I wanted, and I wasn't going to throw it away—no matter how good it felt being with Phin.

I had run out of excuses. Hunched and sullen, I sat in the departure lounge at Heathrow, nursing a beaker of tea. It was five-thirty in the morning, and I didn't want to be there. I wanted to be at home, in bed, soon to begin my nice, safe routine.

I did the same thing every day. I woke up at half

past six and made myself a cup of tea. Then I showered, dried my hair and put on my make-up. I took the same bus, the same tube, and stopped at Otto's at the same time to buy a cappuccino from Lucia.

You could set your watch by the time I got to the office and sat down behind my immaculately tidy desk. Then I'd sit there and savour the feeling of everything being in its place and under control, which lasted only until Phin appeared and stirred up the air and made the whole notion of control a distant memory.

'It's a rut,' Phin had said when I told him about my routine.

'You're missing the point. I *like* my rut.'

'Trust me, you're going to like Africa, too.'

'I'm not,' I said sulkily. 'I'm going to hate every minute of it.'

And at first I did.

We had to change planes, and after what seemed like hours hanging around in airports it was dark by the time we arrived at Douala. The airport there was everything I had feared. It was hot, crowded, shambolic. There seemed to be a lot of shouting.

I shrank into Phin as we pushed our way through the press of people and outside, to where a minibus was supposed to be waiting but wasn't. The tropical heat was suffocating, and the smell of airport fuel mingled with sweat and unfinished concrete lodged somewhere at the back of my throat.

Through it all I was very aware of Phin, steady and good-humoured, bantering in French with the customs officials who wanted to open every single one of our bags. He was wearing jungle trousers and an olive-green shirt, and amazingly managed to look cool and unfazed—while my hair was sticking to my head and I could feel the perspiration trickling down my back.

There were twelve of us in our group. Handpicked by Phin, together we represented a cross-section of the headquarters staff, from secretaries like me to security staff, executives to cleaners. I knew most of the others by sight, and Phin had assured us we would be a close-knit team by the time we returned ten days later. I could tell we were bonding already in mutual unease at the airport.

'Everything's fine,' Phin said soothingly as we all fretted about the non-appearance of the mini-bus. 'It'll be here in a minute.'

The minute stretched to twenty, but eventually a rickety mini-bus did indeed turn up. It took us to a strange hotel where we slept four to a room under darned mosquito nets. There were tiny translucent geckos on the walls, and a rattling air-conditioning unit kept me awake all night. Oh, yes, and I found a cockroach in the shower.

'Tell me again why I'm supposed to love all this,' I grumbled to Phin the next morning. I was squeezed between him and the driver in the front of a Jeep that bounced over potholes and swerved around the dogs and goats that wandered along the road with a reckless disregard for my stomach, not to mention any oncoming traffic.

'Look at the light,' Phin answered. To my relief we had slowed to crawl through a crowded market. 'Look at how vibrant the colours are. Look at that girl's smile.' He gestured at the stalls lining the road. 'Look at those bananas, those tomatoes, those pineapples! Nothing's wrapped in plastic, or flown thousands of miles so that it loses its taste.'

His arm lay behind my head along the back of the seat, and he turned to look down into my face. 'Listen to the music coming out of the shops. Doesn't it make you want to get out and dance? How can you *not* love it?'

'It just comes naturally to me,' I muttered.

'And you're with me,' he pointed out, careless of our colleagues in the back seat.

I was very aware of them—although I couldn't imagine they would be able to hear much over the sound of the engine, the music spilling out of the shacks on either side of the road and the children running after us shouting, 'Happy! Happy! Happy!'

'We're together on an adventure,' said Phin. 'What more could you want?'

I sighed. 'I don't know where to begin answering that!'

'Oh, come on, Summer. This is fun.'

'You sound just like my mother,' I said sourly. 'This reminds me of the way Mum would drag me around the country, telling me how much I should be loving it, when all I wanted was to stay at home.'

'Maybe she knew that you had the capacity to love it all if only you'd let yourself,' said Phin. 'Maybe she was like me and thought you were afraid of how much love and passion was locked up inside you.'

It certainly sounded like the kind of thing my mother *would* think.

'Why do you care?' Cross, I lowered my voice and looked straight ahead, just in case anyone behind was listening or had omitted to put lip-reading skills on their CV. 'We don't have a real relationship, and even if we did it would only be temporary. You can't tell me you'd be hanging around long enough to care about my *capacity* for anything.'

There was a pause. 'I hate waste,' said Phin at last.

I had thought the road from Douala was bad, but I had no idea then of what lay ahead.

After that little town, the road deteriorated until there wasn't even an attempt at tarmac, and a downpour didn't exactly improve matters. Our little convoy of Jeeps lurched for hours over tracks through slippery red mud. We had to stop several times to push one or other of the vehicles out of deep ruts gouged out by trucks.

'This is what it's like trying to get *you* out of your rut,' Phin said to me with a grin, as we put our shoulders to the back of our Jeep once more. His face was splattered with mud from the spinning tyres, and I didn't want to think about what I looked like. I could feel the sprayed mud drying on my skin like a measles rash.

'Of course it's harder in your case,' he went on. 'Not so muddy, though.'

We were all filthy by the time we reached Aduaba—a village wedged between a broad brown river and the dark green press of the rainforest. There was a cluster of huts, with mud daub walls and roofs thatched with palm leaves, or occasionally a piece of corrugated iron, and what seemed like hundreds of children splashing in the water.

My relief at getting out of the Jeep soon turned to horror when I discovered that the huts represented luxury accommodation compared to what we were getting: a few pieces of tarpaulin thrown over a makeshift frame to provide shelter.

'I'm so far out of my comfort zone I don't know what to say,' I told Phin.

'Oh, come now—it's not that bad,' he said, but I could tell that he was enjoying my dismay. 'It's not as if it's cold, and the tarpaulin will keep you dry.'

'But where are we going to sleep?'

'Why do you think I made you buy a sleeping mat?'

'We're sleeping on the *ground*?'

His smile was answer enough.

I looked at him suspiciously. 'What about you?'

'I'll be right here with you—and everyone else, before you get in a panic.'

I opened my mouth, then closed it again. 'Does Lex know the conditions here?' I demanded. I couldn't believe he would have put his staff through this if he'd had any idea of what it would be like.

'I shouldn't think so,' said Phin cheerfully. 'The conditions aren't bad, Summer,' he went on more seriously. 'This isn't meant to be a five star jolly. It's *meant* to be challenging. It's all about pushing you all out of your comfort zones and seeing what you're made of. It's about giving you a brief glimpse of another community and thinking about the ways staff and customers at Gibson & Grieve can make a connection with them.'

I set my jaw stubbornly, and he shook his head with a grin. 'I bet,' he said, 'that you'll end up enjoying this much more than going to some polo match, or having a corporate box at the races, or whatever Lex usually does to keep staff happy.'

'A bet?' I folded my arms. 'How much?'

'You want to take me on?'

'I do,' I said. 'If I win, you have to…'

I tried to think about what would push Phin out of *his* comfort zone. I could hardly suggest he settled down and got married, but there was no reason he shouldn't commit to something.

'…you have to agree to get to work by nine every day for as long as we're working together,' I decided.

Phin whistled. 'High stakes. And if I win?'

'Well, I think that's academic, but you choose.'

'That's very rash of you, cream puff! Now, let's see…' He tapped his teeth, pretending to ponder a suitable stake. 'Since I know I'm going to win, I'd be a fool not to indulge a little fantasy, wouldn't I?'

'What sort of fantasy?' I asked a little warily.

'Do you care?' he countered. 'I thought you were sure you weren't going to enjoy yourself?'

I looked at the tarpaulin and remembered how thin my sleeping mat had looked. There was no way Phin would win this bet.

'I am sure,' I said. 'Go on—tell me this fantasy of yours.'

'We're at work,' he told me, his eyes glinting with amusement and something else. 'You come into my office with your notebook, and you're wearing one of those prim little suits of yours, and your hair is tied up neatly, and you're wearing your stern glasses.'

'It doesn't sound much of a fantasy to me,' I said. 'That's just normal.'

'Ah, yes, but when you've finished taking notes you don't do what you normally do. You take off your glasses, the way you do, but instead of going back to your desk in my fantasy you come round until you're standing really close to me.'

His voice dropped. 'Then you shake out your hair and you unbutton your jacket *ve-r-ry* slowly and you don't take your eyes off mine the whole time.'

My heart was beating uncomfortably at the picture, but I managed a very creditable roll of my eyes.

'It's a bit hackneyed, isn't it? I was expecting you to come up with something a little more exciting than that.'

The corner of Phin's mouth twitched. 'Well, I *could* make it more exciting, of course, but it wouldn't be fair, given that you're going to have to actually do this.'

'I don't think so,' I said, a combative glint in my own eyes. Still, there was no point in pushing it. 'So that's it? Take my hair down and unbutton my jacket if—and that's a very big *if*—I enjoy the next ten days?'

'Oh, you would have to kiss me as well,' said

Phin. 'As to what happens after the kiss...well, that would be up to you. But it might depend on how many other people were around.'

'I'm sure that wouldn't be a problem,' I said with a confident toss of my head. 'So: hair, jacket, kiss for me if you win, and turning up on time for you if I do? I hope you've got a good alarm clock! This is one bet I'm deadly sure I'm going to win.'

CHAPTER NINE

But I lost.

The first night was really uncomfortable, yes, but in the days that followed I was so tired that my sleeping mat might as well have been a feather bed, I slept so soundly.

We spent the next ten days helping the villagers to finish the medical centre they had started a couple of years earlier but had had to abandon when they ran out of money to buy the materials. Somehow Phin had organised delivery of everything that was needed, and I didn't need to be there long to realise what an achievement that was.

It was an eye-opening time for me in more ways than one. For most of the time it was hard, physical labour. It was hot and incredibly humid, and the closest I got to a shower was a dip in the river, but I liked seeing the building take shape. Every day we could stand back and see the results of our labours, and we forgot that our hands were dirty, our nails broken, our hair tangled.

When I think back to that time what I remember most is the laughter. Children laughing, women laughing, everyone laughing together. I'd never met a community that found so much humour in their everyday lives. The people of Aduaba humbled me with their openness, their friendliness and their hospitality, and I cringed when I remembered how dismissive I had been of their huts when I first arrived. When I was invited inside, I found that the mud floors were swept and everything was scrupulously clean and neat.

'Why can't you keep your house like this?' I asked Phin.

The women particularly were hard-working and funny. A few of them had some words of English or French, and I learnt some words of their language. We managed to communicate well enough. I kept my hair tied back, as that was only practical, but I forgot about mascara and lipstick, and it wasn't long before I started to feel the tension that was so familiar to me I barely noticed it most of the time slowly unravelling.

I learnt to appreciate the smell of the rainforest, the way the darkness dropped like a blanket, the beauty of the early-morning mist on the river. I began to listen for the sounds which had seemed so alien at first: the screech of a monkey, the rasp of insects in the dark, the creak and rustle of vegetation, the crash of tropical rain on the tarpaulin and the slow, steady drip of the leaves afterwards.

But most of all my eyes were opened to Phin. It was a long time since I had been able to think of him as no more than a bland celebrity, but I hadn't realised how much more there was to him. He was in his element in Aduaba. He belonged there in a way he never would in the confines of the office.

Wherever there was laughter, I would find him. He spoke much more of the language, and had an extraordinary ability to defuse tension and get everyone working together, sorting out administrative muddles with endless patience. I suppose I hadn't realised how *competent* he was.

I remember watching him out of the corner of my eye as he hammered in a roof joist. His expression was focused, but when one of the other men on the roof shouted what sounded like a curse he glanced up and shouted something back that made them all laugh. I saw the familiar smile light up his face and felt something that wasn't familiar at all twist and unlock inside me.

At night I was desperately aware of him breathing nearby, and knew that he was the reason I wasn't afraid. He was the reason I was here at all.

He was the reason I was changing.

And I *was* changing. I could feel it. I felt like a butterfly struggling out of its chrysalis, hardly able to believe what was happening to me.

That I was enjoying it.

It wasn't all work. I played on the beach with the children, and helped the women cook. One of the men took us into the forest and showed us a bird spider on its web. I kid you not, that spider was as big as my hand. None of us thought of wandering off on our own after that.

Once Jonathan and I took a little boat with an outboard motor and puttered down the river. I felt quite comfortable with him by then. My mind was full of Aduaba and our life there, and I'd almost forgotten the desperate yearning I had once felt for him.

We drifted in companionable silence for a while. 'It's funny to think we'll be going home soon,' said Jonathan at last. 'I'll admit I was dreading this trip, but it's been one of the best things I've ever done.'

'I feel that, too.'

'It's made me realise that I never really knew you before, when we…you know…' He petered off awkwardly.

'I know,' I said, trailing my fingers in the water. 'But I think I've changed since I've been here. I wasn't like this before, or if I was I didn't know it. I thought I was going to hate it but I don't.' I remembered my bet with Phin and shivered a little.

'I know you and Phin are good together,' Jonathan blurted suddenly, 'but I just want you to know that I think you're wonderful, Summer, and if you ever change your mind about Phin I'd like another chance.'

I stilled for a moment. How many times had I dreamt of Jonathan saying those words? Now that he had, I didn't know what to say.

I pulled my hand out of the water. 'What about Lori?' I asked. It wasn't that long since he'd been mad about her.

'Lori's back with her ex. It was quite intense for a while, but I think I always knew she was on the rebound, and now that she's back with him I realise how close I came to making a big mistake.'

So I couldn't use Lori as an excuse to say no, I thought, and then caught myself up. Excuse? What do you need an excuse for, Summer?

'I know I didn't appreciate you when I had you, but I can see now that you were so much better for me than Lori,' Jonathan was saying. 'We've got so much more in common.'

'Yes, I suppose we have,' I said slowly.

He leant forward eagerly. 'We've got the same outlook, the same values.'

It was true. That was exactly what I had loved about him, but why did he have to wait until now to realise it? Frankly, his timing sucked.

'Jonathan, I—'

'It's OK,' he interrupted me. 'You don't need to say anything. I know how things are with you and Phin right now. I just wanted to tell you how I felt—to let you know that I'm always here for you.'

Why did he have to be so nice? I thought crossly as we made our way back. It would have been so much easier for me if he had turned out to be lazy, or a whinger, or even if he just hadn't liked Cameroon very much. Then I could have decided that I didn't love him after all. But in lots of ways I had never liked Jonathan as much as I did then.

Jonathan knew Phin's reputation as well as I did. He wouldn't have said anything if he hadn't thought there was a good chance that my supposed relationship with Phin would end sooner or later.

As it would.

Everything was working out just as Phin had said. It was just a pity I didn't know what I really wanted any more.

There was a party on our last night in Aduaba. We drank palm wine in the hot, tropical night and listened to the sounds of the forest for the last time. Then the music started. There's an irresistible rhythm to African music. I could feel it beating in my blood, and when the women pulled me to my feet I danced with them.

I must have looked ridiculous, stamping my feet

and waggling my puny bottom, but I didn't care. The only time I faltered was when I caught Phin watching me, with such a blaze of expression in his eyes that I stumbled momentarily. But when I looked again he was laughing and allowing himself to be drawn into the dance and I decided I must have imagined it.

I ran my fingers over my keyboard as if I had never seen one before. It felt very strange to be back in the office. My head was still full of Africa, and I had found the tube stifling and oppressive on my way into work that morning.

Unsettled, I switched on my computer, and sat down to scroll through the hundreds of e-mails that had accumulated while we'd been away. It was hard to focus, though, and my mind kept drifting back to Aduaba and Phin.

Phin stripped to the waist like the other men, his muscles bulging with effort as they lifted the heavy timbers into place.

Phin laughing with the children in the river.

Phin looking utterly at ease in the heat and the humidity and the wildness.

He strolled in some time after ten, and all the air evaporated from my lungs at the sight of him. I was annoyed to see that he seemed just the same as always, while I felt completely different.

I looked at him over the top of my glasses. 'I see you didn't invest in that alarm clock,' I said crisply, to cover the fact that my heart was cantering around my chest in an alarmingly uncontrolled way.

'No, but then I don't need to turn up on time every day, do I?' said Phin, not at all put out by the sharpness of my greeting. '*I'm* not the one who lost the bet.'

The mention of the bet silenced me, and I bit my lip. Nothing more had been said about it, and I'd convinced myself that Phin hadn't really been serious. It had just been joke…hadn't it?

Much to my relief, Phin didn't say any more, but went into his office and threw himself into his chair. 'So, what's been happening?' he asked. 'Is there anything that needs to be dealt with right away?'

Grateful to him for behaving normally, I took in my notebook and ran through the most urgent issues. 'Shall I make some coffee?' I said, when I had finished scribbling notes.

'Not just yet,' said Phin. 'There's the small matter of the bet we made.' He smiled at me as I stared at him in consternation. 'I think you owe me.'

It was typical of him to let me relax and then catch me off guard. I should have known he'd do something like that.

I swallowed. 'Now?'

'I always think it's best to pay debts straight away, don't you? Do you remember the terms?'

Drawing a breath, I took off my glasses. 'I think so,' I said.

Now that it had come to it, I felt a flicker of excitement. I met Phin's eyes and wondered if he was waiting for me to renegotiate, and I knew suddenly that I didn't want to do that.

'You were right,' I said clearly. 'I loved it.'

Calmly, I got to my feet and went round the desk to where Phin sat in a high-backed executive chair. He was silent, watching me as I leant back against the desk and very deliberately pulled the clip from my hair, so that I could shake it loose and let it tumble around my face.

How embarrassing, my sensible side was saying. How unbelievably inappropriate. How *tacky*.

It was bad enough making a bet like that with your boss, without playing up to his patriarchal male fantasies. How had I got myself into a situation where I was feeling a bit naughty, a bit dirty, a bit sexy *in the office*?

How could I possibly be turned on by it?

But I was. I can hardly bear to remember it without cringing, but at the time…oh, yes, I certainly was.

I smiled slowly at Phin. 'How am I doing so far?'

'Perfect,' he said, but his voice was strained and

I felt a spurt of triumph, even power that I could have that effect on him just by letting down my hair.

Levering myself away from the desk, I moved closer to him. One by one I undid the buttons of my jacket, even though I was having one of those out-of-body experiences again and screaming at myself, *What are you doing? Stop it right now!*

Phin said nothing, but his eyes were very dark as he watched me, and I could see him struggling to keep his breathing even. When my jacket was open to reveal the cream silk camisole I wore underneath, I leant down and pressed my mouth to the pulse that was beating frantically in his throat.

I heard Phin suck in his breath, and I smiled against his skin, slipping my arms around his neck and easing myself onto his lap so that I could kiss my way slowly, slowly, along his jaw to the edge of his mouth.

'Am I doing it right?' I whispered.

'God, yes,' he said raggedly, and his arms came up to fasten around me as I kissed him at last.

His lips parted beneath mine, drawing me in, and the chair spun round as his hand slid possessively under my skirt. It might have been tacky, it might have been deeply, deeply inappropriate, but it felt so good I didn't care.

I have a hazy memory that I thought I should be in control, but if I ever was I soon lost it. It wasn't as if Phin was in control either. That kiss was stronger than both of us. It ripped through our meagre defences, rampaging like wildfire in the blood, sucking us up like a twister to a place far from the office where there were only lips and tongues, only hands moving greedily, insistently, only the pounding of our hearts and the throb of our bodies and the sweet, dangerous intoxication of a kiss that went on and on and on.

Sadly, the office hadn't forgotten us. The sound of a throat being loudly cleared gradually penetrated. We paused, our mouths still pressed together, our tongues still entwined, and then our eyes opened at exactly the same time.

The throat was cleared again. As if at a trigger, we jerked apart, and I would have leapt off Phin's knee if he hadn't held me tightly in place as he swung his chair back to face the door.

Lex Gibson was standing there, looking bored.

'I did knock,' he said. 'Three times.'

I struggled to get up, but Phin held me tight. 'We're a bit busy here, Lex.'

'So I saw. Good to see that work ethic kicking in at last,' said Lex, who had his own line in sardonic humour when it suited him.

'Did you want something?' Phin countered. 'Or are you just here to ruin a perfect morning?'

'I wouldn't be here if it wasn't important,' said Lex dryly.

That hardly needed saying. Lex rarely left his office. Staff were summoned to see *him*, and could often be seen quailing in Monique's office while they waited their turn. It was unheard of for him to seek someone out himself.

Phin sighed as he released me. 'It had better be,' he said.

My cheeks were burning as I scrambled to my feet, desperately trying to smooth back my hair and rebutton my jacket as I went.

'Um…can I get you some coffee?' I asked Lex. I was mortified at having been caught in such a compromising position but, with that kiss still thrumming through me, probably not nearly as mortified as I should have been. 'Then I can leave you two together.'

'Actually, this concerns you,' he said.

Oh, God, he was going to sack me for unprofessional behaviour!

'Shall we sit down?' said Lex, gesturing at the sofas.

Biting my lip, I sat obediently, and Phin came to join me. We glanced at each other like naughty children, then looked at Lex.

'I believe Monique has already told you that she's expecting a baby?' he began, with a hint of disapproval.

I was so relieved that I wasn't getting fired that

I started to smile—before it occurred to me that something might be wrong.

'Yes, she did. Is everything OK?' I asked in concern.

'No. At least, Monique is all right,' he amended. 'But she's been ordered to rest until the baby is born. Something to do with high blood pressure.'

I could tell Lex wasn't up on pregnancy talk. Not that I was much better.

'Oh, dear. Poor Monique. She'll have to be so careful.'

'It's very inconvenient,' said Lex austerely. 'It was bad enough that I was going to lose her in August, but she went home on Friday and now she's not coming in again until after her maternity leave.'

'So why are you here, Lex?' asked Phin with a hint of impatience. 'Or can we guess?'

'I would imagine you could, yes. Obviously I need a PA immediately—and preferably one who's familiar with my office.'

'Summer, in fact.' Phin's voice was flat.

Lex looked at me. 'Monique told me she'd mentioned the possibility of you replacing her during her maternity leave already. I'd like you to come and work for me now, even if it's only to help me through this immediate period.'

I was finding it difficult to concentrate. I'd been jerked so rudely out of that kiss, and every cell in my body was still screaming with frustration.

'Well...er...what about Phin? I mean...working for Phin,' I stumbled, realising that my concern for Phin might be misinterpreted in view of what Lex had just seen us doing.

'I'm here as a courtesy,' said Lex, looking at his brother. 'I appreciate that you've established a good working relationship with Summer—a little too good, some might say—but your office doesn't generate nearly the same amount of work as yet. It seems to me that you could quite easily manage with another secretary, or share assistance with one of the other directors.'

Phin's jaw tightened. 'I'm not going to get into a discussion about how much work I do or don't do here, Lex,' he said grittily. 'This is about Summer and where she wants to work. I'm sure she's happy to help you over this crisis period...' He looked at me for confirmation and I nodded.

'Of course.'

'But after that it's up to her.'

'That seems fair enough,' said Lex, getting to his feet. 'I'm grateful,' he said to me, and I got up, too.

'Er...would you like me to come now?'

'If you would.'

That was Lex—straight back to work. It clearly

didn't occur to him that I might want to talk to Phin on my own.

I glanced at Phin, who was watching me with an unreadable expression. 'I'll…er…I'll speak to you later,' I said awkwardly.

'Sure. Don't let him work you too hard.'

So there I was, walking down the corridor with Lex to the best career opportunity of my life, and all I could think was that only minutes ago I had been in the middle of the best kiss of my life.

Lex behaved as if nothing whatsoever had happened, and I was grateful. I couldn't believe now that I had actually stood there in front of Phin, unbuttoning my jacket, that I had kissed him like that. But at the same time I couldn't believe that I had stopped.

I was torn: my body raging with the aftermath of that kiss, but my mind slowly beginning to clear. Where would it have ended if Lex hadn't interrupted us? Would we really have made love in the office with the door open? I went hot and cold at the thought. I could have jeopardised my whole career. It had been bad enough Lex finding us like that, without the whole office stopping by to gawp at Summer Curtis out of control with her boss.

Everything was getting out of hand, and I didn't like it.

It was a strange, disorientating day. I slipped

back into place in Lex's office as if I had never been away. Monique was fantastically efficient, which helped. It meant I could pick up where she had left.

Lotty, the junior secretary who had replaced me, was hugely relieved when I appeared. 'I was terrified I was going to have to take over myself,' she confided. 'I like my job, but Lex Gibson reduces me to a gibbering wreck.'

I knew what that felt like. Phin could do the same to me, but for very different reasons.

Somehow I managed to keep up a calm, capable front all day, and I don't think anyone guessed that behind my cool façade I was reliving that kiss again and again.

The more I thought about it, the more glad I was that Lex had interrupted us when he had. I mean, that wasn't *me*, sliding seductively onto my boss's lap. I was cool, I was competent, I was *sensible*.

Although it would have been hard to guess that from the way I'd been carrying on recently. It wasn't sensible to get involved with your boss, to pretend a relationship you didn't have, to make stupid bets with him, to *kiss* him. What had I been thinking? I had put my career—everything I believed in, everything I'd always wanted—at risk. I'd done exactly what I had sworn I would never to do and got carried away by the moment.

How my mother would cheer if she knew.

At six o'clock I made my way back down to Phin's office. My desk looked empty and forlorn already. I knocked on his door.

Phin was on one of the sofas, reading a report. He dropped it onto the table when he saw me in the doorway and got to his feet, the first blaze of expression in his eyes quickly shielded. 'Hi.'

'Hi.'

There was an awkward pause.

'So how's it going?' he asked after a moment.

'Fine.'

Had we really kissed earlier? Suddenly we were talking to each other like strangers. I couldn't bear it.

Another silence. I stepped into the room and closed the door behind me.

Phin watched me warily. 'Somehow I get the feeling you're not about to pick up where we left off,' he said.

'No,' I agreed. 'I paid my debt.'

But my heart twisted as I said it. It had been so much more than a jokey kiss to close a bet, and we both knew it.

I went to sit on the other sofa. 'I've decided to take the job with Lex while Monique is away.'

'I thought you would,' said Phin, sitting opposite me.

'It's a fantastic career opportunity for me,' I

ploughed on. 'And when I thought about it I could see that it would make it much easier for both of us. It would be awkward to carry on working together now.'

'Now?'

'I think it's time to call an end to our pretence,' I said. 'It's served its purpose.'

Phin sat back and regarded me steadily. 'Has Jonathan come through?'

'We had a talk in Aduaba,' I admitted. 'He said he wanted to try again.'

'And what did you say?'

'I said I'd think about it.'

'I see.'

I bit my lip. 'The *Glitz* article has come out. Even Jewel's given up on you.' I tried to joke. 'There's nothing in it for you any more. We should pretend that it's over now.'

'Is that what you want?'

'To be honest, Phin, I don't know *what* I want at the moment,' I said with a sigh. 'It's all been…'

I tried to think of a way to describe how it had felt, but couldn't do it. 'I'm confused,' I said instead. 'You, Jonathan, Africa, this new job…I don't know what I feel about any of it. I don't know what I'm *doing* any more.'

'You seemed to know exactly what you were doing earlier this morning,' said Phin.

I could feel the colour creeping up my throat. 'I got... carried away,' I said with difficulty. 'I'm sorry.'

'Don't apologise for it,' he said almost angrily. 'Getting carried away isn't always a bad thing, Summer.'

'It is for me.' Restlessly, I got to my feet. Hugging my arms together, I went over to the window and looked down at the commuters streaming towards Charing Cross.

'My mother's spent her whole life being carried away by one thing or another,' I told him. 'I was dragged along in her wake, and all I ever wanted was something to hold onto, somewhere I could stay, somewhere I could call home. That's why my job has always been so important to me. I know it's not a high-flying career, but I like it, and I do it well.'

I turned back to Phin, trying to make him understand. 'This morning...that was so unprofessional. When I saw Lex, I thought he was going to sack me. I wouldn't have blamed him, either.'

'He wouldn't have sacked you. I wouldn't have let him.' There was an edge of irritation in Phin's voice as he got up to join me at the window. 'It was only a kiss, Summer, not embezzlement or industrial espionage. You should keep it in perspective. It wasn't that big a deal.'

'For you, perhaps,' I said tautly. 'You don't care about this job. You don't really want to be here. I know you'd rather be off travelling, challenging yourself...there are so many things you want to do. It's different for me. My job is all I've got.'

There was a long silence. We stood side by side, looking out of the window.

'Perhaps it's just as well Lex interrupted us when he did,' said Phin at last.

'I'll find you a replacement PA as soon as I can.'

'There's no hurry,' he said, turning away, restless again. 'I was thinking of taking off for a while. One of the crew on the Collocom ocean race has been hospitalised in Rio, and they've asked me if I could fill in on the next leg to Boston. I just heard today. I said I'd ring tonight and let them know.'

Why was I even surprised? Had I really thought he would persuade me to change my mind? Phin would never be happy to stay in one place for long.

'What about things here?'

'There's nothing urgent. The projects we've set up will keep ticking over, and if not maybe you could keep an eye on them. Otherwise I was just due to do PR stuff, and I might as well do that on a yacht. Gibson & Grieve is one of the race's sponsors, so Lex can't complain—especially not when he's taken my PA away from me!'

It would always have been like this, I realised. Me clinging to the safety of my routine, Phin always in search of distraction. It could never have worked. We were too different. Better to decide that now. Phin was right. It was just as well Lex had come in when he had.

'So...what will we say about our relationship if anyone asks?'

'You could tell everyone you got fed up with me never being around,' he suggested. 'That would ring true. Everyone knows I'm not big on commitment.'

They did. So why had I let myself forget?

'Or you could say that I wasn't exciting enough for you,' I offered. 'Everyone would believe that.'

'Not if they'd seen you take down your hair this morning,' said Phin with a painful smile.

There seemed nothing more to say. We stood shoulder to shoulder at the window, not looking at each other, both facing the fact that it was all for the best. I wondered if Phin was feeling as bleak as I was.

'Well,' I said at last, 'it looks as if it's all change for both of us.'

'Yes,' said Phin. He turned to look at me, and for once there was no laughter in the blue eyes. 'Thank you for everything you've done, Summer. I hope Lex knows how lucky he is.'

'Thank you for all the doughnuts,' I said unevenly.

'They won't be the same without you.'

I wanted to tell him that I would think of him every time I had coffee. I wanted to tell him that I would miss him. I wanted to thank him for taking me to Africa, for making me *feel*, for refusing to let me give up on my dreams. But when I opened my mouth my throat was too tight to speak, and I knew that even if I could I would cry.

'I must go,' was all I muttered, backing away. 'I'll see you before you go, I expect.'

I don't know whether it made it easier or not, but I didn't see him. He sent me an e-mail saying that he had got a flight the next day and that he'd be out of contact for a while.

'I know you're more than capable of making any decisions in my absence,' he finished. *'Enjoy your promotion—you deserve it.'*

I tried to enjoy it. Honestly I did. I told myself endlessly that it was all for the best. I had the job I'd always wanted and a salary to match. I would be able to save in a way I never had before. If I was careful, I could think about putting down a deposit on a studio at the end of the year. What more did I want?

Whenever I asked myself that, Phin's image would appear in my mind. I could picture him in such detail it hurt. That lazy, lopsided grin. The blue, blue eyes. The warmth and humour and wonderful solidity of him. The longing to see him would clutch at my throat, making it hard to breathe, and I wanted to run down the stairs, back to his office, to throw myself onto his lap and spin and spin and spin on his chair as we kissed.

But his chair was empty. Phin wasn't there. He was out on the ocean, in the ozone, the wind in his hair and his eyes full of sunlight. He was where he wanted to be.

And I was where *I* wanted to be, I reminded myself, coming full circle again. I threw myself into work, and mostly people left me alone. There hadn't been any need for an announcement. With Phin gone, and me concentrating fiercely at work, I think most people assumed that we'd split up. They eyed me sympathetically and murmured that they were very sorry. I was just glad not to have to talk about it.

It was very different working for Lex. There were no coffee breaks, no doughnuts. Lex never sat on my desk or held my stapler like a microphone or pretended to make it bite me. It would never occur to Lex to call me anything but my name, and he wasn't interested in my life outside the office.

Not that I had much of one. Anne worried about me. 'You went to all that trouble to get Jonathan back,' she pointed out. 'I don't understand why you won't go out with him now. It's not like he isn't trying. He's always asking you out, and this time he sounds serious. Look at all those hints he's dropped about getting married.'

'I don't want to marry Jonathan,' I said. 'It wouldn't be fair.'

'Because you're in love with Phin?'

I didn't even try to deny it, but there was no point in thinking about Phin. I had to be realistic.

'I do like Jonathan—I actually like him more now than I did when I was in love with him—but if I married him it would just be because he's got a steady job and is ready to settle down. That's not a good enough reason. I know that now. I've got my own steady job,' I told Anne. 'I don't want a relationship for the sake of it. I've realised that I don't need to rely on anybody else to make me feel safe. If security is what I want, I have to make it for myself. I'm earning a decent salary now, and I can think about putting down a deposit soon. I'm going to buy my own place, and then I'll be safe.'

Anne made a face. 'I know security's important to you, Summer, but don't you want more than that?'

I pushed Phin's image firmly away. 'Feeling safe will be enough,' I said.

CHAPTER TEN

OF COURSE, it wasn't that easy. It was all very well to resolve to make my own security and put Phin out of my mind, but how could I do that when he was stuck out in the wild Atlantic? I couldn't think about buying flats until I knew he was safe.

I followed the Collocom race on the internet. I knew six boats had set off from Rio, but they had run into appalling weather. One boat had lost its mast, a crew member on another had been swept overboard in gigantic waves, and I was in such a panic that I actually interrupted Lex in the middle of a board meeting to ask if he knew what boat Phin was on.

'It's not the one you think it is,' said Lex, sounding almost bored. 'Phin's on *Zephyr II*. They've gone to rescue the boat that's lost its mast.'

So he would still be out there in those waves. Offering a belated apology to the board members, who were staring at my desperate interruption, I went back to find out everything I could about the seaworthiness of *Zephyr II*. My heart was in my mouth for four more days, until I heard that the weather had eased and the battered boats were all limping towards land.

As if I didn't have enough to worry about with Phin, my mother announced that she wanted to throw up the precarious existence she had eked out with her shop in Taunton to—and I quote—'become a pilgrim along the sacred routes of our ancestors'.

How she would support herself while criss-crossing the country on ley lines wasn't clear. 'It's all part of the healing process,' she told me, brushing aside my questions about national insurance and rent and remaindered stock. 'This is important work, darling. The galactic core is in crisis. We must channel our light to restore its equilibrium.'

It seemed to me that it wasn't just the galactic core that was in crisis. Her financial affairs were in no better state, and sadly no amount of channelling was going to sort them out.

'Can you believe it?' my mother huffed incredulously when I tried to pin her down about what was happening with the shop. 'They've cut the electricity off!'

That's my mother for you. No problem at all in believing that she has a direct connection to the galactic core—whatever that is—but entirely baffled at the notion that a utility company might stop providing electricity if they're not paid on time.

Is it any wonder I couldn't concentrate on buying a flat?

And, as it turned out, it was just as well.

It became clear that I would have to go down to Somerset and sort things out for Mum. I had encouraged her to rent the shop a couple of years ago. It had seemed like something that would fix her in one place. I should have known that the enthusiasm would pass like all the others.

Things were so busy at work that there was no way I could take time off for the first few weeks, but as soon as I heard that Phin's boat had made it safely to port at the end of that leg of the race I nerved myself to ask Lex if I could have a couple of days the following week.

'Are you thinking of a holiday?'

'I'm afraid not.' I told him about my mother's shop. 'I'll probably need to talk to the bank and her landlord, otherwise I'd just try and do it all in a weekend,' I finished.

Lex looked at me thoughtfully. 'It's unfortunate for you that you're so good at sorting things out. Take whatever time you need,' he said, much to my surprise. I knew he hated it when his PA wasn't there, and he was only just adjusting to having me instead of Monique. 'Lotty will just have to steel herself to deal with me on her own.'

He turned back to his computer. 'I believe all the Collocom boats have made it to Boston,' he said. 'I imagine Phin will be on his way home soon.'

Phin. I felt the memory of his smile tingle through me. 'We're not...it was just...' I stammered, unsure how much Phin had told his brother about the agreement we had made.

Lex held up a hand, obviously to forestall any emotional confession. 'You don't need to explain,' he said. 'I'd rather not know. Have you heard Jonathan Pugh is leaving us? Parker & Parker PR have poached him. It's a good move for him,' Lex added grudgingly.

'I'll still be in London,' Jonathan said, when I congratulated him. 'This doesn't have to be goodbye.'

He insisted on taking me out for a drink to celebrate his new job, and, once fortified by a glass of champagne, he took my hand and asked me to marry him.

'We could be so good together, Summer,' he said.

I looked at him. He was clever, attractive, successful. I had adored him once, and now...now all I could think was that he was a nice man. I remembered how much I'd loved being with him, how I'd loved feeling safe, but his touch had never thrilled me. I had never felt the dark churn of desire when

I was with him. I don't think Jonathan had ever suspected I could feel desire at all until Phin had made him wonder.

I think it was then that I stopped trying to tell myself that I wasn't in love with Phin. I was, whether I wanted to be or not. I said no to Jonathan as gently as I could, and took the train to Taunton feeling as if I had let go of something I had been holding tight for too long.

I felt a strange mixture of lightness and loss—the relief of leaving something old and unwanted behind combined with the scariness of setting off on a new road all on my own again.

My mother was as vague and as charming as ever. She had got a lift into Taunton from the field where she and several others had pitched tepees in order to live closer to nature, and we had lunch together in an organic wholefoods café where tofu and carrots featured largely on the menu. I tried to get her to grasp the realities of giving up the shop, but it was hopeless.

'The material plane has so little meaning for me now,' she explained.

I sighed and gave up. I had been the one who had dealt with all the financial arrangements when she started the shop, and it looked as if I would be the one who would have to close it down.

Still, I was unprepared for quite what a muddle

her affairs were in, and I had a depressing meeting with the bank manager and an even worse one with the owner of the shop, who was practically foaming at the mouth with frustration as he recalled his attempts to get my mother to pay her rent, let alone maintain the property.

'I want her out of there!' he shouted. 'And all that rubbish she's got in there, too! You clear it out and count yourself lucky I'm not taking her to court.'

Mum wafted back to her tepee, and I spent that night in a dreary B&B. I sat on the narrow bed and looked at the rain trickling down the window. I felt so lonely I could hardly breathe.

I had been so careful all my life. I had been sensible. I had been good. I had always said *no* instead of *yes*, and where had it got me? All alone and feeling sorry for myself, in a single room in a cheap B&B, with nothing to look forward to but another day spent clearing up more of my mother's mess.

I thought about ringing Anne, but she was out with Mark, and anyway she was so happy planning her wedding that I didn't want to be a misery. Besides, the only person I really wanted to talk to was Phin.

I missed him. I missed that slow, crooked smile, the warmth in the blue eyes. I missed the energy and humour that he brought with him into a room. I even missed him calling me cream puff, which just goes to show how low I was feeling.

I missed the way he made me feel alive.

Again and again I relived that last kiss. Why had I waited so long to kiss him like that? Why had I hung on so desperately to the thought of a commitment he could never give?

It seemed to me, sitting on that candlewick bedspread—a particularly unpleasant shade of pink, just to make matters worse—that I had been offered a chance at happiness and I had turned it down. I'd been afraid of being hurt, afraid of the pain of having to say goodbye, but I was hurting now, and I didn't even have the comfort of memories, of knowing that I'd made the most of the time I had with Phin.

If he ever came back to Gibson & Grieve, I resolved, I was going to go into his office, and this time I would lock the door. I would shake my hair loose and slide onto his lap again, and this time I wouldn't stop at a kiss. I wouldn't ask for love or for ever. I would live in the moment. I'd do whatever Phin wanted as long as I could touch him again, as long as he would hold me again.

I wrinkled my nose at the musty smell that met me as I opened the shop door the next morning. I had to push against the pile of junk mail and free newspapers that had accumulated since my mother had last been in.

Depressed, I picked it all up and carried it over to the counter. Straight away I could see that someone had broken into the cash register. The only consolation was that they wouldn't have found much money. The stock, unsurprisingly, was untouched. I didn't suppose there was much of a black market in dusty dreamcatchers or vegan cookbooks.

A manual on how to make contact with your personal guardian angel was propped on display next to a pile of weird and wonderful teas. I could have done with a guardian angel myself right then, I thought, riffling through the pages with my fingers as I looked around the shop and wondered where to begin.

Coffee, I decided, dropping the book back onto the counter. There was a kettle out at the back, where the back door had been broken down. I supposed I would have to do something about that, too.

The kettle didn't work. No electricity, of course. Sighing, I went back into the shop—and stopped dead as the whole world tilted and a fierce joy rushed through me with such force that I reeled.

Phin was standing at the counter, with a takeaway coffee in each hand and a bag under his arm.

'Oh, good,' he said. 'I've found the right place at last.'

'Phin...' I stammered. He looked so wonderful, lighting up the shop just by standing there. He was very brown, and his eyes looked bluer than ever. I was so glad to see him I almost cried.

'Hello, cream puff,' he said, carefully putting the coffees down.

I still couldn't take in the fact that he was actually there. I had wanted to see him so much I was afraid I might be imagining him. 'Phin, what are you doing here?'

'Lex told me you were down here trying to sort out your mother's finances,' he said conversationally. 'I thought you could do with a hand.'

'But how on earth did you find me?'

'There aren't that many New Age shops in Taunton, but I've been round them all. I only had one more to try after this one.'

My throat was so tight I couldn't speak.

'It's nearly eleven o'clock,' said Phin, lifting the paper bag. 'I knew you'd be craving some sugar.'

'You brought doughnuts?'

'I thought that was what you'd need.'

No one had ever thought about what I needed before. That was what I had wanted most of all. To my horror, my eyes filled with tears. I blinked them fiercely away.

'I always need a doughnut,' I said unevenly.

'Then let's have these, and we can talk about what needs to be done.'

We boosted ourselves onto the counter. I'll never

forget the taste of that doughnut: the squirt of jam as I bit into it, the contrast of the squidgy dough and the gritty sugar. And, most of all, the incredible, glorious fact that Phin was there, right beside me, sipping lukewarm coffee and brushing sugar from his fingers.

Only last night I'd decided that if I ever saw him again I would seduce him into a wild affair, but now that he was here I felt ridiculously shy, and my heart was banging so frantically in my throat I could barely get any words out. Typical. I didn't even know how to begin being wild.

But right then I didn't care. I only cared that he was there.

'I thought you'd still be in the States,' I said as I sipped my coffee.

'No, I decided to come straight back once we got to Boston. I got home first thing on Friday morning.'

I did a quick calculation. It was Tuesday, so he had been back four days and I hadn't known.

'What have you been doing with yourself?'

'I had things to do,' he said vaguely. 'I didn't realise you were here until I talked to Lex last night.'

And he had come straight down to help me. My heart was slamming painfully against my ribs.

'It must be a bit of culture shock,' I said unsteadily. 'From glamorous ocean race to failed New Age shop in Taunton.'

Phin smiled. 'I like contrasts,' he said.

'Still, you must be exhausted.' Draining my coffee, I set the empty beaker on the counter beside me. 'It was so nice of you to come, but there was really no need.'

'I didn't like it when Lex said you were here alone.'

'I'm fine. Taunton's not exactly dangerous.'

'That's not the point. You don't have to do everything on your own.'

But that was exactly what I *did* have to do. 'I'm used to it,' I said.

'Where's Jonathan?' said Phin, frowning. 'If he cared about you at all, he would be here.'

'I'm sure Jonathan would have come down if I'd asked for his help, but it never occurred to me to tell him about my mother. Besides,' I went on carefully, 'it wouldn't have been fair of me to ask him when I'd just refused to marry him.'

I felt Phin still beside me. 'You refused?' he repeated, as if wanting to be sure.

'Yes, I… Yes,' I finished inadequately.

My eyes locked with his then, and silence reverberated around the shop. 'Anyway,' I said, 'you're here instead.'

'Yes,' said Phin. 'I'm here.'

Our eyes seemed to be having a much longer conversation—one that set hope thudding along my veins. I could feel a smile starting deep inside me, trembling out to my mouth, but I was torn. Part of me longed to throw myself into his arms, but my sensible self warned me to be careful.

If I was going to seduce him, I was going to do it properly. The scenario I had in mind demanded that I was dressed in silk and stockings. My hair would be loose and silky, my skin soft, my nails painted Vixen. I couldn't embark on the raunchy affair I had in mind wearing jeans and a faded sweatshirt, with my hair scraped back in a ponytail.

I wondered if Phin had also been having a chat with his sensible side, because he was the one who broke the moment. Draining his coffee, he set down the paper cup.

'So, what needs to be done?'

I didn't say that he had already done everything I needed just by being there. 'Really just cleaning up and getting rid of all this stuff somehow.' I told him what the landlord had said.

Phin's brows snapped together. 'He *shouted* at you?'

'He was just frustrated. I know how he feels.' I sighed. 'I'd spent the whole day trying to deal with Mum, too. I was ready to shout myself! It's OK now, though. I've paid the rent arrears and settled the outstanding bills so everyone's happy.'

'That must have added up to a bit.' Phin looked

at me closely when I just shrugged. 'You used your savings, didn't you, CP?' he said.

I managed a crooked smile. 'It's just money, as Mum always says.'

'It was for your flat,' said Phin, looking grimmer than I had ever seen him. 'Your security. You worked for that money. You needed it.'

'Mum needed it more,' I said. 'It's OK, Phin. I'm fine about it—and Mum's very grateful. I've freed her up to get on with healing the galactic core, and the way things are going at the moment that might turn out to be quite a good investment!'

Phin's expression relaxed slightly, and I saw the familiar glimmer of a smile at the back of his eyes.

'Anyway,' I went on, 'I've decided to stop worrying so much about the future.' I smiled back at him as I jumped off the counter. 'You taught me that. I'm going to try living in the moment, the way you and Mum do.'

'Are you, now?' The smile had spread to his face, denting the corner of his mouth and twitching his lips.

'I am. You won't recognise me,' I told him. 'I'm going to be selfish and irresponsible…just as soon as I've finished clearing up here.'

Phin got off the counter with alacrity, and tossed the paper cups into the bin. 'In that case, let's get on with it. I can't wait to see the new, selfish Summer.'

I can't tell you how easy everything seemed now that there were two of us. Phin sorted everything. He left me to start packing up and went off to find a man with a van.

He was back in an amazingly short time to help me. 'Somebody called Dave is coming in a couple of hours. He's agreed to take all the stock off our hands.'

'What on earth is he going to do with it?' I asked curiously.

'I didn't ask, and neither should you. Your problem is his trading opportunity.'

We were dusty and tired by the time we had finished. Dave had turned up, as promised, and to my huge relief had taken away all the stock—which wasn't all that much once I started to pack it away. Then we'd bought a couple of brushes and a mop and cleaned the shop thoroughly, and Phin had mended the back door where the thieves had broken in.

I straightened, pressing both hands into the small of my back. 'I think that's it,' I said, looking around the shop. It was as clean as I could make it.

Then I looked at Phin, sweeping up the debris from his repair. I thought about everything he had done for me and my throat closed.

'I don't know what I would have done without you,' I told him.

Phin propped his broom against the wall. 'You'd

have coped—the way you always do,' he said. 'But I'm glad I could help.'

'You did. You helped more than you can ever know,' I said. 'You helped me just by being here. I'm only sorry to have dragged you all the way down to Somerset as soon as you got home.'

'You didn't drag me anywhere,' said Phin. 'I wanted to be here.'

I laughed. 'What? In a quiet side street of a pleasant provincial town? It's not really wild enough for you, is it? I can see you wanting to trek to the South Pole, or cross the Sahara or…or…' What *did* risk-takers like to do? 'Or bungee-jump in the Andes. But clear up an old shop in the suburbs? Admit it—it's not really your thing, is it?'

'You're not the only one who's changed,' said Phin. 'It's true that I used to be an adrenalin junkie, but it took that race from Rio to show me that I could push myself right to the edge, I could face everything the ocean could throw at me—and believe me that was a lot!—but hanging out on a trapeze over the waves in an Atlantic gale was still nothing like the rush I get when I'm with you.'

His tone was so conversational that it took me a moment to realise just what he'd said, and then I felt my heart start to crumble with a happiness so incredulous and so intense that it almost hurt.

Phin was still standing on the other side of the

room, but it was as if an electric current connected us, fizzing and sparking in the musty air. I was held by it, by the look in his eyes and the warmth of his voice, and I couldn't move, couldn't speak. All I could do was stare back at him with a kind of dazed disbelief.

'I thought about you every day at sea,' he said, his voice so deep it reverberated through me. 'It was tough out there, tough and exhilarating, but as soon as we got into port all I wanted was to see you, Summer. I wanted to hear your voice. I wanted to touch you. I suddenly understood what people mean when they say they want to go home. It wasn't about being in my house, or in London. It was just being with you. And if that means spending a day clearing out an old shop, that's where I want to be.'

I opened my mouth, but no sound came out. The air had leaked out of my lungs without me noticing and I had to suck in an unsteady breath.

'I've missed you, Summer,' said Phin.

I felt my mouth wobble treacherously and had to press my lips firmly together. 'I've missed you, too,' I said, my voice cracking.

'Really?'

I made a valiant effort to pull myself together. It was that or dissolve into an puddle of tears and lust. And what a mess that would be.

'Well, apart from your fiddling, obviously.'

A smile started in his eyes and spread out over his face as he took a step towards me. 'I even missed your obsessive tidying.'

'I missed you being late the whole time.' It was my turn to take a step forward.

He came a little closer. 'I missed the way you scowl at me over your glasses.'

'I missed your silly nicknames.'

We were almost touching by now. 'I missed kissing you,' said Phin—just as I said, 'I missed kissing you.' Our words overlapped as we closed the last gap between us, and then we didn't have to miss it any more. I was locked in his arms, my fingers clutching his hair, and we were kissing—deep, hungry kisses that sent the world rocking around us.

'Wait, wait!' I broke breathlessly away at last. 'It's not supposed to be like this!'

'What do you mean?' said Phin, pulling me back. 'This is *exactly* how it's supposed to be.'

'But I want to seduce you,' I wailed. 'I had it all planned out. I was going to be your fantasy again—but this time I was going to lock the office door so that Lex couldn't interrupt us.'

Phin started to laugh. 'CP, you're my fantasy wherever you are.'

'Not dressed like this—all dirty and dusty!'

'Even now, without your little suit,' he insisted. 'You're all I want.'

Well, how was a girl to resist that? I melted into him and kissed him back. 'That's all very well, but *my* fantasy is to seduce you properly,' I said. 'And I can't do it here.'

'I agree,' said Phin, his eyes dancing. 'If I'm going to be seduced, I'd like it to be in comfort. Does it have to be the office? Let me take you home instead. There's something I want to show you, anyway.'

So we picked up my bag from the B&B, dropped the key to the shop through the landlord's door, and headed back to London. Phin's car was fast, and incredibly comfortable as it purred effortlessly up the motorway, but I was so happy by then that I could probably have floated all the way under my own steam.

I was shimmering with excitement at the thought of what was to come, and it was still incredibly easy being together. We talked all the way back. Phin told me about sailing up the coast of South America, about winds and waves and negotiating currents, and about their dramatic rescue mission. I told him about my mother's new plan, and Anne's wedding, and how I'd decided to rent a little place on my own and not tie myself down with a mortgage.

We caught up on office gossip, too. I told Phin about Jonathan's new job. 'It's a big promotion for him.'

'Lex won't be happy, but I can't say I'm sorry he's leaving,' said Phin. 'But then, I'm just jealous.'

It was so absurd I laughed. 'You can't possibly be jealous of Jonathan, Phin!'

'I am,' he insisted. 'I remember how you felt about him. I know how important steadiness and security has always been to you. When you told me you'd talked to Jonathan in Aduaba, it seemed to me that he was offering you everything you really wanted.'

'Is that why you left when I went to work for Lex?'

He nodded. 'I thought it would be easier for you to get together with Jonathan, but as soon as I agreed to go to Rio I knew I had made a terrible mistake. All the time on the boat I thought about you with him, and I hated it. I couldn't believe how stupid I'd been. What had I been thinking? Helping you to get Jonathan back when all along I'd been falling in love with you myself. *Duh.*'

Phin slapped his forehead to make the point. 'And who had I been trying to kid with all that stuff about wanting you to be happy with Jonathan if that was what you really wanted? I was way too selfish for that. I wanted to make you happy myself, and I knew that I could do it if only you'd give me a chance. I had my strategy all worked out.'

'What strategy?' I asked, turning in my seat to look at him.

'You'll see,' said Phin. 'I flew back to London

as soon as we hit land, which gave me the weekend to put the first part of my plan into action. The next stage was to find you and separate you from Jonathan somehow. So I went into the office yesterday, but of course you weren't there—and nor was Lex. I couldn't get hold of him until later, and that's when he told me you were down here on your own. I was partly outraged that Jonathan wasn't here to help you, but I was pleased, too, that you were alone so I could tell you how I felt.'

He glanced at me with a smile. 'Then you told me that you weren't going to marry him after all. You'll never know how relieved I was to hear that, cream puff.'

I smiled back at him. 'It took you going for me to realise how much I loved you,' I told him. 'I knew then that I couldn't marry Jonathan. I thought I loved him, but I didn't really know him. You were right. I loved what he represented. But you knew more about me after that first time we had coffee than Jonathan ever did. He never made an effort to see what I was really like until you made it easy for him. You were the only one who's ever looked at me and understood me. You're the one who's made me realise I can be sensible some of the time, but I don't have to be like that all the time—and I won't be when I seduce you,' I promised.

'I love the fact that you're so sensible,' Phin told

me. 'I love the contrast between that and your sexiness, that you wear sharp suits but silk lingerie. And most of all,' he said, 'I love the fact that I'm the only one who sees that about you. Everyone thinks you're wonderful—'

I goggled. 'They all think I'm nitpicking and irritable!'

'Maybe, but they also know you're kind and generous, and the person they can all turn to when they need help or something has to be done. But I'm the only one that sees the cream puff in you,' said Phin, and his smile made my heart turn over.

'Don't joke,' I said, laying my hand on his thigh. 'I'm going to be channelling my inner cream puff from now on. I hope you're ready!'

Phin covered my hand with his own. 'Don't distract me while I'm driving,' he said, but his fingers tightened over mine and he lifted them to press a kiss on my knuckles.

'I've never been the kind of girl who has an affair with her boss,' I said with a happy sigh. 'I hope I'll be able to carry it off.'

'Perhaps it's just as well I'm not going to be your boss any more,' said Phin. 'We'd never get any work done. But who's going to keep me in order in the office? Have you found me a new PA yet?'

'No. Everyone I've considered has been too

young or too pretty for you to share doughnuts with. I'm looking for someone who's ready to retire.'

Phin laughed. 'I won't eat doughnuts with anyone but you, I promise.'

'It's only until Monique comes back,' I said. 'I'm thinking we could get by if we look after you in Lex's office. Lotty could keep your diary.'

'Sounds good to me,' he said. 'As long as you come down to my office occasionally and lock the door before you take your hair down!'

We had been making our stop-start way along the King's Road, but now Phin turned off into his street. I looked at his house as we pulled up outside. 'There's something different... You've painted the door!' I suspect my eyes were shining as I turned to him. 'It's exactly the right shade of blue. How did you know?'

'Phew,' said Phin, grinning at my delight. 'I have to admit that was a lucky guess.'

I got out of the car, still staring. 'And window boxes!'

'I got a gardening company to do them. What do you think?'

My throat was constricted. 'It's just like my dream,' I said, wanting to cry. 'You remembered.'

'Wait till you see inside!'

I hardly recognised the house. It was immaculately clean, and all the clutter had been cleared away so that the rooms felt airy and light.

I stood in the middle of the living room and turned slowly around until my eye fell on the sofa.

Two cushions sat on it, plump and precisely angled.

I looked at them for a long, long moment, and then raised my eyes to look at Phin.

'They look all right, don't they?' he said.

Taking my hand, he drew me down onto the sofa, careless of the cushions. 'You know that studio you were thinking of renting? I was thinking you could move in here instead. I had cleaners blitz the house yesterday, so I can't promise that it will always be like this—but you could tidy up all you want.'

'Move in?' I looked around my dream house, then back to the dream man beside me, and for a moment I wondered if this really *was* just a dream. 'But aren't we going to have a passionate affair?'

'It depends what you mean by affair,' said Phin, picking his words with care.

'I mean sex with no strings,' I said adamantly. 'I don't want to tie you down. I've learnt my lesson. I want being with you to be about having fun, being reckless, not thinking about the future or commitment or anything.'

'Oh,' said Phin.

'That's what you want, isn't it?'

'The thing is, I'm not sure I do.'

I stared at him.

'I think,' he said, 'that I've changed my mind.'

My heart did a horrible flip-flop, leaving me feeling sick. 'Oh,' I said, drawing my hand out of his. 'Oh, I see. I understand.'

But I didn't. I didn't understand at all. I had just let myself believe that he wanted me as much as I wanted him. Why had he changed his mind?

Phin took my hand firmly back. 'I'm fairly sure you *don't* see, Summer. For someone so sharp, you can be very dense sometimes! I haven't changed my mind about you, you idiot. I've changed it about commitment. I've spent my whole life running away from the very idea of it,' he admitted, 'but that was because I had never found anyone or anything that was worth committing to. Now there's you, and it's all changed. It was all I could think about on the boat. It wasn't that I didn't enjoy the sailing, but this time I wanted you to come home to. I wanted to know that you would always be there.

'So I'm afraid,' he said, with a show of regret, 'that if you want to have an affair with me you're going to have to marry me. I know you're just interested in my body, but I'm so in love with you, Summer. Say you'll marry me and always be there for me.'

I looked back into those blue, blue eyes, and the expression I saw there squeezed my heart with a mixture of joy and relief so acute it was painful. I was perilously close to tears even as exhilarating, intoxicating happiness bubbled along my veins like champagne. It was like stumbling unexpectedly into paradise after a long, hard journey. It was too much, too wonderful. I could hardly take it in.

Unable to tell Phin how I felt, I reverted to joking instead.

'But what about my fantasy to seduce you?' I pretended to pout. 'I was so determined that I was going to live dangerously. You can't have an affair with your own fiancé!'

'If you want to be reckless, let's get married straight away,' said Phin.

'I don't think Lex would like that very much. He's running out of suitable PAs.'

'He'd be furious,' Phin agreed, and grinned wickedly at me. 'Let's do it anyway.'

I pretended to consider. 'I still don't get to have an affair,' I pointed out.

'How about we don't get engaged until tomorrow?' he suggested. 'Then you can have your wicked way with me tonight with no commitment at all. But I'm warning you—that's it,' he said with mock sternness as he pulled me down beneath him. 'One night is all you're going to get, and you won't even have that unless you say yes. So, just how badly do you want an affair, my little cream puff?'

'Very badly,' I said, a smile trembling on my lips.

'Badly enough to stick with me for ever after tonight?'

'Well, if I must...' I sighed contentedly.

Phin bent his head until his mouth was almost touching mine. 'So here's the deal. You seduce me to your heart's content tonight, and then we get married.'

'I get to do whatever I want with you?'

'It's your fantasy,' he agreed. 'I'm all yours. And tomorrow you're all mine.' He smiled. 'Do we have a deal?'

Well, it would have been rude to say no, wouldn't it?

I put my arms around his neck and pulled him into a long, sweet kiss. 'It's a deal,' I promised.

'Good,' said Phin, satisfied. 'Now, about this fantasy of yours...where are you going to start?'

I took hold of his T-shirt and pulled it over his head. 'I'll show you.'

HOUSEKEEPER'S HAPPY-EVER-AFTER

BY
FIONA HARPER

MILLS & BOON

> **DID YOU PURCHASE THIS BOOK WITHOUT A COVER?**
>
> If you did, you should be aware it is **stolen property** as it was reported *unsold and destroyed* by a retailer. Neither the author nor the publisher has received any payment for this book.

All the characters in this book have no existence outside the imagination of the author, and have no relation whatsoever to anyone bearing the same name or names. They are not even distantly inspired by any individual known or unknown to the author, and all the incidents are pure invention.

All Rights Reserved including the right of reproduction in whole or in part in any form. This edition is published by arrangement with Harlequin Enterprises II BV/S.à.r.l. The text of this publication or any part thereof may not be reproduced or transmitted in any form or by any means, electronic or mechanical, including photocopying, recording, storage in an information retrieval system, or otherwise, without the written permission of the publisher.

This book is sold subject to the condition that it shall not, by way of trade or otherwise, be lent, resold, hired out or otherwise circulated without the prior consent of the publisher in any form of binding or cover other than that in which it is published and without a similar condition including this condition being imposed on the subsequent purchaser.

® and TM are trademarks owned and used by the trademark owner and/or its licensee. Trademarks marked with ® are registered with the United Kingdom Patent Office and/or the Office for Harmonisation in the Internal Market and in other countries.

First published in Great Britain 2010
Harlequin Mills & Boon Limited,
Eton House, 18-24 Paradise Road, Richmond, Surrey TW9 1SR

© Fiona Harper 2010

ISBN: 978 0 263 87334 4

Harlequin Mills & Boon policy is to use papers that are natural, renewable and recyclable products and made from wood grown in sustainable forests. The logging and manufacturing process conform to the legal environmental regulations of the country of origin.

Printed and bound in Spain
by Litografia Rosés, S.A., Barcelona

As a child, **Fiona Harper** was constantly teased for either having her nose in a book, or living in a dream world. Things haven't changed much since then, but at least in writing she's found a use for her runaway imagination. After studying dance at university, Fiona worked as a dancer, teacher and choreographer, before trading in that career for video-editing and production. When she became a mother she cut back on her working hours to spend time with her children, and when her littlest one started pre-school she found a few spare moments to rediscover an old but not forgotten love—writing.

Fiona lives in London, but her other favourite places to be are the Highlands of Scotland, and the Kent countryside on a summer's afternoon. She loves cooking good food and anything cinnamon-flavoured. Of course she still can't keep away from a good book, or a good movie—especially romances—but only if she's stocked up with tissues, because she knows she will need them by the end, be it happy or sad. Her favourite things in the world are her wonderful husband, who has learned to decipher her incoherent ramblings, and her two daughters.

**For Sian and Rose,
my darling girls, who I could never, ever forget.**

CHAPTER ONE

ELLIE gave in to the insistent nagging at the fringes of her sleep and woke up. She focused on the display from the digital clock next to the bed.

Two-sixteen—and she needed to go to the bathroom. But it was her first night in an unfamiliar house and she didn't really want to be crashing around in the dark, even if she was the sole occupant.

She punched her pillow and flopped onto her other side, burying her head under the duvet. She could last. Clamping her eyes shut, she shifted position again, wriggling into the mattress. The seconds sloped by in the thick silence. She lay completely still, counting her heartbeats.

Apparently she couldn't last. Bother.

She blinked and tried to see where the outline of the door was in the blackness of the bedroom. The dull green glow from the alarm clock lit the duvet but not much more. The edge of the bed was about as inviting as the edge of a cliff.

Ellie Bond, get hold of yourself! A grown woman has no business being scared of the dark. Even in the kind of huge old house that looked as if it might have ghosts or bats in the attic.

She flung the duvet off and planted her feet firmly on the carpet, but hesitated for a couple of seconds before she stood up and inched towards the wall.

Ouch! Closer than she'd guessed.

Maybe she should have paid more attention when she'd dumped her cases in here, but she'd been so exhausted she'd only managed half her unpacking before she'd fallen into the large, squashy bed.

She rubbed her shoulder and felt along the wall for the door. It was a couple of steps to the left from her point of impact. The antique handle complained as she twisted it millimetre by millimetre. She winced and opened the door slowly and carefully. Why, she didn't know. It just seemed wrong to be too noisy in someone else's house late at night, even if they were away from home.

Ellie leant out of the doorway and slid the flat of her hand along the wall in search of the light switch.

Where was the stupid thing?

Certainly not within easy reach. But as she crept along the hallway the clouds parted and sent a sliver of moonlight through the half-open curtains at the end of the landing. Bingo! She could see the bathroom door, right next to the window. She padded more speedily along the wooden floor, her bare feet sticking to the layers of old varnish.

Relief swirled through her as she scrambled inside the bathroom and yanked the light cord. A few minutes later she opened the door and froze. The moonlight had evaporated and she was left standing in the pitch-dark.

Don't panic, Ellie. Think!

There had to be logical way to deal with this.

'Okay,' she whispered out loud, 'my room is the—' she counted on her fingers '—third on the left...I think.' All she had to do was feel for the doors and she would be back in that wonderfully comfortable bed in no time.

She tiptoed close to the wood panelling, letting her left fingers walk along the surface in search of door fames.

One...

Two...

She meant to creep slowly, but with each step her pulse increased, adding speed to her steps.

Three...

She opened the door and made a quick dash for the bed. Ever since she was a child she'd had an irrational fear that some shadowy figure underneath would grab her ankles when she got close. She'd even perfected a sprint and dive manoeuvre in her teenage years. She decided to resurrect it now.

Big mistake.

She tripped over a discarded shoe and stumbled into a solid wall of…something.

It was warm. And breathing.

Oh, heck.

There was somebody in the house! A burglar, or an axe-wielding maniac…

Her brain short-circuited. Too much information at once. Too much to process. Thankfully, more primal instincts took over. She backed away, hoping she hadn't got muddled and that the door was still directly behind her. But she hadn't made more than two steps when a large, strong hand grabbed her wrist.

Ellie's stomach somersaulted and she froze. Without even thinking about why or how, she lunged at him, whoever he was, and shoved the heel of her hand under his chin, causing him to grunt and stumble backwards.

Mother, I will never moan about the self-defence classes you made me go to in the village hall again!

In the surreal slow-motion moment that followed, she wondered why a burglar would be bare-chested in March, but before the thought was fully formed in her head his other arm grabbed her and he fell, taking her with him. She came crashing down on top of him, and then they lay winded in a tangle of arms and legs on the floor.

Here, he had the advantage. She didn't know how, but she could sense he was taller than her, and if the chest she'd just landed on was anything to go by he had five times as many muscles. Somehow as they'd fallen they'd twisted, and she was now partly pinned underneath him, her legs trapped. She started to wriggle.

I should have paid more attention at those classes, instead of gossiping at the back with Janice Bradford.

Because the man obviously had no intention of letting her loose. In one swift movement he flipped her onto her back, his hands clamping both her wrists and digging them into the scratchy wool rug while his knees clamped her thighs together. The air left Ellie's body with an 'oof' noise.

She flailed and struggled, but it was like trying to dislodge a lump of granite. Eventually she lay still beneath him, every muscle rigid. His toothpaste-scented breath came in short puffs, warming the skin of her neck. Panic fluttered in her chest.

It dawned on her that her original assumption that he was a burglar might be a tad optimistic. Things could be about to get a lot worse.

She had to act now—before he made his next move.

In a moment of pure instinct, she lifted her head and sank her teeth into the smooth skin of his shoulder. Then, while he was yelping in pain, she used every bit of strength in her five-foot-five frame to rock him to her left, getting him off-balance and thereby gaining enough momentum to swing him back in the other direction. The plan was to fling him off her so she could escape.

The plan was flawed.

He tumbled over, all right, but as she tried to crawl away he got hold of her right foot and dragged her back towards him. Ellie tried to stop herself by twisting over and clawing at the rug, but large tufts just came away in her fingers. And then she realised she was travelling further than she'd scurried away. She was being dragged back towards the bed.

That was when she started shouting. A wave of white-hot anger swept up her body.

How dared he?

'Get out of my bedroom!' she screamed. 'Or I'll—'

'What?'

He was angry, but there was something more in his voice—confusion?

Harsh light flooded the room, accompanied by the click of a switch. Ellie peeled her face off the carpet and blinked a few times, desperate to focus on anything that might give her a clue as to where the door was. Her eyes began to adjust, and she made out a tall figure against the pale blue of the wall.

Pale blue? Oh, help! My room is a kind of heritage yellow colour.

She crinkled her eyelids until they were almost shut, and swivelled her head to face her attacker. Through the blur of her eyelashes she saw a pair of deep brown eyes staring at her. There was something about them... Had she dreamt about a pair of eyes just like that before she'd woken up? Half a memory was lodged somewhere, refusing to make sense.

Ellie's chest reverberated with the pounding of her heart and she felt the fire wash up her face and settle in the tips of her ears. He looked as astonished as she felt.

She *had* seen those eyes before, but not in her dreams. They hadn't been scowling then, but laughing, *twinkling*...

Ellie let out a noise that was part groan, part whimper as the memory clunked into place. She started to collect her limbs together and move away.

'I'm...I'm...so sorry! I got lost in the dark...' She shot a glance at him, but his face was still etched with confusion. 'I mean, I thought you were a—a maniac.'

He blinked. Something told her his assessment of her hadn't been dissimilar.

'Mr Wilder... I...'

'I know who I am. Who on earth are *you*?'

She licked her lips—they seemed to have dried

out completely—and cleared her throat. 'I'm Ellie Bond, your new housekeeper.'

One month earlier

Ellie's limbs stopped working the moment she crossed the threshold of the coffee shop. The woman in the red coat was early. She wasn't supposed to be here yet, but there she was, sitting at a table and reading a newspaper. After a few seconds the door swung closed behind Ellie, hitting her on the bottom. She didn't even flinch, mainly because she felt as if she'd swallowed a thousand ice cubes and they were now all jostling for position as they slowly melted, spreading outwards through her body.

The woman's long dark hair almost touched the tabletop as she bent over an absorbing story. Chunky silver earrings glinted in her ears when she flicked her hair out of the way so she could turn the page. Earrings that Ellie had given her for her last birthday.

The woman hadn't noticed Ellie yet, and she was glad about that. She stared harder. Perhaps if she just stood here for a moment, took her time, it would come to her.

Something the woman was reading must have bothered her, because she stiffened and, even though her head was bowed, Ellie knew that three vertical lines had just appeared above the bridge of the woman's nose. That always happened when she frowned. When people had been friends for more than a decade, they tended to notice little things like that about each other without even realising it. The brain collected a scrapbook about a person, made up of assorted images, sensations, sounds and aromas, all of which could be called up at a moment's notice. And Ellie had plenty of those memories flooding into the front of her consciousness right now—untidy college bedrooms, the smell of dusty books in the library, the giggles of late-night gossip sessions…

A fact that only made the current situation more galling.

Ellie couldn't remember her name.

Since the accident, finding the right name or word had become like rummaging around in the cupboard under the stairs without a torch. She knew the information she wanted was in her brain somewhere, but she was fumbling in the dark, not really knowing what she was looking for and just hoping she'd recognise it when she finally laid hold of it.

A waitress bustled past her, and the movement must have alerted her friend to the person standing at the edge of her peripheral vision, because she looked up from her newspaper and smiled at Ellie.

Ellie waved back, but behind her answering smile she was running through the letters of the alphabet, just as she'd been taught at the support group, to see if any of them jogged her memory.

Anna? Alice? Amy?

The woman stood up, beaming now, and Ellie had no choice but to start walking towards her.

Belinda? No.

Brenda?

The chunky earrings bobbed as her friend stood and drew her into a hug. Ellie just stood there for a moment like a rag doll, and then she made a conscious decision to contract her arm muscles and squeeze back. Not that she was opposed to hugging; it was just that her brain was far too busy ferreting around for the right letter, the right syllable, to get her started.

Christine…Caroline…Carly?

Carly. It seemed right and not right at the same time.

A whisper tickled her ear. 'It's so good to see you, Ellie!'

Ellie knew her friend would understand if she just admitted her memory blank. But Ellie was fed up with being *understood*. She just wanted to *be*— to live her life the way everyone else did, without the sympathetic glances. That was why she'd arranged this meeting in the first place.

A familiar sensation washed over her. She imagined it to be what it might feel like if portions of her memory were buoys, chained to a deep and murky ocean floor, and then all of a sudden one freed itself and floated upwards, arriving on the surface with a plop.

Charlotte Maxwell.

'Hi, Charlie,' she said, and finally relaxed into the hug. 'It's good to see you too.'

She tried not to, but as she pulled away and sat down Ellie sighed, deep and hard. Charlie tilted her head and looked at her.

'How are you?'

Ah. How innocent that phrase sounded. How kind and well-meaning.

Ellie had come to hate it. People were always asking her that, normally wearing a concerned expression. Oh, she wasn't fooled a bit. It wasn't small talk. Chit-chat. What people wanted from her when they asked that question was a full psychological and medical rundown.

She smiled, but her lips remained firmly pressed together. 'I'm great. Really.'

Charlie kept staring at her. 'Still getting the headaches?'

'Only occasionally,' she replied, shrugging the observation away.

The wicked twinkle returned to Charlie's eyes as she stood back and looked Ellie up and down. 'You've had your hair cut,' she said.

Ellie automatically raised a hand to feel the blunt ends of her tousled blonde curls. She'd only had it done a few days ago, and she still wasn't used to finding fresh air where there had once been heavy ringlets that reached halfway down her back. The ends now just brushed the tops of her shoulders. It was shorter, maybe a bit younger, and a heck of a lot more manageable.

'I was ready for a change,' she said.

Change.

That was why she was here. She might as well get down to business and ask Charlie the question that had been burning her tongue all morning. If she didn't do it soon she was likely to get distracted and end up going home without mentioning it at all. She opened her mouth to speak.

'I don't know about you,' Charlie said in a grave voice, 'but I can't be expected to indulge in a month's worth of gossip without a side order of caffeine—and possibly a muffin or three. It's just not done.'

Ellie glanced over at the counter then stood up.

'I'll have a...'

Oh, flip. What was the word? She knew she knew it, but it seemed to be speeding away from her, like a dream that was fast evaporating with the last traces of sleep.

'You know...the fluffy, milky drink with powder on top.'

Charlie didn't bat an eyelid, bless her. 'Two cappuccinos, please,' she said to the barista.

Ellie leaned forward and looked at the girl over Charlie's shoulder. 'And a chocolate muffin, please.'

'Make that two.' Charlie turned and smirked at her while the barista rang up the sale. 'That's my girl. Couldn't forget chocolate if you tried.'

If her mother or her sister had said something like that Ellie would have snapped at them, but she found herself laughing at Charlie's sideways comment. Maybe she was too sensitive these days. And she'd wound herself up into a state about meeting Charlie before she'd even got here. No wonder her memory was malfunctioning. It always got worse when she was stressed or nervous.

Charlie understood. She made Ellie's 'condition' seem like no big deal. That one positive thought gave her confidence. She was going to ask her. She was ready.

But the first cappuccinos had been drained and the second round ordered before Ellie finally worked up her nerve. She twiddled the silver locket she always wore between her thumb and forefinger.

'Actually, Charlie, there was a reason I suggested getting together this morning. I need a favour.'

'Anything. You know that.' Charlie leaned forward and rubbed her forearm. 'I'll do anything I can to help.'

Ellie took at deep breath. She was asking for a lot more than the usual sympathetic ear or moral support at social functions. A lot more.

'I need a job.'

Charlie just seemed to freeze. She blinked a couple of times. 'A job?'

Ellie squeezed her bottom lip between her teeth and gave a little nod, but Charlie broke eye contact and took her time while she folded a corner of the newspaper page into a neat triangle. She glanced up once she'd scored it with a long, red fingernail.

'I'm sorry, Ellie. I only need a couple of people in the office, and I've got all the staff I require at the moment.'

Oh, fab. Charlie thought she was asking her for a pity job—one with minimum responsibilities and no challenges. But Ellie couldn't give up now. She was desperate. She stopped fiddling with her locket and folded her hands in her lap.

'No. I mean I want you to put me on your agency's books, preferably for a job where I can live in. I need to…get away from Barkleigh for a while. You must have something I could do? Something that uses my skills? You know I'm a fantastic cook.'

Charlie nodded and said nothing, but Ellie could see her mind working. She made a rather nice living running an exclusive little agency providing the well-off with domestic staff—from butlers and chauffeurs to cooks and nannies.

'But are you…? Can you…?' Charlie wrinkled her nose and paused.

Ellie knew what she was trying to ask, what she really didn't want to put into words. Was the patched-up and rehabilitated Ellie capable of holding down a full-time job? The truth was, Ellie wasn't even sure herself. She thought she was. She'd worked hard to put strategies and coping mechanisms in place to help with the memory and concentration problems that were so common after a serious head injury, but she was shaking in her boots at the idea of moving away from everything familiar and starting again somewhere new.

'I just have to work a little bit harder than everyone else at keeping myself organised nowadays. But I can do this, Charlie. I know I can. I just need someone to believe in me and give me a chance, and you said you'd do anything you can to help.'

Okay, that was playing dirty, but she was desperate. The pained look on Charlie's face was almost too much to bear. She wasn't convinced. And if Ellie had been in her shoes maybe she wouldn't have been either.

For a long time Charlie said nothing, and Ellie thought she might be creating brand-new wrinkles on her forehead with all the mental wrestling she was doing. Then, slowly, the lines faded.

'Okay,' she said, staring out of the window. 'I just might have something. I'll let you know.'

The cottage door slammed. There was something very final about the sound of the old door hitting the door frame. Ellie tried to remove the key from the worn Victorian lock, but it refused to budge.

Today was not going well. Lost keys, a case that wouldn't shut and a pigeon stuck in the roof had already plagued her this morning. If she had been one to believe in bad omens she'd have run upstairs and hidden under her duvet a few hours ago. But the duvet was freshly laundered, waiting for someone else, and the rest of her life had been divided into packing boxes and suitcases. The cottage was now bare of all personal possessions, ready to be rented out by the week. The holiday lettings company had jumped at the chance of a child-friendly property in the picturesque little village of Barkleigh. Other families would build memories here now.

She caught the tip of her tongue between her teeth and resumed her negotiations with the lock. The choreographed sequence of turns, pulls and twists had long ago become a matter of muscle memory rather than conscious thought, and finally the key jerked free. It always did in the end. It just needed a little gentle persuasion.

It was time to leave. Ellie shoved her keys in the back pocket of her jeans and stared through the stained glass panels that filled the top half of the heavy old door. Once, the hallway had been warm and inviting, filled with discarded shoes, coats hanging haphazardly on a row of hooks. Now it was cold and empty, distorted through the rippling glass.

A large drop of rain splashed onto the top of her head. She shuddered, picked up the last piece of luggage, then turned and walked down the path towards her waiting car.

Ellie looked out across the fields. An overstuffed dark grey cloud was devouring the sunshine, heading straight towards her. Another plop of rain dropped on the back of her neck and ran down between her shoulder blades. She increased her speed. The boot of her old hatchback stood gaping and she slung the holdall in the back, slammed the door shut and hurried round to the driver's door. The tempo of the rain increased. By the time she was inside it was drumming an unpromising rhythm on the roof of the car. Warm, earthy smells drifted through the ventilation system.

She glanced at the handbag sitting on the passenger seat. Poking out of the top was a worn blue teddy bear with one eye and bald ears where the fluff had been loved off. The backs of her eyes burned, but she refused to blink, knowing that any moisture leaking over her lashes would feel like acid. The pummelling on the roof of the car magnified, filling her ears and pulling the world away from her down a long, invisible tunnel.

Not now. Today of all days I need to keep it together.

She forced herself to sit upright in the driver's seat and stared blindly into the blurry grey scenery beyond the windscreen, then turned the key in the ignition. The car rumbled grudgingly to life, coughed once, and promptly stalled.

Still she didn't blink, just held her breath for a few seconds, then reached out to stroke the dashboard.

Come on, girl! Don't let me down now.

She pumped the gas a few times and tried again, and when the engine rewarded her with an uneven purr, she released her breath and put the car into gear. She pulled away slowly, rumbling down the country lane, and didn't allow herself the luxury of looking back.

An hour later she was sitting behind a caravan on the motorway. It was only going at about fifty, but she made no attempt to pass it. This speed was fine, thank you very much. Driving wasn't her favourite occupation these days, and she hadn't been on a motorway in a long time. She distracted herself from the haulage trucks passing her at insane speeds with thoughts of fresh starts and new jobs.

Everyone had been so happy when she'd come out of hospital after the accident, sure she was going to be 'back to normal' in no time. And after a year, when she'd finally moved out of her parents' house and back into the cottage, her family and friends had breathed a collective sigh of relief.

That was it. Everything done and dusted. Ellie is all better and we can stop worrying now.

But Ellie wasn't all better. Her hair might have grown again and covered the uneven scars on her skull, she might even talk and walk the same, but nothing, *nothing*, would ever be the same again. Underneath the 'normal' surface she was fundamentally different and always would be.

She focused on the droplets of rain collecting on the windscreen.

Water. That was all those tiny splashes were. Almost nothing, really. So how could something so inconsequential alter the course of three lives so totally, so drastically? She nudged the lever next to the steering wheel again and the specks of water vanished in a flurry of motion.

Thankfully, within a few minutes the rain had stopped completely and she was able to slow the squeaking wipers to a halt. Warm afternoon light cut clean paths through the clouds. Her shoulder blades eased back into their normal position and she realised she'd been clenching her teeth from the moment she'd put her foot on the accelerator. She made a conscious effort to relax her jaw and stretched her fingers. The knuckles creaked, stiff from gripping the steering wheel just a little too tightly.

A big blue sign was up ahead and she read it carefully.

Junction Eight. Two more to go.

She'd promised herself that she would not zone out and sail past the turn-off. Getting lost was not an option today.

The caravan in front slowed until it was practically crawling along. Ellie glanced in her wing mirror. She could overtake it if she wanted to. The adjacent lane was almost clear. Still, it took her five minutes and a stiff lecture before she signalled and pulled out.

She was still concentrating on remembering to exit at Junction Ten, visualising the number, burning it onto her short-term memory, when a prolonged horn blast startled her. A car loomed large in her rear-view mirror. It inched closer, until their bumpers were almost touching, its engine snarling. Ellie was almost frightened enough to speed up to give herself breathing room. Almost.

Flustered, she grabbed at the levers round the steering wheel for the indicator, only to discover she'd turned the fog light on instead. She fought to keep her breathing calm, yanked at the correct lever and pulled into the inside lane. What she now realised was a sleek Porsche zoomed past in a bright red blur.

A sigh of relief was halfway across her lips when the same car swerved in front of her. She stamped on the brake and glared at the disappearing number plate, retaliating by pressing her thumb on the horn for a good five seconds, even though the lunatic driver was now a speck in the distance, too far away to hear—or care.

It had to be a man. Too caught up in his own ego to think about anyone else. Pathetic. She had made a policy to keep her distance from that type of person, whether he was inside a low-slung car or out of it.

She shook her head and returned her concentration to the road, relieved to see she was only two miles from the next service station. An impromptu caffeine break was in order.

It wasn't long before she was out of the car and sitting in an uncomfortable plastic seat with a grimy mug of coffee on the table in front of her. She cupped her hands round it and let the heat warm her palms.

The crazy Porsche driver had flustered her, brought back feelings and memories she had long tried to evade. Which on the surface seemed odd, because she couldn't even remember the accident itself.

But perhaps it was better not to have been conscious as they'd cut her from the wreckage of the family car, the bodies of her husband and daughter beside her. Not that her battered memory didn't invent images and torture her with them in the depths of the night.

She had no clear memories of the beginning of her hospital stay either. The doctors had told her this was normal. Post-traumatic amnesia. When she tried to think back to that time it was as if a cloud had settled over it, thick and impenetrable.

Sometimes she thought it would be nice to lose herself in that fog again, because emerging from it, scarred and confused, to find her lovely Sam and her darling eight-year-old Chloe were gone for ever had been the single worst moment of her existence.

All because it had rained. And because two boys in a fast car hadn't thought that important. They'd been arrogant, thinking those little drops of *almost nothing* couldn't stop them, couldn't spoil their fun.

She looked down at her coffee. The cup was empty, but she didn't remember drinking it.

Just as well.

Brown scum had settled at the bottom of the cup. Ellie shook off a shudder and patted down her unruly blonde curls, tucking the ends of the long fringe behind her ears. She couldn't sit here all day nursing an empty cup of coffee. But moving meant getting back in the car and rejoining the motorway. Something she wanted to do even less now than she had when she'd left home this morning. She closed her eyes and slowly inflated her lungs.

Come on, Ellie. The only other option is admitting defeat and going back home to hibernate for ever. You can do this. You have to. Staying at the cottage is eating you alive from the inside out. You're stagnating.

She opened her eyelids, smoothed her T-shirt down over her jeans, swung her handbag out from underneath the table and made a straight line for the exit.

Back on the road, her geriatric car protested as she reached the speed limit. She filtered out the rattling and let the solitude of the motorway envelop her. She wasn't thinking of anything in particular, but she wasn't giving her attention to the road either. Her mind was in limbo—and it was wonderful.

The sun emerged from the melting clouds and flickered through the tops of the trees. She flipped the visor down to shield her eyes. The slanting light reflected off the sodden carriageway and she peered hard at the road, struggling to see the white lines marking the lanes.

In fact, she was concentrating so hard she failed to notice the motorway sign on the grassy verge to her left.

Junction Ten.

CHAPTER TWO

WHEN she finally arrived, her new workplace was a bit of a surprise. Big shots like her new boss normally wanted their homes to shout out loud how rich and grand their owners were. Yet as she drove up the sweeping gravel drive and the woodland parted to reveal Larkford Place, she discovered a small but charming sixteenth-century manor house surrounded by rhododendrons and twisting oaks. The mellow red bricks were tinted gold by the rays of the setting sun, and the scent of lavender was thick in the air after the rain. The house was so much a part of its surroundings she could almost imagine it had grown up together with the ancient wisteria that clung to its walls.

For the first time since she'd decided to escape from her life she felt something other than fear or desperation. It was beautiful here. So serene. Hope surged through her—an emotion she hadn't experienced in such a long time that she'd assumed it must have been wiped clear of her damaged memory banks with everything else.

The drive swelled and widened in front of the house, a perfect place to park cars. But this wasn't where she was stopping—oh, no. It was the lowly tradesmen's entrance for her. She changed gear and followed a narrower branch of the drive round the side of the house and into a cobbled courtyard. The old stables still had large glossy black doors, and Ellie admired the wrought-iron saddle rest that was bolted to the wall as she got out of her car and gave her legs a stretch.

Once out of the car, she stood motionless in the courtyard and stared at the ivy framing the back door. Wind rippled through it, making it shiver. With measured steps she approached it, pulling the key she'd picked up from the previous housekeeper out of her pocket, then sliding it into the old iron lock. She pushed the wooden door open and peered down a dark corridor.

The excitement she'd felt only moments ago drained away rapidly, gurgling in her stomach as it went. This threshold was where yesterday and tomorrow intersected. Crossing it felt final, as if by taking that step other doors in her life would slam shut and there would be no return.

But that was what she wanted, wasn't it? To move forward? To leave the past behind?

She willed her right leg to swing forward and make the first step, and once she'd got that over with she marched herself down the corridor, her footsteps loud and squeaky on the flagstones, announcing her decision and scaring any ghosts away.

A door led to a bright spacious kitchen, with a pretty view of the garden through pair of French windows on the opposite side of the room.

Ellie turned on her heels and took a better look at the place that would be her domain from now on. It was a cook's dream. The house had been newly renovated, and she'd been told the kitchen fitters had only finished last week. The appliances looked as if they'd walked straight out of a high-end catalogue. They even smelled new.

A long shelf along one wall held a row of pristine cookery books. She wandered over to them as if suddenly magnetised. *Oóh*. She'd been eyeing this one in her local bookshop only last week…

Without checking her impulse, she hooked a finger on the top of the binding and eased it off the shelf. She had plenty of time to explore the house—almost a whole week—before her new boss arrived home from his overseas trip. The wall planner and the sticky notes could come out tomorrow, when her brain was in better shape to make sense of all these unfamiliar sights and sounds. Right now she needed to rest. It had been a long and tiring day and she deserved a cup of tea and a sit-down. She opened the book and flicked a few pages. It was legitimate research, after all...

It didn't take long to locate the kettle, the teabags and even a packet of chocolate digestives. While she waited for the water to boil she wandered round the kitchen, inspecting it more closely. What was that under the wall cabinet? It looked like a...

Oh, cool. A little flatscreen TV that flipped down and swivelled in any direction you wanted. She pressed the button on the side and a crisp, bright picture filled the screen—a teatime quiz show. She'd work out how to change channels later. For now it was just nice to have some colourful company in the empty house, even if the acid-voiced presenter was getting rather personal about a contestant who wasn't doing very well.

She made her tea and hoisted herself onto one of the stools at the breakfast bar, the cookery book laid flat in front of her, and started dunking biscuits into her mug before sucking the chocolate off. Nobody was here to catch her, were they?

Now, what could she cook Mr Big Shot for dinner on his first night back? It had to be something impressive, something to make him want to hire her permanently when the three-month trial period was up.

Ellie suspected she wouldn't have been offered

the job if the man in question hadn't been a) Charlie's cousin and b) desperate for someone to start as soon as possible. Her new boss was something big in the music industry, apparently. She thought the name had sounded vaguely familiar, but she really didn't keep up to date with that sort of thing any more.

Her oldest friend, Ginny, had actually seemed impressed when Ellie had made the announcement about her new job. She'd gushed and twittered and gone on about how lucky Ellie was. Ellie hadn't stopped her, glad that Ginny had been too distracted to ask any difficult questions about the *real* reason for Ellie's sudden need to uproot herself from her comfortable little life and flee.

But she wasn't going to think about that at the moment. For once she was grateful for her brain's tendency to flit onto a new subject without a backward glance, and turned her whole attention to the colourful book on the counter in front of her.

Now, was squid-ink pasta really as stupendous as those TV chefs made out? Or did they just use it because it made the pictures in their glossy cookbooks look good?

The cooking part of the job would be fun. She'd always enjoyed it, and had even taken a few courses at the local adult education college to hone her techniques before Chloe had been born. In the last couple of years it had become almost an obsession. But obsessions were something she could excel in these days, and since she'd been out of the workforce and had a lot of time on her hands it had been a perfect way to keep herself occupied. Funnily, it was the one skill she seemed to have clung on to without any deficit since the accident. She didn't know why. Perhaps that knack of combining flavours and textures was held in a different part of the brain—one that hadn't been shaken and swollen and bruised as the car had rolled and crumpled around her.

There it was again, that feeling that the world was retreating, leaving her in an echoey bubble all on her own. Her fingers automatically found her locket while she tried to distract herself with the book. Initially the print blurred and the pictures refused to stay in focus, but she blinked twice and forced her eyes to work in unison, and eventually everything slid back to normal.

The television was still on low in the background and Ellie glanced at it. The quiz show she'd had half an ear on was over and something else had started. It looked like some red carpet thing that was obviously going to clog up the TV schedule for the rest of the evening. An eager reporter in a low-cut top clutched her microphone and tried not to let on she was shivering in the brisk March wind.

Just then a graphic flashed up at the bottom of the screen. Ellie did a double-take, then lurched forward in an effort to get closer to the television—anything to help her unscramble the images swarming up her optic nerve and into her brain.

'That's—that's him!'

The book lay on the counter, forgotten, and her finger, which had been scanning a list of ingredients, now hovered uselessly in mid-air. She jumped off the stool, walked over to the little TV and used that very same finger to drum on the volume button.

'*Mark Wilder*', the caption at the bottom of the screen said.

Her new boss.

Crumbs, she could see why Ginny had gone all twittery now. He certainly was very good-looking, all ruffled dark hair and perfect teeth. Not that those things really mattered when it came down to forging a long-lasting relationship. Nice dental work amounted to nothing if the man in question turned out to be a shallow, self-centred waste of space. She was much more interested in what a man was like on the inside.

She looked at Mark Wilder again, *really* looked at him. He was about the same age as her. Mid-thirties? Possibly older if he was aging well—and, let's face it, his sort usually did. But who was he beneath the crisp white shirt and the designer suit? More importantly, what would he be like to work for? She stood, hands on hips, and frowned a little. When Charlie had phoned to offer this position she'd been too excited that her plan was coming to fruition to think much about her future employer. He'd been more of an escape route than a person, really.

Suddenly a woman slid into shot beside him—early twenties, gravity-defying bust and attire that, if it stretched in the wash, might *just* qualify as a dress.

Ellie sighed.

Oh, he was *that* kind of man. How disappointing.

The reporter in the cleavage-revealing top didn't seem to be bothered, though. She lurched at him from behind the metal barrier. 'Mr Wilder! Melissa Morgan from Channel Six!'

Oh, yes. That was her name.

This should be interesting. From what Ellie remembered, this woman had a reputation for asking awkward questions, being a little bit sassy with her interviewees. It made for great celebrity soundbites. You never knew what juicy little secrets she might get her victims to accidentally reveal.

Wilder spotted the reporter and strode over to her, his movements lean and easy. In the crowd, a couple of hundred pairs of female eyes swivelled to track his progress. Except, ironically, those of his girlfriend. She was looking straight at the camera lens.

Even the normally cool reporter was fawning all over him. Not that Wilder seemed to mind. His eyes held a mischievous twinkle as he waited for her to ask her question.

'Pull yourself together, woman!' Ellie mumbled as she brushed biscuit crumbs off the cookery book with the side of her hand.

Melissa Morgan blushed and asked her question in a husky voice. 'Are you confident your newest client, Kat De Souza, will be picking up the award for best female newcomer this evening?'

Go on, Ellie silently urged. Prove me wrong. Be charming and gracious and modest.

He increased the wattage on his smile. The reporter looked as if she was about to melt into a puddle of pure hormones.

'I have every confidence in Kat,' he said in a warm, deep voice, appearing desperately serious. But then his eyes did that twinkly thing again. 'Of course, having superior management doesn't hurt.'

How did he do that? Special eye drops?

Of course the reporter fell for it. She practically tripped over her own tongue as she asked the next question. Wilder, in turn, lapped up the attention, deliberately flirting with her—well, maybe not flirting, exactly, but he had to be doing *something* to make her go all giggly like that.

Ellie reached for another digestive without taking

her eyes off the television, and knocked the packet onto the floor. The man seemed to be enjoying the fact that a couple of million viewers were catching every second of his very public ego massage. And what was even more annoying was that he batted each of the reporter's questions away with effortless charm, never losing his cool for an instant.

There was no end to the reporter's gushing. 'I'm sure you are not surprised to discover that, due to your success as one of the top managers in the recording industry today, *Gloss!* magazine has named you their most eligible bachelor in their annual list.'

He clasped his hand to his chest in mock surprise. 'What? *Again!*'

Oh, great. Self-deprecating as well as shy and retiring. This guy was going to be a blast to work for. Just as well Charlie had said he spent the greater part of the year travelling or in endless meetings.

He stopped smiling and looked deep into the reporter's eyes. 'Well, somebody had better just hurry up and marry me, then.' He looked around the crowd. The grin made an encore. 'Anyone interested?'

The reporter blushed and stuttered. Was it just Ellie's imagination, or was she actually considering vaulting the barrier? And Ellie didn't think she was the only one. Something about the scene reminded her of a Sunday night nature programme she'd seen recently—one about wildebeest. A stampede at this moment was almost inevitable.

She flapped her book closed, ignoring the puff of crumbs that flew into the air, and let out a snort.

The reporter stopped simpering and suddenly smoothed her hair down with her free hand. Her spine straightened. About time too, Ellie thought. This woman was supposed to be a professional. How embarrassing to catch yourself acting like that on national television.

This time when she fired her question, the reporter's voice was cool and slow. 'Was it hard to rebuild your career after such...*difficult* beginnings, both in your professional and personal life?'

Her face was a picture of sympathy, but the eyes glittered with a hint of ice. Ellie almost felt a tremor of sympathy for him. But not quite.

Something other than lazy good humour flashed in Mark Wilder's eyes.

'Thanks for the good wishes.' He paused as his stare hardened and turned to granite. 'Good evening, Ms Morgan.' And then he just turned and walked away.

The reporter's jaw slackened. It was as if she'd been freeze-framed by her own personal remote control and all she could do was watch him stride away. The camera shook a little, then panned to include Mr Wilder's companion. Miss Silicone pouted a smile and trotted after her man, leaving the floundering reporter to find another celebrity to fill the gaping space in front of her microphone. She turned back to the cameraman, looking more than a little desperate, and then the picture cut to a long shot of the red carpet.

Ellie shook her head, punched the button on the side of the TV and flapped it back into place under the cabinet. She was starting to fear that this whole new job idea was one of the random impulses that had plagued her since the accident—just another one of her brain's little jokes.

She tucked the cookery book under her arm and tossed the empty biscuit packet in the direction of the bin. It missed.

With a few long strides Mark put as much distance as he could between himself and the trouble his smart mouth had caused him. Flashguns zapped at him from every direction. Suddenly his expensive suit seemed really flimsy. No protection at all, really.

He'd been bored enough to welcome the devilish urge to tease Melissa Morgan, but he'd forgotten that behind the batting eyelashes was an intelligent reporter—one who didn't hesitate to go for the jugular where a morsel of celebrity gossip was concerned. She'd done a number on quite a few of his firm's clients in recent years, and the opportunity for a little payback had just been too tempting. But it had backfired on him, hadn't it? The story he'd wanted her to focus on tonight was Kat and her award nomination, not his own less-than-glorious past.

He glanced at the crowd bulging against the barriers as he overtook an up-and-coming British actress in a long, flowing gown. He should be loving every second of this. It was the life he'd always worked for. What most people sitting in front of their TVs with their dinners on their laps dreamed of—red carpets, beautiful women, fast cars, exotic locations, more cash than they knew what to do with…

So what was wrong with him?

He shook his head to clear the baying of the photographers, the screaming of the crowd, and became aware of determined footsteps behind him.

Oh, heck. Melodie. Ms Morgan must have got him more rattled than he'd thought. He gave himself a mental slap for his lack of chivalry and turned and waited for her. She was only a few paces behind him, and as she came level with him he placed a guiding hand on her elbow.

Melodie's agent had called his PA a couple of weeks ago and asked if he would like to meet her. This was what the love lives of the rich and famous had come to. Relationships were practically conducted in the third person. *My people will call your people...*

He didn't normally respond to requests like this, but he'd needed a date tonight at short notice, and Melodie was young, sexy and stunning—just the sort of woman he was expected to have on his arm at a bash like this. It didn't matter that he suspected she didn't have any romantic yearnings for him when he'd called to ask her out. And that the industry grapevine had confirmed that a certain C-list model was looking to kick-start a pop career.

It was all very predictable. But predictable was good. At least he knew what to expect from this self-serving approach, even if his choice in female companions only inflamed the tabloid gossip about his private life. He hadn't even met half the women the papers had paired him with. And the ones he did date were just like the woman walking next to him: happy to use him for their own ends.

Good for them. It was a dog-eat-dog world and he'd learned one vital piece of wisdom early on: the woman who talked of love and commitment was the one who turned and bit you on the butt when you were least expecting it. He had the scars to prove it.

They moved inside the old theatre. Had they redone the décor in here? It had seemed opulent and elegant last time he was here, but now the crimson walls screamed at him, and the gold leaf everywhere just hurt his eyes.

He hadn't planned on coming to the awards this evening, but duty had called. Or, to be more accurate, duty had cried and pleaded down the phone in the shape of his newest and youngest signing, Kat De Souza.

They reached a flight of stairs and he held back and let Melodie walk up the sweeping staircase in front of him. Her dress was shimmering silver, backless, with a neckline slashed almost to her navel. It clung in all the right places. And Melodie certainly had *places*. Mark did his best to appreciate the view, but his pulse was alarmingly regular. Just another indicator that he was out of sorts tonight. Must be the jet lag.

An usher led them to their table at the front of the auditorium. Kat was already there, with her boyfriend *du jour*. This one was a drummer, or something like that. Mark pulled out Melodie's chair for her and made the introductions, then leaned across to Kat.

'Nervous?'

Her head bobbed in small, rapid movements.

'Sorry I woke you up and snivelled down the phone at you the other day.' She paused to twirl one of her long dark ringlets around a finger with a bitten-down nail before looking up at him again. 'The time differences are so confusing, and I was in a bit of a state.'

He remembered. Technically, although he'd been the one to 'discover' Kat, after he'd walked past her busking on the Underground, he wasn't her personal manager. He was careful not to get too close to his clients nowadays, normally leaving the legwork to his junior associates. He'd been in the business long enough to pay his dues, and had ridden more tour buses and slept on more recording studio floors during all-night recording sessions than he cared to remember. He'd paired Kat up with Sasha, a hip, energetic young woman at his firm who had the potential to go far. But where he'd hoped there would be female bonding, there had only been friction.

In the end he'd decided to step in and take an active interest for a few months—ease the teething process, if you like. Kat was only seventeen, and a bit overwhelmed at her sudden shove into the spotlight. She needed stability at the moment, not constant bickering. A happy client was a productive client, after all.

Mark smiled back at Kat and waited for her to finish fidgeting with her hair. 'Who needs sleep, anyway?' he said, giving her a little wink.

'I'm so grateful you changed your plans and

flew in at the last minute. I'm frantic! I don't know whether I'm more scared of winning or not winning. How crazy is that? And I reckon I need all the support I can get.'

The scruffy excuse for a musician sitting next to her swigged a mouthful of champagne out of the bottle and produced a proud burp. Mark shifted position and tried to block his view of him with the avant-garde floral arrangement exploding from the centre of the table.

Great choice of support, Kat. First class.

Proof, yet again, that his client was young and naive and definitely needed a guiding hand.

With the uncanny knack females had of confirming his opinions of them, Kat reached for the glass of champagne in front of her and swung it towards her lips. Mark's arm shot out in a reflex action that stopped the flute reaching its destination.

'Hey!'

He prised the glass from her fingers. 'No, you don't, young lady! You're underage.'

Kat's chin jutted forward as she had one of her teenage Jekyll and Hyde moments, switching from sweet and grateful to sour and belligerent in the snap of a finger. 'Chill out, Mark! You can't tell me what to do, anyway. You only manage my career, not my personal life.'

Okay, technically she was right. And if it had

been anyone else on his agency's books he would have minded his own business. But it just didn't seem right to sit there and do nothing.

'No, you're right. I can't tell you what to do, but I can *advise* you. It's my job to look after your best interests. It's what I take my fifteen percent for, after all.' He placed the glass out of reach behind the spiky centrepiece. 'Anyway, you don't want to be tipsy when you collect the award later. And I mean *when*, not *if*.'

When in doubt, flatter. It always worked. He raised his eyebrows and waited for the thaw.

Kat's blistering stare softened a fraction. Girls of her age could be fiendishly stubborn. It was just as well he seemed to have the knack of charming each and every female he met, whether they were nine or ninety. Kat continued to glower at him, but he knew he'd won. He would let her back down gracefully without pressing the point further.

'Water is better for my voice, anyway,' she said, lounging back on her revolting boyfriend to give him a defiant kiss.

Mark beckoned a waiter and smiled to himself while his face was hidden.

Six months ago no one had heard of Kat De Souza. Despite her youth, she had a wonderfully mature soulful voice. Not only that, but she wrote the most amazing love songs and played the acoustic guitar to accompany herself. Her pared-down debut single had been a smash hit, catapulting her to overnight fame. His firm's expertise and connections had helped, of course, but she had ten times the talent of some of his other clients. Securing a recording deal had been a breeze. Now he just had to make sure that the pressure and the insanity of the music industry didn't derail her before she got to where she was destined to go.

He watched Kat bite her thumbnail down to a level that surely had to be painful. Mature talent, sure, but she was still just a scared schoolgirl underneath all the bluster. He was glad he'd shuffled his life around to be here tonight.

At that moment a wave of unexpected tiredness rolled over him. He hid a yawn and ignored the jet lag pulling at his eyelids.

It was going to be a long night.

Once Ellie had rustled herself up something more filling than biscuits to eat from the well-stocked larder, she decided to give herself a tour of Larkford Place. Tomorrow she'd get her Post-it notes out and label every door in the house—which was saying something. It seemed as if there were hundreds of them, all leading to rooms and corridors you wouldn't expect them to.

The scraps of coloured paper would be gone

again by the time her boss returned, of course. It wasn't everybody's taste in décor. But in the meantime they'd help her to create some new neural pathways, remember the layout of the house. So, hopefully, when she wanted to cook something she'd end up in the kitchen and not the broom cupboard. She'd had to resort to this technique when she'd returned to the cottage after the accident, which had seemed utterly ridiculous. How could she have lived in a house for almost a decade and not remember where her bedroom was?

But it had all sunk in again eventually. And it would happen here at Larkford too, if she had time and a little bit of peace and quiet so she could concentrate. She mentally thanked Charlie again for organising things so she could have a week here on her own before her boss arrived back from wherever that red carpet was. Had Charlie mentioned New York…?

As she wandered round, she was pleased to find that the inside of Larkford Place was as lovely as its exterior. It oozed character. No steel and glass ground-breaking interior design here, thank goodness. Just ornate fireplaces and plasterwork, high ceilings and ancient leaded windows.

Ellie's jaw clicked as she let out a giant yawn. Fatigue was a normal part of her condition—due to the fact she had to concentrate on things most people did automatically. And today had been a day that had required an awful lot of mental and emotional energy. No wonder she was ready to drop. It was time to check out the housekeeper's apartment above the old stables, so she could crash into bed and become blissfully unconscious.

She pulled a couple of bags out of the boot of her car as she passed it, and made her way up the stairs to her new home. But when she opened the door, the smell of damp carpet clogged her nostrils. And it wasn't hard to see why. Water was dripping through a sagging bulge in the ceiling, and the living room floor was on its way to becoming a decent-sized duck pond. There was no way she could sleep in here tonight.

So she dragged her bags back to the main house, up the stairs and into one of the guest rooms on the first floor. By the time she'd left a message with a local plumber and placed some kitchen pans underneath the damaged ceiling to catch the worst of the dripping water, the yawns were coming every five seconds. She only made it through half of her unpacking before she decided it was time to stop what she was doing and tootle down the hallway to the bathroom she'd spotted earlier before falling into bed.

But as she lay there in the dark, with only the creakings of the old house for company, she found she could close her eyelids but sleep was playing hide-and-seek. Running away from home had seemed such a good idea a few weeks ago, but now she was second-guessing her impulse.

What if she proved Charlie's unspoken fears to be right? What if she wasn't up to the job?

And she *needed* to be up to this job, she really did—for so many reasons.

She'd just about come to terms with the fact that the accident had not only destroyed her perfect family, it had also altered her brain permanently. She would never be the same person she'd been before that day, never be the Ellie she knew herself to be.

Sometimes it felt as if she were inhabiting the body of a stranger, and she could feel her old self staring over her shoulder, noticing the things she couldn't do any more, raising her eyebrows at the mood swings and the clumsiness.

She rolled over and tried another position. Was it possible to haunt yourself? She certainly hoped not. She had enough ghosts to outrun as it was.

She sighed and clutched the duvet a little closer to her chest.

Maybe she'd never be that person again, but this job was her lifeline, her chance to prove to herself and everyone else that she wasn't a waste of space. This was her chance to be *normal* again, away from the judging eyes and the sympathetic glances.

She was just going to have to be the best darn housekeeper that Mr Mark Wilder had ever had.

As the awards ceremony dragged on Mark was proved right. It had been an *incredibly* long night.

Melodie was irritating him. The package was pretty, but there wasn't much inside to interest him. He had tried to engage her in talk about the music industry, but even though she was trying to veer her career in that direction she seemed superbly uninformed about the business.

The show was good, but he had the feeling he'd seen it all before—the pseudo-feuds between cool, young indie bands, the grandpa rockers behaving badly as they presented awards and the hip-grinding dance routines by girls wearing little more than scarves. Well, maybe he didn't object to the skimpy dresses that much, he thought with a chuckle. He was tired, not *dead*.

The only highlight of the evening had been Kat's victory in the 'Best Newcomer' category. Nobody else might have noticed the way her hands shook as she held the supposedly funky-looking trophy, but Mark had. She'd accepted her award with simple thanks, then performed her latest single, sitting alone on the stage except for her guitar and a spotlight. The whole audience had been silent as her husky voice had permeated the sweaty atmosphere. When she'd finished, even the most jaded in the crowd of musicians and industry professionals had given her an ovation.

The remainder of the ceremony was a blur as Mark tried to keep his eyes open. He began to regret the two glasses of champagne he'd drunk. He hadn't eaten since the flight this morning, and the alcohol was having a less than pleasant effect on him. Instead of mellowing him out, everything jarred. All he wanted to do was get home and sleep for a week solid.

The ceremony drew to a close and Kat leaned over to Mark. 'Are you coming to the after-show party?'

Melodie, who was eavesdropping, looked hopeful.

Mark shook his head. 'I'm tired and jet-lagged. I'm going home to bed.'

Melodie looked even more hopeful.

Erm...I don't think so, sweetheart.

It was time to ease himself out of the situation. Melodie would probably be happier at the party, mixing with the boy bands, anyway. He gave her a non-commital, nice-to-have-met-you kiss on the cheek. 'I know I'm being boring, but why don't you join the others at the party? I'm sure Kat and...er...'

'Razor,' said Kat helpfully.

'*Razor* will look after you.'

Melodie weighed her options up for a second, and decided the offer wasn't too shabby after all.

'That's cool,' she said in her little-girl voice and flicked her hair extensions.

Mark slipped away, leaving the theatre by the back exit, happy to distance himself from the muffled roar of the paparazzi as the stars emerged onto the red carpet out front. He fished his mobile phone out of his jacket pocket and called a cab, telling the driver to meet him in a backstreet close by, then ran a hand through his unruly mop of dark hair and made his way down an alley. Only when he had emerged from the shadow of the theatre did he loosen the top button of his shirt and breathe in a luxurious lungful of cool night air.

CHAPTER THREE

So much for sleeping for a week solid. Someone was making a racket on the landing. How inconsiderate could you get?

Mark sat up in bed, cold reality only just intruding on his nice, warm sleep haze.

After the awards ceremony he'd had the urge to get right out of the city, so instead of asking the cab driver to make the short trip to his flat on the river, Mark had made him very happy and told him the destination was Sussex.

There was another noise from the landing. Nothing loud, but someone was definitely out there. He hadn't dreamt it. There was only one explanation. It was after two in the morning and someone was in his house. Someone he hadn't invited because he was supposed to be here on his own. That wasn't good.

Mark jumped out of bed, wondering what he might have to hand in his bedroom that would help in a situation like this, but it was pitch-dark and he didn't have a clue where to start fumbling. He knew his squash racket was in the house somewhere…

But he didn't have time even to reach for the lamp by his bed. Just then the door slammed open. Mark tensed, unable to see who or what had just invaded his bedroom. A split-second later something—someone—barrelled into him.

He didn't have time to think, just reached out and grabbed him. There was no way some snotty youth from the village was going to swipe his silver, or his high-tech audio gear, or whatever it was he was after.

A struggle ensued and he finally got the lad pinned down on the floor. Now what? How was he going to call the police without—?

'Ow!'

A searing pain radiated from his right collarbone. The little runt had bitten him! Actually sunk his teeth in and clenched hard! And now he was getting away, even though Mark didn't remember letting him go. He grabbed for the intruder and was rewarded with an ankle.

Well, it was better then nothing.

Time to take the upper hand. And the first thing was to see who he was dealing with. They were both shouting at each other—although it seemed to be more sounds than words that he was deciphering. He lunged for the bedside lamp and switched it on.

And that was when things really got confusing. Maybe he was dreaming after all.

This was no lad from the village. Not with those soft blonde ringlets and wide green eyes. And she was wearing…pyjamas! He flushed hot at the thought, though he hardly knew why. They were thick brushed cotton and only hinted at the curves beneath. Now, he knew some women could be a little over-keen to meet him, but this was just ridiculous!

And then she started babbling, and in the string of words he heard his own name.

'I know who I am. Who on earth are *you*?'

She looked up at him, breathless and blushing. The only motion he was aware of was the uneven rise and fall of the curves under her pyjama top; the only noise was their mingled rapid breathing. And then she spoke.

'I'm Ellie Bond—your new housekeeper.'

He'd been clenching his jaw in anger, but now it relaxed. His eyes widened as the sleep fog cleared from his brain. She pulled her arms and legs into herself and sat ball-like at his feet, suddenly looking like a little girl. She began to shiver.

Truth was, he had no idea how to handle this. And it was better if she got out of here before he said or did something he'd regret in the morning.

'You'd better get back to your room,' he said.

* * *

She should have known something was up when she'd tripped over that stray shoe. She never left her shoes lying around. And last night had been no different. She'd kicked them off and placed them neatly beside her case before going to bed. At home, her make-up might be spilled all over the dressing table, her jeans might be hanging by one leg over the back of a chair, but she always put her shoes away. Mainly because she only wore something on her feet when absolutely necessary. Her feet liked freedom.

Ellie stretched. Apparently a bulldozer had run over her last night while she'd drifted in and out of sleep—and then had reversed and had another go. There was no point trying to drop off again now. She was an early bird by nature and she knew her body clock would refuse.

She gave up squeezing her eyelids closed and rolled over and looked at the curtains. Dawn wasn't far away. Maybe some fresh air would stop her brain spinning in five different directions at once. She pulled a huge cable-knit sweater on over her pyjamas. Since she didn't own a pair of slippers she tugged a pair of flip-flops from the jumble at one end of her case.

Once she was ready she paused, listening for any hint of movement from the room next door. There was nothing.

Now she was satisfied the coast was clear, she

headed into the hallway and stopped briefly to reassess the scene of the crime, counting the doors on this side of the corridor. Four. There was a small cupboard opposite the bathroom that she could have sworn hadn't been there before.

Not wanting to get caught in her pyjamas a second time, she turned in the opposite direction and went down the narrow staircase towards the kitchen, a room far enough away from the bedrooms for her to finally breathe out and think. Once there, she switched the kettle on and looked aimlessly round the room. The passageway that led into the cobbled courtyard was visible through the half-open door. Her car was sitting out there, ready to go. One of her mad impulses hit her.

What if she just ran out through the door this minute, jumped in her car and bombed out of the front gates, never to be seen again? Tingles broke out all over her arms. The urge to do just that was positively irresistible. It was only six o' clock.

Breathe. Think...

She recognised this itchy feeling for what it was—another legacy of her head injury. It was all very well to know that her impulse control was permanently out of whack, but another thing entirely to tap into that knowledge when you were in the magnetic grip of what seemed like the best idea ever and find the strength to resist it.

She should be thankful, though. At least she was just a bit harum-scarum these days. Some of the other people she'd met during her rehabilitation had it far worse. How could she forget Barry, who didn't seem to realise that grabbing the rear end of every woman he clapped eyes on wasn't appropriate behaviour? Or Fenella, the posh old lady who swore like a trooper if she didn't have an even number of peas on her plate at dinnertime, all lined up in rows? Ellie nodded to herself. Oh, yes. Things could be a lot worse. She just had to keep remembering that.

As if she could forget, when last night's disastrous run-in with the boss was clearly going to get her fired.

She brewed herself a strong cup of tea and opened the French windows that led onto a wide patio. The garden was beautiful in the soft early-morning sunshine. She breathed deeply and walked along the smooth grey flagstones till she emerged from the shadow of the house into the warmth of the sunrise. She skirted the lavender hedge, sipping her mug of tea, and stepped onto a rectangle of lush, close-clipped grass. It was heavy with dew and springy underfoot. Her head fell back and she stayed motionless for a minute or so, feeling the sun's rays on her cheeks and inhaling the clean, pure scents of the awakening garden.

This reminded her of mornings at her cottage years ago. Sometimes she would wake early and sneak out into the garden before Sam and Chloe stirred. The garden had been Ellie's place to centre herself, to pause from the hectic pace of life and just *be*. She would walk out barefoot and let the soft blades of the lawn tickle her toes. Then she would wander about, clearing her head by talking out loud. Sometimes she just rambled to herself; sometimes she couldn't help looking skyward and thanking God for all the amazing things that made her life perfect.

When she returned to the cottage she would be able to hear the machinery of the day starting to whirr—the clattering of toothbrushes in the bathroom, footsteps on the stairs. However busy the day got after that, she carried a sense of peace with her that had been born in the quiet of the day. It had been her secret ritual.

But she hadn't done it for years—not since Sam and Chloe had died. There was no peace to be found anywhere. Did she think she'd find it under a bush in her own back garden? Not likely. And as for God, she'd been tempted to stand outside late at night and scream at Him for being so cruel. They hadn't been on speaking terms since.

Ellie bent down to examine a cobweb glistening between the branches of a small shrub. Beads of moisture clinging to each strand reflected the sunlight like a thousand tiny mirrors.

What was she going to do? She was all alone and in a terrible mess. Her pretty dreams about being independent, free from the past, had come crashing down around her ears in less than twenty-four hours. What a fool she'd been to think she could outrun her ghosts.

A tear bulged in the corner of her eye. She sniffed and wiped it away with her middle finger. Thoughts were scrambling around inside her head, so she stood still and let the spring sun warm her inside and out. Then, when she was ready, she shook off her flip-flops and walked, and talked to the faultless blue sky until the words ran dry.

A floorboard on the landing creaked. Ellie stopped stuffing clothes randomly into bags and held her breath at the back of her throat.

She'd heard noises upstairs some time after noon, and had scurried up here not long after that. It was amazing just how long it could take a person to pack two cases and a couple of smaller bags. She'd made it last all afternoon.

But for once her reasoning panned out: the longer she left it before she saw him again, the less embarrassed she would feel and the easier it would be to handle her emotions when he asked her to leave. It couldn't hurt to delay the inevitable confrontation with her soon-to-be-ex-boss until she'd finished packing and was on an even keel.

She squashed the T-shirt she was holding into the case in front of her and reached for her wash bag. It slid out of her fingers, but she managed to snatch at it, gripping it between forefinger and thumb before it reached the floor. Unfortunately her quick reflexes didn't stop the contents spilling out and scattering all over the rug. With all her limbs occupied just preventing the bag from falling, she couldn't do anything but watch as her tube of toothpaste bounced on the floor, then disappeared deep under the bed.

So much for an even keel. The world was still stubbornly off-kilter and refusing to go right side up.

She lifted Chloe's blue teddy from where she'd placed it on her pillow the night before and pressed it to her face. For a while it had smelled of her daughter, but the scent of strawberry shampoo had long since faded. Ellie kissed it with reverence and placed it beside the case.

She'd only allowed herself a few treasures from home, and they had been the first things she'd pulled from her luggage when she'd unpacked. Propped on the bedside table was a single silver picture frame. The photo it held was her favourite of her and Sam together, taken on their honeymoon. They'd handed their camera to the retired couple in the next hotel room and asked them to take a snap on the day they'd travelled home.

She preferred this picture to the forced poses of her wedding photos. They were laughing at each other, hair swept sideways by the wind, not even aware of the exact moment the shutter had opened. She traced a finger over her husband's cheek.

Her beautiful Sam.

He had been so warm and funny, with his lopsided grin and wayward hair. When he'd died it had been like losing a vital organ. Living and breathing were just so hard without him.

They'd met on the first day of primary school and been inseparable ever since, marrying one week after they'd both graduated from university. Sam had taken a teaching post at the village school and she'd commuted to the City, working as a PA for a big City firm, and they'd saved to buy the rundown cottage on the outskirts that they'd fallen in love with. They'd transformed the tumble-down wreck bit by bit, scouring architectural salvage yards for stained glass, old taps and doorknobs. They had even rescued an old roll-top bath out of one of their neighbour's gardens—removing the geraniums before it was plumbed in.

When the last lick of paint had dried, they had proclaimed it their dream home and immediately started trying for a family. The following spring, they'd come home from the hospital with Chloe, a tiny pink bundle with fingers and toes so cute they'd verged on the miraculous. Ellie had almost felt guilty about being more happy than a person had a right to be.

But one wet afternoon had robbed her of all of it.

Her smile dissolved and she pushed the frame flat and folded the photo up in her pyjamas before tucking it into a well-padded corner of her sturdiest case.

When she'd moved back home after her rehabilitation, well-meaning friends and family had taken one of two approaches—some had wanted her to freeze-frame time and never do anything, the rest had dropped great clanging hints at her feet about moving on with her life. Their insensitivity had astounded her.

Move on? She hadn't wanted to move on! She'd wanted things back the way they were *before*. Chloe's pink wellies in the hallway. Sam bent over the kitchen table marking homework. But that was impossible. So she'd settled for hibernating in the present. But hibernating hadn't taken long to become festering. Perhaps she should be glad that events in the village had forced her to leave.

She zipped up her bulging case, then sat on the edge of the bed and stared at the elegant surroundings.

Her journey had led her here, to Larkford Place.

Unfortunately only a brief pit-stop. She hadn't a clue what she'd do next. She could stay at the cottage for a few weeks if there weren't any holiday bookings. But that would be going back, and now she was finally ready to move forward she didn't want to do that.

However, she didn't really have much choice after last night.

It was time she hauled her things down to the car. She picked up a case in one hand and stuffed a smaller one under her other arm, leaving her hand free to open the door. She tugged it open and froze.

Mark Wilder was standing straight in front of her, fist bunched ready as if to knock.

Mark dropped his hand, stuffed it in his back pocket and pulled out a wad of folded twenty-pound notes. He held them out to Ellie.

'I thought you might need this.'

She stared at him as if he was offering her a hand grenade.

'For the shopping,' he added.

'Shopping?'

'Yes. Shopping. You know, with money…'

He waved the notes in front of her chin. Her eyes moved left and right, left and right, following the motion of his hand.

'Money?'

This was harder work than he'd thought it would be.

'Yes. Money. It's what we use in the civilised world when we've run out of camels to barter with.'

'But I thought...' She fidgeted with a small silver locket hanging round her neck. 'You'd... I'd be...'

Colour flared on her cheeks and she stepped away from him. He looked at the notes in his hand. She didn't seem to understand the concept of shopping, which was a definite minus in a housekeeper. His decision to view last night as an embarrassing one-off started to seem premature.

He stepped through the door frame and followed her into the room. There were cases and bags on the bed. They were lumpy enough to look as if they had been filled in a hurry. The zips weren't done up all the way, and something silky was falling out of the holdall nearest to him. He really should stop looking at it.

Ellie followed his gaze and dived for the bag, stuffing the item back in so deep that most of her arm disappeared. Now he was just staring at a pile of cases.

Cases? He tilted his head. Oh. Right. She thought he was going to give her the sack.

Well, as tempting as the idea might be, he couldn't afford to do that at present. Firstly because he'd never hear the end of it from Charlie, and secondly because he really did need someone here to look after the house while he was travelling. He was due on another plane in less than twenty-four hours and he simply didn't have the luxury of finding someone else. It had been hard enough to fill the position at short notice when Mrs Timms had decided to leave.

Maybe it was time to work some of the legendary Wilder magic and put this Ellie Bond at ease. If he showed her he was laughing off the incident last night, it might help her relax.

Mark waited for her to finish fiddling with the bag, and then pulled a smile out of his arsenal—the one guaranteed to melt ice maidens at fifty paces.

'Well, I'm glad to see you're still in your own room, anyway.' He threw in a wink, just to make sure she knew he was joking. 'With your track record, we can't be too careful.'

Hmm. Strange. Nothing happened. No thaw whatsoever.

'There's no need to go on about that. It's just that I wasn't expecting anyone else to be here, and I'm not familiar with the layout of the house yet, and I just…the moon went in…I counted three instead of four…' The babbling continued.

There was one thing that was puzzling him. If she'd wanted a bathroom, why had she trekked down the hall?

'Why didn't you just use the *en-suite*?'

She stopped mid-babble. *'En-suite?'*

He walked over to a cream-coloured panelled door on the opposite wall to the bed, designed to match the wardrobe on the other side of the chimney breast. He nudged it gently with his knuckles and it clicked open. Her jaw lost all muscle tone as she walked slowly towards the compact but elegant bathroom.

She shook her head, walked in, looked around and walked out again, still blessedly silent. Actually, his new housekeeper seemed relatively normal when she stopped biting and yelling and babbling.

He had a sudden flashback to the night before—to the baggy blue and white pyjamas that hadn't been quite baggy enough to disguise her curves—and he started to get a little flustered himself.

'I have a...bathroom...inside my wardrobe?'

He gave a one-shouldered shrug. 'Actually, it's not quite as Narnia-like as it seems. The wardrobe is that side.' He pointed to an identical cream door the other side of the chimney breast. 'We just had the door to the *en-suite* built to match. Secret doors seem to suit a house like this.'

The look on her face told him she thought it was the stupidest idea ever.

'I thought it was fun,' he said, willing her to smile back at him, to join him in a little light banter and laugh the whole thing off as an unfortunate first meeting. She just blinked.

'Anyway,' he continued with a sigh, 'let's just see if we can get through the next twenty-four hours without something—or someone—going bump in the night.'

'I told you before. It was an accident,' she said, scrunching her forehead into parallel lines.

It looked as if she was tempted to bite him again. Humour was obviously not the way to go. Back to business, then. That had to be safe territory, didn't it?

'Okay, well take this for now.' He placed the money on the chest of drawers while she watched him suspiciously. 'I'm getting a credit card sorted out for the household expenses, and a laptop so we can keep in touch via e-mail. I just need you to sign a few forms, if that's all right?'

She nodded, but her eyes never left him, as if she was expecting him to make a sudden move.

Mark wandered over to the bed, picked up the sad-looking blue bear sitting next to one of the cases and gave it a cursory inspection. He wouldn't have expected her to be the sort who slept with a teddy, but, hey, whatever rocked her boat. He tossed it back on the bed. It bounced and landed on the floor. Ellie rushed to scoop it up, clutched it to her chest and glared at him.

He raked his fingers through his hair. It was time to beat a hasty retreat.

'I'll see you at dinner, then?' He raised his hands

on a non-threatening gesture. An insane image of him as a lion tamer, holding off a lioness with a rickety old chair, popped into his head. He wouldn't be surprised if she growled at him.

'Fine.' It almost *was* a growl.

'Would you join us? I've invited Charlie to dinner, to say thank you for finding me a—'

The word *hellcat* had been poised to fall out of his mouth and he stopped himself just in time.

Not hellcat. Housekeeper! Just try and remember that.

'—for finding me a *housekeeper* at such short notice. I thought it would be a good way to break the ice before I disappear again.'

'Thank you,' she said. Her eyes told him she'd rather walk on hot coals.

Fine. If she wanted to keep it cool and impersonal, he could keep it cool and impersonal. Probably.

'If you could be ready to serve up at eight o'clock…?'

Her eyes narrowed almost imperceptibly.

He backed out through the door and started walking towards the main staircase. Charlie had a lot to answer for. Her perfect-for-the-job friend was perfectly strange, for one thing! He took himself downstairs and sat on the velvet-covered sofa in front of the fire. Jet lag was making it hard to think, and he had the oddest feeling that his conversation with Ellie had just been weird enough for him still to be asleep and dreaming.

She was clearly barking mad. If the 'lost-my-bedroom' incident had planted a seed of suspicion in his mind, their talk just now and what he had seen early this morning had definitely added fertiliser.

His body clock was still refusing to conform to Greenwich Mean Time, and last night he'd dozed, tossed and turned, read some of a long-winded novel and eventually decided on a hot shower to clear his head. On the way to his bathroom a flash of movement outside the window had prompted him to change course and peer out of the half-open curtains.

Down in the garden he'd spotted Ellie, marching round the garden, arms waving. She'd been talking to herself! At six in the morning. In her pyjamas.

Pyjamas.

Another rush of something warm and not totally unfamiliar hit him. The pleasant prickle of awareness from the close proximity of a woman was one of the joys of life. But he didn't think he'd ever experienced it after seeing a woman wearing what looked to be her grandad's pyjamas before. Silk and satin, yes. Soft stripy brushed cotton, no. There it went again! The rush. His earlobes were burning, for goodness' sake!

He'd practically had a heart attack when she'd

charged into him in the dark last night. He'd been in such a deep sleep only moments before he'd hardly known *who* he was, let alone *where* he was. The small frame and slender wrists of his captive might have fooled him into thinking it was a lad he'd held captive, but when the light had flickered on he'd realised he couldn't have been more wrong. It certainly hadn't been a boy he had by the ankle, intent on dragging him down to the local police station. He'd started to wonder if he'd been dreaming. Those soft blonde curls belonged on a Botticelli cherub.

Just then the bite mark on his left shoulder began to throb.

No, not an angel—his instincts had been right from the start. A hellcat.

It would be wise to remind himself of that. He didn't have to like this woman; he just had to pay her to keep his house running. He would keep his distance from Ellie Bond and he would not think of her in that way—even if there was something refreshingly different about her.

Insanity, he reminded himself. *That's what's different about her. A woman like that is trouble. You never know what she's going to do next.*

A yawn crept up on him. He told himself it would be a bad idea to fall asleep again, but there was something very soothing about watching the logs in the fire crackle and spark. He pushed a cushion under his head and settled to watch the flames shimmer and dance.

When he opened his eyes again the flames had disappeared and the embers were just grey dust. Now and then a patch of orange would glow brightly, then fade away again. He pulled himself out of the comfortable dent he had created in the sofa.

From somewhere in the direction of the kitchen he could hear female voices. Was Charlie here already? He looked at his watch. He'd been asleep for more than three hours. He walked towards the dining room and met Charlie, coming to fetch him. His stomach gurgled. His sleep patterns might be sabotaged, but his appetite was clearly on Larkford time.

'Now, don't go upsetting my friend, Mark. She needs this job, and you are not allowed to mess it up for her.'

Hang on a second. He was the employer. Surely this was all supposed to be the other way round? Ellie was supposed to do a good job for *him*, try not to upset *him*. At the moment he was wondering whether his house would still be standing when he returned in a few weeks.

He opened his mouth to say as much, then decided not to bother. There was no arguing with his bossy cousin when she got like this. It had been the same when he'd tried to talk her out of taking a stray kitten home one summer, when he'd been fourteen and she'd been ten. Charlie had worshipped that cat, but he'd never quite forgotten the lattice of fine red marks the animal had left on his hands and forearms after he'd agreed to carry it back to the house for her.

Unfortunately it had taken another twenty years before he'd been cured of the habit of trying to rescue pathetic strays of all shapes and sizes.

Helena had been like that. Soft, fragile-looking, vulnerable. And he hadn't been able to resist her. Something inside him swelled with protective instinct when he came across women like that. And Helena had been the neediest of them all. Not that he'd minded. He would have gladly spent all his days looking after her.

Three months after Charlie had found the kitten, when its tummy was round and its fur had a healthy sheen, it had disappeared and never come back. That was the problem with strays. It was in their nature to be selfish.

So he avoided strays altogether now, both feline *and* female.

Oh, women always wanted *something* from him. But he made them play by his rules, only mixing with women who wanted simpler things: money, fame by association, attention. Those things were easy to give and cost him nothing.

Mark was pulled back to the present by the aroma of exotic herbs and spices wafting his way. Charlie didn't need to steer him any more. The smell was a homing beacon, leading him up the corridor and into the dining room. He dropped into a chair opposite Charlie and waited, all his taste buds on full alert.

There was a glimpse of an apron and blonde hair through the doorway as Ellie disappeared back into the kitchen to fetch the last in a succession of steaming dishes. Mark swallowed the pool of saliva that had collected in the bottom of his mouth. He hoped she wouldn't be too long.

She finally appeared. At least he thought it was her. She was cool and collected and quiet, and set down the last dish in an array of lavish Thai recipes. Not a hint of growling or biting about her.

Good. He was glad she'd pulled herself together.

His stomach, however, didn't care how the transformation had happened. It grumbled at him to just get over it and start shovelling food in its general direction. Which he did without delay.

CHAPTER FOUR

ELLIE dished up. Her heart jumped so hard in her chest she was sure the serving spoon must be pulsing in her fingers. What was happening to her? Mark Wilder had done nothing but walk into the room and sit down and her body had gone wild. She finished doling out the food and sat down, careful to keep her eyes on her plate lest her stampeding hormones concentrate themselves and get ready for another charge.

The man was *insanely* good-looking!

The TV cameras hadn't done him justice at all. No longer did she want to scold the reporter for drooling; she wanted to congratulate her for forming a coherent sentence.

Last night she'd been too shocked to register the weird physiological response he provoked in her, and this afternoon she'd been too angry. At herself, mainly, but she'd vented at him instead. It was her stupid brain injury that was to blame. She'd never had problems with runaway emotions before that.

Now, any little thing could trigger overwhelming frustration, or rage, or despair.

Of course! She'd inadvertently stumbled upon the answer.

Her sigh of relief drew glances from her dining companions. She caught Mark's eye and quickly returned her gaze to the king prawn on the end of her fork while she waited for her heartbeat to settle.

How could she not have remembered?

The doctors had warned her that some people noticed a change to their sex drive after a traumatic head injury. This intense attraction, this wobbly feeling, it was all down to her head injury. She didn't like him *that way* at all, really. It was just her stupid neurons getting themselves in knots because of the damage they'd suffered.

What a relief!

It explained everything. She could never normally be attracted to a man like him—a man so... well, she didn't have words for what he was *so*... But she'd never seen the attraction of bad boys. Who needed the heartache? Give her a man like Sam— warm, dependable, *faithful*—any day. Not a charmer who thought everything with two X chromosomes ought to fall at his feet and worship.

Now she had that sorted out in her head she could relax a little and enjoy the food. But as she ate questions started to float to the surface.

Why now?

Why, after four years of seeming perfectly normal in that department—even completely uninterested at times—had this symptom decided to rear its ugly head?

It didn't matter. Whatever the reason, she needed to get a handle on it. This job was important to her and she didn't want to lose it. She'd just have to read up a bit on the subject, introduce measures to cope with it, just like she had with her other symptoms. By the time he got back from his next trip she'd have it completely under control.

She made the mistake of glancing up at that point, just as Mark smiled at something Charlie said. He wasn't even looking at her, for goodness' sake, but Ellie still felt her body straining at the leash.

Down, girl!

Oh, my. This evening was going to be torture.

Thankfully, she had an excuse to keep herself busy. She would pay attention to the food, and only the food. And when the meal was over she'd plead tiredness and escape to her room. Charlie would understand. She'd have to.

Mark stole a handful of looks at Ellie as the clattering of serving spoons gave way to silence. She kept her eyes on her plate, only lifting them once to dish out another spoonful of rice.

The only information she'd volunteered during dinner had been about the plumbing disaster in the housekeeper's apartment, which cleared up the final mystery of why she'd been sleeping in the room next door to his. She'd barely acknowledged his thanks for organizing the repairs.

So much for 'breaking the ice'. It seemed the dining room was in the grip of a rapidly advancing cold snap. But he wasn't going to push.

Instead, he turned to Charlie and asked after her brother, which led to a raft of hilarious anecdotes about his recent backpacking trip to Indonesia.

Ellie said nothing. It was almost as if she knew she was sitting a few feet away from him but was desperately trying to wish herself invisible, or at the very least make herself blend into the background. Whatever she was trying to do, it wasn't working.

It was odd. She wore virtually no make-up, and the reckless curls were piled on top of her head and secured with a clip, and yet he couldn't stop glancing at her. It must be pheromones or something, because she wasn't his usual type at all.

Not any more, anyway.

A curl escaped from the long silver clip on top of Ellie's head and threatened to dunk itself in her meal, but before it could slim fingers tucked it behind her ear. That tiny hand had packed quite a punch last night. He stared at it, watched her fingers as they pleated her serviette, closed around her fork...

Charlie caught him with his cutlery frozen between his mouth and his plate, eyes fixed on Ellie. She smirked. He retaliated with a warning kick under the table. He knew how much of a blabbermouth Charlie was, and he didn't want her complicating things by teasing him, especially as he and Ellie had reached an icy truce. Besides, there was nothing to tease him about. She was his housekeeper.

Charlie glared at him and leaned underneath the table to rub her leg. A second later searing pain radiated from his shinbone.

'Ouch!'

Ellie glanced up, puzzled by the exchange, and Mark decided to deflect the attention from himself before she realised the food wasn't the only thing that was causing his mouth to fill with saliva.

He could do polite and businesslike. He could behave like a proper employer rather than a best buddy. And, with a sideways look at his cousin, he decided to prove it.

'So... Where are you from, Ellie?'

Ellie chased some glass noodles round her plate. Mark stretched out, then rested his hands behind his head and waited.

'Kent,' she replied quietly.

'The whole of Kent, or one spot in particular?'

'Barkleigh.'

What was that edge in her voice? Was she angry with him?

That was a little unfair. After all, she wasn't the one with teeth marks on her torso. And he'd done his best to wave the olive branch by chatting to her earlier on, and got his head bitten off for his trouble.

Pity. He liked a woman with a sense of humour.

Cancel that thought. She was an employee. He was her boss. He would make polite conversation and help her to feel more comfortable, right? Good. *Here goes...*

'So, what made you decide to—?'

Ellie clattered the empty plates together before he could finish his sentence and vanished in the direction of the kitchen, muttering something about coffee. Mark waited a split second, then grabbed a couple of empty wine glasses as an excuse to follow her. He got the distinct impression he'd said something wrong, although he couldn't think what it might be. His questions had been innocent enough—bland, even.

When he got to the kitchen Ellie was standing motionless near the sink, a couple of dishes still in her hands. She looked lost. Not in a metaphorical sense, but genuinely lost—as if she'd suddenly found herself in alien territory and had no idea of what to do or where to go next. Mark stepped forward to help her, and she jumped as if electricity had arced between them. The crockery leapt out of her arms and smashed against the flagstone floor.

She stammered her apologies and started to pick up the pieces.

'No. It was my fault,' he said. 'I startled you.'

He bent down to help her. She looked across at him as they both crouched beside the kitchen cabinets, picking up the remnants of the dishes. Their knees almost grazed, and whatever had startled her shot through him too. An anonymous emotion flickered in her eyes and she looked away.

When they had finished clearing away the mess, he pulled out one of the kitchen stools and motioned for her to sit down.

'I'll do the coffee.'

Her eyes opened wide, and he could feel the heat of her stare as he turned to the coffee machine.

'Dinner was stupendous,' he said as he placed a cup and saucer in front of her.

'Thank you,' she replied, looking even more surprised.

Suddenly he didn't feel like being the normal, wise-cracking Mark Wilder everyone expected him to be. He didn't want to *dazzle*. Some forgotten instinct told him to pare it all back, leave the charm behind and just talk to her, human being to human being. Actually, he did have something he wanted to ask her, something that might cement them in their right relationship without causing her to take offence.

'Actually, I was wondering if you could do me a favour.'

Her eyebrows raised a notch further.

'I mean, I love exotic food, but there is one thing I haven't had for a long time and I've *really* got a hankering for. I wonder if you wouldn't mind putting it on the menu some time?'

She looked at him, her eyes hooded and wary. 'What's that?'

He looked at floor before giving her a hopeful smile. 'Shepherd's Pie?'

Ellie Bond surprised him once again. Instead of scowling or rolling her eyes, she let go of all the tension she'd been holding in her face and laughed.

The kitchen was silent and empty when Ellie entered it the following morning. Dawn had come and gone, but the overcast sky produced an artificial twilight in the unlit kitchen. The state-of-the-art stainless steel appliances and barren worktop made the place look like a hotel. There was none of the usual clutter that made a kitchen the heart of the home. No family photos. No children's drawings. No pet bowls.

She found a note on the counter from Mark, letting her know he'd already left for the airport. An itinerary was stapled to it, in case she needed to contact him while he was away. She read the note in full, and cheered up instantly when she discovered he'd given her permission to buy anything she needed for the kitchen. Some women loved shopping for shoes; Ellie had a worrying love of shopping for kitchen gadgets—and this house could definitely do with her attention. It needed a food processor and measuring spoons and a griddle... And that was just for starters. It wasn't that there wasn't anything in the cupboards, but most of the equipment fell into the 'pretty but useless' category. The designer grater she'd found had been an odd shape, and they'd almost feasted on grated knuckles instead of grated ginger in their curry last night.

Outside it was grey and chilly, but the grounds of Larkford were still beautiful. Daffodils—not the garish ones, but blooms the colour of clotted cream—had burst through the lawn in clumps and were now whispering cheerfully to each other in the breeze. Wood pigeons cooed in the trees, and the first cherry blossoms were now visible on the silvery grey branches. It was almost a shame to be inside, so she went out for a walk, and continued walking long after the bottom of her teacup was visible.

Taking her cup of tea for a walk became part of her morning routine. On her return to the kitchen she would pass the super-duper, multi-highlighted calendar on the large fridge and mentally tick off the days until Mark returned.

Twelve more days of blissful solitude… Eleven more days… Eight more days…

And she ignored the fact that she felt slightly elated, rather than disappointed, as each day went by.

Mark lounged on a wicker sofa, high on the roof terrace of his hotel's penthouse suite. He was ignoring the traffic rushing round the corner and down Rodeo Drive in favour of the clear blue sky above his head. It had been an extremely long day schmoozing record company executives and their sharp-toothed lawyers in order to finalise the launch of Kat's album in the US, but he'd come away with what he'd wanted from the meeting—eventually. He was very good at schmoozing, after all.

He'd had an invitation to go clubbing this evening, with a rather strait-laced lawyer who looked as if she'd be a whole lot of fun once she let loose, but he'd turned her down. For some reason he wanted to be on his own at the moment. He didn't feel right, and he needed to relax a little and work out why.

Today he felt out of sorts, uncomfortable. As if he was wearing a suit that wasn't cut quite right.

He closed his eyes and sank into the deep cushions of the sofa.

Well, he wasn't wearing a suit now. He'd changed into shorts and a T-shirt as soon as he'd got back to his suite. Unfortunately he still had that same itchy feeling, as if something wasn't quite right. He shook his head and pulled his sunglasses down over his eyes. Even with them closed the sun was still a little bright, burning strange shapes onto the backs of his eyelids.

Slowly the blobs swam and merged, until they solidified into an image that looked suspiciously familiar. In fact it looked suspiciously like his new housekeeper. He snapped his lids open and let the white sun bleach his retina instead.

What was up with him?

This was the third time something similar had happened. He was seeing her everywhere. And he didn't want to remember how sad and lost she'd looked when she'd smashed his best crockery to smithereens. He also didn't want to remember how warm and alive she'd looked when he'd mentioned Shepherd's Pie and she'd thrown her head back and laughed.

Housekeepers weren't supposed to be memorable. They were supposed to fade into the background and just do their job. He knew from personal experience how important it was to keep the lines between personal and professional firmly in place.

Somewhere in the back of his head he heard laughing.

Like you're doing with Kat?

That was different. He wasn't going to make the same mistake with Kat that he'd made with Nuclear Hamster. Stupid name. He'd advised them against it, but they hadn't listened. It was just that Kat was so young, she needed—

Okay, he was starting to act like a big brother towards Kat, but it didn't mean anything. Most importantly, it didn't mean he was setting a precedent of getting too close to his employees. He'd been cured of that fault a long time ago. Which meant he was totally capable of interacting with Ellie Bond without thinking of her as a woman—a woman who filled a pair of striped pyjamas very nicely, actually.

He sighed. He'd be back at Larkford in just over a week.

And Ellie would be there. It was what he'd hired her for, after all.

Suddenly the thought of the two of them alone in that big old house together seemed a little... intimate. He stood up, walked over to the parapet and stared out towards the Hollywood hills. A house like his—well, what it really needed was to be filled with people. Lots of them.

On the day there were only five spaces left on the calendar Ellie got restless. All her tasks were done, and she'd finished the book she was reading. She needed something to do. Something to clean out. Sorting through cupboards and purging the rubbish was a therapeutic activity she rather enjoyed. It made her feel as if she were in control of something for once.

The infamous cupboard opposite the bathroom had become the object of her obsession. As far as she could see it was full of boxes of miscellaneous clutter that had been sent down from Mark's London flat and had yet to be sorted out. She'd found plenty of bedlinen, a squash racket and three boxes of books. The empty shelves in the study came to mind, so Ellie decided to liberate the volumes from the dust and cardboard and put them where they could be useful.

She carried the box down to the study and started pulling books out and putting them on the thick wooden shelves. As she got to the last book in one stack a slip of paper fell out of the pages and wafted to the floor. She picked it up and realised it wasn't a piece of paper after all, but a photograph.

Not any old photograph. It was a wedding picture.

Mark and an anonymous bride.

Well, well, who'd have thought it? The bachelor playboy hadn't always been a bachelor. Bet he'd always been a playboy, though.

She frowned almost instinctively and studied the photograph more carefully. Mark looked younger—maybe in his mid-twenties?—fresh-faced, and very much in love with his beautiful, sophisticated bride. Her expression softened a little. A man who could look at a woman like that *had* something. Exactly what, she didn't know. Maybe he didn't either, because he'd thrown it all away and was living a very different life now. What a pity.

Turning the picture over, she saw the words 'Mark and Helena' scrawled on the back. The date underneath was twelve years earlier. Ellie slid the photograph back into its resting place and put the book on the shelf, feeling a little bit guilty for having found out what she sensed was a secret.

She reached for the next book, but was interrupted by the shrill beckoning of the telephone—the house line, not the one here in Mark's office.

Blast! She'd noticed the cradle in the hall was empty when she'd walked past with the box of books. She'd probably left the phone lying around again, which meant it might be anywhere.

She stood still and listened carefully.

The kitchen.

She raced down the passageway, skidding on the tiles in her socks.

It's in here somewhere!

The ringing was louder now, but oddly muffled. She ransacked a corner of the kitchen near the hob. Nothing! She leant closer to the worktop, then started frantically opening drawers.

Nope. Nope. Aha!

There it was, nestled amongst the wooden spoons. Where else?

She jabbed the button and uttered a breathless hello, then snapped to attention as she heard Mark's deep tones.

At first she didn't listen to the words, the content of what he was saying, because she hadn't been prepared for the way even his voice made her tingle. Oh, why couldn't he have e-mailed her? She wouldn't have had to concentrate on sounding normal if she'd been typing a reply!

Ah, but the phone call might have something to do with the fact she'd forgotten her password and hadn't been able to check her e-mails for a while.

It was just then that she realised Mark had stopped talking.

'Ellie?'

'Uh-huh?'

'Are you…? Is everything all right?' She could hear him suppressing a smile.

Unfortunately she was more than a little breathless—from all the phone-hunting, of course.

'Just...couldn't...find the phone.' She took a gulp of air and managed to croak, 'Can I help you?'

'Yep. I've decided to throw an impromptu party as a kind of housewarming when I get home. Only a few dozen guests—don't worry.'

A few dozen?

'My PA is handling the invites, and I'll get her to send you a list of caterers. We've decided on Saturday.'

'Saturday? This Saturday? That's less than a week away!'

'I know. I've been e-mailing for days, but you didn't reply. Don't stress. That'll be plenty of— hang on—'

Ellie huffed and tapped the counter as Mark chatted to someone on his end of the line. She thought she heard a woman's voice.

None of my business. I don't care who he's with.

'Got to go, Ellie. I'll be back on Friday evening.'

The receiver hummed in her ear.

He hadn't even given her time to tell him that she couldn't possibly organise a party in six days. She'd only just got to grips with the day-to-day running of the house, and the last thing she needed was something that was going to send all that into a tailspin.

However, it didn't seem as if she had much choice. If she wanted to keep this job she would have to cater to her boss's whims, no matter how inconvenient.

Catering.

Was that the best place to start? It was so long since she'd had a social life herself, thinking about planning a party seemed as run-of-the-mill as planning a trek up the Amazon.

She closed her eyes. Remember what you learned at the support group. Don't panic over the big picture. Take things one step at a time. Start with the obvious.

Her eyelids lifted again. The cleaners were coming on Friday anyway, so no problem there. And she could get Jim the gardener to help her rearrange the furniture in the downstairs reception rooms, and the florists in the village could provide some arrangements.

After her initial panic she realised it wasn't that different from what she'd done when she'd worked as a PA in the City after leaving college. Her cantankerous boss had had a penchant for drop-of-the-hat cocktail parties to impress the partners, where he would swan round being all sweetness and light, then return to being a sour-faced grump the next day. If she could create a party to blow Martin Frobisher's socks off, she could certainly succeed with a lovely backdrop like Larkfield.

Yes, but that was *before*…

Shut up, she told herself. It's all there inside your head still. She was just going to have to do a little…archaeology to uncover the buried bits.

She could do this.

Her brain began to whirr with excitement as menu ideas sprang up in her mind. This was her chance to prove to Mark Wilder that she wasn't a loose cannon, that she could do this job.

She reached for the phonebook and flipped it open to 'F' for florists, her smile wide. Passwords could wait for later. For now she would use the phone.

If Mr Wilder wanted a party, she was going to give him a party!

Ellie slipped the straps of the little black dress she'd borrowed from Charlie over her shoulders. She wasn't looking forward to this evening one bit. She'd tried hard to talk him out of it, but Mark had insisted she attend the party—partly to keep an eye on the caterers and whatnot, but partly to 'have a bit of fun'. She'd have much preferred to stay holed up in her apartment with a packet of biscuits and a chick-flick.

She smoothed the bodice of the dress over her torso and looked in the mirror. She turned from one side to the other, scrutinising her reflection. Not bad. The simply cut black dress accentuated her curves, but didn't cling in desperation. She slipped on a pair of strappy high heels—also borrowed from Charlie. Her ankles wobbled as she adjusted to the altitude.

Tyres crunched on the gravel outside. She exhaled wearily. Guests were starting to arrive, which meant it was her cue to go downstairs. While it wasn't her place to welcome the guests, she wanted to make sure that the pair of local girls she'd hired to help with coats and suchlike had retained the pertinent information from their briefing yesterday.

Perhaps she could just stick it out for an hour or so and then slope off when he—when *no one*—was looking.

She left her room and headed for the main staircase. It wound down into a hall that was larger than the living room in her cottage. The banisters were solid oak, and still as sturdy as the day they'd been made. Ellie was rather grateful for them as she made her way down the stairs in Charlie's disobedient shoes. They seemed to have a mind of their own. She watched each foot carefully as she planted it on the next step, and it was only as she neared the bottom that she looked up and caught a glimpse of Mark, standing by the huge marble fireplace, chatting to the first of the arrivals.

Unfortunately she'd discovered when he'd returned home the previous evening that time and distance had done nothing to dilute the sheer physical impact the man had on her. It was pathetic, really, it was. She knew better, knew what sort of man he was, and yet here she was, *twittering* along with every other female in a five-mile radius. She comforted herself with the knowledge that at least she had a medical reason for behaving this way.

She looked over at Tania and Faith, the girls from the village. Neither of them had thought to relieve any guest of a coat or a wrap; they were too busy standing in the corner and getting all giggly over a certain member of the male species.

Ellie forced herself not to look at Mark as she made her way across the hall and reissued her instructions to the two girls in a low, authoritative voice. They instantly sprang into action, relieving guests of their outerwear and delivering the items to one of the smaller rooms on the ground floor where Ellie had set up some portable clothing racks.

The only problem was that Tania and Faith were now so intent on proving themselves efficient they'd both darted off at once, leaving Ellie no choice but to act as hat-check girl herself when the next huddle of guests piled through the door. She approached the group that had just crossed the threshold.

Mark moved forward to greet them at the same time, and Ellie couldn't avoid meeting his gaze. It was like being hit in the chest with one of those

Taser guns. Her heart stuttered, fizzing with a million volts, and she disguised the resultant quivering in her limbs by breaking eye contact and smoothing out a non-existent wrinkle on her dress. All the same, the hairs at the back of her neck lifted, full of static. She just knew he was still looking at her. He inhaled, as if he was about to say something, but before the words left his mouth, another voice gatecrashed the moment.

'Mark, you old dog!' bellowed a good-looking blond man in a dinner jacket, slapping him across the shoulders.

'Hello, Piers,' Mark replied in his good-humoured tone. 'Come in and find yourself a drink. What do you think of my new place?'

'Bloody difficult to find, that's what I say!' he roared, slapping Mark a second time.

Ellie was standing there still waiting to take any coats. She felt like a prize lemon.

'Let me introduce you to this trinity of lovelies,' Piers continued, ushering a group of bejewelled women into the house. 'Carla, Jade, and of course you already know Melodie.'

Of course. Ellie recognised her as the woman from the television. She didn't say anything, but silently willed Melodie to hurry up and hand that pashmina over. Ellie wanted an excuse to make herself scarce.

Mark didn't falter as he offered a polite

greeting to all three women, but Ellie had a sense as she took hold of their wraps and coats that he wasn't as comfortable as his relaxed stance implied. She was just about to scamper away to the temporary cloakroom when the pair of girls returned and relieved her of her only legitimate means of escape.

Then, just to make matters worse, Mark turned to her and asked her something. She saw his lips move, heard the words, but her brain retained none of the information. Why had he done that? She was the help. And she'd actually like to keep their relationship on that footing, thank you very much. Things were complicated enough as it was.

Just then a waitress with a large tray walked past the entrance hall en-route to the drawing room. Caterers! She was supposed to be here in a professional capacity, after all. She would inspect each and every trayful of over-priced morsels and make sure they were just what she'd ordered. She mumbled something about food, not so much to Mark but to the room in general, then fell into step behind the waitress, lengthening the distance between her and the group at the doorway. As she rounded the corner she could still hear Piers's booming upper-class drawl.

'Ding-*dong*!' he said with a whistle. 'Who was that?'

She didn't wait to hear Mark's explanation of her existence, but scuttled away even faster—high heels permitting. The last thing she wanted to do was actually have to talk to people tonight. They would expect her to be dazzling and witty. And if she had ever been dazzling and witty in her previous life she had certainly forgotten by now. Socialising was something other people did. Even the prospect of a night down at the Anglers' Arms in Barkleigh filled her with fear and trembling. In comparison, this party was like purgatory with canapés.

A few dozen guests? Someone had underestimated a little.

The drawing room was like a *Who's Who* of popular music. Wasn't that…? You know, the guy who always seemed to be at number one? And that girl over there—Ellie had seen her latest music video only the other night on TV. Normal party nerves escalated into something far bigger and scarier. It would be really great if she could think of the girl's name—if she could recall *anyone's* name, actually. These were the sort of people who expected to be remembered.

She circled the drawing room, 'fluffing' the

floral arrangements, hoping that no one talked to her and expected her to know who they were. But she wasn't really looking at what she was doing, and more leaves fell off due to her attention than she cared to notice. As soon as she could she slipped out and made her way to the kitchen.

CHAPTER FIVE

THERE was a strange calm to be had amidst the noise and movement of the kitchen. At least in here Ellie knew what she was doing. Her lists and charts were pinned to the cupboard doors, her timetable clung to the fridge door with the help of a few magnets, and waiters and waitresses were all jostling each other, doing exactly as they were supposed to.

It didn't take long before one of the catering company staff appeared with a question, and Ellie found herself busy for what seemed like a half an hour but turned out to be almost two hours. Eventually tiredness washed over her, the mind-fogging fatigue she knew she shouldn't ignore. Dodging dashing bodies and clattering trays suddenly became too much of an effort and she crept up the back staircase. Before she went to her room she carried on along the landing and looked over the banisters into the hall, where the party was still in full swing. She'd done well this evening, and she wanted one last mental picture of her achievement, to cement it firmly in her memory before she fled back to her bedroom and shut the door firmly behind her.

From her vantage point on the landing she watched the glittering crowd ebb and flow. The clink of champagne glasses and jumble of conversation drifted up from below. Surprisingly, she found the sound soothing now she was no longer in the thick of it.

Her eyes drifted here and there, searching. It wasn't until they fixed on Mark that she realised she'd been looking for him. He was the perfect host—she'd give him that. He was charming and smooth, always with a crowd around him. The group he was with laughed at something he said. So he was good company too, it seemed. But he didn't dominate the gathering, forcing people to look at him. They just flowed around him, accepting the good time he offered them.

That woman from the awards ceremony was talking to him now, batting her lashes and jutting her ample chest under his nose. Ellie rolled her eyes. And, funnily enough, when the woman turned to grab herself a cocktail from a passing tray, Mark did a microscopic version of the same expression. That made her smile. It also made her look a little closer.

He smiled. He talked. But every now and then he just drifted off and stared at nothing for a second, until the next excited guest drew him back into the conversation. It was almost as if…

No. That was a stupid idea. Why would someone throw a party if they didn't actually want to be at it themselves?

'What are you doing skulking up here? I've been looking for you everywhere.'

Ellie stopped breathing momentarily as Charlie appeared from nowhere.

'Don't do that!' Ellie whispered sharply, pressing her palm to her chest in an effort to slow her galloping heart. 'And I'm not skulking.'

Charlie stopped smiling and looked concerned. 'You're a bag of nerves,' she said, while giving Ellie's arm a reassuring rub. 'Come on, chill out. It is a party, after all…'

Ellie nodded. 'I know. But I need this to go well. I can't lose this job, Charlie, I can't—'

Without warning her eyes filled, and the party below glittered even harder than before.

'Hey!' Charlie's voice was gentle and her arm rested around Ellie's shoulders, pulling her close. 'What's all this about?'

She took a deep breath. 'Did you tell him…Mark Wilder… about me?'

Charlie's three frown lines appeared above her

nose. 'All I told him was that you were an old friend of mine and I thought you'd be perfect for the job. I wasn't lying, Ellie.'

Ellie scratched at a non-existent mark on the banister with a blunt fingernail. 'No. I mean, did you tell him about how I have problems with… about my…?'

Charlie's voice was low when she answered. 'No, I didn't tell him about the accident or how it's affected you. It's up to you whether you want to share that information with him.'

Okay, so Charlie had believed her when she'd sworn blind she had it in her to be a top-notch housekeeper. Now she just had to prove her right. Ellie's chest rose then fell deeply as she let out a huge breath. 'Right. Thank you.'

A soft look appeared on Charlie's face. 'Do you really think being here, moving away from home, will help you…you know…get over things?'

Suddenly Ellie needed to sit down. Her legs folded under her with the grace of a collapsing deckchair and she grabbed on to the banister with both hands. Charlie's arm appeared, firm and protective, around her shoulders.

'There's more to this sudden desire for a new job than just needing fresh scenery, isn't there, Ellie? Why did you really want to leave Barkleigh in such a hurry?'

Blast. Why did Charlotte Maxwell have to be so perceptive under her devil-may-care exterior? Ellie stared at the milling guests below. Their only problems were deciding which diamond to wear or which sports car to drive.

A feeling of loss washed over her, so deep, so overwhelming that she thought she might just dissolve into nothing right there on Mark Wilder's landing.

Sometimes she wished her brain would just finish the job and give up working all together. Then she could just evaporate. She'd be happy then, feeling nothing, remembering nothing. It was this half-in, half-out thing her memory did that was driving her to distraction.

'I can't go home,' she whispered. 'I just can't.'

'Why?'

'Remember Ginny? Chloe's godmother and my oldest friend?'

Charlie nodded. 'Yes, I remember her.'

Ellie didn't want to say it. Hearing the words spill out of her own mouth would remind her of everything she'd lost. Of everything she longed for.

'She's pregnant.'

She didn't look up. Couldn't.

Charlie's hand stopped stroking her arm and slid down over her wrist until their fingers meshed, Charlie's red fingernails bright against her pale skin. Ellie gripped her hand, hanging on to it as if it would anchor her.

'I know it's awful, but I think if I have to see her every day for the next eight months, seeing her grow bigger, seeing how happy she is with Steve, I might just go *properly* bonkers. I just had to get away.'

She was happy for Ginny and Steve, really she was, but how could she watch them add to their happy little family when her own had been wiped from the face of the earth? It was too... too...*blatant*.

Charlie didn't say anything, just hugged her tight. 'Do you want me to get you anything? A glass of water?'

Ellie shook her head. 'No. I'm just tired. I think I'll just stay here for a few seconds and then go to bed. You go on and enjoy the party.' She nodded to the hall below, where the rather good-looking man she'd seen Charlie with earlier was searching the crowd. 'I think someone's looking for you.'

Charlie smiled, and her eyes never left the man as he moved this way and that. 'If you're sure?' she said.

'I'm sure.' Ellie gave her a shove in the right direction and Charlie headed off down the stairs. The man spotted her, and the look he gave her as she descended was pure magic. Ellie sighed. At least someone was happy.

She moved a little further to the left, so she could

see more of the hall. Mark was still leaning on the mantelpiece, and he had that distant look in his eyes again.

Her mind wandered back to his smile in the wedding photo. She'd seen him smile plenty of times tonight, but not one of those smiles had lit up his face like his smile for the woman in the wedding photo. Where was she now? What had happened? For the first time she realised there were scars beneath his good-humoured persona. From wounds that maybe hadn't fully healed. Her hand flew to the locket around her neck. She knew all about the pain those kinds of wounds could cause.

As if he sensed she was watching him, Mark paused, his glass raised halfway to his lips. And then he turned his head and met her gaze. She froze. Could it be any more obvious she'd been staring at him and only him? She didn't think so.

Still, he didn't look cross. He wasn't smiling that irritating twinkly smile—wasn't mocking her. The other occupants of the room melted away, their conversation drowned out by a loud thudding sound.

Oh. That was her pulse.

Heat crept up her cheeks, but still she hadn't moved. And moving at this point would be a really good idea.

Still staring at Mark, she took a couple of wobbly steps backwards, then turned and fled along the corridor. For some reason she ignored her bedroom door and headed for the back staircase. She needed space, distance. And she didn't think she'd get that with only a ceiling and a couple of walls separating her from Mark Wilder.

The stupid stilettos strangled her ankles as she clattered down the back staircase. She paused at the bottom. No one was around, so she tiptoed down the corridor into the kitchen.

Ellie stole a smoked fish thing off a platter of canapés and popped it in her mouth. As she slid past a waitress carrying a tray of cocktails she pilfered one of those too, knocking it back and shuddering as whatever it was hit the back of her throat.

She edged past the round table near the French doors. An abandoned tray stood on the table, cluttered with champagne flutes, some empty, some full. She plucked one of the full ones and nipped out of her favourite escape route into the garden.

A wave of muffled laughter wafted past her on the clear night air. She took a sip of champagne, but barely tasted it. There was something she had to do first, before she could enjoy it properly.

Her feet were killing her.

She sat on a low stone wall and fiddled with the microscopic buckles. Pretty soon she'd flicked the shoes off and she hooked the satin straps under her fingers and headed into the garden.

The flagstones were cold and rough on the soles of her feet, and she veered in the direction of the lawn and sank her toes deep into it. Heaven! She closed her eyes and took another sip of champagne. The canapé was the first thing she had eaten all evening, and on an empty stomach it wasn't hard to feel the bubbles doing their work.

Funny how parties always sounded more inviting when you were on the outside. All she had wanted to do when she was in there was escape, yet now she was out here she felt strangely alone.

She took a few more steps on the springy grass, letting the blades invade the spaces between her toes. She wriggled them and drained the flute of its contents. Goosebumps flourished on her upper arms as she heard a low masculine voice behind her.

'Caught red-handed!'

A powerful pair of hands clamped down on Ellie's shoulders. The champagne glass slid out of her hand and bounced off her foot. She instinctively ducked down and forwards, wriggling out his grip, then swung round to face him.

He blinked groggily at her. 'What's the matter?' he slurred. 'Don't you like me?'

His name might have deserted her, but she hadn't forgotten this man. The floppy pale hair, the arrogant smirk. She didn't know who he was to

Mark, but if the rest of his friends were like this, he could keep them.

He draped an arm across her shoulders. 'What d'you say we go for a little walk?'

She had to handle this carefully. He might be a pain in the behind, but he was Mark's guest too, so losing her temper would only get her in trouble. 'I'd rather not, thank you.'

His eyes were glassy and his breath reeked of whisky. She carefully peeled his arm off her shoulder. He lost his balance now he wasn't leaning on her for support, his feet sliding on the dewy grass. His smile faded.

'Hey! There's no need to be hoity-toity about it.'

'I didn't... I...' Oh, what was the use? He'd probably take any conversation as encouragement of some sort. The best thing to do was get out of here before she really did get *hoity-toity* with him.

She turned and walked back towards the house. He lumbered after her, stumbling slightly, and managed to grab hold of her arm and haul her towards him.

Something flashed white-hot inside her head. She dreaded these surges of anger, but could do very little to contain herself when they struck. She was going to blow, whether she liked it or not.

'Get off me!' she yelled.

He made a curious gurgle that she interpreted as

a laugh, and clamped her to his chest. His lips made contact with the skin beneath her ear and slid down her neck in a slobbery trail.

'Ugh!'

Enough was enough. No more Miss Nice Guy. She swung Charlie's killer sandals wide and brought them crashing down on his temple.

Mark had suddenly had enough of standing around talking to the same people, having the same conversations he'd had last week. He needed fresh air.

Instinctively he headed for the kitchen, then paused at the threshold. Why had he come this way? He had the feeling he was looking for something but had forgotten what.

Nonsense, his conscience said. You know exactly why you're here...*who* you're looking for.

But it didn't matter. She wasn't there.

So he ducked past the busy catering staff and out of the French windows to the small lawn.

The floodlights on the outside of the house made the dark night even blacker, and it took him a few moments to realise he wasn't alone. A movement at the end of the lawn caught his eye and he made out two silhouettes. He almost grinned and shrugged it off as a couple of guests slipping away to get friendly, but something made him look again.

Piers was up to his old tricks, it seemed. He was

a notorious flirt. The only reason Mark had invited him was because he needed his firm's specialist legal knowledge on a recording contract he was putting together. Still, Piers was relatively harmless, and most of the females in their circle of acquaintance knew how to deal with him. Mark peered deeper into the darkness. Just who was he with this time, anyway?

And then he was running, the sound of his own blood rushing and swirling in his ears. He worked out regularly enough, and his legs were pumping beneath him, but somehow he seemed to make torturous progress, like the slow-motion running in a dream.

The woman Piers was slobbering over was Ellie.

And there was no way he was going to let some jumped-up little twit who worked for his daddy's law firm foist himself on one of his staff. She might not know how to—

Mark almost slipped on the damp grass.

Perhaps she did.

He watched as Ellie gave Piers a first-class whack with her shoes. Piers stumbled and fell on the damp grass, clutching a hand to his head. Mark finally skidded to a halt in front of them and yanked Piers up by his collar. His right fist was itching to make contact with that pretty face. He ought to flatten him for treating Ellie that way.

'Mark, no!'

The panic in her voice was all he needed to make him reconsider. He released the slimy runt and gave him a shove in the direction of the house.

'Go home, Piers. You're drunk.'

Piers wiped saliva from the edges of his mouth with the back of his hand.

'Steady on, Mark!'

He marched towards Piers and stopped inches from his face. Piers might have a reputation for being a ladies' man, but Mark had never suspected how nasty he could be with it. How could a man who appeared so polished during the working week turn out to be such a rat? Once again he'd believed the best in someone, only to be utterly disappointed.

'No. You *steady on*,' he said, with more than a hint of controlled fury in his voice. 'Don't ever set foot in this house again. In fact, don't bother to set foot in my offices again, either. As of Monday I will be seeking new legal representation—you and your firm are fired.'

Piers tugged at his tie and stood as tall as the whisky would let him.

'Now, look here. I could sue you for assault, manhandling me in that way!'

'Yes, you could. And I could tell the paparazzi hiding in my front bushes how you got plastered at my party and tried to grope one of my guests.

I'm sure the partners at Blackthorn and Webb would welcome the publicity, don't you?'

Piers turned tail and lurched towards the house. Mark watched until he was out of sight, then faced Ellie. 'I'm so sorry about that. Are you all right?'

'Fine.' Her voice quivered enough to call her determined face a liar.

'You gave him one hell of a clout with those shoes!'

The shell-shocked expression gave way to a delightfully naughty smile. 'You should have warned him I was dangerous to mess with.'

The fingers of Mark's right hand wandered to the spot near his left collarbone, where she'd bitten him only a few weeks earlier. At the time he'd been livid, hadn't found it funny in the slightest. Tonight, however, he found he couldn't find it anything but, and he started to laugh.

To his surprise, Ellie joined him. Softly at first, with a giggle that hinted she was holding more of it in than she was letting out. But eventually she was laughing just as hard as he was, and the more he saw her eyes sparkle and her cheeks blush, the more he wanted to keep the moment going.

Look at her. When she smiled like that, lost the glare and the frosty expression, she was... Not beautiful. At least not in the way Hollywood and the media defined the word. But he couldn't stop looking at her.

And why would he? She was laughing so hard she'd gone pink in the face and her eyes were squeezed shut. Any minute now he thought she'd keel over. It was adorable. Just as she threatened to make his prediction come true, she clutched at the air to steady herself. Her hand made contact with his upper arm and all the shared laughter suddenly died away.

Ellie looked away and tucked and escaped curl into the clip on top of her head. It bounced back again, unwilling to be leashed. His desire to reach forward and brush it away from her face was almost overpowering, but he'd done that so many times with other women. It would be too much of a cliché.

She looked up at him and shivered.

'You're cold.'

She started to protest, but he swung his jacket off and carefully hung it round her shoulders. It must be the night for clichés. This, too, was something he'd done more times than he could remember too—one of his *moves*, part of the game.

But it wasn't like that with Ellie. She'd been cold, and he'd done something to remedy that. He wasn't playing any games. Mainly because he didn't know what the rules were with her. She made him feel different—unpolished, uncertain—as if he wasn't in control of whatever was going on.

He looked at the warm light spilling from

Larkford's every window. He really ought to get back to his guests.

She moved slightly, and the friction of material between his fingers reminded him he was still holding the lapels of the jacket firmly. He really should let go. But Ellie was looking up at him, her eyes soft and unguarded, just as they had been when she'd stared down at him from the landing.

He'd liked that look then, and he liked it now. There wasn't a hint of greed or artifice in it. And that was a rare thing in his world. It was as if she saw something that surprised her, something that everyone else missed.

He'd seen her skirting the edge of the party, boredom clear on her face. And when he'd turned back to Melodie and the record producer he'd been chatting to he'd suddenly seen the whole gathering through Ellie's eyes, as if he'd been given X-ray specs that cut out the glare and the glitter, revealing everyone and everything for who and what they really were. Not much of what he'd seen would benefit from close scrutiny.

But out here on the lawn everything felt very real indeed. Uncomfortably so. His heart was hammering in his chest—and it wasn't from his race across the lawn.

She was tantalisingly close, her feelings clearly written in her face, floating across the surface. He felt her warm breath on his neck, sending shivers to the roots of his hair. He clenched the lapels of the dinner jacket, pulling her closer until only a molecule of air prevented their faces from touching. Normally he'd go in for the kill now, take the advantage while he had it, but he waited.

What for, he wasn't exactly sure.

The world seemed to shrink into the tiny space between his lips and hers. At least Ellie was aware of nothing but this, nothing beyond it. And, since remembering past or future was a struggle sometimes anyway, she finally let go and just existed in the moment. This particular moment revolved around a choice, one that was hers alone: to flow with the moment or push against it.

She was so tired of fighting herself, tired of pushing herself, of always keeping everything under constant surveillance. Just once she wanted to follow an impulse rather than resist it.

She wanted *this*.

Hesitantly, she pressed her lips against his, splaying her hands across his chest to steady herself. For a moment he did nothing, and her heart plummeted, but then he pulled her to him, sliding his hands under his suit jacket to circle her waist, and kissed her back.

All those women who fluttered and twittered merely at the sight of him would have melted clean away if they'd been on the receiving end of a kiss like this. Every mad hormonal urge she'd been fighting for the last few weeks roared into life and she didn't resist a single one.

It was a kiss of need, exploration...perfection.

She didn't need to think, to struggle to remember anything. And she wouldn't have been able to if she'd tried, not with Mark's teeth nipping at her lower lip, his hands sliding up her back until they brushed the bare flesh of her shoulders. Ellie reached up to feel the faint stubble on his jaw with her fingertips. He groaned and pulled her close enough to feel the muscles in his chest flexing as his arms moved. She let her head drop back when his lips pressed against the tingling skin just below her jaw, and she slid her fingers round the back of his head, running them through the short hair there and feeling him shiver.

A tray clanged inside the kitchen, and the noise cut cleanly and smoothly through the night air. They both froze, and the moment they'd shared shattered along with the glasses landing on the kitchen floor.

There was a horrible sense of *déjà vu* as they stared at each other, neither sure of what was going on and what they should do next.

Mark grasped for words inside his head. *Say something!*

He reached for her. 'Ellie...'

Come on, smooth talker! Where's all your patter now?

She stared back at him, wide-eyed and breathless. Then, before he could get his thoughts collected into syllables, she bolted into the house.

See? Unpredictable. He couldn't have guessed she was going to do that. After all, it wasn't the normal response he got when he kissed a woman—quite the reverse.

He raced after her and burst through the French windows into the kitchen. Precious seconds were lost as he collided with a fully laden waiter. The clattering of trays and muttered apologies masked the sound of her bare feet slapping on the tiles as she tore out of the kitchen and down the passageway that led to the back stairs.

He dodged another waiter and ran after her, only to be corralled by a group of guests.

'Mark!'

He turned to find Kat, looking all dishevelled and misty. Her puppy-dog eyes pleaded with him.

'It's Razor…'

She sniffed, and a single tear rolled down her cheek. Mark looked hopelessly at the staircase to his left, then at Kat, and back to the staircase. Kat hung on to his sleeve. He knew her well enough by now to realise that full meltdown was only seconds away. He put his own desires on the back burner and guided her through the crush in the drawing room to his study.

The boy wonder had undoubtedly been his usual considerate self, and Mark's shoulder was the one designated for crying on these days. He'd resisted that in the beginning, but he was too much of a sucker for a forlorn female to just pat Kat on the head and say, *There, there*.

As he ushered her into the study and shut the door he reasoned to himself that Ellie wasn't going anywhere for the moment. It would probably be better to give her a few minutes before he went after her—some thinking time. So he allowed Kat to spill out the whole sorry story and soak his shirt with her tears.

Ellie sat in the dark, shivering despite the central heating. She couldn't bear to turn on the light and see Sam's picture on the bedside table. Her eyes were sticky with tears and her nose was running. With a loud sniff she toppled back onto the mattress and curled into a ball.

'What was I thinking?'

Oh, but *thinking* hadn't been the problem. It was what she'd *done* that had messed everything up. Thoughts were fleeting, easily lost, erased or misplaced. Actions, however, were a little more concrete. And in this case definitely more memorable.

Just the memory of Mark's lips on hers was enough to make her flush hot and cold again.

How could she have done this to Sam? Wonderful, loving, dependable Sam? She was sure he would have been happy to think she would find someone else and rebuild her shattered life, but Mark Wilder! He was the worst kind of womaniser there was.

She searched the darkness above her head for an answer, desperate to make sense of it all.

But Mark hadn't seemed like a womaniser tonight in the garden, quite the reverse. He'd sent Piers Double-Barrelled packing, backing her up and taking her side, and he hadn't even taken advantage of the situation when she'd been vulnerable and heaving with hormones. She could have walked away…

Maybe it wasn't about Mark. Maybe it was a symptom of her decision to break free, to learn to live again. Perhaps part of herself that she'd thought had died and been buried along with Sam had sprung to life again. She was a young woman still. It was just a healthy interest in the opposite sex, a natural response to a good-looking man.

But that train of thought derailed just as fast as the last one had.

It was only since meeting Mark that she'd been anything but numb. He was a catalyst of some kind. And…and if it was just about pent-up desires, she wouldn't have rejected Piers. He was suave and attractive, but it didn't stop her experiencing a wave of revulsion every time she thought of him.

So she was back to Mark. Her brain was swinging in wild arcs, but it always came back to Mark. What was she going to do about that...about *him*?

His attraction to her was genuine, there was no mistaking that, but it wouldn't last. Men like him didn't stay with women like her. After a couple of months it would fizzle out and she'd be left alone again. And in search of a new job.

She didn't want an affair, or a fling, or a one-night stand. Settling for less than the all-encompassing love she'd had for Sam seemed like being unfaithful to his memory. It would be like losing the Crown Jewels and replacing them with paste and nickel that made your skin turn green. This thing with Mark, whatever it was, it couldn't go anywhere. It couldn't be anything.

She sniffed again and stretched out a little. Why? Why be interested in someone like him? She could say it was the money, or the success, his looks and his charm, but it wasn't any of those things. Tonight she'd glimpsed something else behind the cheeky, boyish charm. Something darker and deeper that resonated with a similar *something* inside her too.

A faint hint of Mark's aftershave drifted into her nostrils. She looked up, half expecting to see him standing there, waiting for her, but the room was empty. Then she realised she was still wearing his jacket. His masculine scent clung to it, and she was reminded of the moment he'd put it on her in the garden.

He'd seemed so vulnerable standing there. For a man who had women drop at his feet on a daily basis he'd almost seemed unsure of himself. Not at all what she'd expected.

She whimpered and covered her face with her hands, even though there was no one there to see her blush.

How was she going to face him in the morning?

CHAPTER SIX

MARK stumbled downstairs some time after ten. He'd intended to get up earlier, but he hadn't dropped off until dawn and then his sleep had been heavy, full of dreams where he was running from unseen predators. He'd wanted to be fresh and calm this morning, to deal with the aftermath of last night's events with just a little panache.

He didn't have to search hard for Ellie, though; he could smell something delicious wafting from the kitchen, and he followed the mouthwatering smell like a zombie.

Well, almost like a zombie. His heart rate was pattering along too fast for him to be considered officially dead. Was he…was he *nervous*?

He'd spent hours last night in his study, going over and over it all in his head. Not that he'd come to any earth-shattering conclusions. He had a housekeeper. She kissed like a dream. That was about the sum total of it.

All he'd done was kiss her. It was hardly a big deal.

All he'd done... He should listen to himself.

If it had just been a kiss, his heart wouldn't be flapping around inside his chest like a fish out of water.

He liked Ellie. And not in the let's-have-dinner-at-the-Ivy kind of way he normally liked women. It felt different. As if this kind of *liking* had a different shape, was a different kind of entity all together.

Now, that was a scary thought.

Like Helena, Ellie was one of those delicate beings, beautiful in their frailty like an orchid or a butterfly. And that made her even more dangerous. He knew he couldn't resist getting drawn in by women like that, finding himself wanting to protect them, to care for them until they were whole again. It was a weakness, he knew, but one that he channelled into his clients these days, by being the best manager in the business. At least they paid him for his devotion.

That kind of woman sucked everything out of a man until he had nothing left to give. And then she took what he'd done, all the tender, loving care he'd given, and bestowed it on someone else, someone who didn't remind her of the pain. Someone who didn't remind her of who she used to be when she was just a shell, empty and hurting.

He couldn't do that again. He couldn't be that for anyone again.

So he would just have to deflect Ellie, dazzle her, and move things back to where they should be—on a purely professional level.

If he could talk a highly strung diva down from demanding three-hundred-pound-a-bottle mineral water that had been blessed by a Tibetan priest in her dressing room, he could surely manage this. And then he would invent a reason to go and stay at his flat in London for a few days. It wasn't running away; it was self-preservation.

'Morning,' he said, overcompensating a little and sounding much too relaxed as he entered the kitchen. Ellie had her back turned to him. She was stirring something in a saucepan on the hob and returned his greeting in a cool, clipped voice, not looking up from the pan.

'What are you doing?'

Ah, yes. This is the smooth wit and banter you are famous for... This will charm the socks off her and sort everything out.

Ellie didn't say anything, just stirred harder.

'It smells great. What is it?'

'I decided to make a big batch of bolognaise and freeze it in smaller portions for quick suppers,' she said in a starchy voice. 'Would you like me to stop and fetch you breakfast?'

That was the last thing he wanted. Far too awkward.

'It's okay. I'm more than capable of getting my own coffee.'

He grabbed himself a mug of coffee and sat down at the circular wooden table near the French windows that led to the garden. Ellie was pushing what he now recognised as beef mince round the pan with a wooden spoon. It spat and hissed, the only sound in the rapidly thickening atmosphere.

He cleared his throat. 'Ellie, listen…'

'Look, Mark, I know where this is going.'

'You do?' He rubbed his nose with the heel of his hand.

'I do. And let's not go there.'

Good. They were reading off the same page. Why, then, had his stomach bottomed out like a plummeting lift?

'Okay,' he said, not trusting himself with anything more complicated. It seemed as if Ellie was doing fine on her own, anyway. She took a deep breath in readiness for another speech.

'You're my boss. You spend your time flitting around the globe and living the high life. And I'm…' She looked at the ceiling, searching for the right word.

'I know I'm your boss—of course I know that—and you're…'

Surprising? Appealing? Unforgettable? Those were the words that filled his head. None of them were the right ones to come out of his mouth, though.

'You're…'

Ellie's gaze wandered down from the heavens and settled on him. 'I'm your *housekeeper*.'

'Right.' That was correct. But it didn't *feel* like the right answer.

She shook her head, her curls bouncing slightly. 'To be honest, you and me, it's just—'

'Complicated?'

She shrugged one shoulder. 'I was going for tacky or predictable, but your word works too.'

Ouch.

'I'm your employee, and I think we should keep our relationship on a professional basis,' she said, turning to face him fully.

'I agree with you one hundred percent.'

He looked hard at her, trying to work out what she was thinking. Her words were telling him she was fine, but her tone said something entirely different.

'You seem upset…'

She waved the wooden spoon in dismissal.

'Upset? I'm not upset!'

'Good.'

She gave him a blatantly fake smile, and returned her attention to the meat in the pan.

'Annoyed, then?'

More frantic stirring.

'Nope. Not at all.' She started jabbing the wooden spoon at the remaining lumps.

Ellie might be different from a lot of women he knew in a lot of ways, but the whole pretending to be fine when she clearly was not was horribly familiar.

'Ellie, I know I may have been a bit impulsive last night, but I don't think we...*I* did anything wrong.'

'Oh, you don't?' she said through clenched teeth.

'No. Do you?'

Now he was totally lost. Why did women have this secret agenda that read like code to normal human beings—men, in other words?

The pan spat ferociously as Ellie added a jar of tomatoey gloopy stuff and mixed it in. She turned to face him and took a step away from the counter, still holding the dripping spoon.

'You're unbelievable, do you know that? You live in a lovely little Mark bubble where everything is perfect. You haven't got a clue what real life is like!'

He thought he did a pretty good job of living life, thank you very much, and he didn't much care for someone he hardly knew judging him for it.

'I don't?'

'No! You don't. Real people have real feelings, and you can't just go messing around with them. You live in this rarefied world where you do whatever you want, get whatever you want and everything goes right for you. Not everybody has that luxury. And you waste it, you know? You really do.'

Something in her stare made him hold back the smart retort poised on his lips. Through the film of tears gathering in her eyes he saw determination and an honesty that was surprising—and not a little unnerving.

Something was very wrong, but as usual he was totally mystified as to what was going on inside her head. Why was she blaming him? He hadn't been the one to start it last night. *She* had kissed him, remember? And he certainly hadn't meant to mess around with her feelings, but perhaps he had…without realising it.

Maybe he *was* clueless. He needed to consider her accusation a little more fully before he gave a real answer.

Ellie made use of the silence to ram her point home. 'I think it's best for both of us if we just put that…you know, the…'

A crack in her anger showed as she desperately tried to avoid using the word 'kiss'. It would have been funny if she hadn't been giving him the brush-off.

'Let's just put what happened last night down to champagne and temporary insanity, okay? I don't want to lose this job.'

He nodded just once. 'And I need to start looking for a new housekeeper like I need a hole in the head.'

Finally she breathed out and her shoulders relaxed a little. 'I'm glad we understand each other,' she said with a small jut of her chin, and turned her attention back to the bolognaise sauce.

She was right. He knew she was right. It was just...

Aw, forget it. He'd spent the last decade fooling everyone—even himself—that he was 'living the dream'. He might just as well return to that happy, alpha-wave state and forget that he'd ever yearned for anything more.

If you can, a little voice whispered in his ear. *If you can...*

Mark disappeared back to London the next day, much to Ellie's relief. But it didn't stop him coming back to Larkford again the following weekend. Or the one after that. During the week she could relax, enjoy her surroundings, but the weekends were something else. Stiff. Awkward. And, although she'd never expected anything more than a professional relationship with the man, now they were operating on that level it just seemed, well...weird.

And that was how it continued for the next month or so.

So, there she was on a Saturday afternoon, hiding out in the kitchen, preparing the evening meal, even though she needn't start for hours yet. But it was good to keep herself busy and out of a certain person's way. Not that it had been hard today. He might be at home, but he was obviously working; he'd hardly left the study all day. They were keeping to their separate territories as boxers did their corners of the ring.

She was still cross with herself for being too weak to control her brain's fried electrical signals. They still all short-circuited every time he appeared. It was as if her neurons had rewired themselves with a specialised radar that picked up only him as he breezed around the house, as calm as you like, while her fingernails were bitten so low she'd practically reached her knuckles.

Blip. Blip. Blip.

There it went again. Her core temperature rose a couple of notches. He was on the move; she just knew it. She stopped chopping an onion and listened. After about ten seconds she heard what she'd been waiting for—footsteps in the hall, getting louder.

She kept her eyes on her work as Mark entered the kitchen. The coffee machine sputtered. Liquid sloshed into a cup. The rubber heel of a stool squeaked on the floor. Silence. The tiny hairs on the back of her neck bristled.

Just carry on as if he's not there.

The knife came down hard on the chopping board—thunk, thunk, thunk—so close she almost trimmed her non-existent nails. She threw the onion pieces into a hot frying pan where they hissed back at her. According to the recipe they should be finely chopped. The asymmetrical lumps looked more like the shapes Chloe had produced as a toddler when left to her own devices with paper and safety scissors.

She sliced the next onion with exaggerated care and flipped the switch for the extractor hood above the hob. It was too still in the kitchen. Too hot. She plucked a papery clove of garlic from a nearby pot.

Only one more left.

That gave her an idea, stunning in its simplicity. She turned to face Mark with what she hoped was a cool stare. He sat looking straight back at her, waiting.

'I need to go out—to get some things I can't find at the local shops from the big supermarket. Is there anything you'd like me to get you that's not on the shopping list?' She nodded to indicate a long pad hanging on a nail where she always listed store cupboard items as soon as they'd run out. She even managed a smile on the last few words, so delighted was she at the thought of getting out of the house and into fresh, uncomplicated air.

He just lifted his shoulders and let them drop again. 'Nope. Nothing in particular.'

Most housekeepers would be glad of having a boss with such an easygoing nature, but the contrast with her own jangled emotions just made her want to club him over the head with his large wooden pepper mill. She strode to the other side of the room and snatched her handbag from where it hung on the back of a chair.

It wasn't more than a minute later that she was sitting in the driver's seat of her car, turning the key in the ignition.

Nothing.

'Come on, old girl!' she crooned, rubbing the dashboard. 'Don't let me down now. You are my ticket out of here—at least for the afternoon.' She tried again, pumping her foot frantically on the pedal. Her old banger coughed, threatening to fire up, then thought better of it. She slapped the steering wheel with the flat of her hands.

'Traitor.'

She collected her bag and strutted back into the kitchen, chin in the air. Mark was still sitting on the stool, finishing his coffee.

'Problems?'

'Car won't start. I'll have to go another day, after I've had the old heap looked at.'

Mark stood up and pulled a bunch of keys from his pocket. 'Come on, then.'

'What?'

'I'll take you.'

'No, it's okay. Honestly. You're busy.'

'No problem,' he said with that lazy grin of his, the one straight out of a toothpaste ad. 'I could do with getting away from my desk and letting things settle in my head, anyway.'

Ellie groaned inwardly. Now the afternoon was going to be torture rather than escape. She followed him reluctantly to his car. It was a sleek, gunmetal-grey Aston Martin. She could almost see his chest puff out in pride as he held the passenger door open for her.

Boys and their toys. What was the theory about men with flash cars?

Mark didn't need to take his eyes off the road to know that Ellie had shifted position and was now staring out of the window. He was aware of every sigh, every fidget. And her body language was yelling at him in no uncertain terms—*back off*!

What if she'd been right all those weeks ago when she'd shouted at him? He'd given the whole thing a lot of thought. Did he live in a 'Mark bubble'? A self-absorbed little universe where he was the sun and all revolved around him? Did he now waltz through life—well, relationships—without a backward glance?

If he did, it hadn't always been that way. His

thoughts slid inevitably to Helena. That woman had a lot to answer for. He'd have stayed by her side until his dying day. Hadn't he promised as much, dressed in a morning suit in front of hundreds of witnesses? Stupidly, he'd thought she'd felt the same way, but it turned out that he'd confused *loyalty* with *neediness*. She'd stuck around while he'd been useful and then, when he'd needed her to be the strong one for a change, she'd walked away.

And he hadn't seen it coming. Before the news had broken, he'd been thinking to himself that Helena had finally reached a place where she seemed less troubled, and he'd even been thinking about broaching the subject of having kids.

But then his first management company had gone belly-up because he'd made the same mistake with Nuclear Hamster. He'd really believed in them, had remortgaged his house, emptied his savings accounts to give them a start in the business. Friends had warned him not to take a cut of the net profit in their first contract when most managers took a percentage of the gross. The album had sold well, but on tour they'd run up huge bills—having parties, chartering private jets—and at the end of the day fifteen percent of no profit whatsoever and creditors knocking at the door meant he'd had to declare himself bankrupt. It hadn't been any comfort at all to know he'd walked into a trap of his own making because he made the mistake of trusting people he'd got close to.

He'd thought Helena's coolness, her distance, had been because she'd been worried about money. Heck, he'd been terrified himself. He'd known how expensive it was to take a rock band to court. But what else could he have done? He couldn't have let one bunch of freeloaders ruin his career and reputation, could he?

All at once the love and care she'd demanded from him for the previous four years had been deemed suffocating, and without the nice lifestyle there hadn't been much incentive to stick around. Helena had declared she needed space, that it was time to stand on her own two feet. You name the cliché and she'd flung it at him.

Of course that hadn't lasted more than two minutes. She'd soon found herself a rich TV executive to pander to her needs and the whole cycle had started all over again. Oh, she'd sniffed around again when he'd won his court case and rebuilt his company, but he hadn't even returned her calls. If she couldn't stand by him through the tough times—through living in a bedsit and eating beans on toast for months, through losing all his so-called friends and business associates—then she didn't deserve even a minute of his attention. He'd surprised himself at his own hardness.

And it gave him a grim sense of satisfaction to know she'd burned her bridges too soon. Half a ton of debts was all she'd been entitled to in the divorce proceedings. If she'd waited a couple of years before she'd bailed she would have done a lot better for herself.

Light drizzle peppered the windscreen. He watched it build into a pattern of dots. A flick of a switch round the steering wheel created a blank canvas where a new and completely different design was free to form.

He turned off the main road into a narrow country lane and determined to concentrate on the road in front of him. The Aston Martin was heaven to drive. Normally he didn't have time to sit back and enjoy it, always hurrying from A to B, always focusing on the destination instead of the journey. Ellie's presence as his passenger made him want to savour the experience.

The trip to the supermarket had been fun, in a way. Spending time with her on neutral territory had been different. She'd relaxed a little. He felt strangely comfortable pushing the trolley along behind her as she'd browsed the aisles, squeezing avocados and reading the backs of packets. Of course he'd had no idea what she was doing half the time, or what she'd make with the assortment of ingredients she'd flung in the trolley, but the fact *she* knew gave her an air of wisdom.

The raindrops on the windscreen got fatter and rounder. They were going to have to get a move on if they were going to get home before it tipped down. The purr of the engine seduced him into going faster. He was pretty confident in his driving skills and was starting to become familiar with these lanes, anticipating the sweep and curve of the overgrown hedgerows as they got closer to Larkford. He glanced at Ellie. She was staring straight ahead, a grim look on her face.

He swung round a corner into a flat, fairly straight stretch of road and picked up speed. He loved the growl of satisfaction as the engine worked harder. It responded with eagerness to every nudge on the accelerator.

The sky darkened and the wild hedgerows whipped past, clawing at the car as if they were jealous. Inside the low-slung sports car the air was full of static. He could almost feel the crackles arcing from Ellie's thigh as he changed gear, his knuckles threatening to stroke the warm denim of her jeans.

A pheasant burst from the hedge in a flurry of feathers. He heard Ellie's sharp intake of breath, and out of the corner of his eye saw her grip the edge of her seat. After he'd braked slightly, he turned his head fully towards her, meaning to reassure her.

'Mark...' The trembling plea hardly escaped her lips.

'It's okay. We weren't going to—'

'Mark...please...!'

The urgency in her voice panicked him. Her face was frozen in stark horror. He looked back down the lane and his stomach lurched as he saw the farm vehicle pulling out of a concealed entrance. He squeezed the brake harder, slowing to a smooth crawl, and allowed the rust-speckled tractor to rumble past them. He pulled away and silently congratulated himself on not even leaving a skid mark on the tarmac.

'Stop the car.' Her voice was faint, but determined.

'But we're almost home.'

Her voice came in breathy gasps. 'I said...stop the car...I want to get out.'

Mark's faced creased into a scowl of disbelief as Ellie scrabbled at the door lever, desperate to free the lock. He pulled deftly into a passing place. Before the car had fully stopped Ellie had popped her seat belt and staggered out of the car, stumbling forward, gulping in damp country air. She was shaking, her whole body quivering.

Mark sat paralysed in the driver's seat, too stunned to move. Then, coming to his senses, he unbuckled himself and ran after her. It didn't take long to catch her as she straggled up the lane, half in a dream state.

He grabbed her wrist and pulled her firmly to him. Her head lodged just under his chin, and for a split second she moulded against him before pushing him away again.

He should have remembered she was surprisingly strong for a woman so soft and rounded-looking. He managed to grab one of her wrists before she darted off again down the middle of the road.

She turned to face him, fury in her eyes. 'I asked you to *stop* the car!'

Her free arm waved around wildly and she pulled and tugged the other, trying to twist it out of his grasp.

Mark stared at her. What on earth was wrong with her? Why such angst over a stupid tractor? Puzzled as he was, he held on to her as gently as he could without letting her run down the lane into oncoming traffic. Ellie swung towards the middle of the road as she attempted to wrench her arm away from him again, all the while pressing a flattened palm to her chest and breathing in shallow gasps.

The nasal blast of a horn pierced the air and Mark grabbed her back out of the path of an approaching car. He stumbled backwards with her until his feet were on the grassy verge, the gnarled twigs of the ancient hedgerow piercing his back.

Ellie's mouth worked against his chest. He could feel her jaw moving, feel the moist warmth of her breath through his pullover. She might have been trying to shout at him, but nothing remotely resembling a word was included in the few noises tumbling out of her mouth. Her tiny hands balled into fists and she punched him on the chest. Twice.

He might not know what was going on here—clueless, as always—but one thing was certain: whether she knew it or not, Ellie needed him in this moment. She needed someone to be angry with, someone to fall apart on. And, hey, wasn't he the most likely candidate to light her fuse at the moment, anyway? He might as well take the brunt of whatever this was.

No way was he about to brush this situation off with a joke. It was time to face the challenge he'd walked away from so many times over the last decade. No amount of sequins or cash would defuse the situation. He was just going to have to be 'real' too. He hoped to God he still had it in him.

She was still trying to push away from him, but now the tears came. She gulped and cried and sobbed as if she'd never stop. He swallowed rising fear at such intense emotion, whispered words of comfort in her ear and waited for the squall to wear itself out. Eventually the sobbing became shallower and she surrendered to it, burying her face in his jumper. All those crying sessions with Kat now just seemed like practice sessions leading up to this moment—and he was thoroughly glad of the training.

How he wished he could do something to ease her pain. It was so raw. Perhaps if he held her long enough, tight enough, something of him she needed would seep through the damp layers between them in a kind of osmosis. He wanted to make up the missing parts of her. Loan her his uncanny ability to shield himself from everything, to feel nothing he didn't want to.

His fingers stilled in her curls as he thought what a poor exchange it would be. He had nothing to give her, really. She could teach him so much more. Her determination, her ability to say what she felt whether she wanted to or not. She knew how to live, while he only knew how to dazzle.

The sky turned to lavender-grey as afternoon retreated. Mark let the thump of his heart beat away the minutes as Ellie became motionless against him, pulling in deep breaths. She peeled her face from his chest, the ridge marks of the wool knit embedded on her hot cheek, half blinded by the thick tears clogging her eyelashes. Mark held her face tenderly in his palms and looked deep into her pink-rimmed eyes, desperate to soothe away the tempest he didn't understand.

Ellie stared back at him.

He could see weariness, despair, the ragged depths of her soul, but also a glimmer of something else. Her eyes were pleading with him, asking him to give her hope.

His voice was soft and low. 'Tell me.'

It was not a demand, but a request. Ellie's lips quivered and a tear splashed onto his hand. Never taking his gaze from her, he led her to the passenger door and sat her on the edge of the leather seat, crouching to stay on her level, keeping her hands tight between his.

Ellie let out a shuddering sigh as she closed her eyes. Her top lip tucked under her bottom teeth. He could see she was searching for words. Her pale green eyes flipped open and looked straight into his.

Her voice was low and husky from crying. 'It was just a panic attack. I get them sometimes... Sorry.'

He wasn't sure he was buying this. A forgotten voice inside his head—his conscience, maybe?—poked and prodded him and dared him not to let this slide. Whatever she needed to say was important. And it was important she said it now. So he did the only thing he could do. He waited.

For a few minutes no one spoke, no one moved, and then she dipped her head and spoke in a low, hoarse voice. 'My husband and daughter were killed in a car accident on a wet day like this,' she said, looking down at their intertwined fingers.

'I'm so sorry.'

Well, that was probably the most inadequate sentence he'd ever uttered in his life, but it was all he could come up with. Lame or not, it was the truth. He was sorry for her. Sorry for the lives that had been cut off too early. Sorry he hadn't even known she'd been married. He squeezed her hands tighter.

'It was almost four years ago now. We were driving home from a day out shopping. I'd bought Chloe a pair of sparkly pink party shoes. She never even got to wear them…'

There was nothing he could say. Nothing he could do but let her talk.

'The police said it was joyriders. They'd been daring each other to go faster and faster… There was a head-on collision at a sharp bend on a country lane. Nobody could stop in time—the road was too wet.'

How awful. Such a tragedy. He wondered how she'd found out. Had the police come knocking at her door? A word she'd muttered earlier came back to haunt him.

We?

He rubbed the back of her hand with his thumb. 'You were in the car too?'

She sniffed and hiccupped at the same time, then looked at him, a deep gnawing ache in her eyes. 'I was driving.'

Mark pulled her back into his arms. He could feel her salty tears on his own cheek, smell her shampoo as she laid her head on his shoulder. He closed his eyes and drank in her gentle fragrance. Her soft ringlets cushioned his face, a corkscrew curl tickling his nose.

'Feel,' she said. At first he didn't understand, but she pulled his hand away from her back and placed it on the right side of her head. Where there should have been smooth bone beneath skin and hair there was a deep groove in her scalp. Mark stroked the hair there too. Gently. So gently.

'The police told me there wasn't anything I could have done,' she said quietly. 'But I don't remember. And it's like having a huge question mark hanging over my life. I'm never going to know that for sure. What if I could have reacted a split second faster or turned the wheel another way?'

She drifted off into silence again.

His voice left him. He'd never imagined...

And he realised how stupid he'd been now. He should have curbed the adolescent urge to show off around her, racing his car down the winding lanes. All this was his fault.

Ellie sighed and relaxed into him. It felt perfect, as if she'd been carved to fit there. In recent weeks he'd not been able to stop himself fantasising about holding her close like this, kissing her brow, her nose, her lips. Well, not exactly like this. But he knew if he gave in to the fierce pull of his own desire now he would desecrate the moment, and he knew it would never come again.

She stirred, pulling back from him slightly to drag her hands across her face in an effort to mop up the congealed tears.

'I'm sorry.' Her voice was so faint it was barely a whisper.

'No. *I'm* sorry. For starting all this in the first place…'

'You couldn't have known.' All the fizzing, spitting irritation she'd held in her eyes every time she'd looked at him since the night of the party was gone.

'Well, I know now. And I am sorry. For anything—everything—I did to upset you. You must know I would never do that on purpose, however much of an idiot I may seem sometimes.'

Her mouth curved imperceptibly and her eyes never left his. He felt a banging in his chest just as hard as when she'd been thumping on it with her fist. He stood up and rested his hand on the door to steady himself.

'Let's go home.'

CHAPTER SEVEN

NO LIGHTS were on in the drawing room. The firelight flickered, playing with the shadows on the wall. Mark sat in his favourite chair and savoured the aromatic warmth of his favourite whisky as it smouldered in his throat. The only sounds were the cracking of the wood on the fire and the laborious ticking of the antique clock in the corner. Ellie had gone to bed early, and he was left to relentlessly mull over the events of the afternoon.

They had driven back to Larkford in complete silence, but it had been different from the combustible atmosphere of their outward journey. The calm after the storm. He hadn't wanted to jinx the easy comfort by opening his big mouth. He hadn't been sure if Ellie was lost in the recent past, or plumbing the depths of earlier memories, and it hadn't felt right to ask.

The vivid evening sky had deepened to a velvety indigo by the time they'd drawn up in front of the house. Mark had carried the shopping in, forbidding Ellie to help, and had suggested she have a long hot bath. He'd realised, as he'd struggled with the dilemma of where to put the dried pasta they'd just bought, that he didn't have a clue where stuff went in his own kitchen. He'd got down to a shortlist of two possible cupboards when he'd heard the unmistakable sound of Ellie's bare feet on the tiles.

'Top left,' she said quietly.

'Thanks,' he replied, shutting the cupboard door he was holding open and walking to another one on the other side of the room. When he put the linguine away next to the other bags of pasta he turned to look at her. She was dressed in a ratty pink towelling robe that was slightly longer at one side than the other. Her hair was wet, the blonde curls darkened and subdued, but struggling to bounce back. Her face was pink and scrubbed, eyes bright. He had never seen her look so gorgeous.

She walked towards him. His heart thumped so loudly in his chest he thought she was bound to hear it. But she didn't stop and stare at him. She didn't laugh. Instead, she was smiling, eyes hesitant but warm. He was hypnotised.

'Thank you, Mark. For everything.'

She was only a foot away from him now, and she stood on tiptoes and placed an exquisitely delicate kiss on his cheek.

'Goodnight,' she said gently, and she headed for the door.

'Night,' he replied absently, still feeling the sweet sting of her lips on his cheek.

Now, hours later, he could still feel the tingle of that kiss. He took another sip of the whisky and rubbed the spot with the tips of his fingers.

At least he understood that tragic look in her eyes now. Ellie was haunted; the ghosts of her lost family still followed her. She had lived through more hurt than he could possibly imagine and yet she had found the strength to carry on living.

He looked back at his own life over the last decade and berated himself for his self-centredness and cowardice. He'd been afraid to let anyone close because he'd allowed one gold-digging woman to discolour his view of the rest of her sex. Instead of moving on and growing from the experience he'd sulked and cut himself off from any possibility of being hurt again, learning to cauterise the wounds with sarcastic humour and a don't-care attitude. He'd taken the easy way out.

Not like Ellie. She was brave. How did you pick yourself up again and keep on living after something like that?

He downed the rest of the whisky and sat for a long time, holding the empty glass. Once upon a time he'd written her off as fragile, but she was possibly the strongest person he'd ever met.

Be careful what you wish for, Ellie thought, as she exited the kitchen through the French windows and took her usual route round the garden. All those months in Barkleigh, longing for breathing space, the chance to be on her own without anyone fussing…

Well, now she had air and space in bucketloads. And for a while it had been good, and she thought she'd escaped that creeping sense of loneliness that had seeped into her bones at the cottage, but it had just followed her here.

Okay, most of the time it was pretty perfect. Like now, when the early-morning sun was gently warming her skin as she wandered a subconscious route round the gardens, her habitual cup of tea cradled in her upturned hands, but sometimes all this room, this space, it was a little…well…

She shook her head. She was just being silly.

It was hardly surprising she was finding life a little solitary. Only a couple of days after the disastrous trip to the supermarket Mark had disappeared, mumbling something about putting a big deal together, and she hadn't seen him for more than a fortnight. She guessed he was staying up at his flat in London, going to meetings all day. She tried not to speculate on what he might get up to at night.

The view of the Thames from his flat must be stunning, the vibe of the warm summer nights exciting, but if she had a choice of living in a crowded city, full of exhaust fumes and scary commuters, and being here at Larkford, she knew what she'd pick.

She kicked her flip-flops off as she reached the edge of the lawn and sighed in pleasure as the soles of her feet met soft grass that was dry, but still cool from the early-morning dew.

It was silly, but she couldn't shake the feeling that Mark was staying away deliberately. Maybe he was embarrassed. He wouldn't be the first person not to be able to handle her unique circumstances. She'd tried to run away from that feeling too, hadn't she? And now it had tracked her down and turned up on her doorstep.

She looked around the garden. The roses on the wrought-iron arches that lined the main path were in flower, a variety with frilly shell-pink petals. The smell was fantastic.

She sighed. Well, if Mark wanted to stay away, she couldn't stop him. It just seemed such a pity he was missing how beautiful his home looked. Every day there was something new to admire in the garden, another flower opening its buds or shooting out new green leaves. Maybe Mark wasn't the sort of person to notice these kind of things, but even if you didn't notice the details you couldn't help but feel rested here.

When she went back inside the house and checked her laptop she found an e-mail from Mark, and this time, instead of giving another boring, bland reply, she decided to add a little bit about Larkford—about the rose walk and how the wisteria on the back of the house was fairly dripping with flowers, how the hazy summer mornings burnt off into hot, bright afternoons. At least he wouldn't miss the magic of his house totally, even if he wasn't here to see it for himself.

Just as she was about to turn the laptop off she heard a ping, announcing the arrival of an e-mail. Thinking it might be from Ginny, informing her of the latest in a long line of pregnancy-related stories about absent-mindedness, she almost ignored it, but at the last minute she clicked on the little window and opened up the message.

She blinked and opened her eyes a little wider. It was from Mark. He must be online right now.

Hi Ellie
Thanks for the update on the plumbing situation. I'm sure you'll be glad to have your own space when the repairs are finished in your apartment. Feel free to decorate as you'd like.
I'm glad the wisteria is stunning and the roses are

happy!!! I didn't realise you were a poet as well as a housekeeper ;-)
Mark.

What a cheek! Still, she couldn't erase the image of Mark's devil-may-care smile as she read it, and she was smiling too when she typed back her reply.

Fine. Now I know my boss is a Philistine I won't bother sending any similar observations with my next message!

Of course he couldn't leave it at that. And a rapid e-mail battle ensued. Ellie was laughing out loud when she finally admitted defeat and switched the laptop off. Maybe he was busy, after all. Maybe this whole 'deal' thing wasn't just an excuse to avoid her.

And that was how communication continued the next week or so. The e-mails got less businesslike and more chatty. Mark always added winky faces made out of colons and semi-colons—Sam would have said that he used far too many exclamation marks—and Ellie forgot her threat not to tell him anything about Larkford and ended up describing the way the wonderful house looked in the pale dawn light, losing herself in the images and getting all flowery about it…

And Mark, true to form, would reply with a

teasing quip and burst her lyrical little bubble, causing her to laugh out loud and send back something equally pithy. She decided it was nice to communicate with someone who didn't remind her constantly of what she'd been like before the accident, who just accepted her for who she was now and didn't patronise her. He wasn't just her boss now; he was an ally.

But she knew he couldn't be any more than that. And that was fine, because that was exactly how she wanted it. Really, it was.

London late at night was stunning. Mark pressed his forehead against the plate-glass wall that filled one side of his living room and used his own shadow to block out the reflection of his flat so he could see the city beyond. Multi-coloured lights blinked on the black river below, endlessly dancing but never wearying.

When he'd bought this place he hadn't thought he'd get tired of this view, but lately he'd found himself wanting to trade it in for something else. Maybe a leafy square in Fitzrovia or a renovated warehouse near the docks?

He decided to distract himself from his restlessness by turning on the TV, but everything seemed pointless, so he wandered into his bedroom, crashed so hard onto the bed that it murmured in complaint, then picked up the book on his bedside table. *A Beginner's Guide to Head Injuries.* Only one more chapter to go and he'd be finished.

He got it now. Why Ellie had moments where she zoned out, why she forgot common words. It wasn't just that she was scatterbrained. Not that it mattered, anyway. And he wasn't entirely sure that *all* of Ellie's unique qualities were down to a rather nasty bump on the head. He had the feeling that even if the head injury could be factored out of the equation she'd still be pretty unique.

He read to the end of the bibliography and put the book back where he'd got it from. He hadn't checked his e-mail yet this evening, had he? And he had started to look forward to Ellie's slightly off-on-a-tangent e-mails. She had a way of making him feel as if he were right there at Larkford, with her little stories about village life and descriptions of which plants were in flower in the garden.

Bluebells.

In her last e-mail she'd said that she'd seen a carpet of bluebells in the woodland at the fringes of the estate. Although he'd never been a man to watch gardening programmes, or take long country walks to 'absorb nature', he'd suddenly wanted to stand in the shade of an old oak tree and see the blue haze of flowers for himself. He wanted to see

Ellie smile and turn to him, as if she were sharing a secret with him...

No.

He couldn't think that way. He liked Ellie. He respected her. Hell, he was even attracted to her—majorly—but he couldn't go down that path.

It had been a long time since he'd held a woman in such high regard. And that was why this was dangerous. All the things he thought about Ellie... Well, they were the basis for a good relationship. Friendship, compatibility, chemistry. But he couldn't risk it. And not just for himself. What about Ellie? He wasn't the man for her. She didn't need someone who would probably cause her even more pain.

He jumped off the bed and started moving. Not that he had any particular destination in mind. He just seemed to get a burst of speed whenever he thought about a certain housekeeper.

And that was why he'd stayed away from Larkford. Because he was scared of what he was starting to feel for her. Yet even then she'd burrowed even further under his skin. Staying away hadn't worked, had it?

He found himself by the window in the living room again, and placed his palm on the glass.

So why was he here? Bored and wishing he was somewhere else? If keeping his distance hadn't worked, he might as well go and enjoy the house he'd bought for himself, because that was what he really wanted to do.

He wanted to go and see the bluebells for himself.

The gentle chiming of distant church bells roused Ellie from her Saturday morning slumber. Almost subconsciously she counted the chimes, not realising when she'd started but knowing the total by the time they'd finished. Eight.

Warm sunlight filtered through the curtains. She half sat in bed and rubbed her eyes. Her mouth gaped in an unexpected yawn. She shuffled herself out of bed, threw back the curtains and drank in the beautiful morning. The plumbing in her apartment above the old stables was now all fixed and she'd moved in. While her little kitchen looked over the cobbled courtyard, her bedroom had a wonderful view over the gardens. They were glorious this morning, bursting with life. She felt decidedly lazy as she watched a bee worrying the clematis beneath her window. It seemed completely unimpressed with her and disappeared into the centre of a large purple flower.

She turned from the window, full of great ideas for an al fresco lunch, and the sun glinted off the picture frame on the windowsill. She stopped to look at it, head tipped on one side. The photo had been taken at Chloe's fourth birthday party. Chloe was grinning like the proverbial Cheshire cat, her freshly lit birthday cake in front of her on the table. Sam and Ellie leaned in behind her, faces warmed by the glow of the candles.

They all looked so happy. She kissed her index finger and pressed it onto the glass where Chloe's smile was. It had been a wonderful day.

The memory came easily and painlessly now. She smiled as she recalled the incessant squealing of little girls and the pungent smell of blown-out birthday candles. Chloe had spent the whole party bouncing up and down in excitement, even when she was devouring pink birthday cake. She remembered Sam's smile later that evening, when he'd silently beckoned her to come and look at Chloe. They'd crept through the post-party devastation into the lounge and found her fast asleep on the sofa, chocolate smeared all over her face and clutching the doll they had given her in her sticky hands.

She'd found it so hard to look at this photo in the past. Even so, she'd kept it on prominent display as a kind of punishment. What she was guilty of, she wasn't sure.

Being here when they weren't. Being alive.

Since their deaths she had lived life as if she was walking backwards—too terrified of the unfamiliar territory ahead to turn and face the future. She'd blindly shuffled through each day, just trying to keep going without meeting disaster again. Pain was to be avoided at all costs. No risk. No attachments. But no love, either. Her smile dissolved completely.

What would Sam think of the way she'd been coping?

She knew exactly what he would say. Her face creased into a frown. She could almost see his hazel eyes scowling at her, the trademark tuft of wayward hair slipping over his forehead.

Life should never feel small, Ellie.

That was what he'd always told her. Despite her secure family background she'd always been a shy child, but Sam had seen beyond the reserve. He'd asked her to play tag while the other schoolchildren had ignored the quiet girl on the wooden bench with her coat pulled round her. She'd been desperate to join in, but much too scared to get up and ask in case they laughed and ran away. But Sam had won her over with his gentle smile as he'd grabbed her hand and pulled her off the bench. Within minutes she'd been running after him, the wind in her hair and a smile beneath her rosy cheeks.

It had always been like that with Sam. He had encouraged her to dare, to believe. To make life count.

'Sorry, sweetheart,' she whispered, the glass misting as she talked to his face in the photo.

She sighed and pulled her tatty robe from its

hook on the back of the door. Since the incident in Mark's car, she'd felt different. Liberated, somehow. Perhaps the whole embarrassing scenario had done some good after all. She'd been clutching on to her grief for so long, and her reaction to Mark's driving had finally provided an outlet—the last great emotional lurch in her rollercoaster stay at Larkford so far.

Ever since she had got here she'd been plunging into some forgotten feeling—panic, shame, anger—desire, even. She'd experienced them all in vivid richness. And somehow Mark Wilder stood in the middle of the maelstrom. Instead of making her feel safe, as Sam had, he made her feel nervous, excited and confused all at once. It was as if the universe had shifted a little when she wasn't looking and she suddenly found herself off-balance when he was around.

Yet he'd surprised her with his understanding and sensitivity. Not once had she felt judged for her behaviour that afternoon. It had been so nice to sink into his strong arms and know that she wasn't alone.

She tied the sash of her gown in a lumpy knot. With a heavy sigh she acknowledged that her relationship with Mark had changed in that moment. A boundary had been crossed as she had stood shivering against him in the lane.

She'd also noticed a change in Mark in the

couple of weeks since he'd started living at Larkford again. But the way he was treating her now made her feel uncomfortable in a completely new way. Now he came home more evenings than he stayed away, even though the hour's drive from London could double if the motorway traffic was bad. He was always witty and entertaining, and she no longer fumed at his humour, but laughed along with it. There was even the odd quip at her expense, but it was a gentle nudge rather than sarcastic teasing.

He obviously thought she was too fragile to be toyed with now. What a pity, because suddenly she was ready to find out if there was an upside to all these impulses and strong emotions she'd inherited from the accident, to see if love and joy and happiness might just be brighter and more multicoloured than they had ever been before.

Ellie was working on a salad for lunch when she heard a car pulling up outside. That was odd. She'd assumed Mark had been sleeping late, because he'd had to attend a function the night before, but that sounded like his car. She blinked in surprise when he strode into the kitchen a few moments later.

'You're up early,' she said, inspecting a bottle of rice vinegar to see how much was left—a complete cover for the fact her insides were doing the tango.

He still made her catch her breath every time he walked into the room, but it was different. It wasn't all about hormones fizzing and pure physical reactions. Somehow those sensations had grown beyond the superficial things they were, and now she sometimes felt as if there was a dull ache inside her chest that grew stronger the closer he was to her.

'I had things to do,' he said.

She noticed the little shopping bag he was carrying with the logo of a high-end electrical store and shook her head. '*More* gadgets?' He was a typical man in that respect.

Instead of giving her a boyish grin and proudly showing off his latest piece of kit, he just looked a little awkward as he nodded his answer to her question.

'Actually, I bought this for you.'

Ellie put the vinegar bottle down on the counter and stared at him. 'For me?'

Mark handed her the bag and she pulled a small glossy box from it. A handheld computer. She stared at it, hardly knowing what to say.

'You got me a PDA?'

He nodded again, still unusually serious and silent. 'You can link it up to the laptop and keep all your calendars and notes with you wherever you go. It even has a voice recorder function. I thought it might be…you know…useful when you need to make a note of something in a hurry, before you forget.'

Ellie felt like crying. She hadn't even thought of using something like this, but it was perfect. Just what she needed.

'Thank you,' she said, her voice wavering. 'Why did you…? I mean, what made you think of getting me this?'

He shuffled backwards. 'Just something I read…'

She frowned at him. Where was the normally cocky and devil-may-care Mark Wilder? Why was he looking so sheepish?

Oh, great. He'd been researching her condition—probably read up on it on the Internet. While it was still an incredibly sweet gesture, it just confirmed that his view of her had changed. Now she was just the poor brain-damaged housekeeper who couldn't keep her facts straight without the help of a bit of technology.

She wanted to be cross with him, but she couldn't rev up the energy. Instead she put the box back in the bag and stowed it in an empty cupboard. 'I'll have a look properly later.'

'You like it? You think it'll be useful?'

He looked so hopeful, so eager, that she couldn't help but smile and nod. 'It's wonderful. It'll be a big help.'

And it would. There was no need to be sad

about a tiny computer just because it signalled what she knew already—that anything more than a professional relationship between them was a total impossibility.

Mark grinned. Suddenly he was back to his old self: cheeky, confident…impossible. Ellie picked up a cook's knife and went back to chopping something—anything—to keep her mind occupied and her pulse even. But after a few moments he walked over to the chopping board and looked over her shoulder. Ellie fanned her face. It was very warm. Had he closed the window? She glanced over at the French doors, but the embroidered muslin panels were still billowing gently.

'What are you cooking?'

Ellie put the knife down a little too quickly. It clattered on the worktop. Despite the fact her brain told her the crush she had on Mark was pointless, the neural pathways carrying that information to her body seemed to have gone on strike.

'Vietnamese salad,' she said, the words tumbling out.

'Which is—?' He waved his hand in a circular motion as her mouth moved soundlessly.

'Chicken and noodles and a few vegetables, with a sweet chilli dressing,' she replied, a wobbly finger pointing to each of the ingredients in turn.

Great! Now she was babbling like a bad TV chef.

His cheek twitched, yet his face remained a mask of cool composure. 'Hot stuff, then?'

Under different circumstances, Ellie would have thought he was flirting with her. Heat licked at the soles of her feet. She swallowed. 'It depends on the size of the chilli.'

The look her gave her was positively wicked. 'And you girls try and tell us boys that size doesn't matter.'

Ellie almost choked.

Mark picked up the half-chopped chilli from the chopping board. 'How hot is this one?'

Ellie tried very hard to focus on the bright red chilli and not on Mark's warm brown eyes.

'Medium, sort of. The small ones are the hottest, funnily enough.'

Stop babbling! He already knows that. Everybody knows that!

She bit her lip and turned to peel the outer stem off a stick of lemongrass.

'Do you want this back?'

She felt Mark's breath warm on the back of her neck as he stood close behind her. She failed to still the tiny shiver that rippled up her spine as she turned slightly to take the chilli back from him.

'Thank you.'

She carefully eased it from his grasp, avoiding brushing his fingers, and offered up a silent *hallelujah* as Mark stepped back and headed for the door.

'I'm going for a shower.'

'Okay. Let me know if you want any of this when you come out.'

He ran his hand through his hair and rubbed the corner of one eye with his thumb. That early-morning start must be catching up with him.

But then she realised what he was about to do. 'Don't put your—'

Mark yelped, screwed his eyes shut tight and slapped his hands to his face. She rushed over to him, wincing in sympathy. She peeled the hand from his face and led him over to one of the breakfast stools, where she ordered him to sit down. His right eye was squeezed shut and watering.

'Try and open your eyes,' she said gently.

'Very funny!'

'I mean it. If you can manage to open them and blink a bit, the eye can do its job and wash the chilli juice away. It works a lot faster than sitting there with your fingers pressing into your eyeballs, making it worse!'

Mark groaned again, removed his hand and attempted to prise his watery eyelids apart.

'Wait there!' she ordered, dashing to the sink and washing her hands vigorously with washing-up liquid and scrubbing under her nails with a little brush.

'Here, let me see.'

She moved in close and delicately placed a thumb on the smooth skin near Mark's eye. He flinched.

'Sorry! Did I hurt you?'

'Um...no, it's okay.'

She gently pulled downwards, helping to open his eye. 'It looks a bit pink. Is it still stinging? Try blinking a few more times.'

'It's fading now, thank you, Nurse. How did you know what to do?'

She blushed. 'You think with a memory like mine that I haven't done this to myself a million times?'

Mark's laugh was deep and throaty. He blinked a few more times, opened his good eye, then attempted to do the same with the other, but it stayed stubbornly at half-mast.

Ellie's partial smile evaporated as she became conscious of the warmth radiating from him. They were practically nose to nose. He was sitting on the stool, one long leg braced against the floor, the other hooked on the bottom rung. She was standing between his legs, only inches from his chest. She knew she should move. Mark was looking back at her through bleary eyes. She picked a spot on the floor between her feet and stared at it.

'You're lucky,' she said, succeeding in inching backwards slightly.

Try not to look at him.

'You only touched the chilli briefly. It would have been much worse if you'd been chopping them...'

Mark caught her hand as she attempted to shuffle back further. She made the mistake of looking up. A soft, tender look was in his eyes, despite the fact that one eyeball was still pink and watery.

'Thank you, Ellie.' The sincerity in his tone was making her feel all quivery.

She managed to shift her gaze to her hand, still covered by his. Static electricity lifted the hairs on her arm.

'That's—that's all right,' she stammered. Her hand jerked from his as she shook herself loose. She turned and headed for the door. 'I'll go and have that shower now, then,' she added.

Perhaps a cold one.

She started to scuttle off down the passageway.

'Ellie...?' he called after her, a laugh underscoring his words.

The urge to keep going was powerful, but she turned and popped her head back through the open door. 'Yes?'

Mark was grinning at her. She had the sudden sinking feeling she didn't want to know why.

'*I* was going to have a shower, remember? *You* were cooking.'

Ellie closed her eyes gently and darted a moist tongue over her bottom lip, trying to work out how to salvage the situation. She looked at Mark with her best matter-of-fact expression. 'Of course.'

For some reason he looked very pleased with himself. He wasn't going to tease her about this for months to come, was he? What if he guessed it was him who had got her all in a fluster?

Once her cotton wool legs had taken her back to the chopping board she set about peeling the garlic, trying to block Mark's view of her shaking hands with her body. She heard the scrape of his stool across the floor as he rose from his seat. Every part of her body strained to hear his movements as he left the room. She stripped the skin off a clove of garlic, leaving it vulnerable and naked, and listened to Mark whistling something chirpy as he bounded up the stairs at least two at a time.

CHAPTER EIGHT

'MARK!'

His head snapped up. Nicole, his PA, stood with hands on hips, a buff folder clutched in one hand, scowling hard. This wasn't good news.

'Huh?'

'What is wrong with you this morning? That has to be the fifth time I've caught you admiring the London skyline while ignoring every word I say. You're making me feel like my old maths teacher, Mrs McGill.'

Mark stopped staring through the glass wall of his office and turned to face Nicole fully. She was right. He hadn't been paying attention. But now that he was she still wasn't making any sense.

'What?'

'She was always throwing chalk at Billy Thomas for staring out the window during double algebra. I mean it, Mark! If you make me sound like Mrs McGill I'm going to do something drastic.'

He hunched over his desk and scribbled feverishly away on the pad in front of him. Nicole flopped into the chair on the other side of the desk and massaged her temple with her free hand.

'What are you doing now? I'm feeling too grotty for your stupid games.'

When he had scrawled a handful of lines, he ripped the sheet off and thrust it in Nicole's direction. She snatched it from his hand and started to read it out loud.

'"I will not daydream in Mrs McGill's class. I will not daydream in—" Very funny!'

He easily dodged her missile as she crumpled the paper into a ball and threw it back at him. He did the puppy-dog thing with his eyes he knew she could never resist.

'Sorry, Miss.'

'You'd better be! You were saying something about pushing the record company for a three-sixty-degree contract for the new band's next deal, and then you just drifted off.'

'Sorry, Nic. I promise I'm listening now.'

He rested his elbows on the desk and propped his chin on his fists, deliberately focusing on her and only her.

'And I need to know what you want to do about this video shoot. We've only got five days before we leave for the Caribbean, and Kat's in a state because Razor went AWOL. The director has changed his mind about one of the locations, and the stylist has had a strop and isn't taking any of my calls.'

Mark did his best to listen as Nicole continued to brief him on the latest string of disasters to hit the upcoming shoot. It had been a nightmare from start to finish. He was starting to wish they'd opted for the other treatment, which had involved lots of time on a soggy moor in Scotland. When they'd set it up he'd been looking forward to going to Antigua. He'd planned on taking a few days off after the shoot—the closest thing to a holiday he was going to get this year.

But now the date was looming close he was starting to wish he could wriggle out of it. He didn't want to leave Larkford. A week on the other side of the planet would be a week away from Ellie. Coming into London was different. He was away for the day, but in the evening he would be stranded on the M25 in the rush-hour traffic with a smile on his face, knowing he was on the way home.

Home. Ellie had made his house a home. He loved arriving back there and seeing a warm glow in the windows instead of faceless black. He would park his car, walk through the door and find Ellie pottering in the kitchen, cooking up something fabulous.

He had started to fantasise that she was there

waiting for him, not because he paid her to, but because she wanted to be.

She worked so hard. Now he'd read up on brain injuries he understood how difficult it must be for her. And she never seemed to want a day off to go home. Perhaps there were too many memories waiting for her there. But it would be good if he could get her to relax now she had the household running like clockwork. He'd even cover the cost of a holiday if he thought she'd accept it from him. He almost felt guilty for jetting off to the Caribbean and leaving her behind.

Maybe there was something he could do about that…

Nicole slapped her folder down so hard that the papers on Mark's desk lifted in the resultant breeze.

'If you're not going to listen, I'm going for a girlie chat with Emma at the end of the hall!'

He was only partially aware of the slam of the door and the meant-to-be-heard muttering as she click-clacked out of the office and down the hallway. He swung his chair round again and continued studying the busy city below. The Thames glinted between the mixture of glass office blocks and the pollution-stained masonry of older buildings.

The last few weeks had been both heaven and hell.

The prickly, reclusive Ellie who had arrived at Larkford in the spring was only a memory. The

Ellie he returned to each night was warm and caring and funny. Clever and resourceful. He loved hanging around the kitchen watching her cook, savouring each bite of the meal and making it last as long as possible to prolong his time in her company. He always felt a little deflated when the coffee cups were cleared away and the mechanical whooshing of the dishwasher was the only sound in the kitchen.

She was still a little shy, but it added to her charm. He loved the way she was totally original—one of a kind.

Mark stood up. The afternoon sun was bouncing off the windows of the other office blocks, giving the whole city a warm yellow glow. He took a moment to process the revelation that had just hit him smack between the eyes.

He loved her.

His stomach lurched as he recognised his own vulnerability. Whether she knew it or not, that fragile woman had tremendous power over him.

But he didn't want to push her, even if he guessed she might be feeling at least some of what he was feeling. He watched a jet puff out its white trail in the clear blue sky, the plane so high up it was only a silver speck in the air. Part of him exulted at the knowledge that she found him attractive, that he put her off-balance, but another part of him ached with the uncertainty of any deeper feelings on her part.

'I need a sign!' he whispered, waiting for something to happen.

But the plane kept on its course, its trail a no-nonsense line. No writing appeared in the sky saying *Go for it*. He scanned the horizon for a hint of divine thunderbolts, but the pale clouds refused to comment.

He continued to ponder his position as he sat behind a truck on the M25 later that evening. The crawling traffic gave him plenty of time for self-analysis. He sat for many minutes trying to predict the outcome of any romantic entanglement with Ellie and decided that prophecy was not his thing. It didn't matter, anyway. Whether she loved him back or not wouldn't change how he felt about her. He would just have to be patient. Wait in this horrible limbo until a sign appeared.

Butterflies wrestled in his belly as he turned the car into his driveway. His pulse quickened as he jumped from the car and bounded up the steps to the front door. As he put the key in the lock a mouthwatering aroma assaulted his nostrils. He followed the trail into the kitchen. Ellie bobbed up from behind the kitchen counter, causing his already racing heart to skip a beat.

'That was good timing! I was just about to dish up. You're much later than you said.'

'Traffic jam,' he said absently, his eyes following her every move. She reached to get a couple of plates from the cupboard and passed them to him.

'Your PA called about an hour ago.'

Ah. He'd forgotten all about Nic, and had left the office without telling her.

'She said she will not be coming back into work until you ring and tell her she is no longer Mrs McGill—whatever that means!' said Ellie, searching for the oven gloves and finding them in the dishwasher.

Mark reckoned an apologetic lunch somewhere nice would probably help. And maybe a big bunch of flowers. Nicole's bark was worse than her bite, and he didn't know what he would do without her. His stomach complained noisily, returning him to the present.

'What's for dinner?'

Ellie opened the oven door and stood back from the blast of hot air before she reached inside to remove a scalding-hot earthenware dish. She looked very pink as she stood straight. If it wasn't for the heat from the oven, he could have sworn she was blushing.

'Shepherd's Pie.'

Mark almost dropped the plates he was holding.

'Thank you,' he mouthed to the ceiling, before following her to the table.

* * *

Ellie was in the chemist's in the village, picking up some supplies, when her mobile rang. The caller ID told her it was Mark, and she took a steadying breath before she punched the button to answer.

'Hello?'

'It's me. Are you busy?'

Ellie looked at the tube of toothpaste, a box of plasters and the hand soap in her shopping basket. 'I'm in the village shopping, but I'll be finished in a few minutes. Do you want me to come straight back?'

'Yes. I've got a bit of an emergency on my hands.'

And, without explaining anything further, he rang off. Ellie stared at the phone. Very mysterious. She quickly paid for the items in her basket and hurried back along the lane to Larkford Place, cutting through the gardens to make her journey quicker.

When she reached the back door and entered the kitchen she found it all quiet. Guessing Mark must be in his study, she dumped her shopping bag on the counter, prised off her trainers and socks—it was too hot for shoes—and headed off to find him.

He was sitting behind his desk listening to someone on the other end of the phone when she poked her head round the half-open door. She coughed gently and he motioned for her to come in and sit down, still listening to whoever it was on the line.

She sat in the small but rather comfortable leather chair on the opposite side of the desk and waited, noticing as she did so that the colour of her painted toenails clashed with the rug. He finished the call without saying much but 'mmm-hmm' and 'bye', and replaced the phone carefully in its cradle before looking at her.

'I have an idea to run past you. I hope you don't mind?'

Ellie shook her head. Although she was a bit puzzled as to why Mark would want her help with what was obviously a business problem.

'I'm due to fly to Antigua at the end of the week and my PA, vital to keeping me organised during what is likely to be a chaotic few days, has come down with the flu. I need someone to fill in for her.'

Ellie studied her toenails again. Tangerine really didn't go with the aubergine shapes on the abstract rug.

'Can't someone from the office fill in?'

'Difficult. The whole place is in turmoil with a newly signed band. Their first single is out this week and it's all hands on deck. Anyone who isn't already with a client is involved in that. I did have two people in mind, but one is on holiday and the other is pregnant and throwing up every ten minutes. I seem to have run out of employees to commandeer.'

Ellie smiled at that. Nobody to boss around? What a hardship.

When she looked up, a wolfish grin was on his lips.

'Well, *almost* run out of employees…' he added.

She didn't like the look of that smile. She felt like Little Red Riding Hood, lost in the woods. Mark's eyeballs didn't move a millimetre as he stared straight at her. Ellie began to shake her head.

No way! Don't you even think it!

He nodded in slow motion as her ringlets bounced from side to side. Without warning he sprang from his side of the desk and bounded towards her. He crouched in front of her and tugged her hands into his.

'I have got one employee who could help me out.'

Her heartbeat accelerated. It was difficult to think whilst looking into those bottomless brown eyes.

'Come on, Ellie. I know you can do this. Charlie told me about how you used to be a PA.'

Ellie tried to stammer *no,* but her mouth refused to co-operate. His eyes looked like a spaniel's. She'd bet this was the puppy-dog thing Charlie had warned her about. It would be like stamping on a poor abandoned animal if she refused. And it would be to help Mark out of a tight spot. She couldn't really do this, could she?

Mark pressed on while he had the advantage.

'Look at the way you run the house. You're quick to pick things up, and you've got bags of initiative. Even with all your challenges you seem to handle any unexpected thing I throw at you. I know this is a different ball game, but I have confidence in you. Please!'

Ellie grabbed the lifeline he had thrown at her. 'The house!' she blurted out.

Mark frowned. 'What house?'

'This one! We can't leave it unattended. Who's going to look after it?' She let out a relieved sigh and relaxed into the padded leather chair, feeling oddly deflated at her own success.

'Mrs Timms could manage for a few days. I've asked her already and she said her daughter would be able to help her out.'

Ellie sat, mouth open, trying to find another valid objection. She'd only just got used to Larkford. To go somewhere else, somewhere completely foreign—literally—and do work she wasn't used to doing. Well, the idea was just plain terrifying. And she hadn't even factored in how difficult it would be to spend days upon end in a tropical paradise working even more closely with Mark.

He was smiling at her, his voice low and rich. Ellie could feel herself slipping. 'Mrs Timms used to work here before you started. Mind you, she wasn't nearly as good—or pretty.' His eyes twinkled. 'And she smelled of peppermints and disinfectant—'

'Mark!'

'I know. Not important.'

He took hold of her hands again, eyes pleading. 'It's only for a few days. I just need someone to handle the red tape while I look after fragile egos and deal with hissy fits—and that's just the tea lady I'm talking about.'

Ellie couldn't help laughing. She suspected he could persuade her that black was white if he put his mind to it.

She folded her arms across her chest. 'I will *think* about it.'

'Basket case!'

Ellie mumbled to herself as she watched the planes taxiing back and forth in the evening haze, her nose pressed hard against the plate-glass wall of Heathrow's first class lounge. The sunset was tarnished by the pollution of the busy airport.

What an idiot to think she could do this.

She turned, leaning back on the cold window to survey her fellow travellers sprawled over the comfy sofas on the far side of the lounge. Mark was chatting to Kat and the other members of her entourage. He looked completely at ease. In fact he'd been looking pretty darn pleased with himself since she'd told him she would fill in for his sick PA at breakfast this morning.

Ellie sighed and banged the back of her head lightly against the glass. She'd made a valiant attempt to say no to Mark's offer, but she hadn't quite been able to bring herself to turn him down.

Of course her decision had everything to do with a free trip to Antigua, and nothing at all to do with spending the next few days with Mark instead of rattling round Larkford Place on her own. At least that was what she'd thought this morning. Somehow the universe had done a one-eighty between then and now. The fantasy of jetting off to a palm tree filled island in a sarong and flip-flops had fallen flat once they had arrived at the airport. Well, slightly before that, Ellie admitted, looking down at her un-flip-flopped feet and sarong-less legs.

She hadn't realised they were going to be travelling with Kat and her 'people'. Immediately she'd gone into tortoise mode, feeling she had nothing much in common with the assorted bunch of strangers. Kat seemed nice—very young, and much shorter than she'd expected.

She studied the other members of the entourage. There was a tall, burly guy with a pair of shades who she presumed was a bodyguard or something. The girl with the funky white-blonde hair had to be a make-up artist or hairdresser. But she couldn't even guess what the others did. The woman in the lurid boob tube could be Kat's personal grape-peeler for all she knew.

The young guy with the pierced nose finished telling a funny story and the whole group erupted into laughter. Ellie's eyes followed Mark's every move as he grinned away, pleased with the reaction. The funky-haired woman put a pressureless hand on his arm as she wiped a tear from her eye.

Ellie frowned and turned back to face the anonymous jets parading round the runway. Her forehead met the cool glass with a delicate thud.

Basket case.

At thirty-five-thousand feet she was still wondering what she was doing with these people. Sure, she'd been on aeroplanes before, but it had been rubber food, cramped leg room and fighting about who had the armrest. Not this. Not champagne and seats you could fit a small family into. It all seemed so foreign—yet it shouldn't. Nobody else seemed to be pining for garish seat covers and lager louts singing football songs.

She felt like an impostor. Any minute now people would start pointing and staring, and she'd be dragged back to Economy, where she belonged. This wasn't her world. What a huge mistake to think she could slide in here with Mark and find it a perfect fit.

However, the outsize chair was definitely comfy, and she sank into it, her eyelids closing of their own accord.

The next thing she was aware of was something brushing her cheek, something soft and slightly moist. She swatted it away without opening her eyes.

'Ow!'

She pulled her eyelids apart with enough force to unstick her eyelashes and squinted at the fuzzy shape in front of her. As it came into focus she realised it was Mark, and his lips were slightly pursed.

'Why are you holding your nose like that?' she asked, shifting in her seat to get a better look.

'I was trying to wake you up when you walloped me.'

'I didn't wallop. I swatted. There's a difference.' She rubbed the spot on her cheek that was still tickling her. 'And how did I end up hitting you on the nose? What were you doing that close?'

In the semi-dark of the cabin she could have sworn his face turned a shade pinker.

'I was just... Never mind what I was doing! I was waking you up because the pilot just announced we'd be landing in half an hour. I thought you'd want to get yourself together.'

She stretched her arms past her head, yawned and looked out of the window. It was so dark out there they could have been flying through a black hole.

'What time is it?'

'Our time or local time?'

'Whichever.'

'Well, it's just after midnight local time. At least we get a few extra hours to catch up on sleep.'

Ellie made a face. 'I think I could do with a whole week!'

He smiled, and she forgot to be grumpy.

'You know, you look very cute when you've just woken up,' he said.

Ellie snorted, then pulled a mirror out of her bag and inspected the damage. Just as she'd thought. All her mascara had migrated into a gloopy lump in one corner of her eye. Very cute.

'You need glasses, then,' she said as she threw the mirror onto her lap and searched for a tissue in a bag pocket.

'Here—let me.'

Before she could refuse he'd whipped a handkerchief out of his pocket with a flourish and tipped her chin towards him with his other hand. He leaned so close all the hairs behind her ears stood on end. She did her absolute best not to look too pathetic as he gently dabbed her eye. Somehow, with him taking care of her like this, she didn't feel so lost.

That incident set the tone for the rest of the journey. When she hauled her cases off the carousel at baggage reclaim Mark was there with a trolley before she even blinked. He shepherded her into one of the cars that appeared like magic out at the front of the terminal and saw her settled at the hotel.

It had been so long since she'd felt like this. Safe. Taken care of. Not struggling to do everything by herself. It was very tempting to give in and forget they'd be home in a few days. And that, technically, she was being paid to look after him.

Ellie shivered as yet another spider scuttled across her foot. The first time one had crawled over her today she'd almost freaked out. Big time. But the cameras were rolling, filming at the first location for Kat's video, and she hadn't wanted to sprint round the set like a lunatic in front of the crew.

Or re-live the incident when they watched the rushes at the end of the day.

Or feature in some TV out-takes compilation next Christmas.

So, although she felt as if she'd imploded with the effort, she stifled the screams, put on a stoic face and stood her ground.

She sighed and ran her fingers through the damp curls sticking to her forehead. The whole crew was packed into a tight knot at the end of an idyllic bay where the narrow beach met the rocks. Ellie was hiding out in the jungle-like greenery that fringed the white-hot sand. Hence the spiders. She'd thought she'd do anything to escape something with eight legs, but the need for shade and even a few degrees less heat had overruled her natural instincts. It was only *after* they'd arrived at the hotel that Mark had explained that summer could be hot and horribly humid on the island. Most of the tourists came in the winter months.

Kat was knee-deep in water, singing along to the track that was due to be her next single. The surf behind her looked mighty inviting. Ellie was fantasising about diving into the sea, acting like a fish and hoping nobody would notice. Nice dream, but in reality she was stuck under the nearest palm tree, wilting, while everybody else did something vastly important.

The heat was making her clothes stick to her skin. Even her skin was sticking to her skin. She longed for the air-conditioned haven of the hotel. Typical of many resorts on the island, the elegant low-rise main building was surrounded by lush tropical gardens and luxurious cabins. She wanted to be doing jobs she knew how to do: faxing things, shredding things. An evil glint flickered in her eyes. She wanted to be stapling things—preferably to Mark's head.

No, that wasn't fair. It was her own fault she hadn't found out what she was letting herself in for. It was the jet lag making her tetchy. And she'd never been on friendly terms with this kind of heat. It made her hair frizz.

The director stood up and bellowed, 'Cut!'

The music died instantly, but Ellie knew the song so well by now that it kept playing inside her skull, pounding against her temples.

The director barked instructions to anyone within earshot.

'Baz, zoom out a little so I can see the sand. Jerry, check that last take to see if the light is still okay. Kat, my darling, could you just move to that rock on your left?' Kat waded obligingly to the rock and took up her position. 'That's it. Can you put one foot on top of it? Good.'

Ellie admired her stamina. They'd all been standing on this beach for most of the day. She'd have dived in and floated away hours ago if it she'd been in Kat's shoes. She massaged her forehead and listened to the pounding of the surf. She'd expected a little time to collect herself after they'd arrived, but it had been straight to work. No lounging by the pool under a yellow umbrella. No sipping coconut-flavoured cocktails in a hammock. Time really was money when video cameras were involved, it seemed.

'Playback!'

The director's yell was like a crack from a shotgun. Birds scattered from the treetops in terror.

Ellie checked her clipboard. All her tasks were done. There was nothing left to do but drift over towards the director and watch Kat's progress on one of the boxy little monitors.

The minute hand on her watch dragged itself listlessly through the next few hours and the sun began to set. They moved position a few times, and each move meant ages of checking the lighting, setting up cameras and other kit. Then Kat would have to sing her song another thousand times, this time in close-up, this time on a long-shot. See? She was even starting to learn the lingo.

Just as the sun had finally set, and Ellie was about to scream with the monotony of it all, Mark suddenly waded into the sea and scooped Kat into his arms.

'Cut!' the director bellowed, impotent with fury.

Ellie could only imagine the myriad expletives scalding the tip of his tongue. He spluttered, searching for the right word to unlock the torrent. Ellie turned quickly to face the trees and hid a smile. The prima donna on this set was definitely not the singer!

Mark said nothing as he carried Kat out of the water, but his eyes were blazing a warning as clear as if he'd shouted it. The director swallowed his rant. Mark unhooked his arm from under Kat's knees and let her bare feet touch the ground in one controlled motion.

'That's a wrap for today, everybody,' he said.

His voice was calm, but everyone from the director to the runners knew that negotiations were useless. The generator coughed to a halt. No one moved.

Ellie broke the tense silence with a scurry of movement. She tugged a fluffy towel out of the bag of provisions she'd hauled along with her and slung it over Kat's shoulders. All that time standing in the water! The poor girl must be prune-like on the bottom half and baked on the top half. She glanced at Mark, and flushed as she saw the flicker of approval in his eyes.

Kat whispered her thanks as they headed to the speed boats that had brought them on the short trip round the coast into the small crescent-shaped bay. It had been chosen because they were practically guaranteed an uninterrupted shoot, with no onlookers or journalists to deal with as it was inaccessible by road.

Mark and Kat headed for the smallest boat, followed closely by Rufus, Kat's bodyguard—or personal protection officer, as he preferred to be called. Ellie trailed along behind, still feeling like a spare part. The rest of the crew concentrated on unplugging and packing the expensive technical thingummy-jigs in foam-padded metal cases. They would follow on shortly, in the larger two boats.

They arrived back at the small marina in the

neighbouring bay and made their way to the cluster of anonymous black people-carriers that were waiting for them in the car park. Mark pulled Ellie back to let Kat and Rufus walk ahead.

'I'm going to wait here for our illustrious director and give him a piece of my mind. If he plans to roast Kat alive in the midday sun tomorrow he's going to have to think again.'

'You act more like her big brother than her manager.'

Mark frowned a little. 'Babysitting the star is part of my job description. On the business side, I wouldn't be doing my job if Kat couldn't finish the shoot.' His matter-of-fact manner softened. 'But you're right. I do feel protective towards her. It's easy to forget she's only seventeen and all her friends are still at school.'

He shielded his eyes with a hand and looked up the walkway after Kat as she slid the back door of the people-carrier open and climbed inside. 'She's a great kid. If she can get through the next couple of years without self-destructing she'll have a long and successful career.' He looked Ellie straight in the eye. 'It would be such a waste if she burns out.'

The compassion in his eyes made something inside her feel very gooey indeed. She'd thought Work Mark would be different—harder, more remote. If it were possible, he was even nicer than Home Mark.

He turned away, stuffed his hands in his pockets and scoured the headland for a hint of the other boats.

'She's had a tough time recently,' he said, and turned back towards her. 'Will you look after her for me while I wait here?'

Ellie rubbed his arm lightly and nodded.

The clouds in Mark's expression were banished by a smile. He planted a feather-soft kiss on the tip of her nose and walked down the pontoons to wait by the empty berths.

That kiss was the cherry on top of the weird feelings she'd been having since they'd arrived in Antigua less than twenty-four hours ago. It was as if she was in a parallel universe where, even though she was working for Mark, the 'employer' and 'employee' labels they'd stuck on themselves had peeled off in the heat, leaving only a man and a woman who were really, really attracted to each other.

CHAPTER NINE

WHEN Ellie reached the car she tapped on the mirrored window, assuming that Kat was taking advantage of the relative privacy to change her clothes.

'Ellie?'

'Yes. Are you okay?'

An exasperated grunt preceded Kat's reply. 'Well, yes and no—it's okay to open the door.'

Ellie eased the sliding door open an inch or two. Kat looked more like a half-drowned cat than a sex kitten. Her eyes pleaded and she wore a weary smile.

'The knot in my bikini top won't come undone.'

'Come here.' She turned Kat to face the other way with the same kind of deft handling that she had used when making Chloe stand still to have her hair brushed. As Ellie set to work on the knot she couldn't help noticing the angry pink on Kat's shoulders.

'You look like you've caught the sun, despite the lotion you slathered on.'

'Great. And I've got to do it all over again tomorrow.'

Ellie released the tangle in the bikini top straps and stood back outside the car as Kat finished changing, leaving the door slightly ajar so she could catch her conversation.

'The director will probably have me snorkelling with sharks or something,' Kat said with a tired laugh.

'I'm sure Mark would have something to say about that.'

'He's great, isn't he?'

Ellie tried not to comment for fear of incriminating herself. She made what she hoped was an ambiguous noise to cover all eventualities, but knew she'd failed when Kat slid the door open for Ellie to climb in. Kat had obviously absorbed some of Mark's mannerisms while she'd been working with him, because that smirk was pure Wilder. Ellie busied herself by doing up her seat belt.

Kat leaned across and whispered in a conspiratorial manner, 'Don't worry. Your secret is safe with me.'

Ellie's eyes jumped from Kat to the back of Rufus's head as he drove the car out of the car park.

'Don't worry about him, Ellie. Rufus knows all my secrets and his lips are sealed—aren't they, Rufus?'

Rufus agreed by remaining silent, his thick neck motionless.

'See?'

Ellie groaned. Was she really so transparent that every passing stranger could read the contents of her head?

'I trust Mark one hundred percent,' Kat said, giving her a meaningful look. 'Some managers sign up young talent and work them like crazy until they drop. Then it's on to the next fresh young thing. But Mark's not like that. He always looks after me.'

Kat looked down at her lap. 'I just split up from my boyfriend. I thought he was perfect. They do say love is blind, don't they?'

Ellie squeezed her hand softly. Kat sniffed.

'It's hard to get over it when I see pictures of him in the papers almost every day. On a beach with some girl. In a nightclub with some other girl. At a premiere with—you get the picture, right? But Mark has been great. I can't count the number of times he's handed me tissues as I told him the latest sob story.' A fat tear rolled down her cheek and she sighed and looked out of the window at the lush tropical scenery. 'Sometimes I wish I could run away for a bit and have a little time to myself to get over it. But just when I think I'm on my own, *bam*! There's a telephoto lens sticking out the bushes. I can see the headlines already: "Kat's Secret Anguish Over Split."'

Ellie felt her own eyes grow wet. Mark was

right. Kat was a great girl, and she lived a difficult life for a seventeen-year-old. When she spoke, there was a croaky edge to her voice.

'My husband used give me a piece of advice that I'm going to pass on to you—'

Kat jumped round to face her, eyes stretching wide open.

'You're married!'

'I *was* married. I'm not now,' Ellie said quickly. 'Long story. Anyway, Sam used to tell me that life should never feel small. I'm a bit of a tortoise by nature, I'm afraid, much happier if I'm all tucked in inside my shell, where I'm safe and warm. But I'm starting to remember that *safe and warm* can be incredibly dull and lonely. Sometimes we've just got to have the courage to step out and live, no matter what happens.' She turned to look Kat in the eye. 'I can see that kind of strength in you. You *will* get through this.'

They hugged as far as the seat belts would allow, then Kat shifted in her seat and stared out the window.

'What happened to...to your...? Did you get a divorce?'

Ellie tried to eliminate any trace of emotion in her voice. 'No. He died.'

Kat's head snapped round. An involuntary hand covered her mouth, trying to catch the words that had already escaped.

'And here's me snivelling about a man who doesn't deserve my tears…'

Ellie's smile was braver than she felt. 'It's okay.'

'When did it…? I mean, how did he…?'

'He and my daughter were killed in a car accident a few years ago.' Ellie glanced down at the date function on her watch. 'In fact, it will be exactly four years in a week's time.'

A tear ran down Kat's face. 'Oh, Ellie!'

'Don't you start!' She pressed the heels of her hands into her own soggy eyes. 'Now you've got me going.'

A small noise from the front seat made them both look up. Did she really see Rufus dab a finger under his eye?

'Does Mark know?'

Ellie nodded. 'About my family? Yes.'

'No, I mean about next Friday.'

Ellie shook her head as the car pulled up under the canopied front awning of their hotel. Rufus got out of the car, leaving it to the valet, and headed round to open Kat's door for her.

Kat continued, despite Ellie's shaking head. 'You should tell him—you ought to, Ellie. He's really sweet and supportive. You know, he even postponed an important business trip to come to an awards thing a couple of months ago. I was petrified—more of winning than of sinking into the background—and Mark cancelled everything to be there for me. You could do with a friend like that right now.'

Ellie had no chance to respond as Rufus opened the door and bundled Kat through the hotel lobby before anyone could mob her. Ellie followed in their wake, taking advantage of the invisible path before it was filled by holidaymakers and bellboys with trolleys. They walked out into the hotel gardens and Kat headed for her cool white cabin with its low tiled roof and wraparound veranda. Ellie stood alone on the terrace steps and watched their progress. Just before the mismatched pair disappeared behind a clump of bushes lining the path, Ellie saw Kat mouth a message to her: *Tell him!*

Tell him? Tell him *what*, exactly? There was so much to choose from.

Tell him it was the first time the dreaded anniversary hadn't filled her with panic? That something had made it different this year, and that he was the something? There was too much to say, and most of it needed to be left unsaid.

She weaved her way back through the bustling lobby, confident in the knowledge that no paparazzi were going to be somersaulting from the light fittings in order to snap *her* picture, thank goodness.

The yellow umbrellas by the pool were calling to her. Time to get intimately acquainted with an outlandish cocktail with pineapple bits and paper parasols. She marched up to the poolside bar and ordered one that came in a glass the size of a small goldfish bowl.

The thick icy liquid struggled its way up the straw and she aimlessly watched the tanned bodies diving into the pool.

Kat was right. Mark was sweet and loyal and dependable—absolutely nothing like her first impressions of him. She'd been so blinkered. But now… Now she could see it all.

It reminded her of the visual neglect she'd experienced for a couple of months following the accident. For a while she'd only been aware of half the things in her field of vision. The weird thing was she hadn't even realised anything was wrong. But she'd found reading confusing, because when she'd read a magazine she'd only seen half of each sentence on the page. And she'd only washed one side of her face. When the nurses had realised they'd developed strategies to help, and gradually, as her brain had started to heal itself, she'd been able to process information from both sides of her visual field again.

Why and how had she chosen to see only half of Mark? And only negative things too? Ellie put her glass down on the bar. She'd made up her mind about him, set its trajectory, before she'd even met him. Her thought patterns had got stuck in one of their grooves yet again.

But now she saw all of him…

Oh.

And she saw all of herself too—all the things she felt for him.

A jumble of images, sensations and smells hit her all at once. As if every moment she'd spent with Mark flashed before her eyes. All her blinkers dropped away and she felt as if she was floating, with nothing left to anchor her to cold, hard reality.

It was quite possible she was desperately in love with him. How could she not have known?

And how had this happened in the first place? He was nothing like Sam, and she'd always expected that happiness only came in that size and shape. How would it work with someone totally different? *Could* it work? Their lives were so different. Could she find joy in his fast-moving, flashbulb-popping world?

Talking to Kat earlier had stretched her conceptions of what being rich, successful and famous was like, had given her a fresh look at life from her side of the lens. Kat was surprisingly human. In fact she was just like thousands of other seventeen-year-olds who cried into their pillows every night because they'd fallen for the wrong guy.

Maybe it wasn't all as impossible as it seemed. Maybe she could have a future with Mark.

Everybody needed love, whether they were rich or poor, somebody or nobody.

Her head swam. Too much pineapple-rum stuff on an empty stomach. This was no time to be thrashing this problem out.

What she needed was a clear head—and a shower.

And with that thought she plopped the straw back into the half-full cocktail glass and walked through the gardens to her cabin, thinking that even if she never qualified for the former she could definitely manage the latter.

A knock on the half-open slatted door of the cabin caused Ellie to jump off the sofa she'd been dozing on. For a second her mind was blank and she was totally in the present, hardly aware of where she was and what she'd been doing to make her so sleepy.

There was another knock, and she swivelled to face the veranda. She knew it was Mark standing out there, knew it in a way that had nothing to do with the height and shape of his silhouette and everything to do with the way her skin prickled in anticipation.

'Come in,' she called out, and then realised too late that she'd been fresh out of the shower when she'd collapsed on the sofa and was still dressed in her old pink robe. Too late to do anything about it now; he was already pushing the door fully open.

She tried to smooth her damp hair down, and pulled at the edges of her robe to get rid of the gap.

'I…er…' He stopped and swallowed. Where was the carefree, free and easy Mark Wilder banter? Probably evaporated in the heat. He tried again. 'I wondered if…if you'd like to grab some dinner?'

'Oh. Okay. That would be lovely.'

Although they'd finished early, the third and final day of shooting had left her absolutely ravenous. On the previous couple of evenings they'd joined Kat and some of her entourage in the rather trendy hotel restaurant. Ellie had enjoyed the gourmet food, but had felt a bit superfluous to requirements.

'I'll just go and get dressed,' she said, pulling herself to her feet.

She wasn't really in the mood for sitting on the sidelines of another round of industry chat and gossip, but the only alternative was sitting alone in her room, and at least this way she got to be with Mark.

As she emerged from her bedroom, wearing a simple long skirt and spaghetti-strap top, she glanced at the clock. 'It's only four-thirty. Aren't we a bit early for dinner?'

'I've been up since six this morning and I'm starving,' Mark said. 'I don't know about you?'

Ellie nodded enthusiastically.

'Anyway, there's something I want you to see first.'

Instead of heading for the hotel restaurant, Mark set off in a different direction, his long legs helping him to stride ahead. She was too busy just keeping up with him to ask questions. He led them into the hotel car park, hopped into a Jeep with a driver at the wheel and sat there, grinning at her, as if he'd done the cleverest thing in the world.

Ellie put her hands on her hips. 'Where are we going?'

She didn't add *alone together*.

'I'm taking you to the best place on the island.'

Ellie looked down at her floral-print skirt and flip-flops. She wasn't really dressed for fine dining. And she was too tired to be on her best behaviour. When she felt all fuzzy-headed like this she knew she was apt to forget words and bump into things more easily.

He patted the seat beside him and gave her a meaningful look. Ellie climbed in, too tired to be bothered to walk back down to her cabin, flop onto her sofa and dial Room Service. At least doing it Mark's way she wasn't going to have to use her legs.

The driver put the Jeep into gear and they rattled their way through the neatly manicured resort, but it wasn't long before they'd left it behind them, heading uphill. The road was lined with palms and aloes and breadfruit trees. Occasionally she saw pretty little clusters of yellow orchids dancing in the light evening wind.

Ellie breathed out and relaxed back into her seat. This was lovely, actually. Although they'd been to three different locations over the island in the last three days, she'd always been too caught up with her clipboard and 'to do' lists, terrified of missing something, to sit back and admire the scenery. This island truly was stunning, everything a tropical paradise should be. The beaches were soft white sand, the sea shades of cobalt and turquoise. If it wasn't all so pretty it would be a giant cliché. But there was something comforting about having her expectations met rather than defied for once.

It was almost a shame that everything was over and they'd be flying back tomorrow. At least she assumed it was tomorrow. If Mark had told her the time of the flight, she'd already lost that bit of information in the maze of her brain.

Looking down the steep hill and out to sea, she asked, 'What time do we need to get to the airport tomorrow?'

Mark didn't answer right away, and eventually she stopped looking at the stupendous view and turned to face him.

'Mark?'

He looked away, studying the scenery through

the windscreen. 'Actually, I'd planned to take a break—stay on for a few more days.'

Oh.

That meant she'd be going home alone. Suddenly all the hours of flying she'd be doing seemed a lot emptier. She nodded, following Mark's lead and looking straight ahead.

Mark cleared his throat. 'And I wondered if maybe you wanted to stay on too? Have a holiday?'

Ellie found her voice was hoarse when it finally obliged and came out of her mouth. 'With you? On our own?'

'Yes.'

There was a long pause, and all the air that had been whipping past their faces, ruffling their hair, went still.

'I'm not ready to go home yet,' he added.

She glanced across at him, and her heart began to thud so hard she felt a little breathless. He didn't look like the normal, cocky Mark Wilder she knew at all. He looked serious and honest and just a little lost.

She had to look away. Scared that she might be imagining all the things she could see in his eyes. Scared this was just another impulse or trick her brain was playing on her.

'Neither am I,' she said softly.

And then the air began to move around them again. They both breathed out at the same time.

After a few moments something tickled Ellie's hand. She didn't look, not wanting to spoil anything. And as Mark's fingers wound themselves round hers she felt something hard inside her melt.

The Jeep climbed higher and higher, the road twisting and turning, and the lush banana trees and palms gave way to scrub and cacti. Now she could see down into the harbour, dotted with the white triangles of hundreds of yachts, and somewhere in the distance she could hear the unmistakable sound of a steel band.

Moments later the Jeep swung round a corner and was parked not far from a few old military buildings, obviously left over from the days of British rule. Reluctantly she let Mark's hand slide from hers as he jumped out of the Jeep and then came round to her side to help her out. They left the Jeep behind and walked towards a huddled group of buildings on the edge of a steep hill.

Unlike the other ruins they'd seen on this part of the island, these had been restored. A crowd was milling around in an open-air courtyard, bouncing along to the calypso music played by a band under a roofed shelter. Mark handed Ellie a plastic cup of bright red liquid. One sniff told her it was rather toxic rum punch, and she sipped it slowly as she swayed to the rounded notes of the steel drums.

Oh, this was better than fancy-pants cooking

and business talk. This was just what she'd needed. She looked at Mark, who was sipping his own punch and smiling at her. How had he known?

'Come on,' he said, putting his cup down on a low wall and holding out his hand.

Ellie shook her head. 'I'm a terrible dancer—really clumsy.' Especially these days, when remembering her left from her right was a monumental effort.

'Nobody cares,' Mark said, nodding towards the more exuberant members of the crowd, who'd obviously been enjoying the punch and were flinging their arms and legs around with abandon. 'You can't look any worse than they do.'

She put her cup down too, laughing. 'I can't argue with that,' she said, and he led her to the uneven dusty ground that served as a dance floor.

Ellie discovered that she loved dancing like this. There were no rules, no steps to remember; she just moved her body any way that felt right. And, unsurprisingly, that involved being in close contact with Mark. He hadn't let go of her hand since he'd led her to the dance floor, and she gripped it firmly, determined not to let it slip from between her fingers again.

As they danced, Mark manoeuvred them further away from the main buildings and towards a low wall. After a rather nifty spin Ellie stopped in her tracks, causing Mark to bump softly into her.

'Wow!'

'Told you it was the best place on the island,' Mark said, as Ellie just stared at the scene in front of her.

The view was stupendous. The sun was low on the horizon, and the undulating hills and coastline were drenched in soft, warm colours. Ellie recognised this view as the one they always stuck on the tourist brochures for Antigua. It had to be the most beautiful place in the whole world. She moved forward to rest her hands on the wall, unaware for a moment that Mark hadn't moved away and that her back was being heated by his chest.

'Will you take a photo of us?'

Ellie looked round to see a sweet young redhead with an English accent holding a camera hopefully towards her. She was standing with a lanky guy in long shorts and rather loud, touristy shirt.

She shrugged and smiled back. 'Okay. Sure.'

The girl beamed at her, handed the camera over, then snuggled up to the violent shirt. 'It's our honeymoon,' she explained, glancing adoringly at him.

'Congratulations,' Mark said from behind her, and Ellie became aware of a slow heat building where their bodies were still in contact.

'You've had the same idea as us, I see,' the girl babbled. 'Get here early to get a good view of the sunset. It's our last night and we've watched every one. We're hoping we'll get to see the green flash before we go home.'

Ellie held the camera up and snapped a picture of them grinning toothily at her.

'Green flash?' she said as she handed the camera back to the redhead.

'It's a rare sight,' the woman said as she checked the photo on the screen and smiled. 'Sometimes, when the last part of the sun dips into the sea, you can see a flash of green light as it disappears.'

Loud Shirt Guy nodded. 'Atmospheric conditions have to be just right. It's all to do with astronomical refraction and—'

His wife laid a hand on his arm and he stopped talking. 'Don't bore them with all that, darling,' she said, laughing. Then she whispered behind her hand at Ellie, 'Honestly, he's a scientist, and sometimes he just doesn't know when to stop.'

Ellie could *feel* Mark smiling behind her. Although how you could tell someone was smiling only by being in contact with their chest she wasn't sure.

'Anyway, we're not watching it for the physics, are we, Anton?'

Anton shook his head, and got a misty look in his eyes. 'Island folklore has it that couples who see it together are guaranteed true love.'

A pang of incredible sadness hit Ellie right from out of nowhere. This couple were so sweet. She remembered being that besotted with someone, sure she was going to have a long and happy future with him. She almost wanted to go and give them both a great big hug, to whisper in their ears never to take the time they had together for granted, never to waste even a second. Instead she smiled at them, feeling her eyes fill a little.

'Well, I hope you see it—and congratulations again.'

They nodded their thanks and turned to watch the sun, now dipping dangerously close to the clean line of the ocean. More people were wandering over to watch the sunset and Mark tugged Ellie's arm, leading her down a path, away from the crowd. The view wasn't quite so breathtaking here, but it was framed by trees and she relished not being hemmed in by lots of people, free to feel all the emotions washing over her without being watched. Her fingers crept up to the locket round her neck and she stroked it as she watched the sun go down.

Somehow Mark had hold of her hand again, and he stood beside her, warming her with his mere presence.

Slowly the air grew thick and silence fell as everyone further up the path concentrated on the wavering orange disc that was now dipping itself into the horizon. Ellie didn't move. She hardly dared breathe as she watched the sun inch its way down.

She hadn't thought it possible, just a few short months ago, that she could love again. But here she was, watching the most mesmerising sunset she'd ever seen, with a man who had turned all her rigid expectations on their heads. But did he feel the same way? Was it even possible this was more than a passing attraction for him? She wanted to believe that the look she'd seen on his face in the car was the truth, but she just didn't trust her instincts any more.

A wayward curl blew across her face and she brushed it away so she could stare harder at the setting sun. He was here with her now, and that was what mattered. Who said love lasted for ever, anyway? She knew better than most that you had to grab the moment while you could. Maybe it was time just to 'go with the flow', as Sam had always encouraged her—as she had been doing when she'd danced to the hypnotic calypso music. Maybe it was time to let life feel something other than small again, no matter what that meant. No matter if *for ever* wasn't part of the package.

Mark leaned forward and whispered in her ear. 'Look.'

The sun was almost gone now, the very last traces only just visible, and she'd been so busy daydreaming she'd almost missed it. Why was it so difficult to live in the moment and not get distracted by wounds of the past or fears for the future? She concentrated hard on the sun, knowing that capturing this moment for her memory banks was important somehow.

And then it happened.

Just as the orange lip of the sun disappeared there was a sizzle of emerald on the horizon. Ellie froze. It lasted only a second or two and then faded away. Mark was standing slightly to the side and behind her. She could hear his breathing, soft and shallow, in her right ear.

Then he began to move, and she moved too, turning to face him.

He looked at her for a long time, a solemn, almost sad expression on his face, and then, just as her mind started to go wild with questions, he leaned in close and kissed her, silencing them all.

Later that evening Ellie wandered on to her veranda alone. She leant on the criss-cross wooden railing and stared in amazement at the confusion of stars jostling for space in the midnight sky. Light from Mark's cabin, a short distance through the gardens, was casting a faint glow on the waving palms, but there was no sign of him.

It had been a magical night—starting with *that* kiss.

By the time they'd returned the short distance up the trail from where they'd watched the sunset the sky had been a velvety dark blue, the sun long disappeared. They'd danced to the steel band, eaten sticky barbecue food with their fingers, and hadn't been able to stop smiling at each other.

Her relationship with Mark had definitely crossed into new territory, but neither of them had brought the subject up, preferring just to live in the moment, rather than spoil it with words and theories.

She wasn't just a fling to him.

The knowledge was there, deep down in her heart—in the same way she'd known after that first day of primary school that Sam's life and hers would always be joined somehow.

There was something between them—her and Mark—something real. Only she didn't have the words to describe it. And for the first time in a very long while the fact she couldn't find the right word, couldn't label something instantly, didn't bother her in the slightest.

The next few days were almost too much for Ellie's mind to deal with. She'd been so accustomed to guilt and pain and misery, clanging round her ankles like shackles, that the light, airy happiness she was feeling took a bit of getting used to. And the glorious island she was on and the wonderful man she was with just made life seem even more surreal.

But who needed real life, anyway?

She'd rather live this dream, where she spent almost every waking moment with Mark. They'd eaten at the most amazing places, ranging from surfside shacks to exclusive restaurants. They'd been sailing and had walked across countless beaches. Some evenings they'd gone out into the bustle of nearby St John's; sometimes they'd just found somewhere quiet to watch the sun set. They hadn't seen the green flash again, but Ellie didn't worry about that. Once must be enough, surely?

And Mark...

He astounded her. He knew her every mood, anticipated her every need. He knew when to hold her tight and when to give her space without her even having to try and get the jumble of an explanation past her lips.

Marrying up this version of Mark with the grinning playboy she'd seen on the television all those months ago was almost impossible. She'd been so blinkered. But, even so, she was sure the way he was behaving wasn't something she'd conveniently blocked out. He was different. More free. He was changing too.

And it only meant she loved him more.

As the week wore on, she felt the shadow of the approaching anniversary looming close on her horizon. With that blocking her view of the sun, it was hard to think about where her relationship with

Mark might go, what it would become when they flew home on Saturday.

She'd just have to get Friday out of the way first. Then she'd be able to think clearly. Then maybe, when the plane took off and she watched the ground drop away, the houses and cars all become miniature versions of themselves, she'd be able to leave her small life behind her once and for all.

CHAPTER TEN

MARK finally spotted her, walking down near the shoreline, kicking the wavelets with a half-hearted foot. He walked to the edge of his veranda and focused more carefully, just to make sure he was right. He was. It was Ellie, looking very much like a lost soul on the deserted beach.

A storm had passed over the night before, and he'd lain awake in the early hours, listening to the creaking of his wooden cabin as the rain had gusted against it, the rustling of the tall palms in the hotel gardens as they curved and swayed in the wind, wondering if Ellie was awake in her cabin too. This morning it was grey, and slightly overcast, but everything was clean and fresh and new.

Normally that was a good thing.

He watched Ellie as she turned to face the wind and stared out to sea, lifeless as a statue. Yesterday he'd thought all his prayers had been answered.

Her smiles across the dinner table had been warm and sweet and just for him.

As they'd headed home the sky had darkened, and by midnight rain had been hurling itself out of the sky with the force that only a tropical storm could manage. He and Ellie had spent their time snuggled up on the sofa in his cabin, watching a bad action movie. He couldn't remember the last time he'd had so much fun.

Yet there had been no glitzy nightclub, no suffocating shirt and tie, no polished mannequin on his arm, laughing on cue at his jokes. Just him and Ellie having a late-night Room Service picnic on the carpet in front of the television. They'd talked about anything and everything, and sometimes nothing at all.

His celebrity-hungry girlfriends would have balked at such an evening. There was no point going out with Mark Wilder unless you were going to be *seen* out with him—and it had better be somewhere expensive! They would certainly have frowned upon scanning the film credits for the most interesting-sounding bit part. Ellie had won with 'second tramp in explosion'. It had beaten his 'teenager with nose-stud' hands down.

Relaxing on the sofa with Ellie snuggled up under his arm, he'd realised that this was what *normal* felt like. He liked it. In fact, he could see himself doing it for a long time to come with her, and he hardly remembered why he had been so terrified of it for almost a decade. Now he had tasted it he wasn't sure he could go back to living without it. It was kind of addictive.

What did that mean?

He tried not to think of the 'm' word, but no matter how he diverted his thoughts they kept swerving back to images of Ellie, dressed in white, a serene smile on her face as he slid a delicate gold band on her finger.

The wind ruffled his hair and his daydreams scattered like the bulbous clouds hurrying towards the skyline. Overnight something had happened. This morning she was withdrawn. No smiles. No bubbling laughter. Today, he hardly existed.

He kicked the railing of the veranda hard. Which was a big mistake—he had bare feet.

What was going on with her? Had she finally taken a good look at him and decided there was nothing more than schmooze and show? Hadn't he criticised himself enough in recent months for the lack of substance in his life?

He raised his foot, ready to take another kick, but thought better of it. Instead he turned and walked through the cabin to his bedroom to get dressed. It was time to find out what was going on, whether the last few days had just been a mirage or not.

Five minutes later he felt the wet sand caving under the weight of his heels as he strode across the almost deserted beach. Ellie was now only a billowing speck in the distance. A remnant of last night's wind lifted her loose skirt as she wandered along the shoreline.

He lengthened his stride.

She didn't hear him come up behind her. She was busy drawing in the wet sand with a long stick. He didn't want to startle her, so he stopped a few feet away and spoke her name so gently it was only just audible above the splash of the waves near their feet.

She stopped tracing a large letter 'C' in the damp sand. Mark's heart pounded like the waves on the distant rocks as he waited for her response. Her head lifted first, but her eyes remained fixed on her sandy scrawlings a few seconds longer before she found the courage to meet his enquiring gaze. The rims of her eyes were pink and moist.

Any words he'd had ready dissolved in the back of his throat. Devoid of anything sensible to say, he held out the single pink rose he'd lifted from the vase in his room. Ellie started to reach for it, then her face crumpled and silent tears overflowed down her cheeks. He dropped the rose and stepped towards her, intent on gathering her up in his arms, but could only watch in horror as she buckled and sat weeping in the sand.

'Ellie? Ellie, what is it?'

He sank down next to her and pulled her firmly into his arms. She tried to answer him, but her words were swallowed in another round of stomach-wrenching sobs. So he waited. He held her and he waited. Waited until the tide turned and the hot flood of tears became a damp trickle. She pushed away from his chest and stood up, shaking the sand from her skirt.

Her voice wobbled. 'I'm sorry.'

Mark leapt to his feet and reached for her.

'Don't be.' He pulled her close to his chest and stroked her wind-ruffled hair. 'Is there something I can do?'

She swept her fingers over her damp eyes and straightened, seeming to have made a decision about something. 'I need to tell you something...' She took a deep breath and held it. 'It's the anniversary today. Four years since...since Sam and Chloe died.'

Her hand automatically reached for the silver locket she always wore. Mark didn't need to be told what pictures it held. He'd had an inkling, but now he knew for sure.

He didn't say anything. What could he say that wouldn't sound patronising or trite? So he just continued to hold her, love her, and hoped that would be enough.

'I didn't mean to shut you out or push you away,' she said. 'I just needed some time to think. It's different this year. So much has happened in the last few months...'

Slowly she unclipped the flat oval face of the locket and showed its contents to him. On one side was a little girl—blonde curls like her mother, as cute as a button. On the other side a sandy-haired man, with an infectious grin and a gleam of love in his eyes for whomever had been taking the photo. It was hard to look at the pictures, because it made him scared that she wasn't ready to move on, but he appreciated what a big step it had been for her to show him.

Ellie stooped to pick up the discarded rose and peeled the crushed outer petals off to reveal undamaged ones underneath. Mark felt ill. What if she was still in love with her dead husband? And how horrible was he for being jealous of him? He was polluting the pure emotions Ellie had provoked in him by thinking this way.

'It was the rose that set me off,' she said, picking up the bud and bringing it to her nose. 'Pink was Chloe's favourite colour.'

He almost thought the conversation was going to end there, the gap was so long, but just when he'd decided she'd lapsed back into silence she continued.

'I didn't get to go to the funeral—I was only barely conscious, couldn't walk, couldn't talk—but my mother showed me the pictures. She thought it would help. Maybe it did.'

She broke off to look out to sea again.

'Chloe had a tiny white coffin with silver handles, and Mum had chosen a wreath made only of pink roses that covered it completely. I planted a bush in the cemetery for her when I got out of hospital.'

Mark felt moisture threaten his own eyelids. She reached out and touched his cheek, stroking it with the fleshy pad of her thumb. 'Thank you for coming to find me. Thank you for never telling me how *lucky* I was to survive. You have no idea how much that means to me.'

How did she do it? How did she think beyond herself so easily? She had every right to spend the day cut off from the world, wallowing as much as she wanted. Ellie had lost part of her life to a fog her brain had created. What must it be like to not have been able to go to the funerals? To never get closure? Part of her must yearn to remember something from those days.

In contrast, he was a coward. He'd *chosen* to forget Helena, forget about love and commitment. And that hadn't helped him heal either. If anything it had just made him more shallow, less brave.

He gazed into her beautiful damp eyes. The pale

green was even more vivid against their slightly pink tinge, and he caught her face in his palms.

'You're amazing, Ellie Bond.'

She lowered her lids. 'I don't *feel* very amazing. I've spent the last few years feeling terrified mostly, and recently—' She looked back at him. The warmth in her weak smile quickened his pulse. 'Recently I've just felt plain old crazy.'

'How can you say that?'

Her lashes lowered and she gave a derisive laugh. 'I would have thought our first meeting would have been ample proof!'

He smiled. 'I think that, despite first impressions, you're probably the sanest person I know. At least you know what's real—what's important. I'd forgotten.'

That made her smile, the thought that someone else might have to wrestle with their memories too, that she wasn't entirely alone in that predicament. Their lips met briefly, tenderly. He could taste the salt from her tears.

'How you survived what you went through I'll never know. Lesser women would have crumbled.'

'But I did crumble. That is until I met—' she stopped and swallowed '—you.' Her voice dropped to a whisper. 'I'd forgotten how wonderful life could be.'

'I still think you're pretty amazing.' He held her

close and his words drifted softly into her ear. 'You don't see it in yourself. That's one of the reasons why I love you.'

She froze in his arms and Mark's stomach churned. Ellie pulled back slightly and scrutinised his face, analysing his expression. He willed his facial muscles to keep still, however much they wanted to collapse. He hadn't a clue what she could see in his face. Honesty, he hoped. All he was aware of was the slicing agony as he waited for her to say something. Anything...

A couple more seconds and he was going to scream.

She blinked away a fresh tear. 'You—you love me?'

Mark recognised that feeling he got in dreams, when he suddenly discovered he'd been walking down the street naked and everybody knew it but him. The familiar urge to bolt was so strong he could taste it. In response, he ground his heels a little deeper into the sand as an anchor.

'Yes. I do. I love you.'

Just as he thought he was going to suffocate on the tension-thick atmosphere Ellie launched herself into his arms and covered his face with a hundred little kisses. At first he couldn't move. He hardly dared ask himself what this meant, hardly dared to hope.

What was that sound?

She was laughing. In between kisses, she was laughing! That was all he needed. He hugged her so tight her feet lifted off the floor. Their lips sought each other out and he lost all sense of reality for a while. When they finally pulled themselves apart rays of sunlight were punching holes in the gruff clouds. He looked at her face, alive with joy, such a difference from the mournful expression she'd worn when he'd first found her. Tears still followed the damp tracks down her cheeks, but he hoped for a very different reason.

At that moment he knew he wanted to love her so completely, so thoroughly, that every speck of pain would be soothed, every wound healed. He might not be able to change her past, but he was going to make darn sure her future was filled with all the adoration and happiness he could give her. He felt strangely unafraid at the thought of for ever.

He linked his fingers in between hers and they strolled back along the shoreline. Every now and then he would spot one of Ellie's random sand doodles. He knew now that the 'C' had been for Chloe. The selfish part of him dreaded seeing a letter 'S'. But he hadn't—yet. Only some squiggles, her name and a flower.

There was another one up ahead he couldn't quite discern. He strained his eyes, trying to read it upside down. When he eventually made it out his heart nearly stopped.

It was an 'M', encased in a gently curving heart.

The words were out of his mouth before his brain had a chance to intervene.

'Marry me?'

What had he just said?

There must still be static left in the air from the storm, because she felt tiny electric charges detonate all over her body. Then a sick feeling of disappointment hit her in the pit of her stomach. She'd heard him say something like this before. She yanked her hand out of his. How could he ruin the moment like this?

'Don't joke with me, Mark.' If he was bright, he'd heed the steely warning hidden in her reply. She turned to face him, expecting to see the trademark grin across his big smart mouth, but it wasn't there.

Another jolt of electricity hit her.

'You're serious, aren't you?'

He scooped her into his arms and kissed her until she nearly forgot the subject of this surreal conversation. Nearly.

'Of course I'm serious!'

She didn't know whether to laugh or cry. Mark started to kiss her again, but she stepped back, holding him at bay.

'Hang on a second, Mark. I can't think straight when you're that close.' She'd thought he'd laugh, but he didn't. She smoothed her wind-blown hair and turned a slow circle in the sand, scanning the horizon for an answer. He came up behind her and hugged her close, his warmth delicious against her cool skin.

'What's there to think about? I love you. Don't you love me?'

'Mark, it's not that easy!'

He nuzzled in close to her neck. 'It could be.'

Could it? Could happiness really be that easy? It was as if someone had told her it was okay to reach out and grab the stars if she wanted to.

For four long years she'd been living in the past. Trying to remember... Trying to forget... Recently she'd actually managed to live in the present, enjoy the moment. But did that mean she was ready to think about the future? That was something she hadn't done for such a long time, she realised, for all her big talk about 'breaking free'. She hadn't really been looking forward when she'd taken the job as Mark's housekeeper; she'd been looking back over her shoulder, running away from ghosts.

But now, standing here on this beach, she was starting to think that the future might be wonderful instead of scary. Today she'd found some peace. And Mark was a wonderful man, so much more than he gave himself credit for. Maybe it *was* that easy. Maybe this was one impulse she should follow one hundred percent, because, boy, she really wanted to say yes.

He turned her to face him without breaking contact, keeping her in the protective circle of his arms. 'Ellie. I love you. I've never felt this way about anyone. Ever. I can't imagine spending another second of my life without you.' In a solemn gesture he took her hands in his, kissed them and lowered himself onto one knee.

Now she knew she really was dreaming! There was no way this could be happening to her. Still, she hoped the alarm clock wasn't going to go off any time soon.

The earnest look on his face made her eyes sting again. 'Ellie Bond, will you do me the honour of becoming my wife?'

She could feel his whole body shaking as she lowered herself to sit on his raised knee and kissed him sweetly, passionately.

'Is that a *yes*?'

Her breath warmed his earlobe as she whispered, 'Yes.'

Mark's ferocious kiss destroyed their precarious balancing act and they both fell onto the sand, tangled but still joined at the lips. Ellie wasn't sure how long they stayed there 'celebrating'. Long enough for the tide to creep in a bit further and take a peek.

'Mark, my feet are getting wet.'

'Do you care?'

'Not really.'

More jubilant celebrations.

By the time the salty water was lapping at the hem of her skirt she surrendered.

'We can't stay here all day, you know.'

Mark fell back into the sand and stared at the vivid blue sky. 'Shame. I was hoping we could just float away to a desert island and never be heard of again.'

That night at dinner they suddenly remembered they needed to think practicalities if they were really serious about getting married.

'What sort of wedding do you want?' Mark asked Ellie as she dug into her creamy dessert, desperately hoping it wouldn't be the three-ring circus Helena had insisted on. Weddings like that felt like bad omens.

Ellie swallowed her mouthful and thought for a moment. 'Something simple.' She dug her spoon into the coconut and rum thing again, but it stopped halfway to her mouth and hovered there, threatening to drop its contents back into the bowl while she considered his question further. 'Something small…private. Just you and me on a sunny day, somewhere beautiful.'

That gave him an idea. 'Somewhere like here?'

Ellie put her spoon back in the bowl and smiled at him. 'That would be perfect! You mean come back in a few months?'

That was exactly what he'd been thinking. But then he thought about all the to-ing and fro-ing, all the hideous preparations and tensions in the run-up to a wedding. That would just spoil everything, ruin the atmosphere of perfection that was clinging to them at the moment.

'How about we get married here? Now. In a few days.' He looked at her earnestly. 'As soon as possible.'

She opened and closed her mouth. Then she made that scrunched-up face she always did when she was trying to process something unexpected.

'We'll have a big party for friends and family when we get back home,' he added. Ellie looked horrified, and Mark remembered the last party at Larkford. He took hold of her hand. '*Real* friends only, I promise.'

'This isn't another one of what *you* think are your hilarious jokes, is it?'

He was deadly serious. How did he make her see that?

'Ellie, I've been hiding for too long, waiting for too long.' He watched as the tension eased from her face and she smiled at him, nodding in agreement. He stopped smiling and looked straight into her eyes. 'I don't want to wait any more.'

She let out a happy sigh. 'Mark, you're asking the right girl, then—because I have this horrible impulse to go along with anything you say, and I just can't be bothered to fight it.'

Ellie stared at herself in the bathroom mirror.

'I'm getting married tomorrow!' she screamed at the idiot grinning back at her. Then she screamed again, just because it was fun. Oh, get a grip, girl! You can't just stand here all day smiling at yourself. You've got some serious shopping to do today. And a fiancé to corner before he disappeared off to do whatever secret things he'd planned and wouldn't tell her about.

One more grin in the mirror for luck, and then she ran out of her bathroom and got dressed in the first things she found in the wardrobe.

The last few days had been madness. Her cheeks hurt from smiling so much. She'd thought she would be flying home days ago, but she was still here in paradise with Mark, and things were going to get even more perfect. She couldn't think about anything else. Her mind just refused to prise itself from that track and she wasn't inclined to let it.

Of course a voice in the back of her head whispered to her, asking her if this was all too quick, asking whether there was unfinished business she needed to sort out first. But she didn't want to listen to that voice, so she drowned it out with a slightly off-key rendition of 'Oh, What a Beautiful Morning'.

Happiness was within her grasp, here and now. She was going to snatch it before the whole dream disappeared in a puff of smoke. No more fear. No more trepidation. Just facing the future with Mark at her side.

But what about the past? the voice said. *What are you going to do with that?*

Ellie belted out the chorus of the song and ran through the garden. She burst through the unlocked doors of Mark's cabin like a miniature whirlwind.

He was in the sitting room, poring over some faxes. His face lit up as he saw her. 'Good morning. And what have you come as today?'

'Huh?' Ellie stopped and looked down, then burst into laughter as she took in her floaty floral-print blouse and her pyjama bottoms.

'I had other things on my mind while I was getting dressed,' she admitted with a wry smile.

'Pyjama bottoms…hmm…' Mark claimed his morning kiss. 'They remind me of the first time we met,' he said, making a feather-soft trail from her neck to her ear.

Ellie flung her arms around him. 'If you really want to recreate our first meeting I think we need to be a little more—how shall I put it?—horizontal,' she said, and let her weight fall backwards, pulling them both down onto the large sofa behind her. 'And you! You should be wearing considerably less!'

'You know I'm not that sort of girl,' he quipped. 'I thought I'd made it very clear. You have to sign on the dotted line before you get to sample the goods.'

'Spoilsport!'

'Only twenty hours to go. Surely you can wait that long?'

'Only just.' She pulled him close for another kiss. 'Just a deposit,' she assured him, making sure she got her money's worth. Both sets of parents and Ellie's brother were due to fly in for the wedding, so they'd planned a meal at the hotel after the ceremony. 'Do we have to stay through *all* of the wedding breakfast? Can't we leave early?'

Mark threw his head back and laughed. He pressed his lips against her forehead as he untangled himself and stood up. 'We won't have to stay long.'

'Five minutes?'

'Three at the most.'

It was her turn to laugh. He walked back to the desk. 'Now, as for the rest of today, you have to go shopping. You can't get married in another outfit like that. Carla, the stylist from the shoot, has faxed me a list of shops in St John's that you can visit for a dress. Thank goodness Antiguan red tape is just as laid-back and flexible as everything else on this island, and I can go and pick up the marriage licence today, once some essential documents have arrived. And, talking of essential elements of our wedding, I have one last surprise for you.'

He grabbed her hand and dragged her with him to another cabin. When they got onto the white-painted veranda he gave her a little nudge in the direction of the open door. Ellie gave him a quizzical look, then stepped inside.

'Charlie!'

Charlie jumped off the sofa and bounced over to Ellie, squealing, and dragged her fully inside the cabin. Then she flung her arms around Ellie's neck and yelled her congratulations in her ear. Ellie was already having trouble catching her breath, and Charlie's bear hug left her practically airless. She patted her friend's back in a pathetic attempt to return the gesture.

'I don't understand. What are you doing here?'

'Do you think I'd miss this? Mark called me the day before yesterday, broke the news, and asked me to fly over with birth certificates and such. I'm a rather stunning, elegant, designer-clad courier!' She did a little twirl just to prove it.

Ellie grinned. 'You're more than that! And the first thing you can do to make up for almost giving me a heart attack is to come dress shopping. It's the least my bridesmaid can do.'

Charlie's high-pitched squeal almost shredded Ellie's eardrums.

Sunrise.

Ellie and Mark walked towards the minister arm in arm as the sun lifted above the horizon. She loved Mark for suggesting her favourite time of day for the wedding. There was something so pure and fresh about the early-morning sun. And it was a beautiful symbol for her life. A fresh start, new hope. Light and warmth where she'd thought there could only be darkness.

Her bare feet sank into the cool, silky sand as they passed the few guests up early to share the ceremony. Charlie and Kat, who'd insisted on cancelling something important to be there, stood beside the minister in their bridesmaids' outfits, smiling at Mark and Ellie as they approached. Charlie looked as if she'd already had to break out the emergency hanky. It was just as well Ellie had insisted she wear waterproof mascara.

Ellie took a deep breath and looked down at her feet. Her softly flowing white chiffon dress was blowing gently round her ankles. Her feet looked almost as creamy as the pale sand. Her toenails were painted a shade of deep pink to match the exotic blooms woven into her hair and in her bouquet. And on her left foot was a white gold toe-ring, beautiful in its simplicity. Mark's gift to her this morning. Just until they got a proper engagement ring, he'd said. But she didn't care; she thought it was perfect.

She wore no other jewellery. Not even her locket. Much as she loved it, she couldn't wear it any more—especially not today. It wouldn't be fair to Mark.

As they reached the minister they halted and turned to face each other. How could she be this lucky? Finding love once with Sam had been wonderful enough, but finding it with Mark was a miracle. She never thought she'd have a second chance. She was so thankful he'd made her see that happiness didn't always come in identically shaped packages.

She almost didn't hear the minister as he started the ceremony, she was so busy staring at Mark. She'd never seen him looking so devastatingly handsome. Her eyes never left him throughout the vows. They might as well have been standing on the beach alone for all she knew. Finally she heard the words *husband and wife*, and the minister gave Mark permission to kiss the bride.

She should have known from the naughty grin on his face that he was up to no good. He lingered a little longer than propriety suggested on the kiss, then swept her up into his arms, hooked one arm under her knees and headed off down the beach with her, leaving her dress billowing behind them and the small band of guests open-mouthed.

'Mark!' she gasped, when he'd gone a dozen or so steps. 'Where are you going? We've still got the reception to get through!'

He slowed to a halt. 'I thought you wanted to disappear as soon as possible after the wedding?'

'I'm tempted, believe me, but we can't leave our guests waiting.'

'Just for you,' he said, and let her legs glide down to meet the sand, then kissed the tip of her nose. Laughing, they walked back to the small group of guests, who were sharing indulgent smiles.

By the time they congregated in the hotel gardens under a flower-draped pergola for their celebratory feast, the sun was glowing gold and fully above the horizon. The hotel chef had been very inventive with the food, and a stunning array of mouthwatering dishes was ready for them. Since the numbers were small they all sat around one large table, sipping champagne and chatting.

After they had eaten, made the toasts and cut the cake, Kat surprised them by picking up her guitar, which had been cleverly hidden behind a planter, and proceeded to serenade them with a song especially composed for the occasion. Tears welled in Ellie's eyes as she listened to the beautiful lyrics.

All my tomorrows are nothing but yours, all my yesterdays my gift to you.

It was the best wedding present anyone could have given them. The chorus stuck in her mind, and she found she was humming it as they prepared to leave for the honeymoon.

'Where are we going, then?' Ellie asked, puzzled, as Mark led her not to the front of the hotel, as she'd expected, but on to the beach. Mark just smiled an infuriating smile that said *you'll see*.

A small speedboat, with a satin ribbon tied bridal-car fashion on the front, was sitting a few feet from the shoreline.

'I thought we'd float away to that desert island we talked about and never be heard of again,' he said, as he lifted her into his arms once again and waded out to deposit her in the boat.

CHAPTER ELEVEN

MARK was as good as his word, Ellie thought, as she rolled sleepily over in bed. Two weeks on their very own private tropical island had been absolute bliss. She snuggled back against him. A heavy arm draped over her waist and his breaths were long and even. Heaven.

The villa they were staying in was small, but luxurious. The local owners brought fresh food and supplies every day, but were discreet enough that Ellie had not caught sight of them yet. She found enough lazy energy to smile as she remembered how Mark had laughed when she had referred to them as the 'shopping fairies'.

If only they could stay here for ever. But today was their last day. Tomorrow it was back to England. She frowned, and snuggled even further into Mark's sleeping body. The last couple of weeks had been like a wonderful dream and she wasn't sure she was ready for the cold grey slap of reality yet. Here they were just Mark and Ellie, besotted newlyweds. No labels, no outside expectations, free to be themselves. The thought of going home made her shiver. She loved Mark desperately, but she had an inkling that getting used to being Mrs Wilder was going to take some effort.

Warm golden light filtered through the sheer curtains. She guessed the sun had been up a while; it was maybe nine or ten o' clock. Her tummy rumbled in confirmation. No wonder! Their half-eaten dinner still lay on the dining table, abandoned in favour of traditional honeymoon recreation.

Wonderful as it is, lying here tangled with my husband, a girl's gotta eat!

She wriggled out from under his arm and reached for her robe. Thankfully she had managed to buy something a little more appropriate for a new bride than her old ratty pink one. The ancient garment certainly didn't come under the category of *sexy honeymoon lingerie*. She'd been astonished when Mark had seemed disappointed she hadn't packed it. Weird. She slung the wisp of ivory silk over her shoulders, only bothering with it because she was afraid of running into the 'fairies'. She left it unfastened and walked away from the bed. A sudden jerk of the sash trailing behind her arrested her progress.

A sleepy voice mumbled from under a pillow, 'Don't go. Come back to bed.'

'I'll be back in a sec. I'm starving!'

'So am I.'

She laughed. 'Why don't I think you've got breakfast on your mind?'

A naughty chuckle from under the pillow told her she was spot-on. In a moment of feminine contrariness she decided to make him wait, and continued her journey to the kitchen. The sash pulled taut as he tried to stop her, but the slippery silk whooshed through the loops and she disappeared out through the door. She laughed gently as she imagined what he must look like with the sash dangling uselessly from his outstretched hand.

'Ellie?' he yelled from the bedroom.

She was still smiling as she reached into the fridge for the jug of fresh orange juice. 'Sorry. Forgot what you said. You'll just have to wait,' she called back, pleased with her own self-mockery.

Mark's effort at secretive footsteps was atrocious, but she pretended not to hear him and readied herself for his attack. She detected a flicking movement out of the corner of her eye, and before she could work out what it was her missing sash looped over her head and dragged her backwards into the hard wall of his chest.

His voice was very nearly a growl. 'I said, Don't go!'

'Mark! I just spilled orange juice all over myself.'

She looked down and watched a bead of liquid travel down her torso towards her belly button.

He loosened the sash just enough to let her turn to face him. 'We'll just have to clean it up, then, won't we?' he said, a truly wicked glint in his eyes.

Ellie sighed as he started tugging her back towards the bedroom. She was pretty sure he wasn't going to fetch a towel.

Ellie wandered outside and sank her feet into the dewy grass. The vibrant green carpet welcomed her feet and she sighed. It was wonderful to be home. She might have lived on in the cottage after Sam and Chloe had gone, but it turned from a home to a shell of bricks and mortar the day they died. She turned and looked at the majestically crumbling manor house. Larkford Place felt like home—but then she'd feel at home in a caravan if Mark was there.

She was surprised at how easy the transition had been. She'd been so worried that she would feel different when they returned from the Caribbean. Over three weeks later she still felt alarmingly peaceful. She'd experienced a strange sense of foreboding on the flight home, but if trouble was looming in the distance it was hiding itself round a dimly lit corner.

She looked at the open French windows and

wished that Mark would stroll through them any second and join her. The curtains rippled in promise, but she knew he wouldn't appear. He was off on business for a few days and due home first thing tomorrow. She'd had the opportunity to go with him. She'd already travelled with him once since they'd been back, but she'd been feeling a bit below par for a couple of days and had decided to stay home and recharge her batteries while Mark flew to Ireland. The idea of sleeping in her own bed rather than a hotel one, however luxurious the surroundings, was too much of a lure. She took a careful sip of her hot tea.

Yuck!

It tasted awful. The milk must be off. She would just have to make a new one. She walked into the kitchen and poured the rest of her tea down the sink, then put on the kettle for a fresh cup. While she was waiting for it to boil she went in search of the offending milk in the fridge.

A row of unopened bottles stood like pristine soldiers in the door. Where was the one she'd used earlier? She moved a couple of items around on the nearby shelf to see if the half-used bottle was hidden away behind something. Nope. Hang on! What were the teabags doing in here?

Oh, well. She popped open a fresh pint of milk and sniffed it, while keeping her nose as far away as possible. No, this one was fine. Having done that, she made herself another cup of tea and sank into one of the wooden chairs round the table. She took a long sip, scowled, then spat it back into the cup. What was wrong with the tea today? It would have to be orange juice instead. She returned the rather chilly box of tea bags to its proper resting place in the cupboard—or would have done if a bottle of milk hadn't been sitting in its spot.

Obviously her absent-minded tendencies were getting worse. She'd been under the mistaken impression she'd been improving recently, but she was clearly deluded. She laughed quietly to herself as she returned the milk to the fridge.

Then she fell silent. These weren't her normal memory lapses. This was something new. Should she be worried about that? She'd never been scatty like this before, unless you counted that time years *before* the accident when…

Oh, my!

Ellie continued staring into the open fridge, the cool air making no impact on her rapidly heating face. When she let go of the door and let it slam closed she realised her hands were shaking. She sat back down at the table, her thirst forgotten, and tried to assemble all the evidence in her cluttered brain. The milk, the tea, the lack of energy—it was all falling into place.

She'd completely gone off both tea and coffee when she'd been carrying Chloe—hadn't even been able to stand the smell when Sam had opened a jar of instant coffee to make himself one. She'd made him drink it in the garden! And then she'd developed an overwhelming craving for tinned pineapple sprinkled liberally with pepper.

Her palm flattened over her stomach. She stood up, then sat down again.

I can't be pregnant! Not already.

She hadn't even considered the possibility, although it would certainly explain her sudden lethargy. A creeping nausea rose in her throat, but she was sure it was more a result of shock than morning sickness.

How could this have happened?

Er...stupid question, Ellie! You spent more time with your clothes off than on on honeymoon. Yes, they'd been careful, but nothing was guaranteed one hundred percent in this life.

She wasn't sure she was ready to have another baby! Life was changing so fast at the moment she could hardly keep up. She needed to get used to being married before she could consider all the possibilities for the future.

And what was Mark going to say?

She hoped he would be pleased, but what if he wasn't? They hadn't even talked about this stuff yet, having been too caught up in a whirlwind wedding and being newlyweds to think about anything sensible.

Calm down! You're getting ahead of yourself!

She didn't even know if she *was* pregnant yet. All she knew for sure was that she'd had a dodgy cup of tea and had misplaced the milk. She didn't have to turn insignificant minor events into a major crisis, now, did she?

Ellie shook her head. Talk about her imagination running away with her. What she needed to do right now was take a few deep breaths and have a shower. Which was exactly what she did. However, all the time she was washing she couldn't shake the nagging voice in the back of her head.

You can't run away from this one, Ellie. You can't bury your head in the sand. But she hadn't been running away from things recently, had she? She'd run *to* Mark, not away from something else. At least that was how it had felt at the time.

She stepped out of the shower and got dressed. She needed to find out for sure. She'd go down to the chemist in the village and buy a test. Strike that. She'd already got to know the local residents, and if the village drums were doing their usual work the news that she might be expecting would be round the village in a nanosecond. The fact that dashing Mr Wilder had married his housekeeper was still the main topic of local gossip. A baby on the way would be too juicy a titbit for the village grapevine to ignore.

She'd be better off going into town and shopping at one of the large chemists. Much easier to be anonymous then. At least when Mark got home tomorrow she'd have had a chance to absorb the outcome herself.

The thought that the test might be negative should have made her feel more peaceful. Instead she felt low at the prospect. If the test *was* negative, she would make a light-hearted story of it to tell Mark over dinner tomorrow. She'd tell him how freaked out she'd been, see what his reaction was, test the waters.

Two hours later she was standing in the bathroom, holding the little cellophane-wrapped box as if it was an unexploded bomb.

You're not going to find out by staring at it.

She removed the crinkly wrapping and opened the box. How could something as mundane as a plastic stick turn out to be the knife-edge that her whole life was balanced on? She sat on the closed toilet lid while waiting for the result, the test laid on one thigh. Two minutes to wait. If someone had told her she was only going to live another two minutes, it would seem like a measly amount of time. How, then, could this couple of minutes stretch so far they seemed to be filling the rest of the day?

First the test window. Good. One blue line. It was working. Then wait for the next window. She waited for what seemed an age. Nothing. She stood up, threw the test onto the shelf over the sink and ran out of the room crying.

All that stress for nothing. She ought to be relieved! It gave her a little more time to think, to plan, to find out what Mark wanted.

Suddenly she wished he was there. She wanted to feel his strong arms wrapped around her, wanted him to hold her tight against his chest and stroke her hair.

She grabbed a wad of tissues from the box beside her bed and blew her nose loudly. She should get out of here, get some fresh air. Perhaps she should pick up the papers from the village shop. Mark liked to read a selection, from the broadsheets to the tabloids, mostly to keep track of what attention his clients were attracting in the press.

She went back to collect the pregnancy test and picked it up, with the intention of putting it in the bin, but the moment she looked at it she dropped it into the sink in shock. The breath left her body as if she'd been slapped with a cricket bat.

The tears must be blurring her vision! She dragged the hem of her T-shirt across her eyes and stared at it again.

Two blue lines?

She took it to the window to get more light. Her

eyes weren't deceiving her. Granted, the second one was very faint, compared to the first, but there were definitely two blue lines. The hormones had to be only just detectable. She could hardly believe it, but there it was—in blue and white.

I'm going to have a baby. Our baby.

Suddenly the rambling old house seemed claustrophobic. She needed to get outside, feel the fresh air on her skin. The garden called her, and she ran down to it and kicked her flip-flops off. Her 'engagement' toe-ring glinted in the morning sun as she stepped onto the grass and began to walk.

A stroll through Larkford Place's grounds should have been pleasant in high summer. The far reaches of the garden, unspoilt and untended, were alive with wild flowers, butterflies and buzzing insects. But Ellie noticed none of it. All she could think about was having a little boy, with a shock of thick dark hair like his father and eyes the colour of warm chocolate.

Was this how she'd felt when she'd realised she'd been expecting the last time? It seemed so long ago now, a memory half obscured by the fog of the accident. But her last pregnancy had been planned. This one was…well, a surprise to put it mildly.

She stopped and looked a bright little poppy, wavering in the breeze. Through the confusion and doubts, joy bubbled up inside her, pushing them aside. She wanted this baby. She already loved this baby—just as much as she'd loved…

Images of golden ringlets and gap-toothed smiles filled her mind, but there was something missing. A word missing.

Her hands, which had been circling her tummy, went still. Just as much as she'd loved…

No. Not now. Not this name. This was one name she was *never* allowed to forget, never allowed to lose. It was too awful. Ellie looked back at the house and began to run.

This couldn't be happening. She couldn't have forgotten her own daughter's name.

Mark burst through the front door with a huge bunch of wilted flowers in his hand. They had looked a bit better before they'd spent two long, sticky hours in the passenger seat of the Aston Martin.

'Ellie?'

No answer. She was probably out in the garden. He almost sprinted into the kitchen. The French windows, her normal escape route, were closed. On closer inspection he discovered they were locked. He ran back to the entrance hall and called her name more loudly. The slight echo from his shout jarred the silence.

Okay, maybe she was out. He was half a day early, after all.

He looked at his watch. Nearly four o'clock. She couldn't be too far away. He'd just go and have a shower, then lie in wait. He chuckled and loosened his tie as he hopped up the stairs two at a time.

But as the afternoon wore on Ellie didn't appear. He ended up in the kitchen, wishing she'd materialise there somehow, and he found her note near the kettle. Well, it wasn't even a proper letter—just a sticky note on the kitchen counter, telling him that she'd gone.

He sat down on one of the chairs by the kitchen table and put his head in his hands.

Not again. She'd seemed so happy since the wedding.

That's when they leave—when they're happy. They don't need you any more.

No. This couldn't happen with Ellie. He loved her too much. More than Helena. So much more. He stood up. He'd be damned if he lost a second wife this way. But if she was really intent on going she bloody well owed him an explanation. He wasn't going to let her waltz off without a backward glance.

The keys jumped from Ellie's fingers as if they had a life of their own. She muttered through her tears and bent to scoop them up from the front step. Thankfully the holiday company had told her they'd had a cancellation this week. The cottage was empty. Perhaps if she went inside it would help.

Although she'd remembered Chloe's name almost the second she'd reached Larkford's kitchen, she still couldn't shake the clammy, creeping feeling of disloyalty and guilt. She'd needed to come somewhere she could rid herself of this horrible feeling of being disconnected from her past.

She slid the key into the lock and started the familiar routine of pulling and turning to ease it open. It was feeling particularly uncooperative today. She gave the key one last jiggle and felt the levers give. The door creaked open.

For no reason she could think of, she burst into tears.

The cream and terracotta tiled hallway seemed familiar and strange at the same time. The surfaces were cleared of all her knickknacks and photos, but the furniture was still *in situ*. Even devoid of personal items it seemed more welcoming than when she'd left on that grey, rainy day months ago.

Ellie hadn't planned to end up here. She just had. An impulse. She walked into the sitting room and slumped into her favourite armchair.

I should never have left this chair. I should have stayed here eating biscuits and never gone to Larkford. Then I would never have forgotten you, my darling girl.

But then she wouldn't have this new baby. And she really wanted it. She clamped her hands to her stomach, as if to reassure the tiny life inside, and her eyes glittered with maternal fierceness.

If Mark didn't want it, then she'd just bring it up on her own.

Ellie shook her head. She hadn't even told Mark yet, didn't have a clue what his reaction would be. She was just making the same mistake she always made: an idea had crept into her head and she'd sprinted away with it like an Olympic athlete, not even bothering to check that she was running in the right direction. Maybe she was so terrified of losing Mark that deep down she almost expected something to come along and demolish it. And at the first hint of trouble she'd been only too ready to believe her luck couldn't hold out.

Sitting here moping was doing her no good. She pulled herself to her feet and started to walk round the house. As she visited every room different memories came alive: Chloe riding her truck up and down the hall; Sam marking homework at the dining table; the kitchen counter where she had made cakes with Chloe, more flour down their fronts than in the mixing bowl. And she realised she'd never been able to do this before, never been able to look at her cottage and see it alive with wonderful warm memories of her lost family.

As she sat trying to process all the new information Kat's song from the wedding drifted through her head:

Yesterday is where I live, trapped by ghosts and memories.
But I can't stay frozen, my heart numb, because tomorrow is calling me...

Ellie guessed the song had been about her break-up with Razor, but the simple lyrics about learning to love again had been so right for their wedding day too. 'All My Tomorrows' was the title. And she'd promised the rest of hers to Mark, willingly. Nothing in the world could make her take that promise back. So there was only one thing to do: she had to go back home—her real home, Larkford—and let Mark know he was going to be a father. Whatever fallout happened, happened. They would just have to deal with it together.

Her instincts told her it was going to be okay. She hoped she was brave enough to listen to them.

She grabbed her keys off the table and took long strides into the hall, her eyes fixed on the front door. A shadow crossed the glazed panel. She hesitated, then walked a few steps further, only to halt again as a fist pounded on the door.

'Ellie? Are you there?'

She dropped her keys.

'Ellie!'

'Mark?' Her voice was shaky, but a smile stretched her trembling lips. She ran to the door and pressed her palms against the glass.

'Let me in, or so help me I'm just going to have to break the door down!'

She patted her pockets, then scanned the hallway, remembering she'd dropped her keys. She ran to pick them up, but it took three attempts before her shaking fingers kept a grip on them. As fast as she could she raced back to the door and jammed the key in the lock. An ugly grinding sound followed as she turned it, then the key refused to move any further. She wiggled and jiggled it, pushed and pulled the door, trying all her old tricks, but it wouldn't budge. The key would not turn in either direction, so she couldn't even get it out again to have another go.

'Ellie? Open the door!' The last shred of patience disappeared from his voice.

'I'm trying! The lock's jammed.'

'Let me try.'

The door shuddered and groaned under Mark's assault, but remained stubbornly firm.

Ellie sighed. 'They don't make doors like this any more.'

Between pants, she heard Mark mutter, 'You're telling me.'

She pressed her face to the stained glass design, able to see him through a clear piece of glass in the centre. He looked tired, disheveled and incredibly sexy. Without warning, she started to cry again.

He stopped wrestling with the door and looked at her through the textured glass. 'We have to talk.'

She gulped. He sounded serious. Was serious good or bad? Good. Serious was good. Please God, let serious be good!

'I know,' she said.

'Why are you here, instead of at home?'

She took a deep breath and turned away from him, pressed her back against the door, then slid to the floor.

'How did you know where to find me?'

'I phoned Charlie in a panic and she suggested I might find you here. I'd already been to your parents' house and your brother's.'

She nodded. Charlie knew her so well. Maybe too well. If her friend hadn't guessed where she was she might have made it back to Larkford and Mark would never have known how stupid she'd been this afternoon. But why had her first impulse been to run? To come here? Did that mean something?

'Ellie?'

She took a deep breath. 'Do you think we got married too fast, Mark? I mean, did we get carried away? Should we have waited?' Everything just seemed so confusing today.

She heard him sit on the step. His feet scraped the gravel path as he stretched his legs out. 'Are you saying you want out?' he said quietly. 'Are you saying you want to come back here for good? I thought you loved me, Ellie. I really did.'

Ellie spun onto her knees and looked through the letterbox. He looked so forlorn, so utterly crushed, she could hardly speak. 'I do love you,' she said, in a croaky whisper. He looked round, and her stomach went cold as she saw the sadness in his eyes.

He tried a small smile on for size. 'Good. Come home with me, then.'

Her fingers got tired holding the brass letterbox open and she let it snap shut. Carefully, because she was feeling a bit wobbly, she pulled herself to her feet. He stood too, and leaned against the door, trying to see her through the multi-coloured glass. Ellie raised her fingers to the clear green diamond of glass where she could see his left eye. It reminded her of the colour of the sunset flash. Of true love. Of coming home.

'I'm sorry, Mark. It's just…I just needed to be somewhere that reminded me of Chloe.'

The green eye staring at her through the glass blinked. She knew what he was thinking. He thought she'd come here to remember Sam too. But while she had unearthed forgotten memories of both the people she'd lost, it didn't make the slightest impact on what she felt for Mark.

'I love you, Mark. And as soon as we work out a way to get this door open I'm coming back home. I promise.'

He nodded again, but she could tell he only half believed her. Another wave of emotion hit her and she began to cry again. What was wrong with her today? 'I don't know why I'm doing this,' she said, half-sobbing, half-laughing. 'I can't seem to get a grip...'

'Perhaps it's the hormones?'

Hormones?

She jumped as the brass flap of the letterbox creaked open again. Something plastic rattled through and clattered onto the floor. Her pregnancy test! She'd left it in the sink. So much for a cool, calm testing of the water on that subject.

'When were you going to tell me?' he asked, his voice going cold. 'I didn't expect to find out I'm going to be a father from a plastic stick. You could have called me at the very least.'

'I *was* going to tell you, but then I...I forgot Chloe's name. And that just freaked me out. I was scared. What if I forget her altogether when this new baby comes along? I couldn't live with myself. You do understand, don't you?'

She heard him grumble something under his

breath. The heavy crunch of his feet on the gravel got quieter.

'Mark!' Ellie ran to the door and pressed her nose against the glass.

No answer. She'd finally scared him away with the ghosts from her past. Her unfinished business had caught up with her.

'Mark!' She sounded far too desperate, but she didn't care.

She dropped the test and flung her full weight against the door. Unimpressed, it hardly rattled. She banged it with her fists, hoping to catch Mark's attention. She needed to tell him how stupid she'd been, that she thought he'd be a wonderful father.

'Mark!' Hoarse shouts were punctuated by sobs as she continued to bang on the door.

She stopped.

No faint crunch on the gravel. No hint of a shadow moving up the path. She used the door for support as she slumped against it, exhausted. He couldn't leave now, could he?

She managed one last hollow plea, so quiet he couldn't possibly hear it. 'Don't go.'

'I'm not going anywhere.'

She spun round to find him striding towards her down the hallway.

'How did you—?'

He nodded towards the back door, not slowing

until he crushed her close to him. His lips kissed her wet eyelids, her nose, her cheeks, and came to linger on her mouth. She might be confused about many things, but here in his arms everything seemed to make sense. When she finally dragged herself away, she looked into his face. All the passion, tenderness and love she had ever hoped to see there were glistening in his eyes.

'Ellie, there is room in that massive heart of yours for all of us. Easily.' He stroked the side of her face. 'Just because we're going to make new memories together—the three of us—it doesn't mean you have to erase the old ones.'

He dipped his hand into his pocket and pulled something out of it. It was only as she felt cold metal round her neck that she realised he had brought her locket with him, and that he was fastening it at her nape, underneath her hair.

Her lip quivered. 'But what if I *do* forget? My brain's not reliable all the time, is it?'

He looked at her with fierce tenderness. 'You won't forget. I won't let you. If you lose a name or a date I'll remember it for you. We're in this together, Ellie. You and me. And I want all of you. We have the future, but your past has made you who you are now, and that's the woman I love.'

She raised both hands and stroked the sides of his face, looking just as fiercely back at him. 'Oh,

I love you too,' she whispered, and pressed her trembling lips to his.

She had one thing left to ask. Just because she needed to be one hundred percent certain. 'You do want children?'

Waiting for his reaction, she swallowed, trying to ease the thickening in her throat.

His hands moved from her back to splay over her still-flat stomach. She laughed. He looked as if he was expecting evidence there and then. He was just going to have to be patient.

'I want it all. I want our baby. I want to change nappies and clean up sick and crawl around on the floor with him. I want to give him brothers and sisters and teach the whole lot of them to play cricket. I want to help our children with their homework, teach them how to drive, give our daughters away at the altar. And I want to do it all with you by my side. Will you do that with me, Ellie? Do you want that too?'

Ellie threw back her head and laughed with joy. Mark always had made everything seem so simple. She was the one who made it all so complicated. She kissed him with a fervour that surprised them both.

Then, for the second time that month, she said, 'I do.'

EPILOGUE

ELLIE crept across the carpet in her bare feet and peered into the empty cot.

'Shh!' A low voice came from a dim corner of the room. 'I've just got him off to sleep.' Mark was pacing up and down, their two-week-old son cradled against his shoulder.

Baby Miles was sleeping the boneless sleep that newborns did so well. His mouth hung open and his brow was tensed into a frown. Mark and Ellie smiled at each other.

'The trick to putting him into bed is to treat him like a stick of dynamite,' he said, sounding like a total expert already as he lowered the infant into the cot with precision. 'One false move and—'

'The explosion is just as noisy and twice as devastating. I know. You've made that joke a hundred times in the last fortnight, and unfortunately I haven't forgotten a single occasion.'

Mark grinned at her, then went back to what

he'd been doing. He eased his hand from under his son's head. They both froze as the little tyrant stirred and made a squeaky grunt. Mark's mask of stern concentration melted.

'I love it when he makes those noises,' he said, reaching for Ellie's hand and leading her from the room. She lifted their joined hands to look at her watch.

'Midnight! Just the right time for a chocolate feast,' she explained, and pulled him towards the kitchen. She delved into the fridge and pulled out a large bar of her favourite chocolate.

He turned the radio on low, and they ate chocolate and chatted until they were both doing more yawning than munching.

Ellie cocked her head. 'Listen, Mark.' He turned the radio up a notch. It sounded deafening in the quiet kitchen. They both looked at the ceiling and waited. When they were sure it was safe to make a noise, she added, 'They're playing our song.'

He started to hum along to Kat's latest single, 'All My Tomorrows'. It had been number one for three weeks already. The music-buying public couldn't seem to get enough of the simple love song, performed with just the expressive huskiness of Kat's voice and her acoustic guitar.

Ellie smiled and remembered the first time she'd heard it. She could almost feel the warmth of the

Carribbean dawn on her skin and smell the hibiscus blossoms. Mark joined in the second chorus. She stood up and ruffled his hair before sitting on his lap. 'Don't give up your day job, sweetie. Kat might have you up on murder charges for doing that to her song.'

Mark pulled a face and Ellie hummed along with the music.

Treasure my heart and keep it safe, and I'll spend all my tomorrows loving you.

Ellie wagged a finger at him. 'Better do as the lady says, Mark.'

'Always,' he said, as he leaned in and stole a kiss.

ROMANCE 2-in-1

Coming next month

ACCIDENTALLY THE SHEIKH'S WIFE
by Barbara McMahon

Welcome to Barbara McMahon's new **Jewels of the Desert** duet. Bethanne is promoted from pilot to princess when she becomes Sheikh Rashid's convenient bride!

MARRYING THE SCARRED SHEIKH
by Barbara McMahon

Rashid's brother, Sheikh Khalid, was the kingdom's playboy until a fire disfigured his chiselled features. Can sweet Ella see the man beneath the scars?

TOUGH TO TAME
by Diana Palmer

New York Times bestselling author Diana Palmer welcomes you back to Jacobsville to meet Bentley Rydel. He lives hard, loves fiercely. This rugged Texan is going to be tough to tame!

HER LONE COWBOY
by Donna Alward

Lily thinks Noah is the most stubborn man she's ever met. Losing an arm doesn't mean he has to lose sight of how strong, brave and loyal he is. Now Lily just needs to convince Noah of that!

On sale 2nd April 2010
Available at WHSmith, Tesco, ASDA, Eason and all good bookshops.
For full Mills & Boon range including eBooks visit
www.millsandboon.co.uk

MILLS & BOON® ROMANCE

is proud to present

Jewels of the Desert

Deserts, diamonds and destiny!

The Kingdom of Quishari: two rulers, with hearts as hard as the rugged landscape they reign over, are in need of Desert Queens…

When they offer convenient proposals, will they discover doing your duty doesn't have to mean ignoring your heart?

Sheikh Rashid and his twin brother Sheikh Khalid are looking for brides in…

ACCIDENTALLY THE SHEIKH'S WIFE
And
MARRYING THE SCARRED SHEIKH

by Barbara McMahon

in April 2010

MILLS & BOON® ROMANCE

is proud to present

THE BRIDES OF BELLA ROSA

Romance, rivalry and a family reunited

Lisa Firenze and Luca Casali's sibling rivalry has torn apart the quiet, sleepy Italian town of Monta Correnti for years…

Now, as the feud is handed down to their children, will history repeat itself? Can the next generation undo their parents' mistakes and reunite their families?

Or are there more secrets to be revealed…?

The saga begins in May 2010 with

BEAUTY AND THE RECLUSIVE PRINCE
by Raye Morgan

and

EXECUTIVE: EXPECTING TINY TWINS
by Barbara Hannay

Don't miss this fabulous sequel to
BRIDES OF BELLA LUCIA!

MILLS & BOON

are proud to present our...

Book of the Month

The Major and the Pickpocket
by Lucy Ashford
from Mills & Boon® Historical

Tassie bit her lip. Why hadn't he turned her over to the constables? She certainly wasn't going to try to run past him – he towered over her, six foot of hardened muscle, strong booted legs set firmly apart. Major Marcus Forrester. All ready for action. And Tassie couldn't help but remember his kiss…

Mills & Boon® Historical
Available 5th March

*Something to say about our Book of the Month?
Tell us what you think!*
millsandboon.co.uk/community

millsandboon.co.uk Community

Join Us!

The Community is the perfect place to meet and chat to kindred spirits who love books and reading as much as you do, but it's also the place to:

- **Get the inside scoop from authors about their latest books**
- **Learn how to write a romance book with advice from our editors**
- **Help us to continue publishing the best in women's fiction**
- **Share your thoughts on the books we publish**
- **Befriend other users**

Forums: Interact with each other as well as authors, editors and a whole host of other users worldwide.

Blogs: Every registered community member has their own blog to tell the world what they're up to and what's on their mind.

Book Challenge: We're aiming to read 5,000 books and have joined forces with The Reading Agency in our inaugural Book Challenge.

Profile Page: Showcase yourself and keep a record of your recent community activity.

Social Networking: We've added buttons at the end of every post to share via digg, Facebook, Google, Yahoo, technorati and de.licio.us.

www.millsandboon.co.uk

MILLS & BOON

www.millsandboon.co.uk

- All the latest titles
- Free online reads
- Irresistible special offers

And there's more...

- Missed a book? Buy from our huge discounted backlist
- Sign up to our FREE monthly eNewsletter
- eBooks available now
- More about your favourite authors
- Great competitions

Make sure you visit today!

www.millsandboon.co.uk

0310_N0ZED

2 FREE BOOKS
AND A SURPRISE GIFT

We would like to take this opportunity to thank you for reading this Mills & Boon® book by offering you the chance to take TWO more specially selected books from the Romance series absolutely FREE! We're also making this offer to introduce you to the benefits of the Mills & Boon® Book Club™—

- **FREE home delivery**
- **FREE gifts and competitions**
- **FREE monthly Newsletter**
- **Exclusive Mills & Boon Book Club offers**
- **Books available before they're in the shops**

Accepting these FREE books and gift places you under no obligation to buy, you may cancel at any time, even after receiving your free shipment. Simply complete your details below and return the entire page to the address below. You don't even need a stamp!

YES Please send me 2 free Romance books and a surprise gift. I understand that unless you hear from me, I will receive 5 superb new stories every month including two 2-in-1 books priced at £4.99 each and a single book priced at £3.19, postage and packing free. I am under no obligation to purchase any books and may cancel my subscription at any time. The free books and gift will be mine to keep in any case.

Ms/Mrs/Miss/Mr_____ Initials _____

Surname _____
Address _____

_____ Postcode _____

Send this whole page to: Mills & Boon Book Club, Free Book Offer, FREEPOST NAT 10298, Richmond, TW9 1BR

Offer valid in UK only and is not available to current Mills & Boon Book Club subscribers to this series. Overseas and Eire please write for details.. We reserve the right to refuse an application and applicants must be aged 18 years or over. Only one application per household. Terms and prices subject to change without notice. Offer expires 31st May 2010. As a result of this application, you may receive offers from Harlequin Mills & Boon and other carefully selected companies. If you would prefer not to share in this opportunity please write to The Data Manager, PO Box 676, Richmond, TW9 1WU.

Mills & Boon® is a registered trademark owned by Harlequin Mills & Boon Limited.
The Mills & Boon® Book Club™ is being used as a trademark.